Xavier Wallace

SHAW SALVATION

Xavier Wallace

Xavier Wallace was born and raised in regional New South Wales, Australia. He attended public primary and high schools, before studying business at the University of Newcastle. He worked in Canberra for the Australian Government in both the public service and politics for over a decade. He has a Master of Politics and Public Policy from Deakin University. Xavier's interests include politics, government, national security, media and communications, philosophy, ancient history and mythology. He is an advocate for equality and human rights, including LGBTI+ rights. Live music, thriller novels and action movies occupy his time outside writing and work. He loves spending time with his family and friends, and his groodle, Atlas.

Xavier Wallace is the author of the Max Shaw spy thriller series.

Dedication

For my niece, Olive, and partner, Ryan.

Acknowledgements

This novel is dedicated to my beautiful niece, Olive. She's still over a decade away from being old enough to read it, but I hope just its existence in some way inspires her to pursue her dreams, and to know that she can do anything she puts her mind to and I'll always be here to support her!

Olive is yet to start school, but I can already see some of my character, Kate 'Alpha' Matthews, in her. She's tough, blunt and a bit ruthless, especially to her older sister, Frankie (who *Shaw Initiation* is dedicated to), but she's beautiful, full of happiness and joy, and has a heart of gold.

Both my nieces make me so proud! They are growing into incredible girls and I can't wait to see what life has in store for them.

I wish nothing, but the best life can offer you! I love you both!

The book is also dedicated to my partner, Ryan. I met Ryan when I was writing my second novel, *Shaw Initiation*, in Newcastle, Australia. He's been an amazing sounding block, and has helped shape ideas and proof the novels over the years. He's also increased my knowledge and understanding of history, among many other subjects. He's provided continual encouragement and motivation, and has helped nurture my love of writing. He's tolerated my occasional grumpiness, supported me through career and job changes, and put up with my love of all things MCU and superhero related.

We made it through COVID, locked in a one-bedroom apartment, and have been together for over six years now, and I just want to say thank you for everything and I love you!

The Max Shaw Spy Thriller Series

Shaw Vengeance

Shaw Initiation

Shaw Confrontation

Shaw Intervention

Shaw Reclamation

Shaw Salvation

SHAW SALVATION

By Xavier Wallace

Sixth Novel of the Max Shaw Spy Thriller Series.

Prelude

The red sandy soil plains stretched on for hundreds of miles. They joined the horizon in a steamy orange blur merging the land and sky. The blue sky was fading into a wash of bright orange, purple and pink streaks as evening began to fall.

The landscape was flat, so flat you could almost see the curve of the earth unobstructed by mountains or hills. The odd tree stood somehow out of place in the harshness of the desert. Termite mounds, small grass trees with their black stumps and thin green leaves, and the sparsely spaced grey salt bushes dotted the endless kilometres of red dust and sand.

The extreme temperature was finally giving way to dusk, but the road still glistened from the melting tar after the day's scorching sun as the heat shimmered off the surface.

The road was perfectly straight. It had been for almost an hour. Every time the drivers though they were reeling in the unwinding road, it just continued to melt into the iridescent horizon. The end of the road seemed non-existent, like a treadmill in the desert. As the kilometres rolled by, the road just kept spooling out from under the setting sun like an endless ribbon pulled from some magic reel.

Every few hundred kilometres the road would open up on either side with signs indicating this section doubled as a landing strip for the Royal Australian Flying Doctor Service. RAFDS was stamped in massive white bold letters on the road, before the barcode like white strips of a traditional runway, then after several football fields played out under the tires, the road narrowed back to an outback highway.

Mobs of emus kicked up red dust as they ran in the distance. Herds of camels milled about, barely visible off to the side of the road in the heat haze.

A dead kangaroo laid baking in the afternoon sunlight as the first police car rushed by with its red and blue lights flashing, before a fully loaded semi-trailer roared past. A second police car followed the truck, which was painted a bright white, though now covered in a thick, uneven coating of red dirt. It had no identifying marks or number plates and the windows were tinted so dark it was almost impossible to see the driver and passenger in the big rig.

From the haze where the skyline met the earth, Alice Springs began to take shape when overhead a huge roar broke the desert calm. A Boeing C-17 Globemaster came in so close its landing gear almost clipped the top of the truck. It touched down in front of the motorcade as the road opened up into a makeshift landing strip. The motorcade didn't slow, but nor did the Globemaster. It easily more than matched their speed as it taxied along the outback highway.

The rear door lowered and two army Bushmaster vehicles rolled out onto the road. They accelerated hard to match the motorcade. Two men in unison in each Bushmaster, opened the top hatches and climbed into the mounted machine gun bays.

Through the window of the front police vehicle an officer was screaming into her radio, then she froze in horror. A line of orange bullets trailed from the top of the Bushmaster ripping into the road surface before tracing a line up into the grill and bonnet of the police car. The onslaught of bullets found the windscreen and the inside of the vehicle was sprayed with blood as the officers were torn apart. The bullets whirled around as the Bushmaster bounced on the remote highway, pounding one after the other into the car, before fire and smoke started to billow from under the hood and it exploded in a huge fireball as the petrol caught fire and the gas tank ruptured.

The wreckage bounced harmlessly off the truck's gigantic bull bar. Ignited petrol sprayed the cabin streaking flames across the front end of the truck.

The second Bushmaster fell back in behind the rear police car. The police officers were frantically radioing for back up and looking over their shoulders at the speeding army vehicle.

The Bushmaster rammed the cop car. The police car collided with the back of the semi and swerved about wildly as the driver tried to wrestle it back under control. The army rig surged forward again smashing into the rear of the police SUV. The driver lost control and veered off the road in a cloud of dust.

Bullets exploded out of the machine gun mounted on the Bushmaster tearing into the metal and glass of the police vehicle. The cop yanked the wheel hard trying to ram the Bushmaster, but didn't really budge. It did however get them tucked in tight enough that the Bushmaster's machine gun couldn't get a clean line of sight at such an awkward angle. The driver seemed to realise this and gripped the wheel tightly trying to hold his line.

The masked machine gunner looked down over the edge of the Bushmaster's roof to assess the situation. He reached down and unbuckled his belt, then pulled two pins and dropped it over onto the windscreen of the police car.

The belt slid down the glass resting on the windscreen wipers, as the masked man dropped back inside the Bushmaster and it pulled away to the right.

The police officers both saw the what was hanging from the belt, but it was too late. The two grenades exploded shredding the police vehicle and erupting in a ball of fire and black smoke. It fell back onto the tar as the Bushmaster left it behind.

The two Bushmasters pulled in alongside the speeding truck and their machine gunners got into position. The masked men flicked the guns over to single shots and took careful aim.

Two shots were instantly followed by two exploding tyres as the bullets hit the front wheels of the white lorry. The truck started to wobble and swerve. Its handling was completely compromised, especially at speed.

One of the Bushmasters drove in front of the truck and aimed the gun at the window. The masked attacker moved his hand up and down telling the driver to slow the truck. He lowered the gun as if signalling they would be spared if they slowed down.

Through the windscreen, he could just see the driver and passenger exchange some tense words.

The truck started to slow.

So did the Globemaster and the two Bushmasters.

Both of the mammoths came to a stop a kilometre apart.

Two men from each Bushmaster jumped down wielding automatic rifles. They aimed at the doors of the semitrailer. One of the men was wearing a cylindrical helmet like the one worn by Australian bushranger Ned Kelly. It had a narrow slit eye hole and was covered in dints. Large bolts were visible in places holding the dark, scratched metal together. It easily covered the wearer's head and neck down to his shoulders.

"Get out of the truck!" Ned Kelly yelled.

"Alright, alright," the driver said, opening the door. "Please you said you wouldn't hurt us."

"I never said any such thing," Ned said as he dragged the driver out and onto his knees on the hot tarmac.

His men on the other side of the truck pulled the passenger out and marched him over to kneel beside the driver.

"Please…" the driver said, but didn't get a chance to finish his protest.

Ned Kelly shot him, then the passenger. They both fell forward as blood ran from their heads into the red sand and dust.

"Let's move," Ned Kelly commanded.

One of the men climbed up into the truck as his comrade unhooked it from the damaged trailer. He drove it off to the side, as one of the Bushmasters was wheeled around. A hitch folded out from under the army vehicle and they connected it to the truck's trailer.

Two of the men from the second Bushmaster dropped a grenade each into their seats. The bushmaster exploded as they ran to join their comrades.

The man who had driven the truck away left a grenade on the driver's seat and it too exploded showering the road and surrounding desert with burning white metal and glass and plastic.

The men climbed on the side rails of the remaining Bushmaster as it towed the trailer down the highway.

The Bushmaster pulled the trailer up into the rear of the idling Globemaster. The men set about fastening it in place as the cargo hold door raised and the Globemaster accelerated down the highway.

The massive heavy lift aircraft lumbered up into the sky as the sun set and a swarm of police cars arrived at the burning Bushmaster and truck.

As the cargo bay doors closed, Ned Kelly took off his helmet and opened his satellite phone. He held the number one for five seconds, then saw the call trying to connect. He raised the phone to his ear, pressing his hand over his other ear to block out the sound of the roaring engines.

"Speak," the gruff voice said on the other end of the phone.

"We have the package, Senator," he said. "On route to our base now."

"Good. This should put a dampener on things for a few days. I'll wire the remaining funds to your account now."

"Thank you, sir."

"Good work."

Chapter One

The wheel on the trolley flickered and squeaked as he walked down the aisle. He picked up a heavy foil bag of muesli and read the back as if he had all the time and not a care in the world.

He placed the muesli into the trolley, then wandered further down the aisle returning the smile of a young woman as she passed with her screaming toddler. An old lady struggled to reach a big bag of flour, so he strolled over and took it down off the shelf for her. She smiled warmly and patted his arm.

"Thank you, young man," she said. "Don't get old. It's bloody terrible."

"You're very welcome," Max said, smiling and nodding. "Have a nice day."

Max Shaw was an incredibly fit man, and while not as strong and agile as he once was, he could still outmatch most on the sporting field or in combat. He'd spent years as Australia's most decorated and elite spy. Those days though were behind him now. Helping old ladies with bags of flour was the closest he'd come to anything dangerous in the last year.

"You too," she said, walking off in search of her next item.

Max slowly gathered his remaining groceries and made his way to the checkout. He exchanged pleasantries with the server, then picked up a copy of the *Canberra Times*.

Government Wins: Election Landslide ran across the top of the page. He smiled seeing the Prime Minister, Ted Sawyer, holding Blake Smyth's hand over his head in celebration. Max folded the paper in half and added it to the conveyor with his other items.

"Thank you," Max said to the checkout assistance as he placed the last bag in his trolley and paid.

Max wheeled the trolley across the rough carpark. Its dodgy wheel continued to flicker and jam as it vibrated over the stones.

Max unloaded his groceries into the boot of his Chevy sedan and closed the lid, then returned his trolley. He strolled across the carpark watching the other shoppers marching in and out of the centre on a mission. The mother and screaming toddler got into their car the next row over as Max climbed into the driver seat of his white sedan and started it. It's big V8 engine roared to life and the radio started.

"The Prime Minister has advised the Governor-General that he has the numbers to form government less than twenty-four hours after the election landslide," the reporter said. *"Discussions are already underway about who will join his Cabinet, but as we can see from the front pages of most of today's papers it is clear the recently elected Member for Canberra, Blake Smyth, will be elevated to the ministry. Rumours are circulating that the former spy master will take on a new role as Minister for Defence and Counter-Intelligence. It would be an incredible achievement for the first openly gay minister to be sworn into the Cabinet. He has the respect of both sides of the chamber and would be a formidable minister. We all remember he entered politics following the disastrous events which unfolded on the international stage just over a year ago when his partner and former colleague, Max Shaw, was arrested and put on trial in The Hague."*

Max hit the volume button, turning off the radio. He didn't need to hear the rest. He had lived it.

As he looked at the screen it lit up. *Incoming call, private number*, it read. A shrill ringtone broke the silence. Max pressed the answer button on his steering wheel.

"Hello," Max said.

"It's me," Hulk said. "How are you, kid?"

"I'm fine, Hulk. How are you?"

"I've been better, Max. That's why I'm calling actually. I need to speak to you."

"Sure. I'm just in the car, but happy to chat."

"I need to speak to you in person, Max."

"Are you in town? I've got some groceries in the boot which I need to get home, but I can meet you after that."

"Jesus. Who would have thought one of the world's greatest spies would be spending his time shopping and playing house?"

"I'm happy, Hulk. After everything I've been through, I'm quite comfortable doing these normal things. You know, I've never really had the chance to do the groceries and mow the lawn, not since I was a kid anyway. This is the life I've helped others live and yes it's been a quiet twelve months, it's better than the alternative."

"Your tone would say otherwise."

"We've been through this. If you're calling to get me to come back, you're wasting your time, I'm afraid."

"We need you, Max. No one can do what you do. I get it. They fucked you over and you're pissed off about it, but you can't keep sitting on the sidelines."

"I'm not pissed off anymore, Hulk. I spent most of my life in the field. I'm finally getting to spend some time away from it all. The death, the lies, the trauma. I can't do it anymore. And, I don't want to do it anymore."

"Just give me a couple of hours. I won't take no for an answer, kid. I need to speak to you."

"Let me think about it," Max said, ending the call.

Max sat for a minute thinking, then reversed onto the road, before driving out of the carpark.

He drove through the treelined streets. The new buds of spring were blooming. The trees which had been bare throughout the cold winter months were coming to life with green leaves and flower blossoms.

Max's house was on quiet street in South Canberra. The houses were generously spaced with large yards and high fences. He had picked the house for the quiet neighbourhood and for its security. He pressed a button on his sun visor and a large steel gate rolled to the side. He drove up the driveway as the gate rolled closed behind his car. His yard was immaculate. The lawn and trees were well maintained, and giant hedges were neatly trimmed. Small blossoming flowers lined the foot paths. Max had had some time on his hands of late and spent the endless hours gardening and listening to music – far from the life he used to live.

Max pressed a second button and the garage door opened. He drove in and parked the car, then gathered the groceries and walked to the side door. He grabbed the door handle. A small green light lit up and there was a soft mechanical buzz and a click which let him know the door had unlocked.

He set about putting the groceries away as his phone started ringing. He closed the fridge door and stopped for a moment to look at the photo on the door of he and Blake at the beach from last summer. He smiled then spun around to pick up the phone.

"Hello," Max answered.

"Prince Charming," Kate said. "Been a while. How's it going?"

"Hi Kate. I'm guessing you don't have time to hear the answer. I take it this isn't a friendly call."

"Why would you say that? I'm always fucking friendly."

"I spoke to Hulk less than thirty minutes ago."

"We need you, kid."

"I'm out, Kate. I don't want to come back."

"That might be the case, but you know I wouldn't be asking unless it was important."

Max didn't respond.

"Max, it hasn't been the same here without you and with Blake going up the hill and Hulk, well, he, he just isn't up to it anymore I'm sorry to say. I need you to head out and speak to him. Can you do that for me?"

"I don't…"

"Please, Max. He needs to see you. I'd consider it a personal favour to me."

"Is that a favour from Kate my good friend or Kate the new Director-General of the Australian Intelligence Service?"

"Can't it be both?"

"Okay, Kate."

"Just promise you'll call me after you've spoken to him."

"I will. Where is he?"

"A chopper is on its way."

Chapter Two

The helicopter landed in Max's front yard. He watched as the wash from the rotors swirled the leaves and dust around. His previously perfect yard was instantly less perfect. He climbed aboard and frowned as the chopper pulled away. He wondered what his neighbours would make of it all. The massive chopper breaking the peaceful suburban life of Canberra's wealthiest residents.

About an hour later, the chopper touched down on the helipad at the Wool Shed – the Australian Intelligence Service's secret training base in western New South Wales.

Max had trained here years ago. He still remembered that winter's morning when Kate had driven him through the gates and up to the old homestead. The fog in the air, the mist from his warm breath, the frost and dew on the lawns. The torture of five a.m. starts and the brutal training regime.

So much had happened since then, but the old place still looked mostly the same. It was an old homestead surrounded by a generous veranda which framed the whole house. There was an old barn and a handful of vehicles and motorbikes parked on the driveway.

The chopper blades slowed as Max opened the door and climbed out. A group of potential recruits were gathered by the boxing ring which sat between the homestead and the shed. They all looked over eagerly, exchanging whispers and looks as they tried to figure out who had made the journey out to the secret base. It must have been someone important, they don't send choppers for just anyone.

Max walked towards them as the instructor at ringside yelled an order to the two recruits in the ring to keep fighting. The pair continued sparing as Max got to the instructor.

"Agent Max Shaw, the Prince himself, returns," Mike Liddle said, shaking Max's hand.

The whispering and looks started again as the recruits heard Max's name.

"What brings you out here?" Liddle asked.

"Hulk called," Max said. "Any idea where he is?"

Liddle pointed over Max's shoulder. Max turned to see Hulk walking across the yard towards them. It had been a few months since Max had seen his old mentor. He looked like he had aged ten years in that time. He was leaning more heavily on his walking stick and was more hunched over. He seemed unsteady on his feet.

Liddle nodded sadly as Max turned back to face him.

Hulk eventually made it across the grounds to them and shook Max's hand. Max noticed his grip was weak. It was certainly a long way from the powerful vice-like grip Hulk had when he had recruited Max. He had also towered over Max with the decades of army training and missions shaping his impressive build. Max tried not to let the shock of the old man's hunched and withering frame register on his face.

"Listen up," Hulk said with the tone and strength of the commander Max remembered. "This here is Max Shaw. Several of the things you will learn over the coming weeks and months were developed thanks to this man's missions and the new tactics he created. Not all of them will be in the 'what to do' pile, a fair share will sit in the 'what not to do' list."

Max smiled and Liddle laughed.

"Regardless, our country and many others have this man to thank for saving their arses," Hulk said.

The recruits all clapped and smiled warmly.

"Any of you think you could take him?" Hulk asked with a wry grin.

The recruits shuffled nervously at the question, not sure how to respond to Hulk's challenge. One by one a few recruits raised their hands figuring it was a test to show their courage. One of the tall recruits in the ring raised his hand and looked down eagerly from the mat to Max with determination in his eyes.

"You, out," Hulk ordered and the taller young man's opponent climbed out of the ring. "Max, let me introduce you to Tom. So far, he is at the front of the pack, but like you he's still got a lot to learn. Want to step in and teach him a thing or two?"

"I didn't come here for this," Max replied, letting his frustration show.

"Fair enough," Hulk said. "Let's head over to the homestead and talk."

The pair started to walk for the homestead with a nod from Liddle.

"Washed up pussy," Tom said, bouncing from foot to foot in the ring.

A few of the recruits chuckled, others paused in silent shock, as Max stopped in his tracks. He looked down at the ground for a moment as Hulk and Liddle both smiled broadly. Max shook his head, then turned back to face the ring. He handed his glasses and phone to Liddle, then slid in under the ropes.

As he went to get to his feet, Tom ran in and kicked him in the ribs. The recruits all gasped at the ungentlemanly act. He wound up for another kick and Max rolled to the side, swinging his leg around and sweeping Tom's leg out from under him. Tom hit the mat with a heavy thud, as Max got to his feet.

"Bit of a dog act," Max said. "Is that really how you want to play this?"

Tom sprung up onto his feet and bounded around like a boxer who had fought hundreds of fights.

"Let's go old man," Tom said defiantly.

Max cracked his neck from side to side and loosened his shoulders, then started bouncing on the spot shaped up and ready. Tom ran forward throwing a haymaker, which Max swatted away easily then he slapped Tom hard across the face. The sound of the slap echoed across the open space. Tom was shocked at the speed of the blow and was embarrassed as his fellow recruits laughed. He ran in again throwing another huge punch, but Max danced to the side and slapped him hard across the other cheek. Again, the sound spread through the otherwise peaceful landscape.

Tom was getting angry and it was starting to show. He stepped forward and unleashed a flurry of punches to Max's mid-section. Max blocked most of the blows with his forearms, but the odd one snuck through. He pulled Tom in close locking up against the ropes. Tom unleashed again. Max used the ropes to bounced back and forth, blocking the attack, then he pushed Tom back and slapped him harder than the first two. Tom dropped to one knee, but leapt up as the embarrassment fuelled his adrenaline. Tom ran in and Max ducked right, letting Tom hit the ropes. He panicked and quickly turned back to see Max moving in.

Max unloaded his own flurry of punches to Tom's mid-section. The younger man blocked several of the punches, but Max was fast and his punches were powerful. Tom was shocked at the speed and force behind the blows. He dropped to the mat and Max backed away as the recruits all laughed and clapped. Max looked over to Hulk and saw the old man smiling.

Tom got back to his feet and Max walked over to shake his hand. He held out his hand, but the younger man swatted it away and punched Max in face. Max stumbled back as the recruits all groaned and murmured at the second ungentlemanly action.

"Not so fucking funny now, is it?" Tom asked.

Max stood and faced Tom. As Tom made his move, Max jumped off his left foot, drew back his right fist and threw a hard right into Tom's face. He landed and let every ounce of energy he had drive up from his heals though his legs and core then out through his shoulder and left fist. The punch struck Tom's face and the young man staggered back then hunched over. Max darted forward with shocking speed and kneed Tom in the face with just enough force to knock him out without doing any permanent damage.

The recruits were all shocked at Max's speed and ferociousness, but they all smiled and clapped having each had to put up with Tom's bullshit for weeks.

Tom laid on the mat unconscious.

"A good lesson for everyone," Liddle said. "There is always someone out there better trained and more experienced than you. Confidence is one thing, but you shouldn't rush in before you know how your opponent fights. What are their strengths and weaknesses, and what can you do to overcome? Liam, Luke, get Tom to the medic. The rest of you can head in and get ready for class."

Two recruits climbed into the ring as Max stepped out.

"Still got it, kid," Hulk said.

"I remember when you kicked the shit out of me in this very ring," Max said.

"A good lesson for you. Same as the one you just delivered to Tom. He reminds me a lot of you actually."

"Why am I here, Hulk?" Max asked as Liddle led the two recruits carrying Tom off. "It wasn't to teach some young recruit a lesson."

"It was actually," Hulk said, pointing to the homestead. "Let's go take a seat."

The pair walked slowly across the lawn and up the stairs at the front of the old house. They took a seat on the porch and Hulk let out a huff as if he had just run a mile.

"There is no easy way to say this, Max, so I'm just going to say it. I've got multiple sclerosis. It's advanced to a point now where it's affecting nearly everything I do."

"Jesus, I'm sorry, Hulk. Are you in any pain or discomfort?"

"I'm managing. I fatigue easily and I've got almost constant pain in my back. My coordination is more often than not out of whack. I've fallen down these bloody steps more than once. My vision sometimes comes and goes, but the worst thing by far is fog. I feel it in my mind. I have difficulty concentrating and I have problems understanding what I am being told and getting it to sink in."

"I don't know what to say."

"It's okay, kid."

"Is there anything I can do?"

"Yes, there is. I need you to come back to AIS," Hulk said as Max went to speak. "Just hear me out. I always thought you would be there to take over field operations and training when I left. Blake was the perfect person to take over AIS and deal with the politicians and run the place. He was living up to my every expectation until he left to run for parliament, which I still don't understand. Why didn't you try to talk him out of it?"

"I did try, but he is his own man and I will do whatever it takes to support him," Max said, unconsciously turning the engagement ring on his finger.

"Well, regardless, he's gone and so are you. AIS is going through a period of change and we risk things falling through the cracks."

"Kate is the new Director-General. I'm sure she will do an amazing job."

"Kate has always been wiser and more of a leader than she lets on. She will do a great job, but she will need help. She can't do it alone. She will need someone she can trust to recruit new people and train them."

"That's why you called me? You want me to take over the Wool Shed?"

"Yes, but I also want you to return to your old job as head of field operations. You will be Kate's number two, deputy director-general responsible for running missions and making sure AIS has the people we need to get the job done. I've been doing it since Blake left, but I can't do it any longer. I'm not the man I was when I recruited you."

"This is a lot to consider, Hulk. I promised I wouldn't come back."

"Who Blake? I'll call him. He'll understand and I think after his promotion to this portfolio, he'll want someone here he can trust. And, who better than his fiancé?"

Chapter Three

The AIS helicopter flew in low over Canberra. It hovered above Max and Blake's front yard, before lowering into a hover just above the grass.

Max jumped out and gave a quick nod to the pilot, who lifted the big bird back into the air and took off as a white BMW sedan pulled into the driveway. The gate rolled to the side and the heavy bulletproof BMW drove into the yard. Blake was sitting in the back talking angrily into his phone.

Max walked to the mailbox and checked it, then walked over to the BMW. The driver and passenger climbed out.

"Mr Shaw," the driver said. "I'm Nick Lovell. The head of Mr Smyth's security detail."

Max shook his hand.

"And sir, I'm Julian Campbell," the passenger said, shaking Max's hand. "One of the security team members."

"Nice to meet you both," Max said. "Since when do backbenchers get security?"

"Well, Mr Smyth isn't really just a normal backbencher. As the former head of AIS he needs security, but the Prime Minister has asked us to provide him with full head of government security."

"Head of government?" Max questioned, as Blake opened his door.

"Hi Max," Blake said. "I see you've met Nick and Julian. The others are on their way."

"The others? What exactly have you gotten yourself into?"

"Well, I'm about to join the Cabinet and the PM thought I needed more security."

"Since when do Ministers get this much security?"

"I'm not just going to be a Minister, Max. I've been asked to be the Deputy Prime Minister."

Max was shocked. Blake had only been in Parliament for around twelve months.

"Don't rush to congratulate me," Blake said.

"I'm sorry," Max said, walking over and hugging Blake. "Congratulations, Blake. I'm just surprised. I have always known you are amazing, but that sort of a rise through the political ranks is unheard of."

"It's all part of Ted's plan to remove the career politicians from the ministry and replace them with people with skills outside politics. He wants to draw from across the public and private sector to put people with real skills in. I'll head up defence and national security. John Sullivan is coming in to takeover treasury."

"The CEO of the Commonwealth Bank?"

"One and the same. It's why I agreed to join them in the first place. Actual people with real skills."

"Well, he's certainly made at least one great choice," Max said, smiling then kissing Blake.

"Thanks, Max," Blake said as another SUV arrived and five federal police officers disembarked and wandered in.

"We'll take up position around property," Lovell said. "You won't even know we are here."

"Thank you, Nick. Let's go inside, Max."

"What was your call about?" Max asked as they walked across the lush green grass.

"What call?"

"When you pulled up in the car. You looked upset."

"There's been an incident in the Northern Territory. A shipment was stolen and it could only have been done by professionals."

"What makes you say that?"

"They took out a police convoy with Bushmasters, then stole the truck with a C-17."

"Jesus."

"Yep. The call was with the outgoing Defence Minister who was not cooperating. He told me it was on a need to know basis and until I was sworn in, I didn't need to know."

"Does he know you used to run AIS?"

"Of course, he's just being an arsehole because they lost. I'll be sworn in soon enough and until then Kate's keeping me updated."

Max fought the urge to ask more questions. It was no longer his responsibility. He needed to let it go. He opened the door and they walked inside, leaving the officers in the yard to secure the perimeter. Blake put his bag down and took off his shoes, jacket and tie as Max walked to the kitchen and took out a bottle of champagne. He popped the cork as Blake walked in.

"I like that sound," Blake said.

"I guess we should celebrate," Max said, pouring two glasses and raising his own. "To the most handsome and appropriately skilled DPM there's ever been."

"Not sure that's much of a competition, but I'll drink to it."

They both took a sip and sat their glasses on the polished concrete benchtop.

"You don't seem that thrilled for me, Max," Blake said.

"I'm sorry, Blake," Max said. "I am. It's just, well, I just worry about you. When you said you wanted to go into politics, well, I just worried about you. You know too much. You've got a target painted on you and that target just got bigger."

"You are very sweet, you know that?"

"I'm being serious, Blake. There are some very dangerous people who you and I have both pissed off, and now you'll be in the public eye. You're exposed. I can't protect you."

"We have a yard full of highly trained security guards, plus you and I aren't without skill in that department. I will be fine."

"I just worry. I couldn't bear losing you."

"I'm not going anywhere, Max."

"Good," Max said as he smiled and took another sip.

"How was your day?"

"Why do I get the feeling you already know?"

"There was a helicopter in our front yard. Do you think they would have let me anywhere near it if they didn't know who it was?"

"I guess not. Do you know where I was?"

"The Wool Shed?"

"Yes."

"How's Hulk? Did he convince you to go back this time? What's this the thirtieth time? He's persistent I'll give him that."

"He's sick, Blake. He's got MS."

"What? Is he okay?"

"He's frail. He told me he has some pretty bad days."

"That must have been hard for you."

"It's harder for him."

"He is your mentor, Max, and a good friend. It must be hard to see him like that."

"I always thought. I don't know. I guess I never thought about growing old. In our line of work, not many get the chance. I never thought I would."

"You will. We will together."

Max smiled as Blake took his hand.

"Well, that's the thing," Max said. "I don't know what to do."

"Do you want to go back?" Blake asked.

"I don't know. This morning was a solid no, but now I don't know."

"For what it is worth, I love having you at home and clearly you enjoy it. Our home and gardens are always so immaculate. But, I can see it in your eyes, you miss it."

"Not all of it."

"What exactly does he want you to do?"

"He wants me to be Kate's second-in-command. Deputy Director and head of field operations. I'd coordinate missions and look after personnel and the Wool Shed."

"But not actually go back into the field?"

"No. I don't think so."

"Well, that sounds okay to me. You'll be able to train the new recruits and help them prepare for what is to come."

"Can I really send these young men to war?"

"Someone has to, Max. You know what needs to be done. It would make me feel better knowing you were there to help get them ready. You can ensure more of them come home alive."

Max just nodded, deep in thought.

"I don't have to make the decision yet anyway," Max said. "I'm being selfish, we should be celebrating the fact I'm engaged to the second most powerful man in the country."

"Well, not until after the ceremony tomorrow," Blake said. "I want you to be there."

"Are you sure? The press has already had a field day with our relationship. They were crapping on about it on the radio just before. They're hung up on it. Not only because you're engaged to a man, but the man from The Hague. They've retried me in the papers a thousand times over."

"The stuff at The Hague is old news now and you were cleared. As for our relationship, let them talk. Let them celebrate, or throw their mud, that the new Deputy Prime Minister is in a loving, gay relationship it's a great thing and can only help this country get over caring who loves who and what people do in their bedrooms. I'm happy to engage in that debate any day to show the world love is love. But, the most important thing is that I love you, Max. You are my fiancé and I want you by my side."

"Then I'll be there."

Chapter Four

"Admiral Smyth, please give your oath or affirmation of office," the Governor-General Admiral Anthony Mills said.

"I, Blake Isaac Smyth, do solemnly and sincerely affirm and declare that I will well and truly serve His Majesty King Edwin the First, His heirs and successors, and the Commonwealth of Australia, according to law, in the office of Deputy Prime Minister and Minister for Defence and Counter-Intelligence," Blake said, before he sat down across from the Governor-General and signed his commission documents.

"Congratulations, Deputy Prime Minister," the Governor-General said after signing the documents and standing to shake Blake's hand.

The flashes lit up the room as the gathered press photographed the pair smiling and shaking hands.

When the other ministers had been sworn and the group photos were taken, Max was introduced or reintroduced to Blake's new colleagues and their families. They had tea on the lawns of Government House and mingled with the dignitaries.

Max had been stuck talking to a gruff old Senator from Western Australia. Kevin Timms was his name. He was a shorter man, pushing seventy, but carried himself with an air of confidence or maybe it was arrogance. He had been in the Parliament for almost three decades and did look likely to leave anytime soon. He was full of questions and thoughts on national security, and prattled on as Max stood and pretended to listen. The Senator had just been sworn in as the new Minister for Foreign Affairs and said he was keen to work closely with Blake to improve our international relations, intelligence and defence. Max had nodded and occasionally corrected the odd fact or two, before the Senator found someone more interesting to talk to and excused himself, much to Max's relief.

Max checked his watch.

"Hello, Max," the Governor-General said, wandering over.

"Your Excellency," Max said, bowing ever so slightly.

The pair had met years ago when the Governor-General was then the Chief of Navy. They had a mutual respect and admiration based on real world fighting experience which vastly differed from the well-healed functions they both now attended with people who would never know their world. One of life and death decision making and warfare.

"I've just been handed a document with your name on it. I figured since you are here, we could sign it together."

"That was fast," Max said.

"I don't think they want to give you a chance to back out."

"And what about you, sir?"

"I'm not in the defence force anymore, Max, so I don't get a choice."

"Well, you still get to sign the papers."

"I do," the Governor-General laughed. "For what it is worth, when I was Chief of Navy, then Chief of Defence, I would have given up a lot to have you on my team. You might have never been a sailor, but you were a hell of a spy. Trained by one of the best soldiers our country has ever produced in our mutual friend, Hulk Scott. It always gave me confidence when you were part of the intelligence chain. I knew you wouldn't give me shit information and that my boys could go into the theatre of war with the best detail we could get. So, the sooner the Prince is back in the game, the better as far as I'm concerned."

"Thank you, sir, that means a lot," Max said, locking eyes with Blake and smiling.

"You must be so proud of him," the Governor-General said, looking over the lawn towards Blake.

"I am. Although I'm not sure about all these politicians."

"I was surprised when I heard he was going to the dark side," the Governor-General said making Max laugh and raise an eyebrow. "I saw you checking your watch before, I feel the same. They are an interesting breed. I probably shouldn't have said that, but it's true. Don't you tell anyone."

"Secret's safe with me."

"Good. I feel better knowing someone like Blake is in there sorting them out. But anyway, let's do this."

Blake walked over when he saw Max raise his right hand into the air.

"Mister Shaw, please recite the oath or affirmation for commissioned officers," the Governor-General said.

"I, Maxwell Kenneth Shaw, promise that I will well and truly serve His Majesty King Edwin the First, His heirs and successors, and the Commonwealth of Australia, as the Deputy Director-General and Head of Field Operations of the Australian Intelligence Service and that I will resist His enemies and faithfully discharge my duty according to law," Max said.

Max and the Governor-General signed his commission documents, then shook hands.

"Welcome back, Agent Shaw," the Governor-General said. "With you two at the helms I feel safer already."

"Thank you, sir," Max said.

The Governor-General smiled and left.

"You made the right choice, Max," Blake said.

"So did you, Blake," Max said. "I'm so proud of you, Deputy Prime Minister. Congratulations."

"Thanks, Max," Blake said, then he kissed Max as the clicks of the cameras and flashes erupted again from the press pack which had been eagerly awaiting the moment.

Max flushed red and turned from the camera.

"You'll have to get used to it," Blake said, squeezing Max's hand.

"You're the politician," Max said.

"And you're my fiancé, but also the deputy head of one of my agencies. We are in the public eye now whether we want it or not."

"Great," Max said, smiling.

"When do you leave?" Blake asked as Max checked his watch again.

"Fifteen minutes."

"Okay, I'll see you in a couple of days?"

"Nothing could keep me away," Max said, making Blake smile and kiss him again to more camera flashes.

The fifteen minutes came and went, and Max's helicopter arrived just down the road from Government House. He climbed aboard and it rose into the sky.

The guests at Government House watched as it turned and headed for western New South Wales.

"Welcome on board, sir," the pilot said. "The Director-General is expecting your call. There is a briefing pack on your new computer which is in the bag beside you. Your AIS ID and weapons are also in the pack. Your access key has also been reactivated and you have full access to our systems."

"Thank you," Max said into his headset. "Can you connect me with Alpha?"

"Yes, sir," the pilot said as Max pulled the tablet computer out and sat it on the seat.

Max heard a series of clicks over his headphones before Kate came on the line.

"Prince Fucking Charming, riding in to save me again," Kate said. "It's good to have you back."

"I wish I could say it was good to be back," Max said, pulling his pistol out of the bag and loading a fresh magazine. "No offence."

"I know it wasn't what you wanted, but we need you, Max. I need you."

"Then I'm here to help."

"Good. I've got your first mission."

"That wasn't part of the deal, Kate. I'm happy to head up field ops and coordinate the missions, but I don't want to be in the field anymore."

"Okay. I respect that. I just thought I would double check."

"What is the mission?"

"A truck full of microprocessors and sensitive equipment was hijacked on route to Pine Gap. It's loaded on your tablet."

Max gathered up his computer and scanned his ring on the sensor unlocking it. He opened the secure app and watched the files download. There were diagrams and schematics of the units and a bunch of IT gear. He had no idea what any of it actually did.

"I've got it," Max said. "Although I'm not really sure what I'm looking at."

"The computer chips run some of our most sensitive military equipment," Kate explained. "Everything from the radar and surveillance systems, through to drones and missiles. This batch was headed to Pine Gap. The Yanks are furious and the Brits aren't far behind them. I'm still looking into what they were going to be used for out there."

"The most secret base we have in the country, I'm sure it was important."

"That's an understatement."

"We know where they are being held?"

"We tracked the plane and think we've found them."

"Good. Who's on our team?"

"The team sheets are on the tablet."

Max closed the schematics and opened the files on the assault team. He saw a couple of familiar faces, but several he didn't know. He flicked to the final file and saw Jonnie 'Bravo' Belluci.

"Bravo's leading the team?" Max asked.

"Yes," Kate said. "He's been our go-to agent since you've been away. He's good."

"I remember. You don't need me on this one. I trust the kid."

"He'll be thrilled to hear it. I'll set up a link at the Wool Shed so you can watch the operation."

"Thanks, Kate. Anything else I need to know?"

"Spend some time at the Wool Shed training and getting back up to speed, then get me as many of those new recruits as you can."

"Yes, ma'am. I'll put them through their paces."

"I'm sure you will."

"I had a good teacher."

"Too fucking right, you did."

"How times have changed, hey? How's life in the office?"

"I'd prefer to be out with you boys any day, but when Blake left and you didn't come back, well, I was the one left to takeover. Certainly not what I expected."

"I hear you're doing great."

"I'm just getting by. The world is changing and we are under constant attack. I'm worried we'll miss something."

"We will do what we can, Kate. I've got your back."

"Thanks Prince Charming. I knew you wouldn't let me down."

"Never."

"It's good to have you back, kid. Let me know when you settle in. I'll call you later."

The call ended and Max smiled. He had originally been hesitant about rejoining AIS, but he had to admit to himself he was happy to hear Kate's voice. He hoped he would be able to help the new recruits and help plan missions. Maybe after all his years of service he could add value without having to go back into the field himself. He had done more than his fair share of killing and lost too many teammates and friends. It was someone else's turn, but if he could help ensure their safety in some way he was going to try.

Chapter Five

The helicopter landed and Max climbed down. He put his overnight bag over his shoulder and carried the pack the pilot had given him with the computer in it.

He walked across the lawn towards the old homestead as he had all those years ago when he had arrived at the Wool Shed for his initiation training.

He climbed the steps and opened the screen door and let himself in.

The original old farmhouse had been built over a hundred years ago. AIS had purchased it decades ago and had since made various upgrades from the massive kitchen and bathrooms through to the multiple structures they had built on the property to train the recruits.

The house itself was ringed by a large wooden deck. Inside there was a ring of rooms with doors which opened on one side out onto the veranda and the other into the large open space in the centre of the home.

In times gone by, long before AIS bought the property, the inner space housed a massive dining room table and grand piano. A room for entertaining and hosting extravagant parties. It was now home to over twenty recruits who each had a small rack for a bed and a chest at the foot of the bed for their belongings.

The opposite end of the room held a number of solid benches and tables which the recruits used as both dining tables and workspaces, with lectures provided by the instructors there daily after physical training.

Max remembered walking in for the first time, young and unsure of himself. It felt like school camp until the realisation set in that he was there to learn spycraft and combat.

He walked around the perimeter looking for a vacant instructor's room. He found one not far from the bathrooms. On his first day of training, Blake had been sitting in this very room. Max had been in a relationship at the time, but there was no doubting he and Blake had a connection from that very moment. He smiled at the thought and walked in.

Max sat his pack down on the table then took his clothes out of his overnight bag and placed them in the cupboard. He tossed the empty bag into the bottom of the cupboard and shut the door.

Max heard footsteps pounding up the steps and across the wooden deck. The screen door creaked open with a metallic grind as the hinges and piston opened. The dozens of footsteps marched along the hallway, until Max saw the first of the recruits spill into the open space.

They were all in their workout gear and looked exhausted. Their shirts were stained, dark with sweat and more than a few looked like they were going to be sick.

Max lent on the doorframe, watching them wander to their bunks. A couple of the recruits grabbed towels and a change of clothes, while others flopped on their beds to rest.

Max saw Liam and Luke enter, the two recruits who had helped Tom from the ring. Liam seemed to be the only one who had noticed Max in the doorway. He locked eyes with him and Liam nodded and looked away, self-consciously.

Tom was last through the door. His eyes carried black and purple bags, and his nose had a white strip of tape over it. He walked over to his bed and kicked off his shoes, boasting to his peers about beating them at this activity or that.

Liddle and Hulk walked in, and both noticed Max straightaway. Liddle smiled and turned to Hulk and he nodded.

"Freeze!" Liddle yelled.

The recruits all stopped in their places.

"Close your eyes," Liddle commanded and the recruits obeyed. "There is something that has changed in this room since we left. Without opening your eyes, raise your hand if you noticed the change."

The recruits shifted nervously. Precious seconds ticked by as Max smiled at Liddle. Max scanned the crowd until three recruits raised their hands.

"Karen," Liddle said, "what changed?"

"The bunks have moved," she said.

"Have they? Tom, I doubt you would have noticed any changes. You were too busy talking yourself up. What do you think changed?"

"The picture of the King has gone."

Max looked across the room to the photo of the smiling monarch hanging on the opposite wall and shook his head.

"Wrong," Liddle said. "Liam, what changed?"

"Agent Shaw is standing in the doorway," Liam said, pointing towards Max without opening his eyes.

"Correct," Liddle said, as Max noticed Tom steal a look. "Although you'll be interested to know he has a new title now, Deputy-Director of the Australian Intelligence Service and Head of Field Operations. Put simply, he's the new boss and only outranked by the Director herself. He will be completing your training and assessing which of you have what it takes to become AIS agents. Hulk and I will continue to be your day-to-day drill instructors."

The recruits shuffled slightly.

"Sir," Liddle said, turning to Max in a show of respect for his new boss and to show the recruits who was in charge. "Would like to say a few words?"

"Thank you, Agent Liddle," Max said. "Stand easy everyone and open your eyes."

The recruits all stood and faced Max as he stepped forward out of the shadows.

"Knowing your surroundings is the most important thing you will ever learn," Max said. "I could have had a gun aimed at your heads and took you out when you walked in. Why didn't any of you react?"

"We didn't see you," Karen offered.

"No, you didn't look."

"We've just been on the obstacle course for hours," Tom protested. "We're fucked."

Max walked down onto the main floor and weaved through the recruits until he arrived in front of Tom. He got right in his face.

"Do you think a terrorist will give two-fucks that you're tired?" Max asked calmly.

"You're not a terrorist," Tom said.

"But I could have been and you walked in here with your head up your arse! Let me tell you all something, there were times when I was in the field where I thought I was going to die. I could feel my body failing and system shutting down from exhaustion. But that didn't stop arseholes from wanting to shoot me or blow up a building. You have to dig deep and find a gear you didn't know you had, because not only does your life hang in the balance, but the lives of hundreds, maybe thousands could be in your hands. There is no excuse for tired. There is no excuse for not paying attention. There is no room for failure. If that sounds too hard for you, then pack your bags right now and fuck off."

The recruits all looked around nervously.

"I'll take it since none of you have moved, you are going to stay. I'll make you this promise, you will be pushed to your limits and beyond by this course, but it will be nothing compared to what you face in the field if you graduate. My job is to make sure that you can handle it and come home alive. If I think you don't have it, you'll be in a car back to town before the sun sets. If you want to do the right thing and quit, if you know you don't have it, I won't try to stop you going now or at any point in the future. But if you are here, you live, breath and shit by my rules, because they might save you someday. Now, Tom here has voiced some concerns about being tired. Anyone else?"

No one dared move, but their eyes darted around. Max turned back to Tom, just in time to see him rolling his eyes.

"You can all thank, Tom here," Max said. "He has a problem with authority and can't seem to control his emotions. You have one minute to be out on the front lawn ready. Move!"

The recruits all ran for their beds and pulled their shoes back on, while others ran for the bathrooms or kitchen to refill their canteens.

Hulk and Liddle crossed the floor and shook Max's hand.

"Welcome back, kid," Hulk said. "I knew you wouldn't disappoint me."

"If I can help them stay alive and get the job done, I'm here," Max said.

"Congrats, boss," Liddle said. "Honoured to have you here."

"Thanks, Mike. It's your show. You'll have the day-to-day with Hulk's support. I'm just here to help."

"Yes, sir."

"Head out and get them into lines."

"Got it," Liddle said, walking out the front door.

"He's a good agent," Hulk said, watching him leave.

"He'd have to be, I know you wouldn't have let him through the door otherwise."

"How was your tea at the Governor-General's place?"

"A mix of pride and worry for Blake, with a hint of extreme boredom talking to some of his new colleagues."

"They are trying on the nerves."

"Tell me about it. I got stuck with Senator Timms for what felt like an eternity."

"Ah, my old friend Senator Timms. He used to put me through my paces on the intelligence committee. I bet he was not too happy to have Ted and Blake sworn into the two most senior roles in Cabinet, especially since he's been in the Senate for what feels like a million years. Entitled prick."

"That's how long I thought I was talking to him for."

"You better get used to it. You'll have to deal with them more in your new role and as Blake's partner."

"I thought I left them behind when I quit working up The Hill."

"Sadly, it's hard to shake them off."

"Great."

"Anyway, fuck them. Blake can sort them out. What's the plan here?"

"I'm going to give the recruits a beasting. A couple of hours should do it, then I'll get a sit rep from Bravo on the microprocessors."

"I almost thought you'd have taken the chance to get on that mission."

"I'm done with field work."

"Fair enough. Having you back at AIS is enough. You'll get this lot into shape, and I have no doubt your advice and oversight of the missions will help save lives. Thank you, Max."

Max nodded and looked around the room to see the remaining recruits scrambling for their gear.

"I'll leave you to it," Hulk said, walking off and leaning on his cane.

Max watched his mentor hobble towards his room and close his door. He marched out on the veranda and saw the assembled recruits in lines on the grass before him, as the last two recruits ran out and down the steps, then found their places on the grass.

Max looked down at his watch. Two minutes and thirty seconds had passed since he gave the order.

"How long did I say you had to get out here?" Max yelled.

"One minute," the recruits replied.

"What?"

"One minute, sir!"

"It took you over two minutes. Drop and give me thirty push-ups, thirty sit-ups, then thirty burpees. In three, two, one. Go!"

The recruits dropped and started their push-ups. It was immediately obvious that their previous workout had pushed them, some were already struggling. The first three recruits spun on the grass into the sit-up position and started. A slow wave rolled over the recruits as one by one they got into position and started their sit-ups. The same three leapt to their feet and started their burpees, as Max took mental notes of the recruits faces and performance, while Liddle took notes on his tablet.

The sun was burning hot as the last of the recruits finished their burpees.

"Take out your canteens," Max ordered. "Inspection."

The recruits all held out their canteens and opened the lids. Max left the veranda and walked down onto the grass.

Row by row he inspected the canteens to see if they were full. Three of the recruits' water bottles were empty or only half full. Max just stared at them, until they poured the remaining water over their heads, having been at the Wool Shed long enough to know the rules. Failing to prepare was preparing to fail. They stood there wet and embarrassed.

"Pair up," Max ordered. "I want you to fireman carry your partner down to the gate and back, then switch. You don't stop until I say. Understood"

"Yes, sir!" the recruits yelled.

"Move!"

The recruits paired up and shouldered their colleagues' bodies, and started for the gate.

"Hurry the fuck up!" Max yelled and the recruits started to run as fast as they could with their fellow recruits hanging from their shoulders.

The recruits did four laps each, then Max called for them to return to their lines. They were exhausted and sucking in deep breaths.

"You, you and you, step forward," Max said, pointing to the recruits with the empty canteens.

They walked forward and stood in front of him.

"Turn and face your friends," Max said and they followed the command. "The rest of you move to the driveway and pick one of the rocks up, then move back into position."

The recruits all ran over to the driveway and picked up a heavy stone each which had been lining the driveway.

"Hold them above your heads, arms stretched," Max said and the recruits all raised the stones high into the air. "Don't lock those arms. You, get another one, that's pathetic."

One of the recruits ran over and switched his stone for a bigger one, then returned to the line and held it above his head.

"Now, you three," Max said to the wet recruits. "Their pain is because of you. You failed to prepare and now they are suffering. Imagine going into mission unprepared. People suffer. Either your team or civilians or maybe even you. Get to the kitchen and fill those bottles. Your friends here can't put those rocks down until you're back. Move!"

The three recruits ran off as nearly every eye followed them. Max studied the remaining recruits. He turned and looked at Liddle who was looking up, scanning then typing notes. Like Max, he was recording who was focused on the job at hand compared to those who were just wishing hateful shit on the others for putting them through pain.

The three returned and presented their filled canteens to Max.

"Back into line," Max said.

Two of the three recruits ran to get stones, while the third ran to the line, before realising his mistake and ran for the stones. One of the recruits at the back, lowered their rock as another went to lower his.

"Did I say you could lower those rocks?" Max asked. "Get them above your heads!"

The recruits all straighten and held the stones high on shaking arms. A couple had closed their eyes to concentrate on focusing their mind, trying to clear away the pain.

As the three recruits raised their stones, Max walked to the left of the homestead and stood on the grass.

"Twenty-seven of you will move over here and gently place the stones at my feet," Max said. "The other three will wait. Move!"

The bulk of the recruits moved towards Max and started piling up the rocks near him. The last of them put their rock down.

"Take a beat," Max said. "Get some water into you. Now, you three, put your stones in the pile, then one by one take a rock from the pile and return it to the driveway. Move!"

The three recruits did as commanded as the others took a drink from their canteens. Tom laughed as one of the recruits dropped a stone.

"Did I say you could laugh, Tom?" Max asked. "Drop your canteen and help put the rocks back."

Tom shook his head, but did as requested and jogged over to the rocks. He picked one up and ran it to the driveway.

When the recruits had taken in some water, Max ordered them back into lines. They looked up to him with a mix of fear and dread. He let them wait a full two minutes in the blazing sun in silence.

"Again," he said and the recruits dropped to start their push ups.

Chapter Six

Jonnie "Bravo" Belluci stood at the front of his four-wheel-drive with a map spread out on the bonnet. He was dressed from head to toe in black combat fatigues. He had dark face paint on and a pair of night-vision goggles sitting up on his head amongst his blond hair. He had a small headlamp on his forehead which cast just enough light to see in the dark night.

His team were similarly dressed, standing in a semicircle around the vehicle. A nervousness ran between them, silently building their adrenaline. It wasn't fear or excitement, just an eagerness to get the job done and done right. They were harnessing their fight or flight energy and channelling it into an easily accessible place to use as soon as Jonnie gave the call. They were ready for action.

"Right, you three take position delta at the rear of the compound," Jonnie said, running his finger over the map to the location. "You two are with me. We're out front. Any questions?"

"How many are we expecting inside?" one of the agents asked.

"We don't know, but we don't think it'll be more than six."

"Heat signatures?"

"The satellites haven't picked up any for a while now."

"That's strange."

"We think they might be shielding the building."

"So, we're going in blind?"

"I'm afraid so. Our job is to scout the building, then call in the cavalry."

The men all looked around at their peers, silently questioning the plan.

"This is what we signed up for," Jonnie said. "To do the impossible. To be the last line of defence. That's what the country needs us to do tonight."

Jonnie pulled another sheet of paper from his pocket and unfolded it on the bonnet.

"This is what we are looking for," Jonnie said, pointing to the new sheet of paper. "Microprocessors. Computer chips. They were headed for Pine Gap. Powerful little units, built in the US. Top Secret tech only the Americans, British and Australia have access to. The Yanks have teams not far from here and so do we. If we find the units, they will come in to secure the area. Got it?"

The men all nodded.

"Good. Let's move."

Jonnie folded the sheets of paper and stuffed them through the open window of his SUV. He led two agents through the thick bushland as three other members of his team peeled off and headed in the other direction.

Jonnie flicked off his headlamp and the world around them fell into darkness. He put his night-vision goggles on, in sync with his team. The landscape shone in an eery dark green, enough to make out the obstacles in their way.

They trekked through the bush, climbing over fallen trees and wading through narrow creeks until they saw the old barn-like shed emerge from the darkness.

Jonnie raised his fist and the two agents stopped behind him. They crouched and watched the old farm compound.

There was no movement and not a sound, bar the occasional bat flying overhead or rustling leaves as the breeze danced through the branches.

Jonnie looked back to his two teammates who shrugged questioningly. He turned back to keep a watch on the area.

"Bravo, we're in position," the delta leader said over Jonnie's earpiece. *"No movement here. It looks deserted."*

"Copy, Delta one," Jonnie said. "We've got the same. Move in for a closer look."

"Ack, Bravo. Moving now."

Jonnie and his team inched forward quickly and quietly, constantly scanning the area with their weapons raised.

Jonnie saw a floodlight on the top of a corner pole and shot it out with his silenced pistol, not wanting the sensor to alert anyone they were there by turning the light on.

They crossed the short distance from the tree line to the fence and entered the yard.

Jonnie reached the shed first and peered through the window. There were six bunks each with a man sleeping in it. Another man was sitting, propped against a wooden crate. He was likely the lookout, but his head was slumped forward. He must have fallen asleep on guard duty.

"Delta one," Bravo whispered into his comms unit. "Sit Rep?"

"Bravo, we're at the rear window," the agent said. *"Visual on six men sleeping in racks inside. No one at the rear of the building."*

"Ack. Seventh hostile inside back to you against the crate. No other contacts visible. Crate fits the description of the one we are looking for. I'll call it in. AIS Command, Bravo here, come in."

"AIS Command, copy."

"Visual seven hostiles. Eyes on the prize. Send back up, we are moving in."

"Roger that, Bravo. Back up is on route. ETA two minutes."

"Delta one, move in."

Jonnie slid the large iron door to the side and stormed into the shed. He put two bullets into the sleeping sentry as his two agents entered behind him and put bullets into the men in the bunks on their side of the shed.

On the other side of the old farm structure, the delta team entered and unloaded three bullets into each of the men in their camping beds on their side.

"Fan out, check the rest of the building," Jonnie commanded and his men started sweeping the shed looking for hostiles they may have missed.

"Clear," one of his men said.

"Clear."

"Clear."

The calls came in from his men. There was no one else inside.

Jonnie heard the engines in the distance of the incoming back up and of the helicopter blades thundering overhead. He knelt down over the sentry, still propped against the crate. Jonnie pressed his fingers into the man's neck and felt the ice-cold flesh of a body which had been dead long before he had fired his shots.

He tore off his night-vision goggles as a laptop computer came to life sitting on top of the crate.

"Sorry AIS, but you're too late," a figure said on the screen. "I had to make some personnel changes and move the microchips."

He was wearing a Ned Kelly style helmet, a long cylindrical metal-like mask, with a narrow slit for an eyehole, shielding his face.

"Hulk's really dropped the ball training you lot," he said. "No wonder the country has turned to shit. But don't worry, that'll all change soon enough."

Ned Kelly was replaced with a countdown timer. Five, four...

"Run!" Jonnie yelled and his men turned to flee.

Two, one...

Jonnie's two teammates reached the door as the explosion rang out. It tore the crate to pieces and the whole space erupted in orange flames and billowing black smoke.

Delta team was entombed by flames and the force threw their burning bodies into the walls.

Jonnie was thrown through the open door. Narrowly missing his teammates and the metal structure as he sailed through the air. His fatigues were on fire as he landed in the dry red soil face first.

He laid still, face down in the dirt, his back on fire, as the backup crews arrived.

Chapter Seven

Max was sitting alone in his room at the Wool Shed. It had been twenty-four hours since he had watched the failed mission unfold. Jonnie was in intensive care and the rest of his team were dead.

AIS were no closer to finding out who the man in the Ned Kelly helmet was and Max was running scenarios over in his mind. He could feel himself being drawn back in, but he was fighting it.

"Nothing you could have done, kid," Hulk said, walking in, leaning hard on his cane. "If you had been there, you'd be in the hospital with him or worse."

"I didn't see it," Max said. "I don't think I could have stopped it, even if I had. But. Shit. I'm not sure I can do this anymore, Hulk. Maybe I've been out of the game too long."

"That's bullshit. None of us saw it. This isn't on you."

"But it is. This is what I signed on for, to help these guys out in the field. How can I do that if I can't see the next move?"

"You've commanded teams in the field before."

"This is different."

"I know you feel responsible for them. I felt the same way every time I sent you into the field. Would you blame me for what happened in the field?"

"No. I had command in the field."

"Then why are you blaming yourself now? Jonnie and his team knew what they were getting into. Sometimes it doesn't work out how we hope it would."

Max nodded silently.

"Any progress on Ned Kelly?" Hulk asked.

"Not yet. Kate has a team on it."

"Well, until she comes back with something, we have a job to do here."

Max followed Hulk down the corridor to an office. It was a room about twice the size of his bedroom.

On one wall was a series of photos of the potential recruits. More than half had lines through their faces. The vast majority of them Max had never seen or met, they had been culled from the program before he arrived.

In the couple of days, Max had been back at the Wool Shed another seven had withdrawn from the course. Liddle had run the thick black marker over their photos ruling them out.

Max took a seat looking back towards the wall of faces. Hulk sat in a big old recliner to his left as Liddle stood and walked over to the wall.

"I have serious doubts about these three," Liddle said, pointing to three photos on the wall. "The psychologist agrees."

"Cut them," Hulk said. "Who else?"

"What about him?" Max asked, pointing at Tom's photo. "Does he have it?"

"He's one of the best. He reminds me of you actually."

"God was I that painful to deal with?"

"Still are, on occasions."

"Who else do you think has what it takes?"

"Tom and Liam are the two best performers," Liddle said, pointing to Tom's photo, before moving to Liam's photo.

"Show me the next five in line."

Liddle pointed out the candidates and explained their backgrounds. One was a university student, selected by tip off from a lecturer, the same way Max came to Hulk's attention all those years ago. The rest were a mix of military and police.

"And the bottom performers?" Max asked.

Again, Liddle strutted back and forth pointing to the bottom five recruits.

"Let's leave them in for now and see how they go today," Max said. "Anything under seventy-five percent is a fail."

"Understood," Liddle said as Hulk nodded in agreement.

"Set up the hostage scenario," Max said, standing. "I'll take the recruits for a run, then meet you over there."

"Got it."

"Hulk, can you please check in with Kate and let me know if they've made any progress?"

"Can do. I'll check on Bravo too."

"Thanks, Hulk. Keep me posted."

"Will do," Hulk said as Max left the room.

He walked out into the main hall where all the potential recruits were milling around.

"Get your training gear on and get outside," Max barked. "Two minutes."

The recruits all scrambled for their gear. A couple were already ready to go and they ran out onto the front lawn. Max walked out after them and stood on the grass with them, stretching.

Max checked his watch as the last recruit arrived on the lawn and started stretching with his peers.

"Thirty seconds," Max said. "Noted."

The recruits all looked at the late arrival and groaned knowing something painful was coming.

Max started bouncing on the spot.

"Follow me," Max said as he broke into a jog.

Max ran down the rocky driveway and down the dusty road, closely followed by the pack of remaining recruits.

After a kilometre, Max stopped abruptly.

"Get down!" Max yelled.

The recruits all downed to their stomachs mimicking his actions.

"Thirty push-ups," Max said, starting his own set.

The recruits started the exercise, falling into rhythm behind Max.

"Thirty burpees," Max ordered, pushing up and jumping to his feet for his first.

The recruits followed suit, completing their thirty burpees, followed by thirty sit-ups and a thirty second plank.

When they finished, Max got to his feet. They were all covered in sweat and dust.

"Let's move," Max said, bouncing on his feet again, before breaking into a run.

They repeated the circuit, after each kilometre. On the fifth, two of the recruits spewed. On the sixth, another three hunched over and hurled up their breakfasts.

Max ran the recruits through the thick bushland that made up the AIS secret training base. They passed a number of the training centres which had been constructed on site from the shooting range to the obstacle courses.

After ten kilometres, they arrived at six storey building. It was constructed from grey concrete and looked like a tower you see firefighters training on. Plain walls and boring concrete, but it was fitted with windows and doors like a normal building. This building was the hostage scenario building. It was equipped with wooden cut outs of terrorists and hostages, and in one of the rooms were a group of real-life people dressed as hostages and terrorists.

"You will be given an MP5 with paint cartridges," Max said as the recruits all stood trying to get their breaths. "You will enter two at time. There are an unknown number of terrorists holding several hostages. Your mission is to rescue the hostages. You two are first. When I say, get to the roof and meet Agent Liddle."

The first two recruits started to run for the building.

"Stop!" Max yelled. "I said, when I tell you to go. Did I tell you to go?"

"No, sir," one of the men said.

"Then what the fuck are you doing?"

"Sorry, sir."

"We haven't finished our circuit yet. Drop now, thirty push-ups."

The recruits all dropped to the ground and started their push-ups as Max walked into the building. He grabbed a bottle of water and walked into the observation room.

Liddle was inside and studiously counting and watching the recruits.

After ten burpees, one of the recruits stopped and sucked in some deep breaths.

"What are you doing?" another asked.

"He's not watching," the recruit said. *"How will he know? I don't want to do any more."*

"I don't think that's real smart."

"I don't think you're real smart," the recruit said, as two others stopped too.

Most of the recruits just powered on, ignoring the exchange.

Liddle typed notes into his tablet as Max wandered out of the room. He grabbed a crate of water and marched out onto the parade ground where the recruits were sitting getting their breaths after the circuit.

Max opened the plastic and started handing out the water bottles. The recruits all gratefully took a bottle, having emptied theirs on the route.

"How'd everyone go with that last session?" Max asked as he wandered through the group.

A few of the recruits looked about nervously, while others just stared at the concrete.

"All too tired to speak?" Max asked.

"It was fine, sir," Tom said.

"Good. What do you think is the most important characteristic of a spy?"

"Ability to keep a secret."

"From whom?"

"The enemy."

"Fair enough," Max said, pointing to another recruit. "What about you? What do you think is the most important characteristic of a spy?"

"Integrity," she said.

"Bingo," Max said. "More than anything a spy needs to have integrity, because without it, how could you ever trust them to get the job done? How could they keep their centre and know what's right from wrong? I mean, would you want someone on your team, protecting your back, without integrity?"

"No," she said.

"So, I'll ask again, how did everyone find that last session? Anything anyone wants to tell me? And, before you answer, I would say that personal responsibility is a major factor in integrity."

The recruits all shuffled nervously. Max just stared as if he had all the time in the world. Eventually one of the recruits who had stopped training put his hand up.

"Yes?" Max asked.

"I didn't complete the session, sir," he said.

"What did you do?"

"I stopped halfway through the burpees."

"Is that what I wanted you to do?"

"No, sir."

"Well, why the fuck are you still sitting there? Get your arse up!"

The recruit jumped to his feet and Max marched over to him, getting right in his face.

"Start again!" Max yelled. "Thirty push-ups!"

The recruit dropped to the ground and started his new set.

"Anyone else?"

Another recruit stood and owned up to their mistake, before Max ordered them to start a new set. He waited patiently for the ringleader to rise and admit his mistake, but he didn't budge. A nervousness hung in the air and even if Max hadn't of seen it with his own eyes, he would have sensed a deception.

Liam got to his feet and Max turned to face him.

"Liam, do you have something to tell me?" Max asked.

"Sir, I can't be sure, but I may have missed one or two reps," Liam said.

"I'm not worried about one or two reps, it's been a big session. I appreciate your honesty. That is what integrity looks like!"

Max pointed at Liam to emphasis his point.

Finally, the ringleader got to his feet.

"I missed a few too," the recruit said, dropping to his stomach to start his push-ups.

Max walked over and stopped in front of the ringleader.

"On your feet," Max said, but the recruit pushed on, ignoring the order.

Max reached down and grabbed him by the shirt dragging him up.

"I said on your fucking feet!"

The recruit stumbled around and took a step back, genuinely frightened of Max's aggressive tone and stance.

"Did I order you to start the circuit again?" Max asked, only inches from the recruit's face.

"No."

"No, what?"

"No, sir."

"Did I tell you to stop the set after only a handful of burpees?" Max said, pointing over his shoulder to the camera on the side of the building. "I was watching the whole time."

"No, sir," the recruit said, lowering his head.

"We can't afford to have people on the team who cut corners. Someone could get killed. But, more importantly, I don't want someone on my team who I can't trust. You're lack of integrity means I can't trust you. You're out. Report back to the Wool Shed. Get your stuff and fuck off out of my program."

"But."

"But nothing. Get out of my sight."

The two other recruits finished their sets and stood at attention as Max turned his focus on them.

"You admitted your mistakes," Max said after a full minute. "You owned it. That was the right thing to do. But if you disobey or ignore my orders again, you'll be following your friend there out the door. Am I understood?"

"Yes, sir!" they both yelled.

"Good. Get to the roof."

The two recruits ran to the building and up the stairs.

"Pair up and await your turn," Max said, walking for the observation room.

Over the next several hours Max and Liddle ran the recruits through the training program. They watched as the recruits in the pairs abseiled into the building and took out the wooden terrorists, before confronting the AIS trainers dressed as terrorists in a large room upstairs in the compound.

Hulk arrived and took a seat beside Max.

"How are they going?" Hulk asked.

"Most of them got through to the last stage," Liddle said. "But missed the sleeper."

"Good. That's what is supposed to happen. To get them thinking."

"Did you do this course, Max?"

"Similar," Max said. "But we had paint bomb boobytraps."

"Dramatic."

"I set one off in the homestead. It exploded and scared the shit out of me. To this day, I still check for trip wires in every doorway. I was covered from head to toe in fluorescent pink paint of figurative death. Hell of a lesson."

Liddle and Hulk both laughed.

"Lesson learnt," Hulk said. "You've got one team to go?"

"Yeah," Liddle said. "Tom and Liam."

"Good. That's why I came over. I want to see this."

Max looked to his old mentor and saw an eagerness in his eyes.

"What is it with these two?" Max asked.

"They've got it," Hulk said. "I can see it in their eyes. Especially Tom. I've been doing this a long time. I think we've found our next two enlistments."

"I guess we'll soon see. Bring them in, Mike."

Liddle radioed the trainer on the roof and the three agents waited, watching the screens.

Seconds later, the footage showed glass shattering as Tom and Liam tumbled through the window. They unhooked their ropes and covered each other as they made their way through the building.

In the first room, they found a wooden cut out of a terrorist holding a hostage around the neck. Tom and Liam both fired a single round each into the terrorist's head. Liam led the small team into the next room. This time the pop up was of a frightened young boy. Liam aimed at the wooden figure, but quickly lowered his gun. A second wooden figure sprung out of the cupboard. An angry looking man with a pistol. Liam fired and the paintballs hit head and chest.

Tom led them up the stairs, eager to show he could do exactly as Liam had done. At the top of the stairs, he went to burst into the room, but Liam held him back. Tom looked furious.

Liam pulled out a telescopic camera and fed it through the keyhole. He checked the little screen and saw a room full of people. Four terrorists standing guard with six hostages sitting at their feet. He showed the footage to Tom and he nodded and signalled he would take the two on the right.

Liam gently sat the camera and screen on the ground, and got into position next to the door.

Tom gave a quick countdown, then kicked open the door.

Tom was through first, closely followed by Liam. Tom fired two rounds hitting the AIS trainers dressed as terrorists on the right. Liam quickly covered his two targets in paintballs, as the terrorists squeezed off rounds of their own.

The paint pellets sailed passed Liam's head hitting the wall behind him. Another three rounds narrowly missed Tom and he turned to see the paint on the wall.

"That was fucking close," Tom said, turning back to the hostages. "Everything is going to be alright, we're here."

Tom started to walk towards the group with a cocky swagger as one of the hostages started to get to their feet. She had been sitting with her back to him and was turning fast as she stood. She was the sleeper amongst the hostages.

Tom saw her just as he felt Liam tackle him. The pair fell to the ground as the makeshift terrorist completed her turn and unloaded multiple paintball rounds into the space where Tom had been standing.

As they hit the ground, Tom opened fire, hitting the now revealed mock terrorist with the remaining pellets in his gun. She staggered back, covered in exploded paintballs. Eleven shots in total. She just shook her head as Tom and Liam got to their feet.

"That is what we would call excessive," Max said, walking into the room with Hulk and Liddle. "What if there was a second sleeper in the group?"

"There's not," Tom said as one of the hostages stood and shot a paintball into Tom's chest.

"Are you sure about that? Pity you're dead, but you didn't have any bullets left anyway. Now, I have to call your mum and your girlfriend and tell them you won't be coming home."

"Shit," Tom said, looking over to Liam.

"I'll definitely be calling Liam's family too," Max said, walking over and turning Liam around.

Three bright orange paint dots ran down his side and back.

"He saved your life," Max said, "but sacrificed his own in the process."

Liam looked down and saw one of the paint marks on his side. The adrenaline meant he hadn't felt them hit and was shocked to see it.

"Hero move, no doubt, kid," Max said. "But your teammate let you down by getting shot after you sacrificed yourself to save him. This was a team activity. You both died. Not sure we can call that a successful mission. Head out and gather the others. Run back to the homestead and get ready for this afternoon's lessons. Go!"

Tom and Liam both ran out of the room and down the stairs.

"Are you okay?" Max asked the trainer who had been pepper with paintballs.

"Yeah, fucking hell they sting," she said. "Is that the last one?"

"Yep."

"Good. I'm going to take a shower," she said as she and the other trainers all walked out.

"Thoughts?"

"They were supposed to fail," Hulk said. "Only way to learn."

"Let's review the lists and make the cuts."

Chapter Eight

The team had assembled in the rear of one of their stolen trucks to discuss the plan one final time. They had all been given codenames for the duration of their time together to maintain some semblance of anonymity, particularly from the authorities.

The guy calling the shots went by the Ned Kelly, following in the infamous footsteps of an Australian bushranger and outlaw from 1870s. Like the real Kelly, Ned was rugged and ruthless. He had a beard, but nowhere near the long bushy mess adorned by his namesake, and his hair was short and neat around the sides, while holding some styled length on top. He was a tall, strong and imposing figure. Clearly fit and athletic.

The first of his recruits to the modern-day Kelly Gang was Joe Byrne. He had boyish features, and was thinner, slightly shorter and less of a dominating figure than Ned. He had blond hair and a swimmer's build.

The two men were in charge of the rest of the crew who were all named after other famous Australian bushrangers. There was Ben "Brave" Hall, Daniel "Mad Dog" Morgan, John "Bold Jack" Donohoe, Alexander Pearce, Captain Thunderbolt and his wife Mary Ann Bugg, and Jessie "The Wild Woman" Hickman.

Brave was a former naval officer. He was a plain man and carried a gruff facial expression and attitude. He had long dark hair in a semi mullet and a thin moustache. He was build like a rugby hooker, short and stocky, but fast and strong.

Mad Dog was the member of the gang who was the closest to resembling the real bushranger. He had a long sharp nose and bushy beard and wild brown hair. He was also quite mad. He loved explosives and was expert in using a huge variety of weapons. He'd met Ned Kelly decades before and their unlikely friendship grew. He'd once been a Federal Police Officer, but now lived a life on the other side of the tracks.

The medical expert on the team was Bold Jack. He had a young Einstein look about him. Greying unkempt hair and an almost comical look in his eyes. He was one of the smartest in the group and had been recruited by Ned to the cause after months of conversation about the troubles the country and the world face, and only possible solution to fixing it.

Pearce was a former junkie who'd spent years on the streets turning tricks to fund his addictions, until Ned had found him. Ned saw the real man and the real pain he'd felt which turned him into the homeless drug addict. He helped rehabilitate him and he'd been Ned's hired muscle since that day.

Ned had given the man they all knew now as Captain Thunderbolt his name after hearing about his exploits escaping a maximum security goal in his youth, similar to the real Thunderbolt. He was far from the gentleman bushranger though, he was tough as nails and merciless in every aspect of his life, bar one, he's devotion to his wife.

The woman they called Mary-Ann Bugg, was his real wife. The pair had met at school and became childhood sweethearts. She was his ride or die and had been the getaway driver from him on many of his sketchy pass dealings. They had almost the same personality, but she was the brains of the couple.

The final member of the gang was The Wild Woman. She was slightly older than the others and had dark tanned skin. It wasn't to the point of leathery, but it was on its way. She'd been in the Army before her dishonourable discharge for theft and assault. She had a no-nonsense attitude and could match it with the men in a canter. She was often the voice of commonsense in the group and several times during the planning of this mission she'd questioned Ned and his goals, but she remained committed to their purpose.

After they finalised their individual missions, they went there separate ways into the night.

The darkness of the cloudy night hung over the old industrial estate. It was warm and still. Not a breath of wind and eerily silent.

An old red brick and corrugated iron factory sat behind a rusted metal fence which was topped with coils of new razor wire. The gates were electronically locked. An ancient looking control panel, covered in dust and grime sat beside it.

Out of the darkness, a man dressed completely in black jogged across the road and up to the control panel. He studied the unit and saw one button which was free from grime and dirt. He raised his gloved hand and pressed the asterisk on the keypad. The dirty dummy control panel folded up revealing an ultra-hi-tech biometric scanner.

Four similarly dressed men, joined their leader at the unit. One of the men reached into his bag and pulled out a severed hand. It has been cut off at the wrist. He past it to his leader.

He pressed it to the biometric sensor and a red glow emanated out under it, before the lock on the gate clicked open. As he took the bloody hand away, the old control panel dropped back into place and the men entered the compound.

Ned Kelly, was through the gate first, closely followed by his number two, Joe Byrne. The other three – Brave, Mad Dog and Bold Jack – followed them onto the grounds.

Byrne ran ahead to the door on the side of the red brick building. A similar control unit hung on the wall, but this time the biometric reader was a retinal scanner. Byrne pulled a small plastic bag from his satchel and held it up to the scanner. A red light scanned across the plastic revealing the bloodied eyeball inside.

As Ned and the others arrived, the door lock released and Byrne pushed it open.

Mad Dog and Bold Jack marched off towards the large roller doors and started getting ready, while Ned, Byrne and Brave headed for the elevator.

The lift was housed in a box which stood boldly as the only real object in the whole complex. It was surrounded by vast open concrete space. Ned pressed the call button and the elevator doors open. He typed a six-digit combination into the keypad and the metal box sank into the ground underneath the old building.

At the bottom, the lift doors pinged open and the gang of three walked out. The lights automatically came on, lighting up the cavernous facility. It looked like a sweeping laboratory covered in white tiles and glass walls. Embossed on the glass was the logo of the Commonwealth Scientific and Industrial Research Organisation or CSIRO.

Ned led them down a corridor until he found the room he was looking for and nodded to the other two. They kept walking as he entered the room.

Ned wandered into the office. He looked around and saw the huge painting of a rolling paddock during a storm. Rain was pouring down over the crop and a bolt of lightning was striking a tree off in the distance.

He walked over and pulled the picture off the wall, revealing a large wall safe. Ned tossed the painting onto the floor and set about opening the safe. He typed in the first code, then a second, before the solid door opened.

Inside there were a bunch of files and a tablet computer. Ned reached in and took them all. He put them into his backpack and left the room.

He walked down the hallway to find Brave and Byrne loading pallets of metal boxes onto two huge elevators with forklifts. Each industrial lift already had two pallets as the two men drove on with a third pallet on each of their forklifts.

Ned climbed onto the lift with Byrne as it started to rise.

The two elevators rose up through the darkness, until the huge metal door folded open in the old industrial building above. The base of the elevators lifted until they were perfectly level and flush with the concrete floor.

Mad Dog and Bold Jack were waiting and opened the roller doors, as two trucks backed into the compound and up to the doors. As they pulled into position, Pearce and Thunderbolt opened the roller doors on the rears of their respective trucks.

Byrne and Brave drove the first of their pallets over and loaded them on the trucks, which sat idling ready to leave.

As they loaded their last pallets, Ned heard sirens in the distance.

"Time to go!" Ned yelled.

Mad Dog climbed into the rear of the truck with Pearce and Bold Jack joined Thunderbolt. Brave pushed the last container in then reversed his forklift back. He climbed down then jogged over to Mad Dog who handed him an AR-15 assault rifle.

Byrne climbed out of his forklift and walked briskly. As he past the back of the truck, Thunderbolt tossed him an AR-15. He walked to the front of the truck and climbed up into the cab into the passenger seat beside The Wild Woman. He looked over and saw Ned climbing up into the cab of the other truck.

Ned gave them the roll out signal as he loaded his rifle beside the woman they called Mary Ann Bugg. Mary Ann hit the accelerator as the roller door lowered on the back of her rig. She drove out through the gates and headed west.

The Wild Woman drove out and headed east.

The empty compound stood in the darkness, before the red and blue lights flashed over it and the sirens broke the night-time silence. The first officers to arrive surveyed the scene, but the two trucks were nowhere to be seen, just an empty old building in an old industrial estate.

Chapter Nine

It was five thirty in the morning. Max sat in the large kitchen at the bench drinking coffee and eating a slice of toast, while reading a briefing on a break in at a secret CSIRO facility.

His mobile started to ring. It vibrated across the bench top.

"Morning, mister," Max said, answering the call.

"Hi, Max," Blake said. "How are you going out there?"

"Things are fine out here. Won't be long now until we put our final list together."

"That's good to hear. How are you settling back in with AIS?"

"It's somehow like riding a bike, while simultaneously being like I've never ridden one before in my life."

"It'll be fine, Max. It'll take a few weeks to get used to it. You've been out of the game for a while."

"That's the problem, Blake. I've been out for too long. The years I spent away are showing. I don't know if I can do it."

"I know you can. They need you. Especially with Jonnie out of action."

"How is he?"

"He was flown here for surgery. I went to see him yesterday. He is still in a coma, but the doctors are feeling good."

"I should have seen it."

"Everyone missed it. You of all people know how this works, Max."

"What if I keep missing things?"

"You won't."

"I wish I had your confidence."

"You can have some of mine until yours returns."

"Anyway, how are you going? How's the new gig?"

"It's going well. A lot to get across, but I'm getting there. My office is coming together. I've pinched a couple of my old AIS staff to come up the Hill, so that's helping."

"I still can't believe you're the Deputy Prime Minister. It's amazing, Blake. Such a massive achievement on so many levels. I'm so proud of you."

"Thanks, Max. I'm still pinching myself. I can't wait 'til you can come home."

"Me too."

"I miss you."

"I miss you too."

"Anyway, I knew you'd be up, so I wanted to call before the day got away from us both."

"It is so good to hear your voice."

"I love you, Max. Have a good day."

"I love you too. Keep an eye on Jonnie, will you?"

"Of course. I'll talk to you later."

"Bye," Max said, ending the call as Hulk walked in and took a seat.

Max poured him a mug of coffee.

"I'm not sure I can think of many days that made me prouder than when I found out you two were engaged," Hulk said, genuinely glowing with a fatherly-like tone which Max wasn't used to. "Blake is my longest serving member of staff and the person I trust most in the world. He has been nothing but loyal and professional. A true friend and confidant. Now the fucking Deputy Prime Minister. Jesus, I didn't see that coming."

"Me either," Max laughed. "You know how I feel about politicians and now I'm engaged to one."

"I grew up in a different time, Max. I've seen so much change in the world. Christ, I've changed so much over the years. Thirty years ago, you couldn't be open about who you were and before that, well, it was a lot worse. I'm ashamed I didn't do more to fight for people like you and Blake."

"You're right, things have changed. We're incredibly lucky, compared to those who came before us. But it's still not going to be easy."

"No, it's not."

"But, we have amazing support networks and friends. Thank you for believing in us and supporting us."

"I always will, Max. You know, I don't speak about this much, but you remind me of my son. He was like you in nearly every way."

"What happened?"

"We had a falling out. I was away so much and stubborn and strict with him when I was home. I didn't see much of him and when I did it wasn't good."

"I'm sorry to hear that. Do you know where he is?"

"He fell in with the wrong crowd and I disowned him. It's the biggest regret of my life. I should have helped him."

"It's not your fault. Sometimes people need to walk their own paths. It's their choice."

"I tried to force him to follow in my footsteps, but it backfired."

"Maybe it's not too late. We have the resources to find him, if you want to see him."

"It's too late. I tracked him down years ago, while you were away. He was certainly not my son anymore."

"I'm sorry, Hulk."

"Don't be, kid. You've been more like a son to me, than he ever will be. I'm not sure I've ever said this to you, but I'm proud of you. You've been through more shit, than anyone I know, but you still keep going. As I said, I couldn't be happier that after all that, you and Blake have found each other. I hope you find happiness."

"Thank you, Hulk."

"Anyway, enough of this emotional shit. What have we got?"

"I was reading the overnight reports. The only one I was really interested in, other than a couple of reports from agents we have overseas, is this one. A secret facility owned by the CSIRO in Adelaide was robbed. I didn't even know CSIRO had secret facilities."

"They have a few. Top Secret research department. Often linked up with the Defence Science and Technology Organisation. Weapons development and sometimes industrial sabotage or defence. They created Wi-Fi and a whole raft of other products we take for granted. Some very smart people there. What did they take?"

"Wollunqua."

"The Rainbow Serpent?"

"Yes, according to the Warramunga Aboriginal peoples from the Northern Territory. Wollunqua is the rain and fertility god. CSIRO named the rain seeding technology they developed after it."

"Rain seeding?"

"Basically, chemicals added to the air and clouds to increase rainfall."

"Why would that be developed in a secret lab?"

"No idea. Kate's tracking down the lead scientist to get some more information."

"Any news on the microprocessors?"

"The Americans think they were all destroyed in the blast. They found enough small fragments in the rubble to feel optimistic."

"And you?"

"It doesn't make sense. Why go to the trouble of stealing them, then blow them up? We saw the countdown on Jonnie's camera. It was deliberately triggered for our arrival."

"I agree, but I don't have any answers."

"Me either. AIS is tracing the signal which set off the attack. We are hoping to back trace it to the source, but I'm not optimistic. Plenty of time's past, they've probably moved on by now. We will find them."

"Then what?"

"I'm going to kill them for what they did to Jonnie."

Max got up grabbed some fruit and began chopping it aggressively. Hulk smiled to himself and took a sip of his coffee. Max was back. He hated himself for dragging him back in when he was just getting his life sorted, but he was the best agent he had ever put into the field and he personally couldn't do it anymore. His illness was taking over and he needed Max. The country needed Max.

Max had given up so much, both willingly and unwillingly, as an agent of the Australian Intelligence Service. His former fiancé had been murdered. His best friend had died after turning traitor. He'd been shot and stabbed, and he had killed countless terrorists, which had turned him cold and brutal in most aspects of his life except for one – his love for his friends and of course for Blake. That love drove him with the deep desire to never let anyone feel the pain he had felt on losing friends and family to terror, and to protect his loved ones. He'd saved the country and the world from both terrorists and malicious state actors alike, and they had thrown everything at him, but he kept turning up and returning fire.

Hulk knew he was personally responsible for all Max's pain. He'd recruited him, trained him at the Wool Shed and put him in the field. He'd supervised him and given him missions, which by all rights he shouldn't have survived. He'd pushed and pulled the strings, and set the course of Max's life on a path to great pain and suffering, but it had all been for the greater good. Max was simply the best agent AIS had ever sent into the field and getting him back in the game would be his legacy. A legacy built on protecting the country he loved and the millions of people in the western world who would never know the sacrifices he and his team had made. He felt guilt, but also tremendous pride, in the man Max had become.

When the potential recruits all surfaced and ate their breakfast, Max took them on a short run, before putting them through their paces on one of the obstacle courses.

By this point in the course, the recruits had been training and studying, and had been tested to their limits for weeks. They were fatigued and some were close to breaking point.

When they returned from the obstacle course, Max surveyed the room. There were only twelve potential recruits left. He worried for a moment he may have cut too many from the program, but he reminded himself of the risks. They were a risk to the operation, a risk to their teammates and a risk to themselves if they couldn't handle it. He was happy with the progress of the final twelve and was leaning towards keeping quite a few of them.

Max's phone rang, interrupting his thoughts.

"Prince," Max said, answering the call.

"It's Alpha," Kate said. "We've got a lead on the Kelly Gang."

"The Kelly Gang?"

"That's what the boys here have taken to calling them, after the leader appeared in the Ned Kelly helmet."

"Got it. What's the lead?"

"We've intercepted some chatter that they may be making a play for the mint."

"The mint. Why?"

"I guess they need the cash."

"It's a secure building and they only make coins there."

"They've been talking about Melbourne. They actually mean the Reserve Bank, not the Royal Australian Mint."

"They definitely won't get in there, but just to be sure, let's double the guards and set up surveillance points in concentric circles out from the compound. We can swoop in if or when they cross the first line."

"I want a team on the ground. If Ned Kelly is there, I want him interrogated on the spot."

"Who are you sending?"

"Well, I was hoping you'd want to do it? Jonnie and his team have us down an assault team. It should be a walk in the park. I've got the local police and feds on the scene already. They'll handle the takedown, you handle the interrogation."

"Okay Alpha, but only because it gets me in a room with the fucker who put Jonnie in the hospital."

"Good. The jet will be there in fifteen minutes. Take the top three with you. Be good to start blooding them in."

"They aren't ready."

"It's observation, not field work. Just ease them into it."

"I'm not sure that's a good idea."

"Noted."

"But do it?"

"Sooner they experience it, the sooner we can put them to work."

"Yes, ma'am."

Chapter Ten

The Gulfstream had taken off from a small airstrip at the Wool Shed and raced south towards Victoria.

Max had reluctantly agreed to take Tom, Liam and Karen with him on the mission. Liddle and Hulk both agreed, they were the top three potential recruits and the most likely to succeed in passing the course.

Max had spent the ninety minutes or so on the plane briefing and preparing the small team for the operation. All three treated the briefing with the respect it deserved and listened intently. They had run scenarios, but this was real life. Max stressed this repeatedly.

After the briefing, he handed over three pistols and three hunting knives, and showed the recruits how to holster them under their civilian clothes, so they wouldn't be seen. He also passed over three laminates which held a photo of each recruit and their names, as well as the crest of the Commonwealth of Australia and the Australian Intelligence Service logo. He told them they were only to be used to get through police lines. They were otherwise not to be shown to anyone.

An AIS Landcruiser was waiting for them at Melbourne's Tullamarine Airport. They climbed in and the driver sped off towards the Reserve Bank of Australia's note printing facility in the city.

Max could feel the anxiety of the recruits in the backseat as they drew closer.

The driver turned into a carpark several blocks from the facility. He drove up to the fourth floor and shut off the engine.

Max climbed down and walked over to a group of police officers all dressed in plain clothes.

Robbie Street was the field commander. Max shook his hand and introduced his team. Street retrieved a map and laid it out on the bonnet of his car.

"Here is the compound," Street said, drawing his finger across the map. "We have a hard border with concrete barriers around the block as an extra layer to the impressive gates and security of the actual facility. Uniformed officers, highly visible on site. They are our last line of defence."

"Good," Max said. "And your team here is ready to go?"

"Yes, sir."

"Excellent, thank you," Max said, turning to face the police officers and his three recruits. "Right listen up. I want everyone positioned around this line."

Max drew a line in a circle around the RBA facility.

"When you see the targets approaching, you call it in," Max said. "We will move backup into position on your location. Do not engage the target. The target will travel through this first line, until they reach the hard border Street just mentioned. At that point, we will close in from behind and seal off the exits."

"We have officers stationed in cars and trucks throughout the area to move into position to block roads," Street said. "Agent Shaw here has operational command. No one moves without his say. Understood?"

The assembled officers all agreed and nodded.

"Good," Max said. "Let's move out."

The larger group broke up into smaller teams, then moved out, careful to put gaps in leaving times to avoid drawing attention.

"Tom," Max said. "Go with Street. Karen move out with that group over there. Liam, you're with me."

"Yes, sir," the recruits all said and moved into position.

Max watched as each group left the garage and walked out into the street. He and Liam looked down as the officers took up positions on corners and near cafes. In their civilian clothes they blended in with the crowd or at least enough to not raise suspicion from passing motorists.

Max and Liam left the parking complex and casually strolled down the road as if they were two mates just chatting on their way to the pub. They passed several of the other units, but didn't acknowledge them. They just kept walking.

Max had chosen a position closer to the RBA, about halfway between the facility and the outer ring of plain clothed officers with a view to the front gate.

Max took a seat at an outdoor table and told Liam to go in and order two drinks. He sat watching the passing traffic and pedestrians, and wondered when they would hit the facility.

A full hour past. Max and Liam nursed their drinks as they waited.

"I think I've got something," Street said over their comms units. *"Small truck. Coming in hot. North side."*

Max turned to his left and looked back up the road to see the small moving truck racing towards them.

"This is Cooper," another officer said. *"We've got incoming too. Small truck. Fast, real fast. West side."*

"This is Johnson," another officer said. *"I'm in the chopper. We've got a bird coming in fast from the south."*

Max's mind was reeling. The Kelly Gang seemed more organised than they had given them credit for, but he thought they would still be able to stop them. He was about to give out the orders, when an explosion rang out from his right. He turned quickly to see the front of the RBA note printing facility ripped open from the inside and engulfed in flames.

"Take them out!" Max ordered over his comms unit, running towards the site and looking back to Liam who was in tow behind him. "Get your gun out."

Max drew his own pistol as Liam pulled his out from under his hoodie.

Behind them, a team of officers, including Tom and Street opened fire on the small moving truck. Its windscreen shattered and the driver was peppered with bullets. The little truck slammed into a nearby shopfront and came to a stop in a shower of glass and tearing metal.

As the team went to move in, the truck exploded and tore huge chunks out of the concrete and brick buildings and the road surface. The shockwave blasted down the roads shattering windows as it raced away from the blast.

Max turned back to see billowing black smoke streaming into the air, licked with orange flames which reached to the height of the building.

"The truck is packed with explosives," Max yelled into his comms unit just as a second blast rang out.

Several blocks away, the second moving truck erupted in the busy street, instantly killing several pedestrians and officers as they moved in. The blast set off a similar wave of shattering glass and towering smoke and flames. Diesel poured out from beneath the truck and quickly caught fire, spreading the flames to nearby cars which exploded from the extreme heat. Matching smoke and flames rose into the street as people screamed and ran for their lives.

Max kept running towards the RBA. The police at the perimeter had started to move in and were shooting at two men who had walked through the devastated space where the front wall had been. The men were both covered from head to toe in metal looking armour. Like the original Kelly Gang, they strode across the path and opened fire back towards the police officers as bullets pinged off their armour. The pair stepped to the side, away from each other, as a small forklift charged through the gap in the wall and out onto the lawn. It was carrying a small shipping container, about half the size of a normal unit.

The forklift sat it down then reversed away from the container, as the chopper came in overhead. It was a modified Tiger helicopter, decked out with all the latest tech and weaponry. It hovered above the container, then fired a missile.

The missile trailed through the air with its distinctive white smoke drawing a line towards its target. The police helicopter didn't have time to react. The missile sliced through the thin metal then exploded.

The chopper was annihilated. Its blades shot off at incredible speed as the hunk of burning and twisted steel fell from the sky. It landed on a car and triggered multiple explosions as fuel and oil caught fire, filling the air with more smoke and flames.

Max and Liam both opened fire at the Tiger, but their bullets bounced off the military chopper harmlessly.

Four cables dropped from the helicopter and Max followed them down to see Ned Kelly and his two co-conspirators on top of the small container. Max and Liam, and the remaining officers took aim and unleashed on them.

The bullets bounced off the metal armour with orange sparks.

Ned returned fire, as the other two attached the cables to the container. When it was secure the Tiger tilted towards Max.

"Oh fuck me!" Max said, grabbing Liam. "Run!"

The pair ran, closely followed by the police officers as a second missile shot out from under the small wing of the chopper. It slammed into the road where they had just been standing and detonated. It tore up the tarred surface and shattered the concrete barriers. Geysers erupted as water mains burst and towering clouds of dirt ruptured up, before showering everything and everyone beneath.

The shockwave threw Max and Liam forward, as two officers behind them disappeared in the flames. Another three officers were violently thrown like ragdolls into the nearby cars and buildings.

Max laid on the road. His head was aching and his ears were ringing. He rolled onto his back and saw the helicopter rising into the air with its stolen container hanging below. The three men on the container all held tightly to their nearest cable. Max saw Ned and felt as if he was looking straight at him, then Ned saluted him, still wielding his gun, before the chopper raced off across the sky.

Max gingerly got to his feet. Liam was laying at his feet. He had a deep cut on his forehead and had lost quite a bit of blood. Max dropped to his knees and took his own jumper off. He used it to hold the cut closed on Liam's head.

Tom arrived with Street ten paces behind him.

"Fuck me, that was intense," Tom said, his excitement and adrenaline pumping. "Fuckers must have been in the building already. We didn't see that coming. Shit. Whoa."

Max just looked up at him without saying a word. Tom looked down and saw Liam for the first time.

"Oh shit," Tom said. "Is he okay? What happened?"

"He needs an ambulance."

"They're on their way," Street said, arriving out of breath from trying to keep up with Tom. "Are you okay?"

"Not exactly," Max said, looking back to Tom. "Where is Karen?"

"Don't know."

"Go find out."

"Yes, sir," Tom said, running off.

"They weren't ready," Max said, shaking his head. "They shouldn't have been here."

"Tom was on point, Max. He took out the driver with the first shot. The rest of us shot a corpse. He took control and held us back from the truck, and got me into cover as it went up. He was ready."

Max just nodded and looked back down to Liam.

An ambulance arrived as other emergency service vehicles drove through the area looking to help. Two paramedics climbed out and took over from Max. They set about patching him up, before taking him to hospital.

"Agent Shaw," Tom said over the comms unit. *"It's Tom. Karen is fine. A bit shaken up from the blast, but she's okay. Same can't be said for the others here. Jesus."*

"Ack," Max acknowledged. "Both of you get back over here."

"Okay, on route."

"Agent Shaw?" a security guard said as he approached.

"Yes," Max said.

"This is Ian Auld the CEO of the facility."

"Agent Shaw," Auld said, holding out his hand to shake Max's. "You're in charge I understand."

"That's right," Max said, holding up his blood-soaked hands to excuse him from shaking hands. "What did they take?"

"Fifty million dollars."

"Jesus."

"That's not all. They also have the designs."

"What designs?"

"The detailed designs of our currency. It means with the right process, it would be almost impossible to tell real money printed here with counterfeit money they print."

"Best case scenario?"

"They print money for themselves to use and get rich."

"Worst case scenario?"

"They print billions, flood it into the economy and drive-up inflation. Hyperinflation would crash the economy."

Chapter Eleven

"It's been a while since I studied economics," Mad Dog said as he swung back on the old office chair.

"You don't have the brains to have studied economics," The Wild Woman said to the laughs of the others. "And primary school math doesn't count."

"Well, explain it to me."

"Oh shit, I don't have any crayons and butcher's paper, nor do I have the patience to teach your dumb arse."

"Just quickly give me the high-level overview. Two-minute briefing."

"Okay. Imagine you have one hundred dollars in your wallet."

"Yep."

"Then overnight the RBA prints lots of money, thousands of one hundred dollar notes and puts them into circulation. It means the next day your hundred dollars is worth less, because there are so many more hundred dollars out there."

"But it's still a hundred dollars."

"Yes, but the same hundred dollars doesn't have the same buying power."

"Hey?"

"He'll never get it," Bold Jack said, standing by the fridge sipping a coffee.

"Okay how about this? If you print more money and circulate it through the system, it means there is more money for people to buy stuff, right?"

"Yeah."

"But if there isn't enough stuff to buy, because now everyone has lots of money and starts buying up everything, then the prices go up. Simple supply and demand. Demand from people to buy stuff goes up 'cause they've got cash to spend, but supply goes down 'cause more people are buying stuff, meaning there are less things to buy and production and imports haven't increased to keep up. It means the people selling things, will put the prices up because the items are rare and people are willing to pay for it."

"But couldn't the country just import more shit from China or wherever to sell or start producing more?"

"You can't set up factories overnight. Can't get ships here in hours. And, even if you could where are the workers to stack the shelves and sell the products? A massive flood of money into the system will cause hyperinflation. A big enough inflow will crash the value of the dollar and eventually collapse the economy. All because what you bought yesterday for one hundred dollars costs more than one hundred dollars today. Got it?"

"Yea, yes," Mad Dog said sheepishly. "Got it."

"Bullshit," Bold Jack said and everyone laughed again.

"Luckily, I didn't hire him for his brains," Ned said, walking into the room. "Mad Dog's got other skills. You all have skills and motivations which have brought you here. We are about to achieve what most people would believe is unthinkable. We will take this country back to the stone age, then we'll move on to the next country and the next, repeating our missions over and over until we create balance."

"A lot of people are going to die," Joe Byrne said, looking around the room to his fellow travellers. "It's time to leave all your doubts behind. Time to pledge yourselves to the cause. Time to do what we must to save the world."

The assembled team all nodded, collectively agreeing with Byrne's statement.

"Let's do this," Ned said, walking over to the fireplace and drawing the long metal rod from the coals.

Ned rolled up the sleave on his left arm and pressed the glowing red hot brand to his forearm. His skin smoked and blistered as the brand took hold. He clenched his teeth, but didn't make a sound over the sizzling of his own flesh.

He pulled the brand off and drove it back into the coals to heat it again, then walked over to a drum of water.

"I won't do it to you," Ned said, pushing his red and swollen arm into the drum of water. "You must do it yourselves to show your commitment to our cause. Who is next?"

There were a few anxious looks, before The Wild Woman leapt from her chair.

"Pussies," she said, walking over to the fire and drawing the brand. "For humanity and the earth."

With that, The Wild Woman pressed the brand to her skin and clenched her jaw letting the iron permanently mark her arm.

She tossed the iron back into the fire and walked over to the drum and doused the burning skin in the water.

As the heat and pain started to calm, and the others lined up to brand themselves, The Wild Woman withdrew her arm from the bucket and looked down at her forearm.

In cursive script her red and blistered skin read, *pro humanitate et terra*.

For humanity and the earth.

Chapter Twelve

"This isn't good enough!" Max spat into the phone. "I want to know who these people are. They are outsmarting us and outclassing us at every turn. I want to find them and take them out."

"Agent Shaw," an AIS analysis said, *"we are working as hard as we can to identify the people responsible for the attacks. We will find them."*

"They know we are onto them and they know our moves. Start with current and former agents of the AIS and our sister agencies. There has to be someone in there with inside knowledge."

"Yes, sir."

"Don't let me keep you," Max said, ending the call. "Fuck."

Max paced in the small office at the Wool Shed trying to piece it all together.

On the wall, the photos of the recruits had been condensed into a small band on the right. Ten candidates remained and they were listed from the best to worst down the wall. The recruits who hadn't made the cut had their photos removed.

On the left, taking up three quarters of the wall were CCTV print outs of Ned Kelly and his gang. They were all wearing masks or some form of face covering, while they had grainy footage of a woman driving a truck outside the CSIRO lab. The AIS analysts were working to clean up the image and get an ID.

The wall also held photos of the stolen items – the microprocessors, the money and the note designs, and the cloud seeding tech, Wollunqua.

"Agent Shaw?" a security agent said over the intercom.

"I'm here," Max said. "What is it?"

"Sir, we have an incoming helicopter. Callsign AIS, double one, eight, seven. Are they cleared to land?"

"Occupants?"

"Two scientists from CSIRO and an AIS pilot."

"Confirmed?"

"Yes, sir. It left Canberra on schedule with no course deviations."

"It's cleared for landing. Stand down perimeter defences."

"Yes, sir. Ten minutes out."

"Thank you."

Kate had tracked down the lead scientists of the Wollunqua project and had ordered them to brief Max on it. AIS agents had collected the scientists and marched them straight onto the chopper.

Hulk walked into the room as Max stared blankly, his mind whirling and calculating, as he tried to connect the dots.

"Australia's fascination with bushrangers has always amazed me," Hulk said, taking a seat and pointing his walking stick at the photo of Ned Kelly on the wall. "Take this son-of-a-bitch, he's a cop killer, a thief, a criminal. Nowadays, people would be screaming in the streets to lock him up. But a romanticised version of history tells us, he was the victim of police persecution. He turned to violence against the police after a particularly vicious encounter with the constabulary in his own home and the arrest of his mother. He vowed to get vengeance against those who wronged her. He was only a teenager when the troubles began. He was the man of the house after his father died after a stint in gaol. You know, his dad was a convict transported to Australia from England. Anyway, it's a compelling piece of history regardless of which side you fall on."

"You seem to know a lot about him," Max said, staring at the picture.

"I used to read stories about bushrangers to my son," Hulk reflected. "When he was little, he had a picture book which really glamorised them as national heroes. As he got older, I chose to read him more accurate accounts of what happened, but he always took Kelly's side. He became his childhood hero."

Hulk stared blankly, lost in his own thoughts, as Max turned around to face him. He saw the sadness in his eyes and wandered over to sit beside him.

"What happened between you two?" Max asked.

"He was working for me," Hulk said, shaking his head. "I had just established the civilian spy organisation within Defence, a precursor to what we know as AIS now. He fit the bill to come on board as a recruit. He had finished his training and was about to post out for his first solo mission in the field. He was about to move to Sydney, so had moved back in with my wife and I until his place was ready. One day he got home early and he saw me in the lounge room with another woman. It wasn't what he thought. She kissed me, nothing more. I would never betray his mother. I know how it looked, but he wouldn't listen. He attacked me and I broke his wrist. It was just, reflex."

"Jesus."

"We were at the hospital when I finally got his mother on the phone. She left work and was on her way to the hospital when she got into an accident. A drunk driver sideswiped her, forcing her car off the road. She hit a concrete pillar under the Government House overpass on Adelaide Avenue, just past the Lodge in Canberra. She died three days later in the very same hospital."

"And he blamed you for her death?"

"Yes. But I don't blame him. In fact, I agree with him."

"You can't hold yourself responsible for a drunk driver. It was their fault."

"Yeah, but she wouldn't have been on that road if it wasn't for me. I called her and told her what had happened. She was angry with me, not about the woman, but about our son's wrist. She was speeding and when the car hit her, she lost control. It was my fault, Max."

"You can't blame yourself, Hulk."

"I've spent a lifetime blaming myself, kid. Everything I have done since has been powered by a desire to right whatever wrongs I could, because I couldn't right this one. You of all people should understand that."

"I do," Max conceded, lowering his head and pausing to reflect.

Max had done the same thing himself. Distressed, devastated and abject anguish from the death of his fiancé, Max had thrown himself into his work. His ruthless pursuit of terrorists was fuelled by a desire for revenge and vengeance, while protecting others from having to endure the pain he felt. He was driven to save them from heartache.

"What happened to your son?" Max asked after a several beats.

"I was due to be posted out to Afghanistan. I arranged for him to stay with his aunty, my wife's sister, while he got himself back on track. I dropped him off and said how sorry I was, but he was shut off from the world, almost catatonic. A few weeks after I arrived in Afghanistan, I got a letter from his aunt. He was missing. He'd run away and she was distraught. I was heading up missions with the SAS and our new intel group in the Middle East. I couldn't leave. I did what I could to find him. I sent men I trusted in Canberra to find him. They eventually found him. He was selling his body, being used by politicians and senior public servants, and countless others, as a sex slave to make money to fund his drug addiction."

"Jesus, Hulk. I can't imagine what you went through."

"It was nothing compared to what he went through. I'd failed him. My tour ended a few years later and I came home. I went to find him and the man I found was no longer my son. He was a shell, a ghost. I had tried to get him help for years. I sent people to help, but he had refused it. He wouldn't refuse me. I got a couple of my guys and we abducted him off the street. We forced him into a van and to a safe room I had built in my house. Over the next few months, I got him the medical help he needed. We detoxed him and rehabilitated him as best we could, but even after all that, my son was gone. When he was sober and sane enough to make his own decisions, he chose to leave. I offered him money and support, but he refused it. He went back and fell in with the wrong crowd again. I confronted him, but he wanted nothing to do with me. Eventually, he got himself shot. He died alone on a cold winter's night in a gutter in Sydney."

"I'm so sorry, Hulk."

"A couple of years later, I got the Government to remove the spy agency from Defence and I created the AIS. I have spent every second since building what we have here. It's my legacy. I built it to honour him and to somehow make up for my failings."

There was a knock on the door and an aide walked in.

"I'm sorry to interrupt, but the CSIRO men are waiting in the mess," he said.

"Thank you," Max said as the door closed again. "AIS has been responsible for saving this country and millions of lives, on many occasions. It is an honour to work for you and in this agency, and it is a legacy I promise we will honour and strive to protect."

"Thank you, kid," Hulk said. "Now, let's go hear what they have to say."

Max and Hulk made their way out to the mess hall in the centre of the homestead. They took their seats and introduced themselves to the scientists, and the head of the CSIRO, Professor Lee Lewer.

"Why have they got your tech, Professor?" Max asked, bluntly.

"I guess our security wasn't good enough," Lewer offered.

"Clearly, but I meant what do you think they are going to do with it?"

"I've been thinking about it on the way out here. Not that I could really think on that noisy, flying death machine."

"Professor."

"Sorry. I just don't like helicopters."

"You're a scientist. Trust the science."

"Ah, touché. I shall keep that in mind."

"Professor, to the point, please."

"Right, I think they want it for nefarious means."

"Elaborate. How could they use it?"

"It is designed to disperse silver iodide into the air to create rain. It is quite ingenious actually, very exciting. It…"

"Professor."

"Sorry, very simply, the silver iodide clings to the water molecules in the air or the clouds, and makes them heavier. The heavier particles then drop, forming rain."

"How is that nefarious?"

"It's not. But, I was thinking about some work we've been doing with the Defence Science and Technology Organisation. DSTO has been working on an idea of using the technology to lace the rain with chemicals to enhance crops."

"Why would DSTO want to help grow crops?"

"It's a humanitarian solution. After war or peacekeeping efforts, countries often struggle to rebuild. This would help accelerate the recovery by reestablishing the agriculture, providing secure food supplies."

"Again, this doesn't sound nefarious, but I'm guessing if you could use it to grow crops, you might be able to use it to destroy crops?"

"Exactly. That's why DSTO had us developing it in a secret laboratory. They lied to me and I am very upset about it."

"Professor, you can worry about your issues with DSTO another time. What can these terrorists do with Wollunqua?"

"Well, it's just a theory, but I was thinking about a mix of silver iodide and something like glyphosate or even ammonia. It would have to be high doses and maybe even a special compound, but basically you could create a version of acid rain. Maybe even more toxic than what we consider acid rain which occurs today."

"Acid rain."

"Yes. Acid rain can eat sandstone and wear it away over the course of a decade or two. It's the reason we make most outdoor metal structures out of stainless steel these days, because it can essentially eat normal metal and cause it to deteriorate within only a few years. Coal and gas, fossil fuels emit nitrogen and sulphur into the atmosphere in huge quantities and can lead to acid rain."

"But you think Wollunqua, can what, supercharge this process?"

"Potentially."

"Jesus. What could they target with it?"

"It depends on the compound they use. Glyphosate or ammonia in high doses could target food crops, disrupting food security. Another compound could be used against government facilities or other targets to weaken structures over time."

"What about people?" Hulk asked.

"People?"

"What if they targeted people?"

"Again, depending on the compound, a form of acid rain on people could lead to anything from rashes and burns to lung diseases or even cancer."

Chapter Thirteen

Max padded into the bathroom barefooted, trying to do up his tie, while brushing his teeth. He held back his tie as he rinsed his mouth, before checking himself out in the mirror. He ran his fingers through his hair as Blake walked in.

"Come on, Max," Blake said, impatiently, "we are going to be late."

"It'll be okay," Max said. "I'm nearly ready. Anyway, aren't you the guest of honour? They won't start without you."

"Still. Hurry up."

"Okay, okay. Just got to find my jacket and throw on some shoes and socks."

"Where's your head at, Max?" Blake asked laying Max's suit jacket down on the bed beside him as Max pulled on his socks.

"I'm chasing a ghost."

"Ned Kelly?"

"Yes."

"We've got teams looking into it. They will find him and then you can go get him. There's nothing more you can do until then, and I need you here."

"Don't you think we are overdressed to be going to a concert?"

"It's one of my first major events as DPM. I wanted to look the part."

"I think we should at least ditch the ties, matter of fact, I think you should wear a t-shirt. Show off your body. You're young and fit and hot, especially compared to the other politicians you work with. And, it's a concert, not a Cabinet meeting. Relax, show you're one with the people."

"Okay," Blake said after a brief pause. "T-shirts, but keep the jackets."

"Deal."

Max and Blake quickly changed, and jogged out to their waiting vehicle and security detail. The driver greeted them as they climbed in and sped off towards the concert.

"I've got a meeting in the morning with DSTO," Blake said. "I'll be asking for a please explain from them on Wollunqua."

"Good," Max said. "They need to answer for their piss-poor security, among other things."

"Indeed. I've also ordered the security to be increased around our defence bases. We can't afford them getting hold of any more tech."

"I'd increase it at our contractor sites too."

"Already taken care of."

"Good," Max said, turning and smiling at Blake. "You look great by the way."

"Thank you," Blake replied with a warm smile. "Right back at ya."

They kissed as their motorcade turned into the grounds of the winery. In the distance, a rolling field had transformed into an outdoor concert hall with a massive stage at the far end. The sun was beaming down onto the crowd through holes in the clouds as the screens broadcast footage of the motorcade arriving.

Max could hear the crowd cheering and Blake squeezed his hand.

"Is that for you?" Max asked.

"It's for us," Blake said. "Apparently we're rockstars."

"Or they think we're the band."

"Guess we'll soon see when we open the door."

"Applause turns to sneers in an instant."

"Let's hope not," Blake laughed.

The car pulled up near the stage and they waited for the all-clear from Lovell, Blake's security leader. A camera crew was waiting and beaming live footage of them up onto the screens. The crowd cheered when they saw Blake.

"Guess it won't be sneers after all," Max said, smiling broadly.

"My Chief of Staff told me we're a celebrity couple now, Max," Blake said. "The head of a spy agency turned politician and his spy, outlaw, mysterious fiancé. He said we're breaking the mound and a symbol for the LGBTI community."

"Well, don't let it all go to your head. You are a politician after all. They'll hate us again at some point, especially you."

"Probably right, but let's enjoy it while it lasts."

Max nodded and smiled, as Lovell opened Blake's door. The car was instantly filled with the thunderous applause and cheers of the crowd. Max saw Blake smiling and waving to the crowd. It was a world away from the life they used to live, hiding in the shadows.

Max climbed across and followed Blake out the door. Lovell smiled at him, appreciating his discomfort in the limelight.

"You'll be fine," Lovell said, patting him on the shoulder.

"I'd be more comfortable in your shoes," Max said.

"I'm sure you would be, sir," Lovell said and Max frowned. "Sorry, I'm sure you would be, Max."

"Thanks, Lovell. Keep your eyes open."

"Of course. Enjoy the afternoon."

Blake reached back and took Max's hand, and the crowd cheered. Max could feel their eyes boring into him, as if they were each trying to glimpse a part of his soul. He had never felt more uncomfortable in his life, but he felt Blake's reassuring hand squeeze his and it instantly calmed him.

The pair took a small staircase up to the stage and were met by an Australian artist who had been performing as an introduction for the main event. Max had no idea who she was. She had finished her set and introduced Blake and Max to the crowd to the applause of those assembled on the picturesque rolling lawns. Max saw the vines winding their way up over the hills in the distance as the clouds rolled in and the concert lights took over.

Max rolled the sleeves up on his jacket as Blake took to the microphone.

"Hello, Hunter Valley!" Blake yelled into the microphone sending the crowd into a frenzy. "I've always wanted to do that! It is fantastic to be here and to be supporting local artists, like Eleanor Grace, isn't she amazing?"

The crowd clapped and cheered for the artist who had welcomed them onto the stage. Max smiled and clapped, and she nodded her thanks to him and held her heart while waving to the crowd.

"Her new album is on repeat in our house," Blake said, and Eleanor nodded and smiled in thanks. "What a talent. I know you're all here to see the main event, the Byron Riders…"

The crowd cheered and whistled.

"I know, I know. Another band on constant repeat on my Spotify! But I wanted to take this opportunity to tell you a little bit about what the government is doing…"

The crowd booed and Max smirked.

"I know, buzz kill," Blake continued, "but I promise it's good news. I'm proud to announce the Government is investing $250 million to support local musicians and creative artists to get their works onto the international stage."

The crowd clapped politely as Eleanor jumped up and down in excitement, building them up again.

"But that's not all, we…"

Max looked across the crowd and up the hill in the distance. A small speck had appeared on the horizon and looked to be getting closer. He struggled to see what it was, but something didn't feel right. He stepped forward, level with Blake, trying to get a better look, as Blake continued addressing the crowd.

"Ah oh," Blake said, looking over to Max. "I must have been talking too long, he's come to shut me up."

The crowd laughed, but Max ignored them, trying to focus.

"Ladies and gentleman," Blake said, "may I introduce you to my fiancé, Max."

Max heard his name and turned to Blake, before smiling shyly and waving to the crowd to their applause. Blake continued to talk, but Max was gone again, focusing hard. He felt the hairs on the back of his neck raise. He turned to Lovell who was looking off into the distance, searching for whatever Max was looking at, then he saw it. Lovell turned to see Max and ran towards the stage yelling into his comms unit.

On the far side of the stage, another federal police officer was running up the stairs, as Max grabbed Blake. Blake's smile and excitement vanished in surprise and shock as Max marched him towards Lovell.

The crowd was concerned and a couple of people screamed as the feds reached Blake and Max. They starred as the small group ran towards the waiting motorcade.

Max and Lovell shoved Blake into the backseat, as Blake yelled asking what was happening.

The bulletproof door closed and Max tapped the roof and it sped off with one of the remaining security vehicles just as a huge arial drone swept in low over the crowd. The initial screams and chaos broke way for laughter and excitement as the drone released thousands of one-hundred-dollar bills into the crowd.

The gathered mass of revellers tripped over each other and fought to grab more and more of the bills. As they scrambled, Lovell and Max watched as the drone did a fast loop to come in again over the crowd. People were excited waiting with open arms for the drone to fly over again, anticipating another cash drop.

A small door opened under the drone and the people cheered.

The drone came in low and just before it reached the crowded fields, it started spraying a water like substance from the small door which had opened. The people's faces were turned skyward and they copped the spray right across their faces.

The people at the rear instantly began to scream in agony. A wall of shrieks and sorrowful groans rolled forward towards the stage, like an horrendous Mexican wave of pain.

Max and Lovell dived clear, as the drone flew over. Max felt the substance lightly mist over his skin. He felt it burning and could feel it filling his lungs. Even the small amount of mist he had inhaled was like pepper spray. He couldn't imagine the pain the crowd was in.

Lovell was wiping his eyes and groaning, as Max grabbed him.

"Don't rub your eyes," Max said. "You'll push it in. Breath and get control. Has the back up security car got a full weapons kit?"

"Yes," Lovell managed to say, as the crowd on the far side of the grounds started to flee in panic. "I need to unlock it."

"Okay," Max said, standing him up and helping him navigate. "Let's move."

Max helped Lovell get through the crowd to the waiting security vehicle. Lovell opened the rear door of the Land Rover, but couldn't see the keypad. His eyes burned and blurred from the mist.

The drone was doing another fast turn and coming back for a run on the far side of the grounds.

Max ripped the cover off the keypad.

"What's the code?" Max asked.

"I can't see the keypad," Lovell said.

"Just tell me the code."

"Six, nineteen, thirty-one, four."

Max entered the code and a draw slid out from under the rear door. It held an array of weapons, but Max found the only one suitable, a sniper rifle. A Izhmash SV-98 to be exact. His eyes were starting to burn, but he pressed on. He climbed up onto the roof of the Land Rover and extended the tripod on the barrel of the gun, resting it on the roof. He tried to control his breathing, but his lungs felt like they were on fire.

He sighted the drone as best he could and chambered a round, then he fired and chambered a second.

The first bullet sailed past the drone harmlessly.

He fired again and chambered a third round.

This time the bullet slammed into the nose of the drone as it began its approach. Max saw the hole it had torn in the nose of the drone, as the spray began.

The fleeing crowd were covered in the mist and started screeching and crying out within seconds, as Max fired his next shot and chambered a round.

The third shot hit the drone's closest engine. The bullet drove in through the thin metal skin and bounced around inside the engine. Black smoke billowed out and through the scope, Max could see the hints of a flame.

He fired again.

The bullet flew into the rear of the damaged engine as the drone began its turn. This time the flames were obvious. The engine burst into fire and the smoke tripled, but the drone kept flying. It was making yet another turn to come in again for another attack.

Max fired three shots as quick as he could. The first hit the front of the drone and only dented it. The second two found their mark. They exploded through the wing and more importantly the fuel tanks. The drone started leaking avgas and as the big unmanned aircraft made its turn, the stream of fuel fell into the flaming engine, igniting it.

The drone exploded. Fire and smoke shot out as it fell towards the earth. Pieces of the fuselage dropped as the big bird started to come apart.

Max stood up to watch it slam into the earth with a thunderous thump.

He climbed down to find Lovell pouring water in his eyes to flush them. He then helped Max wash his own face and eyes. The screams and moans from the concert field were sickening. Fire and other emergency services were starting to arrive and Max ordered the firies to start their hoses to wash everyone down. He told other emergency service personnel to take people down to a nearby creek and dam to rinse the toxin off.

Max walked into the field with Lovell towards the burning wreckage. Max stopped at a piece of the metal fuselage.

"It can't be," Max said.

"What?" Lovell asked.

"This company no longer exists," Max said as he grabbed the metal panel and showed it to Lovell, before tossing it back into the dirt.

It bounced and sat in the black soil proudly displaying its old faded Northstar Defence Industries logo.

Chapter Fourteen

"I thought it was supposed to seed the cloud and make it rain, not spray directly onto the crowd?" Max yelled into his headphones over the noise of his helicopter.

"That was the design and it could still be used for that purpose," Lewer said through Max's headphones. *"But by spraying it into the crowd like they did ensured an especially high concentrate of the compound."*

"You don't have to tell me that, I was there. Are you any closer to identifying the compound? I mean, should we expect any long-term side effects?"

"It looks to be a type of cytotoxic chemical, basically a toxin which attacks the body's cells. The venom of some snakes and spiders share similar structure, but the more scientifically aligned make up of the compound would be that of mustard gas – albeit a weak or watered down version than that used by the military. It also seems to have an acid or some corrosive element in it, which we're trying to isolate."

"Isn't mustard gas a gas?"

"No, it's actually very interesting. It is a mist or water-like droplets. In warfare it is usually coloured with a yellow or orange tinge, but it is actually clear and looks like water."

"If it was seeded into the clouds, what would it have done?"

"It would have ensured a large spread of the toxin, over a longer time."

"What were the final injuries on the ground?"

"Some of the poor people there were covered in blisters and burns, others have severe blistering of the lungs. Six people are in critical condition and three people died at the scene from heart attacks. There are countless others in serious condition, particularly suffering from acute nervous system issues, shaking in the arms and hands, problems with brain function and mobility."

"Is it going to last? You know, long-term."

"We think we can isolate the cause and develop a shot to reverse the damage."

"Timeframe?"

"Days, maybe weeks."

"Okay. Thank you, Professor. Keep working and reporting in. Alpha are you there?"

"We think it could have been a warning," Kate said coming on the line and disconnecting Lewer. *"A statement. We've got this and we're prepared to use it. Either that or they got the mixture wrong."*

"It's hardly comforting either way. Alpha, do you think Blake was the target?"

"We can't rule him out, Prince. Too coincidental."

"I agree. I want his detail increased."

"Already done. He now has the same protection as the Prime Minister."

"Good. What about the drone? What can you tell me?"

"Only the location which you are on route too. We nationalised Northstar years ago and shut down its remaining operations. Clearly there was a black site off the books."

"And what's happening at the site?"

"Satellite images from an hour ago show no heat signatures. It's an abandoned World War II airbase. Nothing there."

"But we are certain the drone launched from the base?"

"Yes."

"Can we rewind the footage to see how it got there?"

"We are working on it, but it looks like you'll arrive before we do."

"Okay, I'll take a look around and get back to you."

"One more thing, Prince. I've sent a couple of the recruits and some support."

"Not sure I'll need them if the site is abandoned."

"I know, but I want to be sure."

"Roger that."

"Prince, how are you feeling?"

"I'm okay. I only got a small dose compared to the others who were in the field."

"Still. Keep an eye on it. I need you at full strength."

"I'll be fine."

"Okay, but I want you to get checked out, when this is done."

"Roger that."

"I mean it, Max."

"I'll see the Doc this afternoon."

"Good. Thank you, Prince. Good luck and Godspeed."

Max clicked off the headset and told his pilot to gun the engines.

While on route, Max changed into his tactical gear and checked his weapons. He felt a slight tremor in his hands, not for the first time today, but he just shook and squeezed them. He'd be fine.

When they arrived, the pilot circled the old airfield. It looked deserted and rundown. The old hangers and huts which lined the facility were rusted and caked in decades of grime and red dirt.

"Take us in," Max ordered and the pilot found a spot to the north of the facility.

The chopper touched down and the pilot started winding the engines down. As the whirling engines started to slow, a bullet sliced a neat hole in the front windshield of the helicopter. It hit the pilot's visor, shattering it, before slamming through his forehead and into his brain. It continued through the back of his helmet and seat, and buried itself into the metal structure about a foot from where Max was crouched in the rear.

Max dived to the ground instinctively as the pilot's body slumped over on the controls.

Max dared to raise his head to look through the windscreen, looking for the sniper, but it was no use she was well hidden.

A second round smashed into the helicopter. Max heard the thunk above his head. The sniper was aiming for the engines, he presumed to stop him from escaping, but then he saw the purplish hue of the avgas running down over his windows.

"Get out of the chopper!" a voice commanded over a speaker system outside the helicopter, *"or the next bullet ignites the gas and we watch the country's greatest spy roast."*

"Fuck," Max said to himself.

He looked around, but there was nothing but the base in the direction of the sniper and vast bushland and desert behind him. Even if he made it to the tree line, he wouldn't get far.

Max opened the closest door and watched as the fuel streamed down from the opening. He stepped through the avgas and out onto the airfield, moving quickly to put some distance between himself and the helicopter.

A crack rang out from the distance and a puff of dirt a metre in front of his feet exploded from the heavy sniper round.

"That's far enough, Agent Shaw," the voice said over the loudspeakers. *"Drop your weapons and kick them away."*

Max dropped his MP5, pistol and knife into the dirt and kicked them off to the side. His laser-like focus was still staring ahead, searching for the sniper, then he saw a figure emerge from the tree line at the far end of the airbase. She was completely decked out in camouflage and carrying a massive sniper rifle. It looked almost as long as she was tall.

The Wild Woman rested the bulk of the gun on her hip when she got closer and aimed the barrel at Max.

"Turn around and walk," she commanded.

Max did as she asked, he turned around on the spot and started forward slowly. He could hear The Wild Woman's footsteps getting closer, but he knew she was still out of reach. The dry dirt and bitumen of the airstrip crunched under his feet, until he reached the end of the old runway. He took another step expecting the soft loose texture of the powdery red dirt, but instead he felt solid steel. He stepped harder listening to the hollow echo below him.

"Clever boy," the Wild Woman said. "Take another four steps."

Max complied and he heard the woman's steps again fall just short of his reach behind him. She keyed her radio.

"We're on the pad," she said.

"Roger that," came the muffled reply.

Max turned around to face the Wild Woman.

"Did I tell you to turn around?" she asked.

"No, but I just wanted to see the face of my captor," Max said. "What happens now?"

"You shut up, for one."

There was a mechanical sound beneath them, then the metal platform lowered into the earth. It was a huge elevator, like one you would see on an aircraft carrier for raising and lowering planes onto the deck. A couple of storeys down, Max learned just how right that was. He stared out at huge underground hanger. It was mostly empty, but there was one remaining drone and what looked like three large surface missiles in the wide space.

As the elevator reached the bottom, two men jogged over and tried to place him in handcuffs. Max spun and slammed his fist into the face of the first man, who stumbled back. He grabbed the wrist of the second one, but felt the strength leave his grip and his hands began to shake more violently. Max fell to the floor and the two men slammed him into the ground, before handcuffing him.

They dragged him up and led him into a side room as the Wild Woman watched on. Max counted nine other terrorists getting the missiles and drone ready for launch. He also saw a number of bunks at the far end of the facility. Clearly, it had held more men than were currently on deck. Max wondered if this had been their base of operations for a long period. They looked like they were moving out.

One of the men sat him in an old office chair and taped his feet to the wheeled base and recuffed his hands behind the chair back. His shaking stopped when he sat down.

The Wild Woman walked into the room and smiled.

"Sorry we won't be able to speak for long," she said. "I've got stuff to do and by the looks of it, you've got other things to worry about. That chemical shit they sprayed on you looks like it's doing a number on you."

"What exactly is happening here?" Max asked, ignoring her jibe. "You guys moving out?"

"We were in the process of moving out, when we saw your helicopter approaching. Seems you found us sooner than we had anticipated. Now I need you tell me how long we've got. Are you on your own?"

"You killed my pilot, so I guess I am."

"Are you expecting backup?"

"Are you?"

She marched over and punched Max in the face. His head fell to the side and he smiled to himself, before looking up defiantly.

"Do you really think you can break me?" Max asked. "Do you know who I am and what I've been through?"

"He's expecting backup," she said into her radio and Max looked up to see the crew all increase their pace.

One guy ran for a forklift and set about moving the missiles onto the elevator platform.

"Is that what you needed the microprocessors for?" Max asked. "You killed a military unit for a handful of missiles?"

"And two drones," she replied watching her men. "You'd have to agree the first one was effective."

"All it did was give up this location."

"We anticipated as much. That's why it's not the only one."

"Where are the others?"

"You think I'd tell you that? Good one."

"So is this the game plan? Lure people in with counterfeit cash then gas them?"

"It will be a fascinating psychological test for people. They will hear about the concert, but will they still be tempted to make a grab for the cash? Why not, right? Only a couple of people died, maybe it'd be worth the pain and shaking hands for some to get to the cash? That is, of course, unless the gas mix changes for the next attacks."

Max felt his concentration drop and he lost focus. His vision blurred and he shook his head to try to clear it.

"You got a good dose of the chemical, didn't you?" she asked noticing Max's face. "More than you've let on. It's disorientating, isn't it?"

"I don't know what you're talking about," Max lied, regaining some focus.

"I think you do."

"What are you planning?"

"I'm not telling you that, don't be stupid. I'm just telling you there will be more and they may not be as nice as the first one."

"You've only got one more drone. I shot down your first, someone else will take out the second."

"Maybe, it won't matter though. Our plans are bigger than this."

"You seem like you're itching to tell me."

"I'm eager for you to see them eventuate. We've been planning this for a long time. What you see here is just what's left. The people will be afraid to leave their homes. The country will never be the same again."

"I've heard that before."

"But this time, we won't fail. As I said, we've been planning this a long time. It's time to return the world to the people. Pro humanitate et terra. This world has lost its way. We need to start again."

"Start again?"

"Rome must burn for Rome to rise, pro humanitate et terra," she repeated showing Max the brand on her arm. "For humanity and the earth. Anyway, I've got to go. Hopefully your back up arrives soon. This would be a cold, dark place to die alone, taped to a chair."

"You're just going to leave me here like this?" Max asked as the Wild Women turned and started walking for the door.

"In the event your team does arrive and figure out how to get you out, tell Hulk he failed," she said as she looked back over her shoulder and smiled without stopping.

"Hulk?" Max yelled. "What's he got to do with this? He's retired."

The Wild Woman just walked on.

Max watched as the crew dragged the drone onto the elevator and they all rushed onto the platform beside it as the Wild Woman arrived. She gave Max a little wave, all of her fingers moving up and down in their own time. She laughed, then ordered the lift to rise.

As the lift blocked the tunnel of light from the outside world, the lights went out and the basement facility went dark. Max willed his eyes to adjust to the minimal light from a distant red light glowing dimly. He was still feeling the effects of the chemical coursing through his system, but the darkness was all encompassing. He felt nauseous.

He kicked his feet trying to loosen the tape. They hardly bunged, but ever so slightly each kick was giving him some minimal wiggle room.

Above him, Max heard the sound of rolling thunder. It was muffled, but Max could tell it was a C-17 Globemaster. They were going to load the weapons and flee.

He kicked with more intensity, thrashing about in the chair. Max could hear the old chair groaning and he stopped kicking, and started bouncing up and down, stomping down hard on the old plastic base which held the wheels. He could feel the plastic weakening and cracking. He thrashed about again as he bounced, until the plastic rod holding his right foot broke away from the base.

It was still taped to his combat boots, but at least he was partially free. He jammed the plastic arm under another spoke on the base of the chair and used it to leverage against the tape, until his boot ripped free. He stood up and kicked the chair over, using the back of the chair to leverage against the tape on his other foot, until it tore and he was free.

He sat on the floor and dragged himself awkwardly through his own handcuffed arms, so they were now in front of him. He looked around the room, but found nothing useful.

He walked out of the room into the large hanger. It was essentially empty, they had cleaned it out. He followed the walls looking for an escape route. He could feel a tightness in his chest and he was breathing heavily, but he strode forward.

Max saw a door under the red light. It had to be an exit, so he started to jog, when the light stopped glowing and the hanger fell into complete darkness.

He froze in place. Trying to visualise the room. He tried to remember the distance and direction of the door.

He walked towards the wall to his left, reaching out trying to find it in the darkness. It was further than he expected. When his finger hit the concrete wall, he walked quickly to his right, feeling his way waiting to hit the door. Again, it took longer than Max had thought, but eventually his fingertips ran over the cold steel door. He felt around for the handle, grasped it and pushed the door open.

As he hoped, it contained a fire escape leading up to the surface. A tiny light at the top was enough to show the way.

Max bounded up the stairs two and three at a time, racing for the exit.

When he reached the top, he paused for a moment to get his breath. The effects of the chemical attack were coursing through his veins and felt nauseous again. He took a brief moment to control his beating heart, before opening the door. There was a guard waiting in the small office and he got a shot off at Max, as Max launched himself forward and tackled him to the ground. The gun dropped from the guard's hands as he took hold of the handcuffs locked around Max's wrist, pulling them to the side to give himself a clear path to Max's face. He drew back his fist and hit Max in the face.

With each punch, Max's anger grew. When he saw an opening, he threw a vicious headbutt, busting his attacker's nose. The guard fell back holding his face and Max capitalised pushing him back and wrestling to get on top of him.

Outside the shack, Max could hear more guards approaching. He heard them over the sound of the C17 idling at the far end of the bush runway. They were getting closer.

He punched the guard in the face, then wrapped his thumbs under the chain of his handcuffs and punched down either side of the guard's neck. The chain went tight and dug into the guard's windpipe. He kicked and clawed at the chain as his face went from red to purple. Max was pressing down with all his upper body strength, listening to the guard's footsteps on the gravel outside, closer and closer they came until they reached the small hut and kicked open the door.

Max rolled to the side, off his attacker, as two bullets slammed into the already dead terrorist. He grabbed the pistol which had fallen to the floor earlier and kept rolling.

He stopped on his back, took aim at the three guards in the doorway and fired three quick shots.

The first two found their marks and dropped the first two guards. The third hit the last goon in the shoulder and he stumbled away.

"Get out of here!" he yelled back to the C17. "He's free!"

The Wild Woman spun around to see his face explode. He dropped to the ground, revealing Max, pistol in hand.

"Get us in the air!" she yelled, running up the loading ramp of the Globemaster.

Max ran towards the big cargo plane, which was starting to taxi. He looked around, knowing once it got to a rolling speed he wouldn't catch it on foot.

He searched as he ran and sighted an old dirt bike. He holstered his pistol and ran hard for the bike. He jumped onto the hot seat, which burned from the sun. He kicked it hard trying to start it, but it wouldn't kick. He tried again and again, until the big plane raced past him. He kicked it again and it revved to life.

Max pushed it into gear and spun it around to give chase. He rode hard, with one hand on the throttle and his other hand resting on the middle of the handlebars, which was as far as they could reach with the cuffs on.

He accelerated hard, half blind from the red dirt being kicked up by the enormous aircraft.

From behind, Max heard shots ring out. He snuck a look back to see four of the Wild Woman's crew chasing him in two small Jeeps. They were firing at him, even though she'd left them behind.

Max couldn't reach his pistol, but even if he could, his handcuffs meant he couldn't return fire. There was only one choice and he made it. He accelerated, redlining the dirt bike.

A gunshot rang out above the chaos. It was a powerful crack.

Max looked back to see a jet black Porsche four wheel drive powering down the runway after them. An AIS agent was standing up and firing a massive sniper rifle through the sunroof. Max watched as a bullet slammed into the back of one of the driver's heads and instantly sprayed the windscreen with blood. The little Jeep left the road smashed through one of the huts lining the old airfield, before it exploded into flames.

Max smiled and powered on, leaving the remaining Jeep to his colleagues who had arrived to back him up. He looked ahead to see two guards at the rear of the Globemaster firing at him. Dirt kicked up in front of his tyres and he swerved giving them a harder target.

As Max looked up at the two shooters, the one of the left levelled his gun at Max. Just as he was going to swerve again. The left shooter's chest exploded. He fell to the ground, before sliding down the still open cargo hold ramp and into the dust.

The shooter on the right was stunned and Max saw his opening. Max hit the ramp and accelerated up at full speed towards the remaining shooter. A metre away, the shooter turned back to aim for Max, but was hit hard by the bike and thrown up over it. Max had jumped at the last minute and landed on the loading ramp. He had rolled to the side, but managed to get a grip of the metal door. He didn't see the bike hit the shooter, but did see the effect. The shooter landed on the ramp only inches from Max and tumbled towards the dirt runway speeding away beneath them.

The bike had sped on and slammed into a cargo crate. It crumbled and threw fuel all over the cargo hold and the crew.

The shooter managed to get a handhold at the last second and he was hanging on with all his might. His whole body was dragging along the dirt and he was screaming, trying to pull himself up the ramp. He managed to get a higher handhold and pulled himself forward, but his legs were still dragging.

Max rolled to his right, putting his feet in beside the shooter's head. The shooter grabbed Max's legs, trying to claw his way up, but also to stop what was about to happen. Max kicked his hands away as the shooter became more and more desperate. Max saw the panic in his eyes, but he didn't hesitate. He kicked the shooter in the face, then stomped down on the top of his head.

The shooter rolled off the ramp and was swallowed up by the red dirt, ragdolling along the ground until he went under the Jeep, almost flipping the little four-wheel drive.

Max crawled and dragged himself onto his feet, as the big plane started to angle towards the sky. He ran forward as one of the crew arrived. They threw down their gun, because they were covered in fuel and couldn't risk sparking a flame.

He ran towards Max, but Max felt the plane tilt preparing for take-off and lunged forward for a cargo strap. He caught it, as the big attacker over balanced and toppled to the ground. He had been coming for Max and as he fell, he caught Max's leg. Max clung onto the strap with both his hands, still only able to use his legs to fight. He kneed the big man in the jaw, then wrapped both legs around his head and neck, and squeezed hard. He stood up with Max on his shoulders, his arms around, Max's legs. Max was still hanging onto the strap, but he managed to get himself into the right position and started working his attacker's neck, crossing his legs behind his head and squeezing, trying to cut off his oxygen supply. The terrorist started tapping on Max's leg, begging for relief. Max held on, until he fell to his knees. Max placed one of his boots on the shoulder of his weakened attacker then sprung forward, pushing down hard with all his weight.

The terrorist tumbled back bouncing once on the ramp, before cartwheeling out and falling towards the ground which was rushing away beneath them. Max saw him hit the ground, just as the second Jeep spun wildly off the road and crashed into a tree. The AIS Porsche pulled up and Max turned back to see what was waiting for him inside the plane.

He couldn't see the crew, but he could hear them. He ducked behind a cargo crate and waited as the plane rose into the air.

"Where is he?" the Wild Woman yelled from the front of the plane.

"I can't see him," one of her men said, arriving at the rear of the plane. "He must have fallen."

"Don't guess! Find out! Search the plane!"

Max released two straps on the cargo crate he was crouching behind and it slid along the floor gathering speed towards the ramp. It hit the guy at the rear of the plane and swept him out, just as another terrorist arrived to see it.

"Jesus Christ!" he yelled.

"What happened?" the Wild Woman yelled.

"One of the cargo boxes came lose and hit him. He's gone."

The man was staring over the edge of the ramp, as Max crawled under the drone, which had been folded to fit in the hold. He quickly removed the cover and took out one of the massive batteries, then he ripped a handful of wires out figuring the more damage the less likely it would be it would be able to fly again. One of the wires was stiff enough for him to use to unpick his cuffs. He was happy to be free of them finally.

Max kicked the battery hard and it slid out from under the drone, using the steep angle of take-off and gravity to do the work. It only missed the terrorist at the rear of the plane by a couple of inches. He watched the battery sail over the edge, as Max rolled out and scrambled forward.

He found a spot to hide from his attackers, behind the two missiles they had managed to load before he arrived, but the guy at the rear of the plane could still see him plainly.

Max looked at the missiles. He knew the type and build. They had to be triggered to detonate. They could sit in burning fuel for hours and not explode. Max also saw they had parachutes attached so they could be dropped without them exploding.

"Hey!" the guy from the rear yelled.

Max turned and fired his pistol. The bullet hit the man in the face and he backflipped out of the plane as his clothes burst into flames from the motorbike's petrol.

One of the nearby crew had heard the gunshot and ran towards Max's position. He waited until he saw her knife welding hand come around the missiles.

Max whipped his pistol down onto her hand and she dropped the knife. He grabbed her wrist as she came around to engage him. He cuffed her wrist to the crate the missile was being transported in. She looked at him with ragging eyes, as he pulled the parachute cord.

The parachute quickly flapped towards the rear of the plane, before it filled with air and dragged the missile crate and the screaming terrorist handcuffed to it out into the blue sky.

"You are tenacious Agent Shaw, I'll give you that," the Wild Woman said. "They were right to try and take you out at that concert!"

"Yeah, well you missed arsehole," Max yelled back. "I'll find you all and take you out."

"And how do you expect to do that? My team is closing in on you. There is no escape. Soon you'll be falling from the plane with no way to stop me, let alone our wider team."

"Well, you're right about one of those things," Max yelled back before buckling his vest to the remaining missile crate and pulling the parachute cord.

As the parachute flapped towards the ramp, Max took a deep breath to steady his heartbeat and looped his left arm through the crate.

"What the fuck? Don't let him escape," the Wild Woman yelled as her crew rushed Max's position.

The first guard arrived and Max fired four shots into his chest. He fell back as his vest caught fire and Max aimed around the crate and fired his pistol dry into his crumpled motorbike which burst into flames as he was ripped free of the plane at incredible speed when the parachute inflated.

The explosion inside the plane ruptured a fuel line. Avgas started spraying all around the cargo hold, until it too caught on fire. The Wild Woman watched as the flames raced up the liquid fuel until it sucked inside the ruptured lines. Explosions burst from the lines as the fire raced along inside, feeding it with more oxygen and increasing the fire's speed, until it found the main tanks.

The C17 exploded in a violent fireball and immediately started raining huge chunks of flaming metal. Max watched as the plane's pieces fell harmlessly into the red sandy desert. The drone had broken free and it too fell for the earth in a burning wreck.

Max's missile crate was two metres from the earth and he took a breath, hoping he was right about the missiles not being armed. It hit the ground hard and toppled over. He breathed out and laughed as the dirt settled around him, and the parachute collapsed and billowed gently in the breeze.

He unbuckled his vest and rolled off the missile, before cutting free the parachute which flapped about and tumbled in the wind, then he leant on the missile crate watching as the black Porsche arrived. He could feel his hands shaking again.

"Good to see you, kid," Max said as Jonnie "Bravo" Belluci stepped out of the performance SUV. "I knew there could only be one person able to take those shots."

"And I knew there could only be one bloke insane enough to try the shit you just pulled," Jonnie said smiling.

"How are you feeling?"

"I'm ready to avenge my team and get these arseholes. Should I be feeling anything else?"

"You sound perfectly healthy to me and I'm glad to hear it. I could use your help."

"Including with that," Jonnie said, pointing to Max's left arm which he was cradling.

"It's dislocated," Max said as Jonnie arrived beside him, taking his arm.

Jonnie felt the shaking and saw how pale Max's face was.

"This is going to hurt like fuck," Jonnie said.

"I know," Max said, through gritted teeth, "ain't the first time."

"The trick is to…" Jonnie said as he popped Max's arm back into place. "The trick is to not tell the patient when you're going to do it."

"Thanks, I think," Max said clearly in pain.

"You're welcome."

Max reached out to steady himself on the crate.

"Are you okay?" Jonnie asked.

"I think that chemical shit they spray us with might be having a mild effect."

"Medic!"

"I'm fine," Max said, waving away the medic. "I just need a minute."

"Are you having other symptoms?"

"I'll be fine, kid. Did you get my other package?"

"She's in the car," Jonnie said, still not convinced Max was okay. "I've got a team en route to collect the missiles and assess the wreck."

"Good work."

"What's next boss?"

"We go find these arseholes and stop them."

"Yes, sir!" Jonnie said, leading Max back to the car.

Before they got there, Max began to shake violently. He fell to the red dirt and convulsed as Jonnie yelled for medical support.

Chapter Fifteen

Brave threw a mug of coffee at the wall and it shattered. The black coffee dripped down the wall as ceramic pieces showered the floor and bench.

"She knew the risks," Mad Dog said. "She dies a hero."

"She didn't need to be there!" Brave ragged. "He could have left anyone else. He's always hated her and you. Well, she schooled you a hundred times. I'm sure you don't care!"

"I do. She was a bitch to me, but I didn't take it as a bad thing. I respected her and took it as a bit of banter. I know you're pissed, but you have to put it behind you."

"Fuck you! She's lying in the middle of nowhere. Abandoned by her team. How can I move on?"

"You can move on by focusing on the plan," Ned Kelly said, walking into the room. "Brave's right. She knew the risks and still volunteered to stay back to get the last of the weapons out. She also knew she could manipulate them if they got to her. She planted seeds. She did her job. You should be proud."

"Volunteered, my arse. You asked her to stay."

"I'm going to let this slide because you are upset, but don't take this as a sign of weakness. Another outburst and I'll put a bullet in your head. Even if I did order her to stay, that would have been my order and it would be done. I'm in charge here, not you."

"I have to go and find her. What if she's alive?"

"It's impossible. She was on board the plane when it crashed. She's dead."

Brave thought for a moment and went to speak, but stopped himself.

"She was a good solider and a loyal and smart one at that," Ned said. "She'll be missed."

Brave looked him up and down, then marched out of the room in anger and torment.

"These were just the distractions," Ned said to his remaining crew. "Keep your eyes on the prize. AIS will be tied up for days chasing dead ends. It's always been the plan to throw them off course. The chemical attack, the money, the mint, it's all misdirection. The Wild Woman knew that and she knew her job, now all of us need to do ours."

"Yes, sir," they all said.

"Joe stay behind for a minute, the rest of you can go. Get to work."

"What's up?" Byrne asked as the others left the room.

"I need you to keep an eye on Brave. This has clearly knocked him off course. I don't want his shit to spiral out of control. Review his tasks and keep him focused, and if he loses track, you know what to do."

"Why are you asking me to do this?"

"You're the only one I trust and you're the only one who knows the full extent of our plans. You know what this means to me."

"To us," Byrne said, taking Ned's hand.

"Careful," Ned said, pulling his hand away. "I don't want the others to know."

"We've been together for a long time now, why does it matter if they know?"

"I don't want them to know anything about us. It'll make it harder for people to trace us, if any of them get caught. The less they know the better."

"That's why you separated Brave and the Wild Woman. If it went wrong, which it did, then at least that solved another problem."

"Yes."

"What's left of the intelligence services will hunt us and the less they all know the better. If they pair up, it could be easy to find them."

"So we'll have to separate?"

"No, that's exactly what I'm trying to say. If they don't know we are together, then we'll be safe."

"I understand. I don't ever want to be apart. This is killing me, but I'll do it. The short-term pain of not being with you will be worth it in the long run when this is all done."

"Exactly."

"That's all I care about."

"Me too," Ned said, smiling.

"What about Mary Ann?"

"My contact tells me AIS have her."

"What are we going to do?"

"I'm thinking about it. She didn't know as much as The Wild Woman, so at least that's something."

"Can you track her location?"

"Yes, but I haven't turned it on yet. I didn't want them to find the bug. They would have searched her for sure and the signal would have been easy enough to find. I think I'll give it a few more hours then turn it on and we'll go from there."

"Okay. Let me know if I can help."

"I will. Now get back to work or they'll start talking."

The man they called Joe Byrne left the room as Ned pondered his next moves.

Chapter Sixteen

Max woke in the medical room at the Wool Shed.

"How you feeling, kid?" Hulk asked from the chair in the corner of the room.

"What happened?" Max asked.

"You had a mild seizure. Doc says the chemical in your system is stronger than originally anticipated. She also says you would have known that."

"I had some minor trembles and weakness," Max conceded.

"They've given you a couple of shots to balance you out, but they still haven't worked out a cure yet."

"I understand."

"They said you should take it easy."

"But?"

"But we all know you too well. Doc said you can can go back out there, but you need to monitor your symptoms. If they get worse, you need to get to a hospital."

"Got it."

"Good."

"Hey, Hulk, let's not tell Blake."

"He'll be pissed."

"He'll be fine and so will I. I don't want him to worry."

"Fair enough. So, are you ready to speak to the woman?"

"Has she said anything?"

"Nothing useful."

"I'll get changed and come over."

"Okay, kid. Take your time."

Hulk struggled to his feet, before leaving the room.

Max took a moment to catch his breath and gather his things.

Mary Ann sat in the cold darkness of the old iron shed on the grounds of the Wool Shed. She was cable tied and taped to a cold steel chair and was shivering from the wintery night air.

She had parachuted to the ground handcuffed to the missile crate. Liam, Karen and Tom had been doing supervisory shifts in rotation. She had dislocated her shoulder too, thanks to the force of the parachute, but was otherwise fine.

Max walked into the observation room watching Tom and Mary Ann. She was clearly getting under his skin. He was shifting on his feet and occasionally pacing to distract himself from her constant complaining and questioning.

"Where are we?" Mary Ann asked. "How can you do this to me? I'm a citizen of Australia, I have rights."

Tom paced again and rolled his eyes.

"If you let me go, I will make it worth your while," Mary Ann said in a seductive tone. "How long have you been here? I bet it's been a while since you've had a break and been with a woman. Probably not even enough privacy to sort yourself out in a place like this. I could help you with that. Just come and untie me and we could be together."

"And what exactly do you think would happen then?" Max asked walking into the shed to Tom's relief, which was clear on his face. "You are hundreds of kilometres from the nearest town and surrounded by guards. You wouldn't make it, even if you did get the drop on my colleague here."

Mary Ann stopped responding instantly and her demeanour changed. She knew Max was in charge and wouldn't take any of her shit. She knew what came next was going to be pain, until she broke. Ned had trained her and their team well.

"You and your comrades seem well-equipped and trained," Max said as he wandered over to face her. "I'm guessing at least one of you, if not others, has some military experience or maybe even covert ops skills. If I'm right, you will know what comes next."

She didn't flinch.

"You see I have been in that chair before," Max said, pulling his shirt up over his head to reveal bullet wounds and torture scars from his long career in intelligence operations."

Even Tom stopped pacing and studied Max's scarred body.

"I've inflicted thousands of times more pain and suffering, than the scars I carry," Max said, pulling his shirt back on. "I know what hurts and I know what works. I will eventually get what I want from you. Save us having to go through all that. Tell me who you work for and what you are trying to achieve."

Mary Ann was seriously considering it, but there was still some hesitation in her eyes.

"I can see you are frightened of your boss," Max said, unzipping a small case to reveal a needle and small glass vial. "He should be the least of your worries right at this moment. But I can assure you, he won't find you and he won't hurt you."

Mary Ann was too focused on the little vial, so Max proceeded to fill the syringe with the clear contents of the small flask. He flicked the syringe and squirted some of the liquid out to remove air bubbles.

"Last chance," Max said, walking over and sticking the needle in Mary Ann's neck. "Tell me what I need to know."

Max could see the conflict in her eyes. He knew she was trying to tell herself she could cope with the pain, but she wasn't confident. He could feel her cold skin under his fingers and could see the goosebumps on her neck. He could sense her deep discomfort from the needle in her neck. He dragged the needle to the side slightly to remind her it was there. She squirmed as much as she could without wanting to move the needle herself.

Max depressed the plunger and the liquid pumped down into her neck. He pulled the needle out and showed her. She had panic in her eyes, which was replaced after a few seconds with confusion as nothing happened.

"I thought it was supposed to work straight away," Tom asked, walking over. "Shouldn't she be screaming in pain by now?"

Max didn't budge. He kept his eyes locked on Mary Ann's. Tom stepped right in next to Max as Mary Ann's complexion changed. She turned red and started to sweat and shake. She gritted her teeth and her eyes looked almost sorrowful as the pain began to take hold.

Tom stepped back as she began to trash about in her seat and scream.

Max grabbed him and pulled him back in closer.

"You have to watch this," Max said. "No textbook can prepare you and no scenario we can put you through will be anything like what the real thing is. This is it. Can you handle it?"

Tom's usual bravado had vanished, but Max saw it returning. He stepped forward and watched Mary Ann scream in pain, shaking trying to get away.

After almost a full minute, the pain calmed down and Mary Ann slumped in the chair, bathed in her own sweat. She was exhausted.

"That was only five millilitres," Max said. "Fifteen risks cardiac arrest and twenty will kill you. Want another five?"

"No," Mary Ann managed to get out, shaking her head and crying.

"Who is he and what does he want?"

"I don't know his real name. We were all assigned names from the Kelly Gang."

"What is your goal?"

"Change."

"What change?"

"Lasting and permanent change."

"Is that what this means?" Max asked, pointing to her forearm and the fresh brand.

"It means for humanity and the world."

Max pulled out the vial and needle again, and set about drawing another five millilitres into the syringe.

"I'm telling you want you want."

"Not fast enough. What change do you want? What exactly do you mean by for humanity and the world?"

"We want a world free from capitalism, free from defence and intelligence systems, and borders and division. We want to see a thriving environment, less pollution and a return of nature."

"How does what happened in the Hunter Valley help your cause?"

"It is symbolic. People's lust for money led them to only pain and suffering. It was also a warning shot to the government to let them know we are serious. I'm sure your fiancée got the message."

Mary Ann made the mistake of smiling when she mentioned Blake. Max slammed the needle into her neck and depressed the plunger for the second time.

"Blake might have gotten your message," Max said, grabbing her by the neck. "Now it's time for you to get mine. I will fucking kill you and every one of your friends if you come that close to him again."

Mary Ann's smile rapidly faded as the serum took hold. Her screams and pain were amplified by the remnants of the first shot still in her system which doubled the effects.

Max held her throat refusing to let her eyes leave his. Max saw the pure fear in her eyes and he knew he had broken her. She saw nothing but death and fear in his eyes.

"How do I find them?" Max asked as the convulsions stopped.

"Find Joe Byrne and you'll find, Ned," Mary Ann said. "They're lovers. We aren't supposed to know. They keep it secret, but I figured it out months ago. Joe hasn't quite let go of his old ways, he still goes to bars and hooks up with strangers when he gets the chance. Ned would be furious if he knew."

"Where can I find him?"

"Melbourne is his favourite city. I'd try there."

Max turned back to the mirrored observation room.

"Send in, Arthur," Max said, before turning back to Mary Ann. "You're going to give the agent as full and detailed description of Joe Byrne and any other details you have on him. If I think you are lying or taking too long, I will come back in here and give you the full ten mills. You will suffer incredible pain before dying in agony from heart failure. Understood?"

Mary Ann just nodded. She was defeated.

Chapter Seventeen

The Prime Minister's motorcade rolled through the intersection at speed. The police escorts had blocked the traffic to allow it through. Police motorbikes played their game of leapfrog blocking intersection after intersection, until the motorcade passed, then they would race on to their next intersection.

It was unusual for the Australian Prime Minister to have such high security, but AIS and the federal police had agreed to ramp it up while there was a constant threat from the Kelly Gang.

Blake was riding in the Prime Minister's car.

"What is the best guess on what they want?" Ted Sawyer, the Australian Prime Minister asked.

"We don't have to guess, sir," Blake replied. "One of the women apprehended has told Max. They basically want nature and communism to reign here in Australia first, before taking over the world."

"What a bunch of horseshit. Their utopia doesn't exist and would never work."

"I think there is something more to it."

"Like what?"

"I don't know. Just a gut feeling."

"Well, that's why I brought you in, Blake. There's no one better to be in your position and advising me and the Cabinet. Trust your feelings and keep us informed."

"Yes, sir."

"You don't need to call me sir, Blake. You're not the head of AIS anymore and not a public servant. You're the Deputy Prime Minister. We are equals. Call me Ted."

"Yes, sir. Ted it is. It'll take some time to adjust, but I'll get there."

"I'm counting on it."

"So, this event. I'll say a few words on the project then introduce you?"

"Yes, then we'll take some questions. I'll do news of the day and general talking points. You handle the project."

"Done."

"I'm glad you're on board, Blake. You're going to be a great minister."

"Thanks, Ted," Blake said as the car pulled into the grounds of the defence contractor.

"Let's go get 'em," Ted said as the door opened and he stepped out.

Blake followed as they were met by the CEO and Chair of Hamilton Hunter Hughes, a major defence contractor, which also went by Triple H. They all shook hands before the CEO led the two politicians down to the parade ground.

There was a crowd assembled, including numerous journalists and camera crews. Two small, but impressive looking tanks sat proudly to each side of the narrow stage.

Blake and Ted were shown the unmanned ground attack vehicle. A woman in army fatigues started the tank using a small handheld tablet and did some basic manoeuvres, before accelerating the tank away to put it through its paces.

The CEO led the pair and the media up to a viewing platform. The tank rolled fast through an obstacle course, splashing through mud, wading through water and quickly ascending and descending the manmade hills on its tracks.

It then turned to face a massive range and an alarm rang out, before the cannon on the tank shot a huge round from its barrel smashing through a long lick of flames. A makeshift target at the end of the range exploded and dirt and dust kick up from the massive crater.

The crowd all clapped as the CEO indicated they should all move back to their seats. She led the politicians onto the stage and showed them to their seats, before taking to the podium.

"The future of warfare is here," the CEO said, raising her hands and clenching her fists. "No longer do we need to put our troops in harm's way. We now have drones for the air, land and sea."

The crowd applauded again.

"It is my great pleasure to welcome the Prime Minister and Deputy Prime Minister to Hamilton Hunter Hughes. I would especially like to acknowledge the Deputy Prime Minister and Minister for Defence and Counter-Intelligence and acknowledge his military and intelligence service to our nation. Ladies and gentlemen, please join me in welcoming to the podium, Admiral Blake Smyth."

The crowd clapped as Blake shook hands with the CEO.

"Thank you, Kerry, for your warm welcome," Blake said. "And thank you for this morning's demonstration. Drones will never replace the need for our brave men and women to don our uniforms and serve our country, but projects like this unmanned ground attack vehicle will go a long way to defeating our enemies and minimising our risks. People often question our ongoing investment in defence and national security. They believe our nation would be better served by investing in other worthy causes, such as health and education. Now I agree governments must invest in those important areas, but we cannot be complacent on national defence. I have dedicated my career to protecting this country and our allies from those who would do us harm. And yes, there are plenty out there who would like it if our people, culture, races and religions were wiped from the face of the earth. Some are foreign powers or are backed by foreign powers. But the threat of terrorism remains at an all time high. These terrorists are both foreign and domestic. We must be prepared for all scenarios and that's why I am such a strong supporter of this project. The Government has invested one point five billion dollars in this project alone and we will be increasing our defence capital expenditure over coming years to around three percent of GDP. Our government is preparing for the worst, while hoping for the best, and we are unwavering in our commitment to national security. It is now my great honour to introduce our Prime Minister and my friend, Ted Sawyer. Please join me in welcoming him to the stage."

Blake joined the crowd clapping the Prime Minister as he made his way towards the podium.

As Blake turned to watch the Prime Minister pass, there was a long crack in the distance and Blake saw Ted get spun around on his heal. Instinctively, Blake lunged forwarded and tackled the Prime Minister to the ground. He rolled him over, then dragged him towards the back of the stage as a second crack echoed over the panicked and fleeing crowd.

Blake saw the bullet slam into Ted's leg and he screamed in agony. Blake dragged Ted over the back of the stage onto the concrete as a third gunshot echoed out and he saw the Chair of Triple H's head explode in a shower of red mist and her body crumple to the ground.

"Jesus Christ," Ted said. "What the fuck is going on?"

"Someone is doing their best to kill you, sir," Blake said, assessing Ted's wounds.

"Where the fuck are our details?"

Blake stole a quick look for the police guards. Half were scrambling towards the shooter but were being held back by gunfire, while the other half were running for their location. Blake saw an agent trying to get into the Prime Minister's car, but his head flew back as a bullet hit it.

"Why the fuck are they out of the car?" Blake asked himself.

Four feds reached them and two took Ted's arms getting ready to move him.

"Give me a gun," Blake demanded.

"No, sir," the head of the PM's detail replied. "You're a civilian now."

Blake grabbed his hand and twisted it into an unnatural position, before disarming him.

"I'm cleared now," Blake said taking the lead. "Follow me."

Blake led the small group towards the cars, pausing to check the way occasionally and to return or provide cover fire.

A gunshot rang out and slammed into the concrete in front of them and they dived for cover. Blake sat there thinking, then settled on a course of action.

"I can't let you do that," the head of detail said.

"You don't know what I'm thinking," Blake said.

"Sure I do. You AIS boys don't give us enough credit. Let me do it."

"No. You have a job. Get him to the car."

"My job is to protect you too."

"Not today it's not."

Blake ran firing hard at the area where he thought the shooter was, trying to draw his fire.

It worked. Shots rang out, hitting the concrete behind Blake, but then he heard three more shots in quick succession and turned back to see Ted take two shots – one to the body and the other to the head. Blake knew he was dead instantly. He leapt for cover as another large round cut a massive hole in the concrete pillar he ducked behind.

He looked around for support but found none, until he sighted the small tablet on a nearby seat. He ran hard and fast, and scooped it up, before diving over a concrete planter box, full of blooming lavender and rosemary.

Blake unlocked the tablet and within seconds the second tank came to life and started rotating its turret. He waited for a moment to see something, anything which would give up the shooter's location. Then he saw it, an orange muzzle flash. Blake quickly checked the feds were at a safe distance, then fired the cannon.

The massive round exploded from the barrel and the small tank rocked and its long burst of flames shot out. The round shattered the trees in the distance and levelled a large clearing, leaving a massive crater where the gunmen have been laying. Blake wasn't sure, but he thought he saw a burst of red mist amongst the dirt.

Chapter Eighteen

"I, Blake Isaac Smyth, do solemnly and sincerely affirm and declare that I will well and truly serve His Majesty King Edwin the First, His heirs and successors, and the Commonwealth of Australia, according to law, in the office of Prime Minister," Blake said, before he sat down across from the Governor-General and signed his commission documents.

"Congratulations, Prime Minister," the Governor-General said, shaking Blake's hand.

"I wish it could have been under different circumstances, Your Excellency," Blake said solemnly.

"So do I, Blake. Ted was a good man and he had grand plans for this country. That duty and responsibility now falls to you."

"Yes, sir."

"You know better than most that we are in crisis. The country needs a leader and you're it. I have every faith in you, Blake, and I know you will lead us through it."

"Thank you, sir. I will do my best."

"I've seen you at your best, that will do."

The two men shook hands again as the private swearing in ended. Blake climbed on board the bulletproof BMW and his motorcade sped down the long treelined road in Yarralumla heading for Parliament House.

When Blake arrived in the Prime Minister's courtyard, he was met by staff from both his office and the former Prime Minister's office. They walked him through the next steps, including the calls which had been received from various leaders from around the world with sympathies and congratulations.

"I don't have time for them now," Blake said.

"The Americans and British will need phone calls in the next couple of hours," his Chief of Staff said. "They will want a personal update on the situation. You have to call them as a matter of urgency."

"Put a prioritised list together and start lining up times. I also need to speak to Max, the Cabinet and the media, not necessarily in that order."

"Agent Shaw has been calling repeatedly."

"With any updates?"

"No, sir. These were personal calls."

"Find five minutes so I can call him before the press conference. I need an update on the search."

"That won't be necessary, sir."

"Why's that?"

"He's arriving any minute."

"He's come in from the Wool Shed?"

"Yes, sir. There was a lot of swearing and well, let's just say he is on route."

"Show him straight in when he gets here."

"Yes, sir. Would you like to read the remarks we have prepared?"

"No. I won't be needing them. I'm just going to talk for a bit."

"Are you sure?"

"Yes. Thank you though."

Blake walked into his office and closed the door on the faces of his advisers. The last few hours had been a whirlwind. He had spoken to Ted's wife and children. To most of his cabinet colleagues and the leader of the opposition. The Governor-General and even the King himself. His colleagues were already jockeying for positions and offering their support for his leadership. He had been sworn in as Prime Minister as was protocol for continuity of government, but he was yet to be formally elected leader of his party. The more political and aspirational among his colleagues saw an opportunity and it turned his stomach thinking about them all tripping over themselves to get a better job for themselves. Ted had only been dead for a couple of hours, certainly not days or weeks, and it was like he was never even there for some of his supposed friends.

Blake remembered how much he disliked politicians and for the first time tasted regret in his choice to join parliament. If he did become leader officially, he would seek to weed out that ugliness in politics.

The door to the prime minister's office burst open and Blake heard the protests of his personal assistant.

"It'll be fine," Max said, storming in and shutting the door behind him.

"Max, you look great," Blake said, registering Max's suit and tie, and momentarily forgetting all that was pilling up on his shoulders.

"Are you okay?" Max asked, ignoring the compliment and walking over to Blake.

"Yes, I'm fine," Blake responded, hugging Max. "Did you get my brief?"

"Yes. Only the one shooter?"

"I think so."

"And you killed them with a tank?"

"Yep."

"Good."

"Any leads?"

"A few."

"What are they?"

"AIS will follow up."

"And what will you do? Continue at the Wool Shed and let them sort it out?"

"No. I'm taking over your security detail."

"You are not."

"I can't protect you if I'm not right here with you. So, I'm staying put."

"I'll be fine, Max. I've got an amazing team."

"Tell that to the last guy. He's the one in the morgue, riddled with bullets."

"And you really think they haven't re-doubled their efforts and increased my security since?"

"That's not the point."

"I know what you think you are doing is right, but I'm the Prime Minister now, at least for now, and I need you back at work."

"You mean back, back, don't you?"

"You're already back, Max. You're the only one who hasn't seen that yet. It's time for you to embrace it. We need you."

"I need you. I can't lose you."

"You won't. And you know I meant the country needs you."

"We've given everything to our country, Blake. We don't need to give our lives. You are the Prime Minister now and your predecessor would agree, that's a fucking risky job, especially while these nut jobs are still out there."

"Review the security detail with Kate, make sure you're comfortable, then get back to work."

"Yes, sir."

"Don't be a smartarse. I can't handle that today."

"Sorry."

"I know you are worried and I have to say I am too, but not for me. For the country, if we don't find these people."

"I understand. How are you?"

"It's a lot to take in."

"I can only imagine."

"You used to work here, you get it."

"I left though remember. Fucking politicians. No offence."

"You don't have to tell me. Ted's not even cold and the sharks are circling."

Max steadied himself on the back of a leather chair. He looked down at the floor as Blake saw his knuckles turn white.

"Are you okay, Max?"

"I'm fine."

"You're not. What's wrong?"

"Just a few little effects from the Hunter Valley."

"You're still having symptoms?"

"It's nothing."

"Have you seen the medic?"

"Yes. I'm fine."

Max let go of the chair having regained his faculties and stood tall. He saw the look on Blake's face, but gave him a reassuring, but dismissive nod.

"Are you going to stay on?" Max asked, changing the subject.

"That'll be up to the party. I've gotten a lot of support, so we will just wait and see."

"Do you want it?"

"I think I can make a difference."

"Then you have my full support, Blake. Whatever you decide I'll be with you."

"Thank you," Blake said, kissing Max as the door opened interrupting them.

"Apologies, sir," the personal assistant said, her cheeks reddening in embarrassment. "The press are waiting."

"Thank you."

"Time to go feed the vultures," Max said.

"Will you come with me?"

"I guess," Max agreed reluctantly.

Blake squeezed his hand and then walked out into the courtyard to the flashes of hundreds of cameras and the shouted questions of the press pack.

He walked to the lectern as Max took a position just behind him to the left. Max's cold eyes scanned the journalists as Blake raised his arms to quieten them down.

"At twelve thirty-two p.m. the Prime Minister, Ted Sawyer, was assassinated," Blake said. "The Australia Intelligence Service and Australian Federal Police, along with a number of other agencies and investigations teams are onsite at the facility. I want all Australians and our friends and foes around the world to know that we will not rest until we have found his killers and brought them to justice. There is no where on this planet these animals can hide. So I say to them, run all you like, but don't celebrate your win today. You haven't won a thing for tomorrow every shadow you see could very well be one of our elite spies or special forces members who will snuff you from existence."

"I spoke to Trisha Sawyer this afternoon and join with her in her grief," Blake continued. "I passed on the thanks and sympathies of our grateful nation. She is with her family and she has asked for privacy, and I ask the media to respect this request. On a personal level, I want to say Ted was a great friend and a great leader, and he will be dearly missed. He had a dream for this country and I hope in some way I will be able to help deliver his legacy."

"On logistics and other matters," Blake went on, "I have been sworn in as Prime Minister in accordance with our continuity of government policy. The party will meet in the coming days to elect a leader. The Cabinet and ministry remain in place until after that meeting. Government continues and our nation will too."

Blake finished his remarks and the journalists all started shouting their questions.

"I'll take a few questions," Blake said, raising his hands again to calm them down, "but you'll be patient and civilised."

The press pack did settle slightly, then Blake pointed to one of the journalists.

"You have only been Deputy Prime Minister and even a member of parliament for a short period," the journalist stated, "what makes you think you are fit to serve as Prime Minister? Can the country be confident in your ability to lead us through this crisis?"

"If anything, I am the best placed to manage this crisis. I managed the Australian Intelligence Service and worked with the agency for decades. I held the rank of Vice Admiral of the

Australian Navy until I joined the parliament. I have served in both management and on the front lines of defence and our intelligence services. The blood of our enemies and of our brave soldiers, sailors, airmen and women, and agents stains my hands and my soul. I carry the scars of battle and the burdens of my decisions, and I am ready to lead this nation through this crisis and to bring Ted's killers to justice."

"Will you stay on as leader following the party meeting?" another journalist yelled.

"With respect to Ted's memory, it's not a decision I have taken or will even publicly speculate on today. I will say it will be a matter for the party room and I will make the relevant announcements when it is appropriate."

"Do you have any leads on the Prime Minister's murderers?" a journalist rushed out.

"We are working on a number of leads and for obvious reasons I won't be announcing those in this press conference. I will repeat though that we are confident we will find those responsible and bring them to justice."

"Is there any truth to the rumour you were the one who killed the assassin, with a tank no less?" a journalist yelled from the back.

"There will be a full investigation and I won't comment any further until it's released."

"How does it feel to be the first openly gay prime minister?" one of the press yelled.

"It's not relevant, especially today," Blake fired back bluntly. "My sexuality doesn't define who I am, what I do or how I do it. I do want to thank Max for his love and support throughout my career and his ongoing love and support in this role, including here today in what is one of the darkest days in our nation's history."

"Max! Max!" a journo from the back yelled. "Agent Shaw do you have any thoughts?"

Blake stepped to the side and let Max step forward.

"On what?" Max asked coldly.

"Your fiancé's rise to the top job and the hunt for the terrorists who helped get him there."

"Blake has dedicated his life to serving this country. There is no one more capable and no one I'd rather have leading us. There is no one who could do a better job and he has my full support. As for the terrorists, you can hide behind your masks and make your threats. You can lie, cheat, steal and even kill, but know this, you can never be safe. No longer can you walk this planet free from my gaze and my desire to kill you. I'm coming for you."

Max stepped back and the journalists all looked around amongst their own number as Blake stepped forward.

"That's it," Blake said. "I'll keep you updated on the situation as it unfolds. Thank you."

The pair left through the doors behind them as the press continued to shout questions.

Chapter Nineteen

Max sat in the comfortable business class seats on the AIS private jet. He had reviewed Blake's security detail and once he was as satisfied as he could be, he left on Blake's request.

There was a knock on the thin door and Max looked up.

"Sorry, sir," Liam said, entering the small cabin, "do you have a moment?"

"Yes, of course," Max said. "How are you feeling?"

"It's still sore to touch," Liam said, softly touching his bruised and stitched forehead.

"It will be a for a few days, but it will heal."

"And what about the mental scars?"

Max put his phone down on the desk and looked Liam in the eyes.

"Sorry," Liam said, turning back for the door. "I shouldn't have said anything. Sorry to disturb you."

"Stop," Max said, standing and walking to the door.

He invited Liam into the room and gestured for him to take a seat as he closed the door.

"Why don't you tell me what's on your mind?"

"It's just," Liam hesitated. "I can't stop thinking about seeing those men and women torn apart by bullets and the explosion. Every time I close my eyes, I can see them. I can smell the smoke and flesh. I can hear their screams and the sirens."

He paused and Max could tell he was reliving the attack on the Reserve Bank in his mind.

"I'm not sure I'm cut out for this," Liam admitted.

"Nothing will ever prepare you for what you saw and experienced. We can tell you what it is like and try to explain it, but until you live it and breath it yourself, the words wouldn't do it justice. I would be more worried if you didn't feel like this."

Liam looked up for the first time with tears welling in his eyes.

"It means you're one of the good guys."

Max walked over and put a hand on Liam's shoulder as the younger man let a tear roll down his cheek.

"This job isn't for everyone. It wasn't for me either. I sat across from my instructors like you are now and said the same things as you are now. They told me I had the skills they needed to stop more people from dying. They told me I could find the people responsible for these atrocities and make sure they could never hurt anyone again. And I know what you're thinking, they manipulated me and you're probably right. But I felt a burning inside myself. It was part anger and part fear. I knew at my very core I couldn't let the bad guys win. The pain they inflicted needed to end and I knew I had the skills to stop them. I couldn't sit by and let them win. Now you have a choice. I'm not going to sit here and pressure you one way or another, only you can make the choice. I want you on my team and this only proves it to me, but if you don't want it, I will respect that and you can go. But if you choose to stay, you must find a way for the hurt you are feeling to fuel your desire for revenge, for retribution and to help those who can't defend themselves. Channel it, harness it, embrace it, but never, ever forget it. Keep your love and kindness in your heart – that's the only way to protect yourself and keep you grounded, and make sure you stay as one of the good guys."

Liam wiped away a tear and breathed deeply. His body language changed.

"I want to get them," Liam said.

"Good. I need you. But promise me this. Promise you will always come and talk to me if you need to. Don't think you are on your own. We are a team. You got that?"

"Yes."

"And you promise?"

"I do."

"Good. Head back to the conference room, when you are ready, we'll go over the plan once more before we land."

"Got it. Thank you."

"Of course."

Max gathered his files and phone, and left Liam in the room to compose himself.

Max grabbed the handrail which ran along the wall under the window. Every muscle in his body was tightening and he started to sweat.

He stopped in his tracks. Something wasn't right. He turned and struggled along the wall to the medical bay and collapsed in the chair.

"Jesus, Agent Shaw, are you okay?" the doctor asked.

"I don't think so," Max said, trying to control his breathing.

The doctor called for a nurse and the two medical professionals set about hooking Max up to various machines. The nurse drew two vials of blood and rushed to a nearby computer and started testing it.

"I was exposed to the chemical in the Hunter Valley," Max said.

"Have you been experiencing symptoms since?" the doctor asked.

"Yes. They gave me some medication at the Wool Shed."

"Others from the event are experiencing light-headedness, headaches, nausea, fatigue and muscle spasms. Are you experiencing those?"

"Yes."

"The symptoms have progressed in others. They're getting worse, not better."

"What's the bottom line?"

"I can give you something to manage the symptoms, similar to what they gave you before, but there's no guarantee it will cure them. The most likely thing that will happen is a short reprieve before the symptoms return."

"Give it to me, Doc, and keep me posted on a long term solution."

"If there is one," the doctor said.

Max just starred at the doctor.

"They're working on it," the doctor said. "The ANU lab is in overdrive, so is the medical research team at Newcastle Uni. I'm sure they will figure it out."

"Monitor it will you?"

"Of course," the doctor said as he plunged a needle into Max's shoulder.

Max almost instantly felt better as the shot did its job.

"Thanks, Doc."

"Keep an eye on it. If you feel the symptoms worsening, let me know."

"Can't you just give me more of that?"

"It's full of adrenaline, among other things. Too much will start to affect your heart."

"Fabulous."

"I recommend you get some rest."

"That's not happening," Max said, getting to his feet. "Thanks though."

Max walked out of the medical bay. He joined the small team in the conference room and they walked through the game plan, before the sleek plane touched down and taxied to the private AIS hanger.

The team had made it to the city and were set up in a hotel across the road from one of Melbourne's most popular gay nightclubs, The Grey Area. They had watched people come and go for hours, but the tempo was picking up as the night rolled on.

Max sent Jonnie, Tom and Karen into the bar, and continued to watch the growing line outside for anyone matching the detailed drawing compiled from Mary Ann's description of the man they called Joe Byrne.

"Max," Liam said, "I think that's him."

"Let me see," Max said, walking over and taking the binoculars Liam offered. "Where is he?"

"He just joined the line. White jacket."

"I see him," Max said as he studied the man's features. "Grab the camera and take a few snaps of him. Get a close up on his face if you can."

While Liam took some photos of the man they suspected as Joe, Max called Hulk and asked him to put Mary Ann on the phone.

"Show her the photo," Max said. "Is it him?"

"Is this your mate, Joe Byrne?" he heard Hulk ask.

"Yes, that's him," Mary Ann's voice confirmed.

"Got it. Thanks, Hulk."

Max ended the call without needing to speak any further.

"Let's move," Max said to Liam, before keying his comms unit to speak to Jonnie. "Bravo, you copy?"

"Prince," Jonnie replied, *"I copy."*

"He's on his way in," Max said as they started down the stairs. "Observe only."

"Ack, Prince. Observe until you arrive."

Max and Liam walked over to the line. There were about six people in the line between them and Joe. They idly chatted like lifelong friends, watching Joe shift impatiently ahead of them. He was average height, maybe five, ten. Light brown, almost sandy blond hair. Not conventionally handsome, but there was something about him. Max figured he was about thirty, but he had younger boyish features and he was clearly very fit and athletic. It didn't look like he was here with anyone.

The bouncer checked Joe's ID, then opened the rope to let him through.

"Through the door now, Bravo," Max said under his breath. "White jacket."

"Got him," Jonnie replied. *"Tom is on the far side and Karen is on the dance floor."*

"I see him," Tom added.

"Me too," Karen said, slightly out of breath.

"Don't make it obvious. Keep your distance. Don't make unnecessary or too long eye contact."

Max and Liam showed their IDs and were waved through by the bouncer who told them to have a good night.

"Got you coming through the door, Prince," Jonnie said from his seat on the lefthand wall of the venue with a wave.

Max walked over to Jonnie and the pair hugged like long lost friends, while Liam made his way to the bar to buy them drinks.

Max and Jonnie sat with their backs to the wall watching Joe weave his way through the crowd.

Liam arrived with the drinks and handed them over, before heading onto the dance floor to keep Karen company.

They traded turns of sitting, buying drinks, dancing for quite a while, before Byrne made his move. Max watched him intently, studying the man and reading his intentions. If Mary Ann was right, Byrne would be looking to hook up with one of the men in the club, either at the venue or take him home, but Max was betting on it happening here.

Joe kissed his dance partner's neck, then the pair made out aggressively amongst the crowd. They weren't the only ones doing it. In fact, some of the couples were well beyond first base and edging closer to the others throughout the venue. The rules were somewhat more liberal in gay bars. Alcohol flowed in high volumes, but so did cocaine and pills. Inhibitions were all but non-existent and it was nothing to see couples having sex in dark corners and hallways, as well as in the back rooms.

Max saw Joe take his new friend by the hand and drag him towards the back of the venue.

"Okay," Max said over his comms unit to his team, "they're making their move. Who's closest?"

"I am," Tom said. *"Want me to follow?"*

"Hold your position. I'm on my way."

"Have fun," Jonnie laughed with his radio on so Tom could hear.

"What's that mean?"

"You'll see."

Max arrived at Tom's side and acted as if he was drunk. He transformed instantly into an over the top flirt, catching Tom off guard.

"Hey there, handsome," Max said, rubbing his hand down Tom's chest.

"What are you doing?" Tom asked under his breath.

"You're going to need to play along if we have any chance of getting back there."

"Jesus."

Max wrapped his arms behind Tom's neck and passionately kissed him. Tom was shocked to start with, but eventually realised he needed to get into character. Max grabbed him by the hand and pulled him down the dark corridor.

Max giggled excitedly like a drunk regular at the club. He wolf-whistled and slapped a guy's naked arse as they passed. The guy was getting a blow job in the hallway and he moaned as Max slapped his arse. Tom's eyes went wide on seeing the various couples and throuples, and others actively engaging in all types of sexual activity in the hallways and the room at the back of the club.

"What happens when we get to our position?" Tom asked nervously.

"That depends on how long it takes," Max replied.

"How long what takes?" Tom asked, but Max didn't say anything.

He felt Tom's palm getting sweatier and he thought he could feel him shaking.

"You'll be fine," Max said, squeezing his hand.

Max found a dark spot along one of the walls, a few metres from Joe and his one-night lover. They were getting hot and very heavy, as Max lent back hard on the wall with his shoulders, and pulled Tom in for another kiss.

Max let the charade go on for a few minutes, then spun him around, pressing Tom's chest against the wall.

"Wait," Tom said, very convincingly and loud enough for others to hear.

He turned back to face Max. Max smiled at Tom, then slapped himself and fell to the floor. There were gasps of shock and the moan and other various noises paused.

"Oh my God!" Max said from the ground. "How dare you hit me!"

People started to scramble to help Max and scold Tom, including Joe's friend who reached out to help Max to his feet.

Tom left the room in a hurry as people yelled at him and asked the darkness if Max was alright.

As he was getting up, Max pretended to slip and his hand hit Joe's leg. Joe stepped back having felt a minor pain, but helped Max up all the same. Max thanked him quickly, not letting his face into the light.

"I'm fine," Max said. "You all just keep having fun, lucky devils! I'm going to find me a real man!"

There were some laughs and words of encouragement as he skipped out of the room.

"Tracker planted," Max said into his comms unit. "Clear out. Take a lap then get to the hotel."

Max walked back through the smoke-filled club, as the lasers danced around the room and strobe lights blinked incessantly to the heavy beat of the music. The bouncer opened the door for him, thanked him for coming to the club and told him to be safe and enjoy his night. Max nodded and walked off into the dark night.

Chapter Twenty

"Where have you been?" Ned asked through Joe's tinny mobile phone speaker.

"I'm still in Melbourne," Joe replied. "I was arranging our next shipment."

"Pearce is dead."

"I figured."

"Really?"

"Yeah, I saw the news. It's pretty hard to miss the death of the Prime Minister and reports of the new one killing the assassin with a tank."

"Why didn't you reach out?"

"I figured that the bigger risk was an intercepted call. Although I guess that's gone out the window with this call. I just got on with my mission."

"I don't need your sass."

"I didn't mean to sound sassy, I'm just really tired."

"Why?"

"I went to a club last night."

"Do you really think that's wise given everything that's happening?"

"I just needed to let my hair down. Don't worry, I only had a couple of drinks then went back to the hotel."

"I think we need to keep a lower profile."

"You're probably right. That'll be the last time, until all this is wrapped up."

"Good. Thank you. Sorry I'm just under a lot of pressure. I wish you were here."

"I'll be there soon enough. But don't worry about me. I know what I need to do."

"Just finalise it and get back here."

"I will. Can't wait to see you."

"Me too. When can I expect you?"

"Sometime tomorrow. Probably about lunch time."

"Good. Be careful. See you tomorrow."

"I will. See you then."

Joe ended the call and felt a pang of guilt for sleeping with some random guy last night, but what was he to do. It had been weeks since he and Ned had been alone together. He had needs.

He gathered his things into a small backpack and headed out the door.

He strolled aimlessly through the neighbourhood admiring the street art and nodding hello to locals as he walked. He checked his watch and saw he had an hour until the meet, so he slowed his pace and started his circuitous route to the location.

When the hour clicked over on his watch, he walked into the old abandoned train tunnel. He stepped lightly and dodged the various water filled potholes and trip hazards. A few hundred metres into the tunnel, it opened up into an old station which was no longer in use. The old stained tiles where covered in graffiti and old advertisements from the decade it last operated as a working station.

There were three men and one woman standing on the platform. He climbed up the stairs and looked his contact in the eyes.

"It was only supposed to be you," Joe said.

"I know," the woman said in a heavy Russian accent. "But I wasn't sure you would hold up your end of the bargain. I see I was wrong."

She waved her hand and the three men all walked back a few metres.

"It's nice to meet you again," she said offering her cheek which he kissed.

"And you. Should we get straight to business?"

"Do you have the microprocessor?"

"Do you have the files?"

"Are we really going to play this game?"

"I'll show you mine, if you show me yours."

"How exciting," she said, clicking her fingers.

One of the men stepped forward and past her an old iPhone.

Joe took a small plastic box from his backpack and they exchanged the packages.

He looked impatiently at her as she opened her little box.

"Oh I am sorry," she said, barely amount to able to contain her excitement. "The access code is one, four, two, zero, nine, eight."

Joe typed the code into the small phone and the screen unlocked. He scrolled to a secure app and entered the same code. A map of Australia appeared and he zoomed in on various locations. When one was large enough, he clicked it and the blueprints for the location appeared. He found a second file with a long list of names and locations. He scrolled until he found one he recognised. Satisfied, he put the phone back in his pocket.

"Spasibo," Joe said.

"Thank you too. It is a pleasure doing business with you."

"Let's not be strangers."

"You can call me anytime," she said seductively.

"I just might," Joe said with a smile.

As he turned to walk away, there was a series of deep thumps followed by the sound of cans sliding along the tiles. Joe and the Russians all looked down to see the small cylinders slide between them, before a blinding white light shot out in all directions with a deafening blast. The group clutched their eyes and ears in pain, and stumbled from side to side.

Both Joe and the Russian woman were clutching for their own weapons. The Russian managed to get one shot off, before the pistol dropped from her hands.

Chapter Twenty-One

Max wandered the Melbourne streets occasionally stopping to look in a shop window. He bought a coffee and slowly sipped it from the takeaway cup as he meandered about.

The earpiece he was wearing just looked like any other ear buds on the pedestrians who were busy moving about the city listening to music or podcasts. But his was broadcasting a live stream from AIS headquarters in Canberra.

"All units the target is making his way onto Hume Street," came the report. *"Prince, hold your distance. He's doubling back."*

Max recognised his callsign and took a moment to look in a real estate agent's front window at properties for sale. He didn't risk looking in the direction of the target. He knew he was walking back towards him, looking for anyone who might be following him.

"Closing in, Prince," the AIS analysis watching the tracker on a monitor in Canberra said. *"Twenty metres."*

Max opened the door to the real estate and walked in, as his target walked past without giving him another look. Max grabbed a brochure and busied himself reading it, keeping one eye on the window tracking his target across the road.

"Can I help you, sir?" an overly eager man in a tight blue suit asked walking towards him.

"No, thank you," Max said. "Just wanted a brochure."

"We got other listings online and I'd be more than happy to show you through them in my office."

"No, the brochure is fine for now. Thanks."

Max grabbed the door and went to leave.

"Wait," the real estate agent said, chasing him to the door. "Here's my card. If you need anything at all, my mobile number is on there. And so is my email."

Max closed the door before the man could finish his sentence and walked off following the target at a distance.

This game continued for around an hour, before the target straightened his course.

"Prince, he looks like he is moving into an industrial park," the analyst said. *"You might want to hang back. There aren't too any other pedestrians around."*

"Ack," Max replied, slowing his walk. "Bravo, how far out are you?"

"Two blocks behind you," Jonnie replied. *"Thirty seconds."*

"Hold at one. I think he's about to move in."

"Ack. Moving now."

Max snuck along the railway lines, using the old cars and shipping containers for cover as he watched Joe slip into the darkness of the old railway tunnel.

"Any chance we have surveillance in the tunnel?" Max asked.

"No, Prince," the analyst said. *"It's too old. There is a platform a couple of hundred metres in, but it was abandoned before CCTV."*

"That's got to be where he's headed."

"Unless he saw you. Could be a trap."

"Could be, but I don't think he saw me. Bravo, let's move."

"Right behind you, Prince," Jonnie said.

Max drew his silenced pistol and waited by the tunnel entrance for Jonnie to arrive.

A black van stopped a few metres away and Jonnie jumped out, followed by a small team of agents and the three recruits.

"Bravo, with me," Max ordered. "The rest of you hold here, until we give you the green light."

The assembled team were kitted out in full combat gear. They all nodded their agreement.

Max and Jonnie moved into the dark tunnel. They were quiet, but quick. Occasionally they stopped to listen for movement, in case it was a trap, then proceeded on.

Ahead there was a dull glow from the old platform and Max started to recognise voices.

"Do you have the microprocessor?" a Russian woman asked.

"Do you have the files?" followed in what could only be Joe's voice.

"This is Prince," Max whispered into his microphone. "Green light, fast and quiet to the platform."

Max and Jonnie inched closer to get a visual, and saw the pair exchanging small objects. They watched as Joe unlocked the phone and scrolled through it.

The team arrived as the pair were exchanging pleasantries and saying their goodbyes. Max gave the signal and three of his team members stepped forward, and pumped small underbarrel launchers which thumped out flashbang grenades.

Max watched the cans bounce at Joe's feet, before covering his own eyes and ears, waiting for the explosion.

It reverberated through the tunnel and as the wave raced past Max he sprung into action with Jonnie at his side. Max ran up the stairs as Jonnie ran along the track in front of the platform. They both took out a bodyguard each, before turning their weapons onto the third who was hit simultaneously with four bullets and dropped to the floor beside his comrades.

Joe and the Russian woman were staggering around the platform, both trying to bring up their own guns. Max pistol-whipped Joe in the side of the head, knocking him out cold. And Jonnie fired one round into the Russian woman's leg. She fired one shot, before she fell awkwardly to the ground and her shiny silver pistol scattered across the tiles.

Max and Jonnie both held the targets in their sights as the rest of the team came onto the platform. Two of the team members flexicuffed the two prisoners while two others checked the three bodyguards were dead and searched their bodies for IDs and anything else which could be useful.

"Secure the phone and the microprocessor," Max commanded, pointing to the two objects. "And search their pockets and bags."

Max looked around the dark space and saw Tom on his knees near the tracks. Jonnie saw too and ran over.

Max jumped off the platform to find Tom looking down at Karen who had a bullet tear in the side of her neck and was losing blood quickly. Tom was holding the wound together as best he could, but there was so much blood. Karen was trying to say something, but she couldn't get the words out.

"AIS this is Prince," Max shouted. "We need an ambulance here now!"

"Roger that," the analyst said. *"They're on route."*

Chapter Twenty-Two

Liam cringed as he listened to Max describe in graphic detail the torture he was going to put Joe through if he didn't start talking soon. He thought he saw some level of fear in the young terrorist's eyes, but there was more than a hint of defiance, or maybe it was disbelief and shock.

Tom for his part was wide-eyed and taking everything in. Liam couldn't work out what his colleague was thinking, but he seemed almost too eager. Too keen to witness whatever horrible interrogation techniques were about to be deployed.

They had arrived at the Melbourne safehouse over an hour ago and their adrenaline was still pumping.

Jonnie and his team had taken Karen to the hospital. She was in an induced coma awaiting surgery. Jonnie would be due back at the safehouse soon and Max wanted to get started on extracting information from Joe. He also wanted to continue Liam and Tom's training, so they stayed.

"Normally," Max said, standing in front of Joe, "I'd start off with something easy, like your name. That way we can get to know each other. We would stretch the session into hours, maybe even days, until you broke and told me everything I need to hear. But I have a feeling. Call it gut-instinct. That you and your friends are about to ramp this up and I don't think I have the time to slowly break you. Do you know what that means?"

Joe said nothing. He just kept looking straight ahead trying to mentally prepared for what was to come.

"It means we need to step this up quickly to get results. I can tell just by your body language, that you have some form of training. You've probably been told how to get through the torture and hold out as long as you can. I can see the wheels turning in your mind. I've sat in that chair before too, too many times, and I can tell you that nothing really prepares you for the pain. And, even if you make it through the first few rounds, everyone eventually breaks. So, how would you like to proceed? Pain or pain-free?"

Joe looked up in almost tearful defiance. Scared, but trying to will himself into embracing the pain. Rebellious, yet not confident. Max could see every conflict he was experiencing. He was putting the pieces together. He knew Joe didn't want the pain and more importantly he knew Joe wanted to test both of them. He wanted to see what Max was capable of, but he also wanted to see how much he could take. He seemed to want to experience some pain, maybe out of loyalty or guilt for getting caught, or maybe to justify breaking in the end – at least he had tried.

Max thought one dramatic action was more likely than not to break his prisoner. It would tick all the boxes, then he'd start talking. Some broke through fear of torture. Others needed to be tortured for hours or days. He figured Joe would talk soon enough with some encouragement.

"I've told you all the things I will do to you," Max said. "I think you get it. I will do whatever it takes, even if that means sending you back to your boyfriend in little pieces."

Joe's eyes widened on the word boyfriend, but before he got the chance to think about what Max knew and how he knew it, Max drew his knife and slammed in down through the top of his foot.

The pain was instantaneous and extreme. Joe screamed as two of his toes were severed from his foot. He thrashed about hopelessly trying to break free of his bonds, but he wasn't going anywhere. His arms and legs were tied tightly to the chair, and two more lengths secured his torso.

Max speared one of the toes with his knife and held it in front of Joe's face.

"You killed several of my men," Max said calmly. "You killed and injured others at the concert, and you attacked the man I love. You've killed and injured dozens more stealing weapons and equipment. You are a fucking terrorist. A complete piece of shit and I will cut every one of your fucking toes off, then your fingers and anything else that might get your attention, until you tell me what I need to know."

"You're a psychopath!" Joe spat.

"Maybe, but I get results. You have twenty seconds to start talking or you'll be lucky to walk properly again anytime soon. You've already lost two toes and in fifteen seconds, you'll lose another one. Ten seconds."

Max saw the fear in his eyes.

"Five seconds," Max said, flicking the toe off onto Joe's lap. "Three, two."

"Okay!" Joe yelled. "Okay, fuck! What do you want to know?"

Liam had turned away, but gingerly turned back to look at Max who had driven the knife into the floor an inch from Joe's foot. Tom was smiling ear to ear.

Max noted the expressions on both their faces, but couldn't waste any time worrying about their mental states. There'd be time for that later.

"Where is the rest of the gang?" Max asked.

"A few hours drive from here."

"Where?"

"Wilsons Promontory. The old lighthouse and compound."

"What's the plan here? You've stolen military equipment and tried to sell them to Russia. You've stolen military drones and money printing equipment. You killed the Prime Minister. What's the connection? What's the end game?"

Joe laughed through gritted teeth and shook his head to himself.

"Want to tell me what's so funny?"

"He's been one step ahead of you the whole time. He knew you'd spend hours trying to piece it together. Wasted hours looking for some rhyme or reason for what he was doing, all the while missing what was right in front of you."

"And what's that?"

"He's better than you. Better than all of you."

"Who? Ned?"

"Yes."

"Why does that matter?"

"Because that's what this whole thing is all about."

"Being better than me?"

"And AIS."

"So you've waged war on the country simply to try to tear down the AIS?"

"It's his legacy and yours."

"Who's legacy? Ned's?"

"No, General Patrick Scott's. You might know him better as Hulk."

Max grabbed Joe by the neck with crushing force, until Joe started to turn blue.

"What's Hulk got to do with this?" Max asked, slightly loosening his grip.

"You wanted to know the end game. Well, he's it."

Max stared at Joe trying to piece it all together, searching his mind for a connection.

"His son," Max finally said.

"Bingo," Joe said, looking past Max to Tom.

Max turned around and saw Liam unconscious on the floor, fractions of second before the butt of a pistol came crashing down on his face and his world went black.

Chapter Twenty-Three

Tom stepped up and levelled his gun at Max's face.

"No!" Joe shouted. "Your father wants him alive. He's part of the plan."

"I hate this fucking prick!" Tom spat. "I've wanted to put a bullet in his face since the moment I met him."

"I know. You did well. Convincing them you were on their side can't have been easy."

"Especially when you see the way Hulk and the golden child here get on. Max is his real son."

"They'll all get what they deserve. Our plans are nearly complete. Put the gun away and untie me. You're going to need to help me walk."

Tom holstered his pistol and leant down to retrieve Max's knife which was still pierced into the floorboards. He used it to cut away Joe's ropes, then gathered his clothes and sat them within reaching distance.

"I'll find a first aid kit while you get dressed," Tom said, walking out of the room.

"Thank you," Joe said, struggling to pull on his shirt.

Tom gave Joe an injection of painkillers and antibiotics, then bandaged his foot.

"I can't believe he cut off my toes," Joe said, spitting on Max. "Fucking psycho."

"We'll take them with us," Tom said, helping Joe up. "One of the others can reattach them when we arrive."

"I saw you smiling like a fucking idiot when he did it too."

"I wanted to pretend I was on board with it all."

"I think he saw through it."

"Bullshit."

"Doesn't matter anyway. He's out for now."

"Come on old man, let's go."

"Old man? I'm not that much older than you."

"Don't remind me, stepdad."

"Not sure I like that title."

"Well, you can deal with it or stop fucking my dad. Your choice."

"You have to remember, no one knows about our relationships, including you and your dad's connection, and mine and your dad's relationship. It's important we keep it that way, because when we're done the gang will all go their own ways and it's best they don't know anything real about us."

"Got it. Let's just get on the road."

Tom helped Joe out of the small cottage and out into the street. The pair hobbled along until they found Max's car. Tom climbed in behind the wheel after helping Joe into the passenger seat. He pressed the ignition button, but nothing happened.

"What the fuck?" Joe asked.

"It worked for him," Tom said. "I don't know why it won't work for me."

"Do you have the keys?"

"No, it doesn't use normal keys. It's an AIS car, so it uses our access keys. Our rings."

Tom took off his ring and polished it, then tried again, but the car didn't start.

"Fuck."

"Go and get his," Joe barked. "We need to move."

"Shit, okay," Tom said, climbing back out of the car. "I'll be right back."

"Hurry up."

Tom sprinted back towards the house. He ran up the small footpath and through the front door. As he stepped into the bedroom which had been Joe's torture chamber, he saw an unconscious Max and felt his blood rising. He could kill him and Joe would never know. He felt the blood pumping in his ears and rush of his pulse, but thought better of it. It wasn't part of the plan, as much as he wished it had been.

Tom reached down and pulled Max's ring off his finger, causing him to stir slightly. Max moaned and Tom felt his muscle tense in his arms. He was coming around.

"Shit," Tom said to himself.

He stood up and quickly marched for the door. As he got to the front gate, Jonnie arrived and was surprised to see him.

"What are you doing?" Jonnie asked.

"Just grabbing something from the car for Prince," Tom scrambled to get out. "How's Karen?"

"I only dropped her off, but looks like she'll pull through."

"Good."

"How's the progress inside?"

"Slow. I'll let him fill you in, I better go get that thing."

Tom started to walk off, not registering Jonnie's intrigued look.

"What do you have to get?" Jonnie quizzed as Tom started to pick up his pace. "Tom. What are you really doing?"

Tom hesitated for just a second, then ran.

Jonnie's intense gaze followed the AIS recruit, then his heart pounded in his chest. He turned and looked back at the house. He had a decision, give chase or check on Max.

He drew his pistol.

"Tom, stop!" Jonnie yelled.

Tom turned back briefly to see the pistol levelled at him, before drawing his own gun and firing.

Jonnie dived to his left behind the garden fence for cover as a second gun fired in the distance. He heard the shots, then the bullets slamming into his own car across the footpath. The bullets tore into the front grill of the four-wheel drive and green coolant started gushing onto the tar. They were immobilising his car.

Jonnie snuck a quick look around the fence and saw Joe firing wildly into his car. Jonnie fired off two quick shots. The first hit Joe through the passenger window of Max's car and lodged in his shoulder. Joe dropped his gun and climbed back into the car and closed the door he had been using as a makeshift cover. Jonnie could see and hear him yelling at Tom to get in.

The second bullet grazed Tom's face, tearing a hot red streak from his nose down his cheek to below his ear. The shock on Tom's face was evident. He'd been only centimetres from death.

Joe started yelling again, breaking Tom's gaze. Tom climbed in the car and the massive V8 engine kicked into gear, then roared as Tom wheeled it out onto the street.

Jonnie ran for his car, but as expected, it wouldn't start. He slammed the door in frustration, before calling for back up and putting an alert out for Max's car.

He ran for the house, with his pistol still drawn. He cleared room by room, until he found Max and Liam on the floor. Max was coming too and Jonnie sighed in relief.

"Max," Jonnie said, shaking his old friend. "Max, can you hear me? Are you okay?"

He could feel Max's body starting to respond and so he slapped him hard across the face to speed it up.

Max's eyes opened instantly and he lunged forward, before realising it was Jonnie.

"Tom," Max managed to say. "That little fucker."

Max turned to see the empty torture chair and swore again. He waved Jonnie off as he tried to help him up.

"I'm okay," Max said. "What about him?"

Max pointed to Liam and Jonnie crawled over to him. He checked and found a weak pulse.

"He's alive," Jonnie said, checking for any obvious injuries. "I can't find anything broken or any wounds."

"Must have been a needle."

"What? How can you be sure?"

"It was silent. I didn't hear a thing. Anything else would have made a noise in the struggle or when he hit the ground."

Jonnie searched Liam's neck and found a small red dot where Tom had inserted the needle.

"Motherfucker," Jonnie said, showing Max the tiny spot.

"Did they get away?"

"Yeah. Shot my car up, so I couldn't pursue. AIS are searching for your car now."

"My car?" Max asked feeling his hand and noting the absence of his ring. "That arsehole. I disabled his access key, because I didn't trust him, so he stole mine. We need Alpha to shut it down."

"I'll make the call."

"Thanks. I've got another one to make."

Max retrieved his phone and dialled the number. On the third ring it answered.

"Got anything out of him yet?" Hulk asked through the tiny speaker.

"Nothing good," Max said.

"Let's hear it."

"It's William, Hulk. He's William."

"Who's William?"

"Ned."

"William who? I'll look him up in the system."

"No, Hulk. You don't understand. It's your son, William."

"What?"

"I'm sorry, boss. Ned Kelly is actually William Scott."

"That's impossible. He's dead."

"Joe told me and I have no reason to doubt it."

"He's got to be fucking with us. Maybe it was a mistake bringing you back in. Maybe you have been out of the game too long, if you so easily fall for fucking bullshit!"

"It's not bullshit, Hulk. I asked him what this was all about and started talking about your legacy. I think they want to destroy AIS's reputation by randomly attacking sites without any connections. They are trying to keep us off guard, while the public loses confidence in us. It's misdirection, forcing us to chase a shadow and waste time trying to connect dots which don't exist."

"I'm not convinced, but more importantly, my son is dead, Max. He overdosed years ago. I buried my boy, along with all my shame and heartache."

"I'm sorry."

"Don't be sorry, be better."

Max heard the line go dead.

Jonnie turned back to Max and handed him his own phone, pausing briefly to put a consoling hand on Max's shoulder in an unspoken gesture which let Max know he had heard everything and knew it was hard on him.

Max looked down at the phone and saw Kate's private line was connected.

"Alpha," Max said.

"How you going, Prince Charming?" Kate asked. *"Jonnie told me he found you knocked out on the floor."*

"It's not the first time, but hopefully it's the last. It's not pleasant."

"Fuck, I remember. Been awhile, but I remember how much it sucks."

"I'll be fine."

"Good. Why don't you tell me what you know?"

"We need to increase security at the Wool Shed and put a protective detail on Hulk."

"Jonnie told me. Are you sure it's William?"

"Yes."

"Fuck. I helped train him, before he went off the rails. I helped get him clean, but he ended up throwing it all away. I remember his funeral. Hulk was a shell, completely devastated. His life was destroyed. He'd lost his wife, which he saw as his fault. Then, in his mind, he failed her again by losing their son.

He was broken. He has spent his whole life since trying to right those wrongs. Finding people like you to train, to build AIS and do good in the world."

"He's done that."

"It's never been enough. AIS is his legacy and we're all filling the void left by William."

"So how is he still alive?"

"I have no fucking idea. It wasn't an open casket, so it's possible he wasn't in the box."

"I need to find him."

"We will."

"No, I need to find him. I'm back, Alpha. I'm taking over as lead agent in the field. I'm going to put a bullet in that little prick Tom's head, then I'm going to take this whole group apart."

"Let me know, whatever ever you need, is yours."

"Thanks, Kate. You can start by giving me a full schematic of Wilson's Promontory, a team and a helicopter."

Chapter Twenty-Four

The helicopter came in low over the sweeping coastline. Below Max could see the roaring waves crashing into the cliffs and rocks, while others rolled and broke over the white sands of the southern Victorian coast.

"Listen up," Max shouted into his headset's microphone. "The most likely scenario is they are no longer here, but it could be a trap. They could have left booby traps or even troops on site for us to find. Problem is it's our only lead. Bravo will lead a team of six from the northern entrance and I will lead our team from the southern, ocean side up into the property. We will sweep the lighthouse and the first two structures on site. Bravo's teams will handle the others. Move quickly, but smartly. Watch your step, watch your backs and don't trust anything or anyone. Understood?"

"Yes, sir," his team responded in unison.

"Good. Weapons ready. We're nearly there."

The evening was starting to close in as the helicopter neared Wilson's Promontory. The lighthouse or lightstation was on the south-east point of the peninsula. The rest of the area was a nature reserve, a massive national park, littered with hiking trails and camping grounds. The reserve was a natural habitat for numerous native species, but more recently had become a favourite place for dear. The park often had to close for several months a year to cull the dear to control their numbers. It had been closed for several weeks, meaning the area was free of members of the general public. At around twenty kilometres from the nearest town, it was the perfect quiet spot away from prying eyes to run their operations.

There were six structures on the island, including a spectacular lighthouse built in the mid-1800s. While one of the buildings was officially the lighthouse keeper's, in practice, modern technology meant the lighthouse keeper didn't need to stay on site, so the whole compound was available to be hired out as holiday accommodation. It still operates as a safety beacon to help ships navigate the Bass Strait, as an important back up, if the ship's modern navigation equipment were to fail.

"Bravo," Max said. "Thirty seconds out."

"Roger that, Prince," Jonnie replied. *"We're aligned."*

"Good luck, mate."

"You too. See you down there."

Max's helicopter rose up the face of the cliff in front of the lighthouse and circled to the right. When Max was sure the area was clear, he signalled for the pilot to land.

Max threw open the door and he and his team disembarked. They moved quickly up the grass slope and took cover behind an ancient stone wall as the helicopter climbed again to give them a real time visual from overhead.

Max watched it climb into the air, then saw the pilots scrambling. The big bird lurched backwards violently.

"SAM, SAM, SAM," Max heard one of the pilots yell through his earpiece, as a white streak cut through the sky above his head.

The white line raced towards the chopper, until the missile exploded on impact.

The hulking mess of fire and steel fell from the sky, trailing heavy black smoke as the av-gas burned. Orange flames lit up the darkening area and the heat radiated from the burning wreckage.

Max and his team moved away, trying to keep the wall between them and the compound for cover.

"Prince," Jonnie asked. *"You still with me?"*

"Still here, Bravo," Max replied. "Chopper's toast though."

"Trail leads to the top of the lighthouse behind you. We're on the ground moving in."

"Got it."

Max turned around to face the wall and gathered his breath to steady himself. When he was ready, he sprung up, sighting in the massive light structure at the top of the tower. He quickly found what he was looking for, a small surface to air missile or SAM turret being manned by one guy who was moving it towards Jonnie's chopper.

Max lined him up and fired three shots.

The terrorist fell forward knocking the turret off target, before falling from the lighthouse and slamming into the ground seventy feet below. The missile shot from the turret on its new trajectory and exploded on impact with the roof of the nearest house. Glass, wood and brick blasted out in all directions, showering the whole compound with lit debris, as flames took hold of the old building.

Max heard gunfire at the other end of the compound and knew Jonnie and his team were moving in.

"On me," he yelled to his troops, who all switched the safeties off on their weapons and held them to their shoulders scanning for targets.

Max pointed at two of his men and pointed the lighthouse. Those two moved towards the big structure as he pointed to another two agents and send them towards the smaller house on the right.

"You're with me," Max said. "Are you up for it?"

"Yes, I'm right behind you," Liam said.

"Good. We're going in there."

Max pointed towards the building which had been hit by the missile, then started walking briskly across the green lawns towards the burning building.

He kicked open the door and smoke billowed out and up into the sky. He took a quick look back at Liam and the pair nodded to each other then entered.

The whole place was full of smoke and burning debris. Flames were starting to take hold of the curtains and bookshelves, and the furniture was starting to smoulder. The paint and artworks were beginning to blister from the heat.

A section of the roof has collapsed in and Max could see someone trapped under it. They weren't moving and were likely dead, so he kept moving.

As he opened the door into the next room, a bullet slammed into his bulletproof vest. Max stumbled back behind the wall trying to get his breath back from the heavy impact. His lungs burned as they dragged in the smoke-filled air and he started to cough. Liam put a hand out, but Max waved him off and nodded that he was fine. But, it wasn't true. His lungs were already in pain from the chemical attack, so the smoke was having twice the impact it would have had on a normal day. If there was such a thing as a normal day.

Max stole a look around the doorframe and saw two men hunkered down behind a solid stone bar. He loosened off two shots and the bullets slammed into the wall above the terrorists' heads as they both ducked behind the bar.

Max was about to reach for a flashbang, but before he got the chance one went sailing past his head. He watched it bounce off the bar and into the wall, before it fell behind the bar. He turned back to Liam as the pair took cover.

They didn't have to wait long. The grenade exploded filling the room with light and sound. The two men from behind the bar came up firing wildly, holding their eyes in pain.

Max fired one shot, through the temple of the first guy. As he was moving to take the second guy, Liam fired and put a bullet through his face. The two terrorists hit the ground and the two agents entered and scanned the room.

There were maps and schematics on the tables, and weapons. Guns, knives and explosives.

"Photograph what you can," Max said, pointing to the table, "then meet me in the next room."

"Got it," Liam said, pulling out his phone and clicking away as Max moved for the next door.

There was one guard left in the room. He had a massive shard of glass sticking out of his chest. He was gasping for air and held a blood-soaked gun in one hand, while the other tried in vain to push a section of bookcase back against the wall.

He levelled his gun at Max, but Max was too fast. He fired two shots and put the guy out of his misery. As he fell, the section of bookcase he'd been leaning on, swung back open.

Max quickly marched towards it and flung open the hidden doorway. A metal spiral staircase trailed down into the earth below the house. Max tried to listen, but couldn't hear any sounds from below. He willed his eyes to adjust to the darkness, but they burned from the smoke and he couldn't get them to focus.

Liam joined him at the top of the hidden stairs and the pair quickly exchanged nods, then Max led them down the steps.

At the bottom, they found a tunnel. It was relatively new. One way led back towards the beach. The other in the opposite direction towards the front of the compound.

"Head that way," Max ordered. "Watch your back and be ready for anything."

"Will do," Liam said as he started to leave.

"Wait!" Max said, jumping forward and grabbing Liam's shoulders.

Liam was slightly confused, but then Max pointed to his feet. Liam had stopped only an inch from a thin metal tripwire. Max observed the wire and traced it back to the wall. A small claymore mine sat nestled against the wall. Max disabled the wire and mine, then told Liam to be careful.

Liam was a mix of emotions. Embarrassed he'd missed it. Thankful Max had saved his life. Nervous for his solo mission towards the beach. Determined to get it right.

Max patted him on the back, then turned back to the dark tunnel.

Max heard Liam's footsteps getting further away as the pair separated.

It wasn't long before Max found his own tripwire. He cut the wire and disabled the mine, then headed on, constantly scanning ahead and looking for targets and tripwires.

He walked through the dark tunnel scanning for hundreds of metres, disabling two more mines along the route.

At the far end, he found a ladder leading up. It was impossible to tell what was waiting at the top in the heavy darkness, but Max made the choice to climb. He moved rung by rung, stopping occasionally to listen for any sign of movement.

As he approached the top, he threw out two flashbangs, wanting the element of surprise on his side. No sooner had the second one exploded, then Max was up and out of the tunnel scanning the space for targets, only to be met by darkness and calm.

He was standing in a massive shed. There were a couple of big semi-trailer trucks and a shipping container, but it was otherwise empty.

"Bravo, come in," Max said into his microphone.

"Prince, where are you?" Jonnie asked.

"A few hundred metres behind the northern entrance. There was an escape tunnel. I'm in an old shed they've been using as a warehouse. I'm about to start the search."

"We're all clear on this end. One casualty, multiple dead terrorists. Otherwise empty handed."

"Find Liam. He took the tunnel in the other direction. I'm guessing it led out onto the beach. He's got some photos you need to get to Kate."

"Roger that. I'll send a couple people your way to help the search."

"Appreciate it. Oh and Bravo, watch out for tripwires. There's claymores everywhere."

"Copy that."

Chapter Twenty-Five

Tom helped Joe through the door.

"Jesus," Bold Jack said. "What happened to you? Someone step on your toes dancing at the nightclub?"

"Fuck off," Joe replied.

"Woah, sensitive!"

"Do I look like I'm in the mood for your shit?"

"I'm just trying to lighten the mood before you see him."

"Is he pissed?"

"They got away, so yeah, he's not in a great mood."

"We set the traps."

"But," William said, walking into the room, "they got away."

"The arsehole you sent with the SAM missed."

"You were on the ground, you had command."

"I told him to shoot the fucking chopper, what more could I have done? He let the first one drop off the agents, before he took it out."

"The first one?"

"Yeah, that's the other thing, there were two of them! And he only took out one, before he got shot and fell to his death."

"In fairness," Tom interjected, "I'm pretty sure he was dead before he hit the ground."

Joe looked sideways at Tom.

"Helpful, thanks."

"And what's your story?" William asked.

"I killed one of the recruits and got him out of there," Tom said, tilting his head towards Joe. "But not before Max had some fun."

Tom tossed the small plastic bag to William. He caught it and looked inside to see Joe's toes.

"Take him to see Thunderbolt," William said, throwing the bag back to Tom. "He's in the back, then get back here. I want a full debrief, including on Hulk and what they know."

Thunderbolt was the team medic. He had a makeshift operating room at their base of operations and quickly set about working on Joe's foot.

A few hours later, William walked into the room. Joe was coming to and he told Thunderbolt to leave the room.

"You told him who I was," William said, sitting on the chair beside the bed.

"Yes," Joe replied. "That's what you told me to do."

"I know. You planted the seed and led him into the trap, but I see now the people I sent with you weren't up to it."

"They found the secondary traps too. We only just got out. I'm sorry, Will."

"It's Ned, while we're here," William said, looking over his shoulder. "It's okay. It's just a reminder of what we are up against."

"How'd he take it when you told him?"

"I think he was surprised, but he's hard to read."

"Doesn't matter. All that matters is the old man knows now."

"He'll probably die in shock."

"He's too stubborn for that. No, I'm going to have to kill the old prick."

"Did Tom give you what you needed?"

"Mostly, but it's not important right now. How are you feeling? I can't believe he let them actually cut you."

"He smiled when it happened. I think part of him enjoyed it. That's beyond any normal daddy issues. I don't think he likes us being together."

"I've been training him since he was about nine. He was never going to be completely normal."

"Especially with the mother he had."

"Jealously is an ugly colour on you. It was two decades ago. You need to let it go."

"Just saying, she went from your saviour to a complete loon within months."

"Don't have to tell me that. I lived it."

"Anyway, do you think you can operate?"

"I can drive, but I don't think I'll be running anytime soon."

"I'll see what Thunderbolt can do."

"Thanks."

William stood to leave, but Joe grabbed his hand and squeezed it tightly.

"I'm glad you're okay," William said softly, not looking back.

William walked into the main quarters.

"Get him whatever painkillers are needed to get him back on his feet," William said. "I need him at full speed."

"I'll see what I can do," Thunderbolt said, "but I'm not sure he'll be at full speed for a few days at least."

"Do what you have to."

"If he damages the toes further, they might come off permanently."

"I don't care, as long as he can get though the next couple of days."

"Understood."

"Are we still going through with this, Ned?" Bold Jack asked. "We've got two dead. One captured by AIS. Another one missing half a foot. We're running out of people, the plans need to change."

"Dan is here now," William said, pointing to Tom.

Dan was a reference to Dan Kelly, Ned Kelly's bushranger brother.

"He'll step in to fill the gaps," William said. "He's got more training than the rest of you. He'll fit in well. Plus, there's no way Thunderbolt would let us leave Mary-Ann in custody. We've got to get her back."

"So, we're going to get her now?"

"No. We have one more thing to do first. It'll throw them off their game."

Thunderbolt walked back into the room.

"I just heard from one of my old contacts," he said. "The AIS recruit didn't die. She's in the hospital."

William turned to Tom.

"I thought you said you killed her," William stated.

"I thought I had," Tom replied.

"You thought wrong."

"Doesn't matter. She doesn't know anything."

"A dead recruit was part of the mission. Don't you get it? It's all psychological warfare. Every piece adds to the puzzle. Every action adds to their mental anguish. Every fucking small part plays a role in the bigger game. We can't break them if we keep making mistakes."

"I'll do better next time."

"No, you'll fix your mistake now."

"She'll be surrounded."

"Get it done. I don't want excuses."

William's thoughts were interrupted by his phone.

"I have to take this," he said, turning his back and walking out of the room. "Hello, Senator."

"How is the plan progressing?" the Senator asked over the phone.

"We've had a couple of setbacks, but I think you will agree we have delivered."

"You have certainly created some chaos and you killed that weak prick, Sawyer. God how that man ever became PM is beyond me. But, I just had a call from the Russians who were very upset they didn't get the microchip."

"AIS turned up and disrupted the handoff."

"I don't need to tell you that it was part of the plan."

"No, you don't. And I don't need to tell you, I could give two fucks about your plan."

"We are in this together. You get your vengeance against AIS and your father, and I get what's been out of reach to me for too long."

"I do appreciate the significant investment you have made and I aim to keep my end of the deal, but don't think for one minute that gives you any sort of command or influence."

"I could take you down at any minute. You're not the only team I have in the field."

"Let's not do this. You and I both know that you have more to lose than I do. I could also kill you with my eyes closed. So why don't you go back to doing whatever it is you do up there on the red carpet and leave me alone to get the job done?"

"Keep me updated," the Senator demanded abruptly before cutting the line.

"Fucking piece of shit," William said, staring at the call ended screen.

He knew in that moment the Senator would try to have him killed when this was all over. He made a mental note to clean his tracks.

Chapter Twenty-Six

Tom sat in the car watching the busy entrance. It was a revolving door of people. Hundreds coming and going constantly.

He impatiently waited for a tall nurse to exit and make his way towards the parking lot.

Tom climbed out of his car and fell into step not far behind the middle-aged man. He checked over his shoulder, watching for any sign someone might have noticed him.

As the nurse approached his car, the blinkers flashed and a soft beep heralded the car was unlocked. He reached for the back door and threw his bag inside, as Tom arrived behind him. Without warning, Tom punched him in the back of the neck, right at the base of the skull. The force knocked him out and he fell forward slamming his head on the roof of the small SUV.

Tom used his falling momentum to push him into the backseat.

He quickly checked no one was watching or coming towards him, then climbed into the backseat with his unconscious victim.

Tom pulled the door closed, then started to undress the man, before undressing himself. As he started to pull on the nurse's clothes, he started to wake. Tom grabbed him by the back of the head and chin, and with a violent whip snapped his neck. The body fell lifeless onto the back seat.

He pulled the scrubs on and fixed his stolen security tag to his shirt, then put a surgical mask over his mouth and nose. The ID wasn't anywhere near a perfect match, but with the mask it would be enough, he thought.

Tom climbed out of the car and made his way across the carpark to the entrance of the hospital.

Inside the disinfectant filled his nostrils, along with an assault of musk from the huddled masses waiting to see the emergency staff. He walked through the crowd and behind the nursing station and picked up a patient's chart.

Tom took in the chaotic surroundings as he scanned faces to see if anyone was paying him too much attention. He calmed as he realised it was too frantic for anyone to really care what he was doing.

He cast his eyes over the names on the whiteboard. Patients were listed by room number as well as entry times and doctors assigned to them. He smiled behind his mask as he found Karen's name and room number.

One of the other nurses starting barking orders and told Tom to get to work and stop just standing around. He nodded quickly and headed off down the hallway.

He checked the room numbers as he went. It wasn't in this hallway, so he scanned the boards hanging from the roof and followed the arrow pointing to the cluster of rooms Karen was in.

Tom saw a uniformed police officer outside in the hallway. He guessed she was guarding Karen's room, so he made show of entering a number of patients' rooms along the long hallway as if he was doing the rounds. The officer noticed him, but didn't pay him much attention.

He said hello to the officer as he entered the room opposite Karen's and checked the machines and chart of the two patients.

"How's it going?" Tom asked.

"Pretty quiet compared to you guys," the officer said. "Don't know how you do it."

"You get used to it. I don't know how you do your job and I don't think I want to trade."

"Especially today, it's pretty dull just sitting here."

"I bet. Anyway, I better get back to it, before the angry boss comes down here and chews us both out. Can I go in and see the patient?"

"Sure. Just let me check the names."

Tom felt his heart skip a beat as the officer grabbed a clipboard, before turning back to look at his ID. She scanned the page on the clipboard and found the corresponding name from the ID. She looked back up and he wondered if she would ask him to remove his mask. There was a moment's hesitation, but then she waved him through by opening the door for him.

As the door clicked closed behind him, Tom took a deep breath and turned to face Karen. She was lying in the bed, hooked up to various pieces of medical equipment. Tom didn't know how any of it worked and he was momentarily struck by how peaceful Karen was, then he smiled knowing just how helpless she was. He knew it wasn't very sporting to kill a defenceless woman in her sleep, but he figured it was a good way to go.

As he approached the bed, Karen's eyes opened and he froze. She blinked a few times as she tried to see who was there.

"Who is it?" she struggled to get out.

"It's okay, Karen," Tom said. "I'm just a nurse here to check in. How are you feeling?"

Karen's eyes widened in fear and recognition. She knew Tom's voice in an instant and reached for the alarm button.

Tom lunged forward. The pair's hands found the white cord at the same time and both scrambled trying to claw their way to the red button, before the other. Tom pulled out his silenced pistol and pointed it at Karen's forehead.

"Stop," he demanded. "Just stop."

Karen had the red button under her thumb, but on seeing the pistol she decided not to press it.

"You tried to kill me," she said. "And you tried to sabotage the mission."

"I did. And now I'm here to finish the job."

"Max is going to kill you, you know."

"He can try," Tom said, readying to squeeze the trigger.

Karen's eyes darted for the door and she smiled. Tom fell for it and turned to look. Karen grabbed the silencer and dragged it quickly off her head, and hit the red button. Tom pulled the trigger as he was turning back to face her and the bullet spat from the barrel and drove itself into the pillow. Karen's free hand was already moving. She grabbed the vase of flowers beside the bed and slammed them into Tom's face. Water, glass and flowers rained down, as she tried to climb out of the bed.

"You fucking bitch!" Tom screamed as blood and water soaked his face.

The door to the suite flew open and the officer entered with her gun drawn.

"Put the gun down," she demanded, lining Tom up.

He let it dangle on his finger, as the officer grabbed her radio.

"Officer Jenson to 187 Command," the officer said, "Command, do you copy."

"Roger, Jenson," the radio squawked. *"Command here."*

"I need…"

The silenced pistol had swung back into Tom's hand and he pulled the trigger. The bullet sliced through the air and tore a neat red hole in the officer's cheek. She blinked and Tom saw the moment of realisation in her eyes, before she collapsed at the knees.

As Jensen hit the ground, her gun bounced off the tiles and slid towards Tom and Karen. Karen lurched forward, trying to get to it, but the various cables attached to her body made it difficult. She fell to the ground in a tangled ball of wires and tubes. She wrestled with them, ripping them free, while trying to crawl to the gun.

Tom shuffled forward and kicked the officer's gun, just as Karen's finger tips touched the handle. The gun clattered its way across the tiles as the voice on Jensen's radio got louder, more worried and impatient for an answer.

Karen found a shard of glass on the floor and rolled over, stabbing it down into Tom's thigh. She smiled as he staggered back, but it was short lived joy.

The bullet cut through the skin and bone like butter. It tore through her brain and exploded out the back of her skull, showering the white walls with blood, bone, hair and brain matter.

"Bitch!" Tom spat as he limped back and ripped the glass from his leg.

He could hear footsteps marching down the hallway and knew he needed to move. He darted out into the corridor and fired five shots. The first two hit the lights and roof above the team of medics coming towards him. The third hit a woman in a long white coat in the shoulder and she fell to the ground, clutching her wound and screaming in pain. The fourth and fifth bullets hit the angry nurse who had told him to get back to work earlier. One hit her between the eyes and the second went right into her heart.

Panic and trauma spread quickly with the fear. People started running for their lives. Chairs and furniture tumbled as patients and staff alike scrambled trying to flee.

At the end of the next corridor, Tom grabbed a cowering doctor and forced him into a small supply room at gunpoint.

"Painkillers and bandages now!" Tom yelled, pointing with his gun at the wound in his leg.

"Okay, okay," the doctor said. "Please, I have a wife and kids. Please don't kill me."

"Patch me up and I won't hurt you."

The doctor started to rifle around on the shelves looking for what he needed. He cleaned the wound as best as he could through the ripped pants, which Tom had refused to remove in case he needed to move quickly. He added gauze and wrapped the bandage tightly around the outside of the pants.

"You'll need to redo this later," the doctor said.

"You think?" Tom snapped. "Dick. Where are the painkillers?"

"They aren't in here. They're down the hall with the antibiotics and other medicines."

"Take me there."

Tom pushed the doctor in the back with the pistol and the pair made their way down the hallway to the medical supply room. The doctor tried the door, but it was locked. A frightened nurse was trembling behind the glass.

"Open this fucking door!" Tom demanded, but the nurse shook her head in fear and buried her face in her arms. "Open the door or I'll shoot this guy in the face."

The nurse looked up hesitantly seeing her colleague and friend, and the worried look on his face.

"It's okay, Amanda," the doctor said. "Open the door, so I can get him the medicine he needs, then he'll leave us."

She studied them both in absolute panic.

"It'll be okay," the doctor said. "He doesn't want to hurt either of us."

Amanda was crippled by fear. Tom had had enough. He shot at the glass, but it didn't break. It crackled on impact, but it was reinforced.

"That won't work," the doctor said. "It's a secure room to protect the supplies."

"You have five seconds to open this door," Tom said to both the medical professionals. "Four."

"Amanda, please open the door."

"Three."

"Amanda, please!"

"Two!"

"Okay," she said getting to her feet gingerly.

"One!"

Amanda jumped forward and opened the door. Tom pushed the doctor forward and shut the door behind them.

"Sit there and shut up," he said, pointing to an office chair. "And you get the drugs now. Hurry up!"

Amanda sat, as the doctor ran to get the glass vials and a syringe.

"Give me a solid dose," Tom said. "I need to be able to move without pain."

The doctor was about to reply, but thought better of it. He plunged the needle into the vial, extracted the clear liquid, then stabbed it down into Tom's leg. He repeated it with the second vial of antibiotics.

"Take these," the doctor said, handing Tom a packet of tablets. "When the pain comes back, take two every four hours and don't take them for more than twenty-four hours."

"Thanks, Doc," Tom said, pocketing the pills. "You're a good man."

Tom fired a single bullet into the doctor's heart and he collapsed as Amanda started to cry. Tom turned the gun towards her and fired. The bullet went through her hand and into her face. She fell and blood started pooling around her, as Tom left the room.

Tom ran as fast as he could on his injured leg. He couldn't feel a thing. Whatever the doctor had given him was strong.

As he burst through the front door, two police cars were coming down the road, lights flashing and sirens blaring. He ran for the nurse's car and pulled open the door. He quickly hit the ignition button and the car came to life.

He threw it into reverse and accelerated out of the park as one of the police cars pulled up. The officers hadn't seen him, so they ran into the hospital.

The second car arrived, they'd obviously seen him, as he put his own in drive.

The officers drew their weapons and aimed for his front window. Tom could see them yelling as he hit the gas. The car sprung from the spot with surprising speed for the little engine SUV. He pressed the window button, put his arm out and started firing at the officers. Bullets hit their car and one officer dived for cover, but the second officer wasn't so lucky. He had frozen in fear. He managed to loosen off a bullet which hit the windshield of Tom's car, but it hammered into the passenger seat harmlessly.

Tom clenched the wheel, then crashed the SUV right into the officer. The bumper smashed into his knees and he fell forward denting the bonnet, as his head thumped on the thin metal. Tom watched him bounce over the windshield, heard him tumble over the roof, then saw him crash down onto the pavement in the rear-view mirror.

Chapter Twenty-Seven

Max sat in the comfortable chair on the Gulfstream across from Jonnie. They had print outs of the photos Liam had taken on the table between them and they had spent the best part of an hour trying to brainstorm ideas on locations.

The schematics were only partials. The edges and some sections hadn't escaped the flames of the burning house.

The phone on the table rang. Max reached forward and pulled it up to his ear.

"Hi," Max said.

"Hi, Max," Blake said. *"I called because I just heard. How are you feeling?"*

"I'm okay. Just trying to figure out these schematics."

"I meant about Karen. I'm sorry to hear what happened."

"She's tough as nails, she'll be okay."

"Oh. You don't know, do you?"

"Know what, Blake?"

"There was an attack at the hospital. Multiple injured. At least three dead medical staff. One dead police officer and another being rushed to surgery, but the doctors aren't confident."

"What happened to Karen?"

"They killed her. I'm so sorry, Max. She fought him off and got a good shot at his leg with a shard of glass, but she wasn't up to the fight given her injuries. He killed the officer protecting her too."

"Who?"

"Kate's still looking at the footage. He had a mask on, but it sounds like it might have been Tom."

"Fuck."

"I'm sorry, Max."

"I'm going to kill him. Weak prick, killing a defenceless victim in a hospital bed. Fucking coward."

There was a loud explosion over the line.

"What the fuck was that?" Blake yelled.

"Blake, are you okay?" Max asked. "What's going on?"

"We're under attack!"

"Where are you?" Max asked, putting the phone on speaker so Jonnie could hear.

"I'm in the motorcade. We're on the Bungendore Road, heading back into Canberra from JOC."

JOC was the Headquarters of the Australian Defence Force's Joint Operations Command which was buried under the hills outside Canberra. Essentially, it was the war room and one of the most secure locations in Australia.

"Talk to me. Tell me what's happening."

"Jesus. They've taken out the police escorts. They're in the bushland surrounding the road. They're firing at the remaining vehicles, including this one. Get us out of here, Nick!"

"Keep talking to me, Blake. Keep the line open."

"Give me your weapon, Julian."

"I don't think that's a good idea," Max heard the security guard say in the background.

"We're not going to keep having this conversation. Give me a weapon."

"Here."

"What's this?"

"It's the access key. It opens the weapons storage, next to you."

"Blake, talk to me," Max said.

"I'm unlocking the weapons cache in my car."

"Are you moving?"

"No, we're pinned down."

"Get those guns out."

"I'm trying. The car is bouncing around as Lovell tries to get us out. We're wedged between the other security vehicles."

"We're coming for you, Blake. Hold on."

Max jumped out of his seat and started for the back of the plane. Jonnie didn't need to be told, he ran to the front of the plane to talk to the pilots.

Max pulled open the door as the Gulfstream banked and started to descend. He walked into the small storage room and started gathering his kit. He restocked his vest and loaded his weapons. He was still in his combat gear.

"Blake?" Max asked.

"The vehicle's nearly free," Blake replied. *"Feds from the car in front of us have piled out, they're taking heavy fire and a couple have gone down. They're holding them back in the bush for now."*

Max holstered a pistol to each thigh, then put his hunting knife in a sheath on his belt. He added extra magazines to his vest and belt, then placed a couple of grenades in the vest. Finally, he slid a mag into his MP5 and chambered a round, before putting three extra clips in his vest.

"Oh fuck," Blake said. *"Another agent down. What's our plan, Nick?"*

"Get this car unstuck and drive like the wind back to the Lodge," Lovell said.

"I'm scrambling support," Jonnie said as Max started pulling supplies down for him. "They're coming from both sides – JOC and Canberra."

"They better hurry."

When Jonnie was geared up, they pulled on sleek black backpacks and moved to the door in the main cabin.

The co-pilot was standing at the door waiting.

"One minute," the pilot said.

"Who was that?" Blake asked. *"One minute to what? Back up?"*

The pilot opened the door and wind rushed in.

"What's that sound, Max?"

"We're on our way too," Max said as the pilot nodded and he leapt through the open doorway, closely followed by Jonnie.

Blake sat two pistols on the backseat next to him, then handed Campbell a loaded MP5. He then loaded a second MP5 and chambered a round.

"How many of them are there do you think?" Blake asked.

"Got to be twenty of more," Campbell replied.

"Concentrated on our right, right?"

"I think so, sir."

"Tell the men in the forward vehicle to take cover on the left and focus their fire on clearing the lefthand side."

"Yes, sir," Campbell said, clearly not used to taking these kinds of orders from his protectee.

He radioed in the command and watched through the bulletproof windshield as the men moved.

"Call command," Blake said, "and tell them to get the soldiers from JOC to circle in behind the guys on our right."

More agents fell as Campbell called in the orders.

"We need to help," Blake said, moving to the left-hand door.

"No, sir," Lovell said. "I can't let you do that."

"You can and you will."

"No, sir. This is a bulletproof vehicle and you're safer inside."

"I can't just sit here while our team is dying."

"I'm sorry, sir, but that's their job. Let them do it or the lives we already lost will mean nothing. They sacrificed themselves to protect you."

Blake knew he was right, but after a career dedicated to being the one to risk his life for others, he felt guilty and helpless.

More agents fell and the scene was suddenly eerily quiet, then Blake saw a man stride out of the bushes with what looked like a laptop strapped to his waist. He watched as the man used the control unit to pilot a four rotor drone over his head.

The drone sped through the air, before falling into a hover above the bonnet of Blake's car. It dropped a small package, then rose up into the air.

Blake focused on the small black package on the bonnet. If it was a bomb of some sort, who knew what damage if could do. Blake was confident the car could take a lot of punishment, but a high yield explosive could do the damage.

Lovell got the car free finally and accelerated away. He weaved through the bodies and burning debris, just as the small package started to shower bright white and orange sparks into the air. It was burning at tremendous heat and melted its way through the bonnet, before chewing right through the plastic shield over the engine and starting on the engine itself.

The car only managed to make it another one hundred metres before the thermite charge cut through and into the engine block, completely destroying it. The big BMW rolled to a stop as Lovell angled it at ninety degrees to provide some cover if they needed it.

The three men looked back towards their flaming motorcade or what was left of it as least. Then the remaining attackers strode up onto the bitumen. They fired rounds into any agents still conscious, killing them where they laid, before turning to face Blake.

They walked with purpose towards the disabled car.

"Get ready," Blake said.

"I'm sorry we failed you, sir," Lovell said.

"I'm not dead yet."

Blake watched as the approaching attackers all stopped in their tracks. The ones on the left suddenly ran to the right, and the ones on the right similarly darted to their left. Blake was puzzled, until two simultaneous explosions rang out on either side of the group.

Burning hot metal shrapnel tore into the attackers, dropping several and scattering the others. The remaining men, clambered to their feet, but soon started to fall one by one, as if they had been struck by some sort of invisible lightning.

Blake could see the Army vehicles in the distance closing in. He turned to face the city to see a column of large black SUVs speeding towards him.

Out of nowhere, a Bushmaster roared over a small hill and raced across the paddock. It sliced through the thin wire fence and sped up onto the road, before slamming at pace into the side of Blake's BMW.

Four men exited the vehicle and retrieved a large metal battering ram, like the police use to open doors for a rushed entry. One of the men ran to the rear of Blake's car and put a small hunk of plastic explosive onto the glass.

"Shit, get down," Lovell said as Blake moved further into the vehicle trying to get clear.

The explosive fired and the thick bulletproof glass cracked and spiderwebbed across the back of the car. The second attacker leapt onto the boot and swung the striking device once, twice, three times into the window, before it cracked and fell away.

Blake was ready and levelled his MP5 at the attacker, but before he got the chance to fire, the attacker's chest was assaulted by barrage of bullets. They tore him open and he gushed blood from the wounds as he fell from the boot and onto the road.

Blake watched as two thick soled combat boots past the window, before a man in black combat gear touched down on the road. He unclipped his parachute and let the wind take it. It billowed and flapped in the breeze, as Blake watched Max take down two more attackers with his MP5. On the other side, Jonnie landed and went to work on the last of the terrorists.

Two men rushed back to the Bushmaster and slammed the doors closed. Max fired but the bullet bounced off harmlessly. The Bushmaster reversed back and as it was making its turn, Max ran and jumped onto the big military vehicle.

He climbed up onto the roof and made his way to the hatch. He opened it and dropped a flashbang in. The blinding light flashed through the windows and out through the hatch, and the sound from inside the big vehicle, while muffled by the armour on the outside, was catastrophic to the vehicle occupants.

Max dropped down into the cabin and put three bullets into Bold Jack as he was clutching one ear and shielding his eyes with his arm.

Mad Dog tossed his gun at Max's feet and put his hands in the air.

"Good choice," Max said, slamming his gun into Mad Dog's face and knocking him out.

Chapter Twenty-Eight

"This failure is unacceptable," the Senator said. "I can't believe you missed him again."

"I imagine from your comfortable office it's easy to see how things should or could be done," William said. *"But for those of us in the field, we understand that every mission carries risks, especially when you are up against one of the best intelligence agencies in the world."*

"You were trained by them."

"And they have endless resources at their disposal as well as state of the art equipment."

"I've given you everything you've asked for. Money, equipment, intelligence and access to worldclass systems. I'm sick of your excuses. Get the microchip to the Russians and take out Blake Smyth. I don't want any more excuses."

The Senator didn't wait for a reply, he ended the call and sat the phone down on the marble benchtop. He turned off the running water he had been using to muffle the sound of his voice in the old mansion.

He looked himself up and down in the bathroom mirror. Considering he was pushing seventy and hadn't slept in two days, he looked okay. He actually felt like he was in the prime of his life and better than he'd ever felt. Plus, if William could deliver, he was but a heartbeat from realising his lifelong dream.

He straightened his tie, unlocked the door and walked out into the hallway. He had chosen a bathroom at the far end of the old home and his boots clunked down hard on the creaking floorboards.

At the end of the hallway, two federal police officers greeted him warmly and opened the sliding doors for him.

"Minister," one of the officers said, holding the door open. "They've just started. Your seat is opposite the Prime Minister on the righthand side of the table."

"Thank you," Minister for Foreign Affairs, Senator Kevin Timms said, walking through and taking his seat.

"Senator," Blake said, waving to Timms's seat, "thanks for joining us. Please take a seat. I was just explaining, I've gathered half the Cabinet here at the Lodge. The rest of our colleagues are in the bunker at Parliament House, who join us via video conference on the screen. I've asked them to hunker down for continuity of government purposes, should any further incidents arise. As we know, the terrorists have successfully carried out a number of attacks, including the assassination of Ted Sawyer, the Prime Minister. What some of you will be hearing now for the first time is that only two hours ago, they made an attempt on my life too."

There were audible gasps around the table and from the conference speaker, and murmurings in the room.

"Please," Blake continued.

"Are you okay?" the Social Services Minister asked.

"Yes, I'm fine. Thanks to the dedication, and sadly, the sacrifice of men and women from the federal police and AIS. They risked and gave their lives for me, and I will never forget them or their sacrifice. I have personally called their next of kin to express as much and the thanks of our nation. These men and women are heroes, and I would ask you all to stand and join me in a moment's silence."

Blake and the Cabinet, and all the security guards and staff stood, and bowed their heads.

"Thank you," Blake said, motioning for everyone to take their seats.

"Are we any closer to finding these scumbags?" Timms spat with his trademarked gruff demeanour. "I mean what the fuck are AIS and the feds doing?"

Blake looked across the room to see Max standing in full combat gear behind the senator. A frown of both anger and embarrassment flashed across his face.

"Kate Matthews, the Director-General of AIS, is here and is happy to provide an update to the meeting," Blake said. "But let me just say, AIS is working tirelessly to find and bring this group to justice."

"Excuse me, Blake, but you must see your loyalty to AIS is an issue. We need to dispassionately look at whether Ms Matthews and the AIS is up to the challenge. She certainly wasn't my pick for the top job when Hulk Scott left the role. Maybe it's time to start asking these questions."

"I would respectfully disagree," Blake said, seeing Max's anger rising over the Senator's shoulder. "Kate is one of the best agents we have ever had and I don't think there is a better person for the role, but that brings me on to the first topic of business. We need to consider continuity of government and management of AIS at the Cabinet level. I need someone with experience to oversee it. I am clearly a target and while I have confidence in AIS and the other agencies, we need to be prepared. I need to nominate a new Deputy Prime Minister. I also agree there is a perception of a conflict between my role and my former role, so to hit two birds with one stone, I am recommending to you all that Senator Timms be appointed as Deputy Prime Minister and Minister for Counter-Intelligence. He will retain his position as Minister for Foreign Affairs until this crisis passes to provide some assurances and comfort to our allies. We don't need any more upheaval at this time. I want to run a true Cabinet style government. This isn't a dictatorship, so I want everyone to have a say. So, let's hear it."

It was fair to say there was a split opinion amongst the Cabinet on Blake's choice for deputy. Max actually laughed at a comment from the Minister for Defence, who said Timms didn't know his arsehole from his elbow, particularly in light of airing his thoughts previously on Kate.

"Why is Agent Shaw in the room?" Timms snapped on hearing the laugh. "He's covered from head to toe in weapons and given your relationship, I have to say it is quite intimidating having him standing behind me and snickering."

"After the attack on my motorcade," Blake said as dispassionately as he could. "We have agreed that Agent Shaw will take over as head of my security detail, until we bring these terrorists to justice.”

“Have we?” Timms asked. “Blake, as the new Minister for the AIS, I’m not so sure that’s a good use of our resources.”

“You’re not the Minister yet, Kevin, and it’s Mister Prime Minister, while we are in session.”

Max smiled watching the senator squirm uncomfortably at being pulled into rank. But Max’s enjoyment was short lived. His face harden and turned with purpose to determined action, as an explosion rang out outside the windows.

“Lock us down!” Max ordered as he leapt over the table towards Blake who was already on his feet and moving with his training kicking into gear. “Get the Cabinet members to their dedicated saferooms!”

Federal agents scrambled dragging the ministers to their feet, knocking over furniture to the shouts and screams of the elected officials and their staff.

The door slid open and Kate was standing there shouting orders.

“They’ve breached the gate,” she said as Max dragged Blake passed.

“They’re persistent, you’ve got to give them that,” Max said as the three ran for the ground floor saferoom.

“This is one of the most secure buildings in the country right now. It’s fucking ballsy, I’ll give ‘em that.”

Max entered the sitting room. It had a large fireplace, an old chesterfield lounge and two big leather sitting chairs. A bookcase ran the length of the room and one of the AIS agents was standing at an open Murphy Door, a hidden door in the bookcase. It hid the first of the saferooms in the old mansion. There was another one upstairs near the Prime Minister’s bedroom and a third one in the basement. All the Cabinet members were allocated to one of the rooms in the event of an attack. Blake was to go to which ever one was closest.

Max turned to pull Blake through the door as an explosion tore the window and exterior wall apart. The sitting room was instantly engulfed in flames and billowing smoke, as glass, wood and concrete were thrown violently around the room. The AIS agent at the Murphy Door was hit with a concussive force which sent him tumbling back against the bookcase. Books, shelves, trinkets and gifts from world leaders, and the agent all fell to the ground.

Max was thrown through the door and took out both Blake and Kate. The three tumbled across the foyer as the first wave of men, led by Tom, entered the sitting room. He smiled seeing Max, Blake and Kate, trying to get to their feet and levelled his AR15 at the trio.

Kate reached out and grabbed the MP5 which was still slung over Max's back. Without freeing the strap, she fired through the open door at Tom. He took a round in the vest, but manage to jump for cover. One of his men wasn't so lucky. Kate drew a bead on him and fired. Four bullets hit their mark and the attacker fell.

It was enough to force the others into cover and to give Max the time he needed to get to his feet. He swung the MP5 around his shoulder and fired a few more shots into the sitting room as a warning.

"Get him upstairs," Max yelled for misdirection over the gunfire echoing out around the grounds, while pointing downstairs to Kate.

She stepped forward and took Max's pistol from his left thigh holster and a spare mag from the back of his belt.

"Max," Blake said, back over his shoulder as Kate dragged him towards the stairs. "Come on."

"I'll be right behind you," Max said as the pair headed down the stairs for the basement secure room.

Max backed away from the door, providing cover as the remaining staff and ministers ran for their lives.

He heard Tom yell that the Prime Minister had been taken upstairs and smiled to himself. He allowed Tom to see him head for the stairs and run up the first couple, firing wide, hoping he would give chase.

At the mid-point on the staircase, Max dropped to one knee and opened fire on three men as they came through the front door of the Lodge. All three men fell, as a bullet sailed past his head and slammed into the massive painting on the wall. Max threw three flash grenades, one at the sitting room, one out the front door and the final one at the sliding doors of the Cabinet room they'd been in only minutes ago.

The blinding lights and deafening concussive sounds of the flashbangs drowned out the other raging gunfire and screams for a few seconds of calm. Max used those precious seconds to slip behind the painting into a concealed passage. He clicked the hidden door back into place only a few seconds before he heard Tom and his team running up the stairs on the hunt for Blake.

The secret passages led throughout the house. They connected all the rooms as a means of escape or to get to the panic rooms if needed.

Max took a narrow staircase down towards the basement. He moved quietly, but with purpose. MP5 against his shoulder waiting.

He stopped at the bottom of the steps, listening intently for any signs of activity on the other side of the wall. Max knew there was a massive fake storage locker on the other side, so he wasn't confident he would be able to hear them either way.

He gently pressed the door which served as the back wall of the storage locker. It clicked and he slowly opened it, happy to see the locker doors facing out to the room weren't open. He climbed into the locker and pulled the hidden door closed behind him, then stopped to listen again.

There were at least two men in the basement, which served as the anti-room to the basement panic room. He tried in vain to look through the slats cut into the metal doors, but could only see rough shadows.

He focused his thoughts, took a deep breath, then softly opened the locker door an inch.

From outside the locker, all you could see if you were looking was the small black tip of the MP5 barrel.

One of the men saw it, but too late. The last thing he saw was the mussel flash as Max squeezed the trigger. Max used the confusion of their fallen comrade to completely open the door and step out into the room. He put a bullet into each of the men. One he had seen as a shadow across the room and the other a new arrival from the main staircase.

Max marched quickly across the room to the main stairway and fired three shots up towards the landing, warning off any new attackers, then quickly drew a grenade from his vest.

He sat the grenade between the leg of a chair and the wall, and angled the chair so any incoming attackers would have to move it to enter the basement.

Once he was satisfied, he turned back and faced a small bust on a dusty shelve in the corner and nodded.

He heard a click to his left and moved quickly to the hidden door of the saferoom. He knew the bust had a camera and the feed was live in the panic room. Blake and the others would have been watching.

Max pushed the door open, then darted in, before quickly closing it behind him with a click.

Several staffers were huddled in one corner trying to collect themselves. Blake and Kate were at the security console watching the various feeds from around the house. Timms and two other ministers were standing and exchanging heated words just out of earshot, but Max could see them wildly gesturing to the final figure in the room.

Tied to a chair was the Kelly Gang's Mad Dog, who Max had captured following the attack on Blake's motorcade.

Max walked over to Blake and Kate.

"I take it they're not happy we have him here," Max asked, nodding towards the politicians.

"Fuck no," Kate said. "They carried on a lot when we got in here. You'd think they forgot all the bullets and explosions from two minutes ago. Fucking politicians."

Blake raised an eyebrow at Kate.

"Shit," Kate said. "You don't count. You're not one of them."

"Still," Blake said. "Best to tone it down given the previous conversations about us."

"What fucking conversations?"

"Don't worry about it," Max said. "What's the situation?"

"Most people made it to the panic rooms. A few staff are still unaccounted for and the Minister for Health. We think they're in the kitchen."

"We can't see them?"

"No. The only place they could be is the walk-in fridge. Unless they've found some other hiding spot. Kate, scroll back the camera in the kitchen and see if we can get a confirmation on that."

"They won't last long in there. It'll be too cold and they'll want to come out."

"My thoughts exactly."

"Confirm the location and I'll go get them."

"Are you sure?"

"I'm positive."

Their conversation was interrupted by Timms as he marched over demanding answers for why a terrorist was tied up in the Prime Minister's official residence.

"He's here to be questioned," Max said, dismissively.

"Questioned?" Timms said. "You mean tortured."

"I mean questioned. If you're going to be the new boss, you are going to have to get used to our methods."

"I am your boss and I demand you."

"You'll demand nothing," Blake snapped, cutting off the senator mid-sentence. "You're not the Minister yet or my Deputy. At this rate, you may never be. I suggest you bring your temper down a few degrees. Take a breath and let us handle this."

"But."

"No buts. Shut the fuck up."

Timms went to continue but was pulled away by one of his staff.

Mad Dog sat watching with a quiet grin on his face.

Max locked eyes with him and the cold stare wiped the smile from his face.

"What's the end game?" Max asked his prisoner. "Why are you targeting, Blake?"

Mad Dog stared off blankly, but Max had had enough. He stormed over and punched him in the face. His head flew back violently, then slumped to the side. Neither Kate, nor Blake flinched in anyway. Timms, the other ministers and staff did though.

Mad Dog's groggy head tilted forward and he hocked a bloody golly into Max's face.

Max wiped the spit from his eye with his anger at almost boiling point. He drew his knife to the murmurs of the staff and politicians, and just as he was about to slam it down through the terrorist arm, Kate spoke.

"She's there," Kate said, pointing to the screen. "Kitchen. Walk in fridge. They'll find her soon enough if we don't get her."

Max didn't break his stare with Mad Dog, but he holstered the knife.

"We'll finish this soon," Max said, turning back to Kate. "I'll get her."

"I'm coming with you."

"No way."

"You work for me."

"And you're the Head of the AIS now, Kate, not a field agent. This is why you brought me back in. You need to keep him safe and find these fuckers."

"He's right, Kate," Blake said, reluctantly. "Let him go."

"I won't be long," Max said, checking his weapons.

He glanced at each of the little screens trying to get a lay of the land and locations on the terrorists.

"Be careful," Blake said softly.

Max just nodded and unlocked the saferoom door. He slipped out into the basement, then started for the stairs.

He stalked ahead with athletic grace even after all these years. His footsteps fell quietly on the old floors as he searched with his MP5 and laser-like focus for anyone who might want to kill him.

He moved his makeshift flashbang trap to the side and re-sleaved it in his vest. On the stairs he found two terrorists waiting and two bullets spat from the MP5's silencer into their faces. He bounded up the stairs and was passed the two dead men just as they hit the ground.

Max ran across the foyer and dived through the Cabinet Room sliding doors, as bullets exploded from guns behind him and slammed into the walls puffing the plaster board on impact. He scrambled for the side door, firing back behind him at the advancing terrorists. As they stumbled for cover, Max fled through the door running for the kitchen.

His movements had aroused the attention of two other terrorists, but they both fell as one of the federal police guards opened fire on them. They both fell, but not before one of them got a shot off. It hit the fed in the chest and he coughed blood as he fell to his knees. Max nodded in a sign of respect to his fellow agent, before the life drained from his eyes.

Max didn't stop, he couldn't, they were still coming.

In the hallway which ran to the back of the old house, Max found a terrorist creeping slowly along the wall towards the kitchen. He snuck up behind him clamped his hand hard over his mouth, then slid his knife into the guy's neck.

Max took his whole dead weight on the handle of the knife and ducked into a small cutout in beside a bookcase.

As the chasing terrorists entered the hallway, all they saw was one of their comrades leaning against a wall. They approached cautiously, whispering to their colleague. They asked if he'd seen Max. As they got closer, they started to realise something was wrong, but it was too late. Max dropped the knife and the terrorist slummed to the ground. His friends followed him with their eyes to the floor. It was just enough time for Max to trace a line of bullets across the narrow hallway. The three men were cutdown where they stood.

Max ducked his back out to see one of the men choking on his own blood, still clawing for his fallen weapon. Max stepped out, levelled his gun and fired one shot straight through the terrorist's right eye.

He moved across the hallway and braced behind the doorframe for the kitchen.

"AFP, AFP, this is AIS, do you hear me?" Max asked forcefully, but quietly through the door.

A few seconds passed.

"I hear you, AIS," the police officer replied. "But, how do I know you are who you say you are?"

Max threw his MP5 through the door and heard it clatter across the floor. He then stepped through the doorway with his hands in the air.

The fed stood cautiously from behind the kitchen bench.

"Thank God," the fed said. "I've been guarding the door. The Health Minister is in the fridge. I wasn't sure anyone would come. I thought we were done for."

"I saw you on the CCTV," Max said, reassuringly as he picked up his MP5. "Only the Health Minister in there?"

"Yep. Not sure if everyone else got through, but the explosions blocked our way to the saferoom."

"It's ok. Let's get her out and get moving."

Max moved forward, but felt the now familiar shakes returning to his hands.

"Not now," he said to himself.

"Are you okay?" the Health Minister asked, joining them in the kitchen.

"Not exactly," Max said as he fell to his knees.

Chapter Twenty-Nine

"You can't torture this man," Timms protested as Kate set a knife down on the table. "Not here anyway."

"That's your argument?" Kate asked. "Just don't do it in this building? In case your narrow mind missed it, the building has been taken over by terrorists who came here to kill you. This piece of shit is one of them."

"This is official government property. You can't do it here. It's against the law."

"You really are something, you know that? All bluster and bravado when the cameras are rolling, but when you see it firsthand and in the flesh, you turn to water."

"Kate, check this out," Blake said from the small monitor in the corner.

"What is it?" she asked, turning her back on the senator and walking over to Blake.

They both stared intently at the monitor. Blake was pointing and they were both watching and discussing how Max had taken down several terrorists. He was now talking to one of the federal agents. They watched as he retrieved a cold and shaking Health Minister, Susan Black, from the fridge, but then Max fell to his knees. Black and the Federal Officer rushed forward to help him up. Blake's heart skipped a beat. Clearly, Max hadn't been quite truthful about the effects of the chemical attack.

"What are you doing?" one of the staffers asked from the far corner of the room. "Hey, what are you doing?"

Blake and Kate didn't register it to start with, but with the follow up question they turned to face the room.

Mad Dog's tape had been cut from his wrists and he was now wielding a small silver pistol. Timms was standing beside him with a pocketknife.

"He cut the tape," the staffer said, as Mad Dog fired a shot.

The round hit Kate in the neck. Blake turned in pure horror to see Kate clutch her neck as blood started to pump between her fingers. He caught her as she fell to her knees. She laid back into his arms, staring up at him.

"Fuck," she said softly. "Guess I'm out of practice."

"Too much time behind a desk for both of us," Blake joked.

"I'm sorry I failed you."

"You have nothing to be sorry for, Kate. You didn't fail me, you've served your country with pride and dedication, and more importantly, you've always been an amazing friend."

"Prince Charming is coming to rescue you. Look after each other."

"We will," Blake said, unable to hold back the tears for his long-term friend and colleague.

Kate slumped in his arms and the tears openly flowed down his cheeks.

"So touching," Timms said. "I've got to say, I didn't think we'd get her too, but I am thankful for it."

"You will pay for that," Blake said.

"I don't think so."

"What do you want?"

"There's only one thing I want and that's for you to die."

Blake watched as Mad Dog stood, now free of his restraints, and opened fire killing the two ministers and moving the pistol towards the three staff in the room. They screamed and cried as Blake leapt forward and crash tackled Mad Dog.

The pair wrestled on the ground trading blows as one of the staffers ran to help. He dived onto Mad Dog's back and for the briefest of moments it seemed they had the upper hand.

Timms stepped forward and plunged the knife down hard into Blake's back. Mad Dog quickly regathered his pistol and shot the staffer between the eyes.

Blake turned back in pain to Timms.

"What a sad day for the nation, yet another Prime Minster cut down," Timms said. "The country's going to need a strong leader to bring us together and set us on the right path."

"That's what this is about?" Blake asked. "You want my job?"

"Among other things. And the whole Cabinet saw you appoint me as Deputy. They'll know I had your blessing to take over. They'll hardly protest your final orders."

Blake fell back awkwardly. He could feel the wave of unconsciousness clouding his vision and mind. He was slipping and he could no longer fight it.

He passed out in a pool of his own blood.

A short time later, Max arrived, helped to the room by the Health Minister and Federal Police Officer. They found the door of the saferoom wide open. He signalled for Black and the officer to hold their positions as his adrenaline kicked in.

Max stepped quickly into the room and immediately saw Blake. The sticky red blood was pooled at his back. He ran forward in sheer panic and checked for a pulse.

"Get in here!" Max yelled back through the door.

Black was horrified by the scene before her. The federal officer dushed forward.

"Find the first-aid kit," Max pointed, his hands covered in blood. "In the second cupboard."

"Is he going to make it?" Black asked, arriving by Max's side.

"I'm not going to let him die," Max said, determinedly. "Pull the door closed."

The fed passed Max the kit and he quickly tossed the contents onto the floor, as Black ran back to the door and pulled it closed, locking it.

Max's hands searched for the small vial. He finally found it and a syringe, and hurriedly withdrew the clear liquid into the syringe. He punched it down into Blake's chest and depressed the plunger.

He waited for a few seconds before he started CPR.

"You know where the blood is?" Max asked.

"Yes," the agent replied, turning back for the cupboards.

"Get it."

"Blood?" Black asked. "They have blood storage in here?"

"Not exactly," Max said as he furiously pumped on Blake's chest.

The agent returned with the synthetic blood. It was purely to be used for emergencies to carry oxygen through the blood stream until real blood could be replaced.

Max stopped the CPR and listened. He felt Blake's neck and was overcome with thanks as he found a weak pulse.

"He's got a pulse," Max said.

The fed was already assembling the small synthetic blood drip. Max took the needle end and stabbed it through Blake's skin and into a vein in his hand. The officer helped get the fake blood flowing, while Max cleaned up the wound on Blake's back and set about stitching it closed.

When he was finished, he was finally able to fully take in the rest of the room. He saw the dead staffers and ministers at the back of the room, and felt overwhelming failure.

He turned back to face the others, where he found Black kneeling beside the body of one of his lifelong friends, Kate 'Alpha' Matthews. Max's crushing guilt turned into catastrophic sorrow. He staggered over and fell to his knees beside her and cried.

"She's dead," Black said. "I'm so sorry, Max."

Kate had trained him alongside Hulk at the Wool Shed. She'd been on his team and constant reliable soldier for years. She was possibly the strongest and most courageous person he knew, and he instantly knew it was the worst thing that could possibly happen to a warrior of her standing. To be cut down without the chance to die fighting, she would be fucking livid.

Max felt the anger rising in his body and he jumped to his feet and grabbed the nearest chair and smashed it into the floor repeatedly until it broke apart. Black stepped back in pure fear at his rage. He tossed the back of the chair against the wall and roared in pain, letting out his emotions.

When he calmed down, he saw the officer at the monitor.

"They're leaving," he said. "Back up will be on the scene soon. We'll be able to get the Prime Minister to hospital and secure the building."

"No," Max said. "They think he's dead. We need to relocate him or they'll come back to finish the job."

"He's not stable enough to move."

"He's a fighter. He's going to have to be."

"I agree with the officer," Black said. "I don't think we can move him. I think we should wait for back up and paramedics."

Max thought about it for a moment, Black was a doctor after all. He leant down over Blake and ran his blood covered hand tenderly on the side of Blake's face. He saw the short sharp breaths he was taking and knew they were right. But he needed to get him to safety.

Eventually, the back up did arrive and the federal agents moved through the building clearing each room as they moved. Max waited until they had left the basement, then made his move.

He ducked out through the door and pulled it closed again. He made his way upstairs, then out the back door to find a row of ambulances and police vehicles.

"Help, please," he shouted to two nearby paramedics. "Bring your stretcher."

They did as requested and followed him into the house with a carry stretcher and their medical bags.

He led them down into the basement. Black opened the door for them and they gathered around Blake.

"Jesus," one of the paramedics said. "It's the Prime Minister."

Max explained the wounds and the treatment, as the medical officers set about attaching leads to Blake and assessing the injuries.

"I need him to be dead," Max said to the shock of the two medics. "Just until we get him to the ambulance. They think they killed him and if he's alive they will try to kill him again, I just know it. I need you to help cover our exit, so I can get him to a safehouse."

The officers exchanged nervous looks.

"Do you know who I am?" Max asked.

"Yes, sir," one said. "I've seen you on the news with the Prime Minister."

"He's my fiancé and I love him more than anything in the world. I'm doing this for his safety, but also because I think his government has been compromised."

"How do you figure?"

"There's a missing body."

"What?"

"The Foreign Minister was in here at the time of the attack and he's not here now. I think he's involved."

"Holy shit," Black said, realising for the first time the gravity of the situation.

The federal police officer moved back to the monitor and started scrolling back the footage until he found the scene. Max was right, Timms was talking to the terrorists as they were leaving. It looked like he was giving orders. When the police arrived, he hurried over to them pointing back at the Lodge and playing the survivor card.

"That son-of-a-bitch," Black spat.

"We don't know who else is involved," Max said. "Right at this moment, the only people I trust are right here in this room."

"What do you need us to do?" one of the paramedics asked.

"I need you to carry him out with a sheet over him. We'll all follow and get in the ambulance with you and leave. I need you stabilise him for a bit of a journey and the good doctor here is going to help you."

"We'll do what we can."

Black nodded softly, realising there was no other option.

Chapter Thirty

They pulled the ambulance into the old cobweb covered shed and shut off the engine. A few birds in the distance were the only sounds for miles.

The paramedics gathered their supplies as Max and the federal officer carried Blake across the old driveway and into the old country homestead outside Bungendore.

They made their way to the master bedroom and set up a makeshift ward for Blake.

Max left the medical team to work on Blake and walked back into the lounge room to find Black with a small photo frame in her hand. She was studying it intently.

"His name was Lachlan," Max said.

"You both look so young and happy," Black said.

"We were."

"Do you mind if I ask what happened?"

"I happened."

"What do you mean?"

"He died, because of me. Because of my job."

"I'm sorry, Max. I had no idea."

"Don't be. It's not a story we normally share and it was a long time ago."

"That doesn't stop the hurting."

"It's not the only scar I carry."

"What is this place?"

"It was our home. Well, it was going to be. I bought it to surprise him as a wedding present. We just didn't get the opportunity to actually get married."

"And you've kept it all these years?"

"I threw myself into my work and was away for a long time. I just never got the opportunity to get rid of it. When I was out of the country, Blake looked after it for me. I guess he never had the heart to sell it either."

"It's spotless."

"A cleaner comes in regularly. I guess I was hoping one day Blake and I would move in here."

"I'm sure he would love that. He loves you very much."

"I love him more than anything."

Max looked at the photo of Lachlan sadly.

"He would want you to be happy, you know? He'd be happy you found love again."

"I know."

A few hours passed and they made small talk, as Max tried to sort through his next steps.

Liddle and Hulk arrived with a small AIS medical team.

Max shook Liddle and Hulk's hands and introduced the others.

Liddle and Black left the two spies to talk.

"You look like hell, kid," Hulk said. "He'll be okay. We've got the best of the best on the payroll. Even our worst doctor is still one of the best in the country. He's in good hands."

"They killed Kate," Max said softly, revealing the terrible news to the old spymaster for the first time. "I'm sorry, Hulk."

The old man looked genuinely upset. It was the first time in decades Max had seen his mentor show any emotion other than his usually gruff persona or anger. He saw the tears momentarily well up, then retreat.

"She was one of the best," Hulk said. "She went out serving her nation and I couldn't be prouder of the person she became."

"She was a great person. I can't believe I let this happen."

"Kate was a fucking great agent, Max. If they got the drop on her and Blake, you could have been lying there dead too. There's nothing you could have done."

"Maybe."

"Look at me, Max," Hulk said, pulling Max's shoulder. "Don't blame yourself for this. Focus that pain on getting these arseholes. If Kate was here, what would she say?"

"She'd say don't cry for me, Prince Charming. Go kill those motherfuckers."

"Exactly," Hulk agreed and they both smiled at the thought.

There was a long pause as the two men's smiles faded and they considered the impact of those words. The last time they spoke, Max had hold Hulk the leader of the terrorist group was his one and only son. Max couldn't guess the pain the old man was in knowing that truth.

"We need to find them," Max said. "And find out what's going on here."

"You don't need to pussyfoot around it, Max," Hulk said. "If you're right and it is William, then he's a dead man walking. My son died years ago and whoever he's become is not the boy I raised or the agent I trained. You, Kate and Blake are my family."

Max let a single tear stream down his face as the old man patted him on the back.

They spent some time working on leads and tried to paint a picture of everything they knew.

The Governor-General had called and asked Hulk to temporarily resume his role as Director-General of AIS until a replacement was found for Kate. The two old military men shared a strong and storied history and relationship. They ended the call with Hulk warning that not all was as it seemed. The Governor-General heard the message loud and clear, and knew he would be filled in when the time was right.

Hulk rallied the troops at AIS and worked across agencies to hunt for those responsible for killing the Prime Minister. They let that rumour spread and the news media were in overdrive with speculation and fear. Two Prime Ministers dead and an escalating series of terror attacks. The country was at war with an invisible enemy. There was panic in the streets.

Amongst the carnage, the party had appointed Senator Kevin Timms as leader and he was due to be sworn in any minute as Prime Minister.

Hulk poured himself half a glass of whiskey in a solid glass tumbler. He took a drink, then sat the glass down heavily on the table beside Max. He walked over to his bag and retrieved a small box.

He wandered back over and handed Max the box.

"I wanted you to have this," Hulk said, taking a seat and another gulp of whiskey.

"What is it?" Max asked opening the box.

"This was given to me when I first became a spy."

"It's a survival bracelet."

"I wore it every day for years and I want you to have it."

"Thank you," Max said, taken back by the gesture.

"It's the closest thing I have to a family heirloom. It's got a watch and compass, survival cord, torch. The works. I also had the boys in R&D make a few modifications over the years."

"Is that right?"

"Yeah, carbon fibre knife, alarm and a small charge too."

"This is old school."

"Ain't no school like it. We didn't have all the high-tech shit that you guys use today, but that bracelet got me out of a lot of scraps back in the day."

"Thank you," Max said, genuinely touched.

"You guys have been like family and I want you to have it."

Max wrapped the cord of the bracelet around his left wrist and admired it. He let his fingers run over the cord and the watch face.

There was a quick knock on the door, before Liddle burst in.

"Sorry to interrupt," Liddle said.

"What is it?" Hulk asked.

"It's Blake, he's awake."

Max shot out of his chair and was out the door, before Hulk had a chance to reach for his walking stick.

He jogged down the hallway and into the room. He marched to Blake's side and took his hand, as Blake opened his eyes and smiled softly.

"How are you feeling?" Max asked.

"How many dead?" Blake asked.

"Don't worry about that now."

"How many, Max?"

"Twenty-five, including two of your ministers, several staff and police."

"I've got to address the nation. They need to see me. I need to assure them everything is going to be okay."

"There's a little complication with that."

"What?"

"I need you to get better."

"I'll be fine, Max. What is the complication?"

Blake was becoming more alert and started to take in his surroundings.

"Where are we?"

"Bungendore."

"What? Why?"

"They think you're dead and I want it that way."

"I don't understand."

"Do you remember what happened?"

Blake looked blankly for a few seconds at Max. He was searching his memory trying to remember, then it hit him like a tonne of bricks.

"Kate," he said sadly letting a tear run down his cheek, before the anger rose in his throat. "Timms!"

"What happened?"

"He let the terrorist we were holding free. The terrorist shot Kate then Sally and Henry, and the staff we had in the room. I tried to stop him, but Timms stabbed me. It must have been his gun. It was a small nickel-plated pistol. Jesus. Where are they now?"

"We don't have a location on the terrorists."

"And Timms?"

"This is the part you're really not going to like."

"It's not bad enough already?"

"He's about to be sworn in as Prime Minister."

"What?" Blake said throwing back the sheets and trying to sit up.

"What are you doing?"

"I've got to stop him."

"Then they'll know you're alive and come for you again."

"So be it."

"We can't let him takeover."

"The wheels are already in motion. We don't know how deep this goes, where they all are or their endgame. I need you to recover, while I find them all and take them out."

"And what damage will Timms do in the meantime?"

"We'll cross that bridge as we get to it. But for now, we need to uncover his network."

"He's right, Blake," Black said, walking into the room. "The country needs you, but we've got to find these people first and take them out."

"Susan, what are you doing here?"

"Max rescued me. We've been talking about how to handle things and I've come to realise he is completely right. We've got to uncover the conspiracy, then take action."

"Take action?"

"Max is going to kill every last one of them."

Blake thought about it for a few moments, before Liddle came into the room.

"You're going to want to see this," Liddle said, holding up his tablet computer.

"We're standing by for the new Prime Minister, Kevin Timms," the news anchor said. *"He has just been sworn in by the Governor-General and will address the media in. Oh wait, here he is now walking to the podium. Here is the Prime Minister."*

"Good evening," Timms said. *"It is with incredible sadness that I assume the role of Prime Minister in these circumstances. Our nation is facing a crisis. We've had two assassinations on our soil in recent days, including Prime Minister Blake Smyth, who served the nation with distinction in the Royal Australian Navy and at the Australian Intelligence Service before his untimely death. My thoughts are indeed with his family, although I'm afraid I have further bad news on that front. As you are all aware, Prime Minister Smyth was in a long-term relationship with this man."*

Timms held up a photograph of Max so the cameras could see it.

"This is Agent Max Shaw who was recently reinstated as a senior agent at the AIS. Our police sources have confirmed that they believe Mr Shaw was part of the terrorist group which led the assault on the Lodge. It is unclear what his intentions were in leading such a vicious attack, but what we do know is that he killed the Prime Minister and many others, including his boss, Kate Matthews, the Director-General of the AIS. My advisers have informed me that they believe Mr Shaw was not working alone. They have evidence that Mr Shaw has been in contact with Patrick Scott and Michael Liddle, as well as several members of parliament and our police and intelligence services. I have asked the police to begin making arrests and I have instructed the Governor-General to close the AIS with its vast powers to be transferred to the Federal Police. I have also instructed the Governor-General to commission a private contracting firm, Alexander Industries, into the public service to run a full review of operations between the intelligence and policing agencies. William Alexander is here from Alexander Industries. William, would you like to say a few words?"

The room fell deathly quiet as William Scott took to the lectern beside the new Prime Minister. He was the dead spit image of his father, just thirty years younger.

"While I can understand people may see this as an unusual appointment," William said, *"we live in unusual times. The very people and agencies we trusted to protect us have turned on us. They have let the terrorists win. They have killed our friends, our colleagues and our leaders. But no more. Enough is enough. There is no place they can hide from us and we will find them. My promise to the new Prime Minister and to all my fellow Australians is that Alexander Industries will not stop until these people are brought to justice, one way or another. With this in mind, we are recommending a nationwide curfew be brought into effect immediately."*

"Jesus," Blake said, trying to sit up. "I need to stop this."

"We don't know who we can trust, Blake," Max said. "We need to keep you safe and regroup."

"They're about to tell every agency we've got to hunt you and Hulk and Mike. William and his crew will lead the charge and if I get killed in the process it won't matter because I'm really dead. It's not too late for me to stop this."

Blake reached for his phone and started scrolling for a number. He found the Governor-General's mobile and hit call. Three long beeps echoed around the room as the call failed to connect.

The newsfeed on the tablet computer in Mike's hands froze and then displayed an error message. No signal.

The lights went off and the room fell into darkness.

"They're here," Max said.

Mike and Hulk both sprung into action, and checked their weapons. Max did the same.

"I guess they know I'm alive," Blake said.

"What's going on?" Black asked.

"They're coming to fucking wipe us out," Hulk said, coldly.

"Oh my God. What are we going to do?"

"I've got a friend not far from here. He'll be on route. Until then, we've got to move. We're sitting ducks in here."

"Can you walk?" Max asked.

"I think so," Blake said, already half out of bed. "Give me a gun."

"Let's get to the shed," Max said, handing Blake his pistol and getting under his shoulder to help him stand and walk. "If all else fails we take the ambulance and make a run for it."

"It's as good a plan as any."

"Mike and I will hold them off, while you get Blake to the shed," Hulk said as Mike eagerly nodded.

"Thank you," Blake said, knowing it would be useless to argue with his old boss.

"Go," Hulk barked.

"Here," Max said to one of the paramedics. "You guys help, Blake. I'm staying with these guys."

The paramedics jumped on either side of Blake who again was too weak to argue with Max.

The paramedics led Blake and the small group, including Black and the AIS medics, to the rear of the house. Blake counted a few beats and told them to hold their position.

A few seconds passed, before gunshots rang out at the front of the old home and he told them to move.

Max, Hulk and Liddle had sighted the incoming attackers and started firing to distracted them and draw their fire.

Hulk was at the front door, taking cover behind the frame. Mike was behind a concrete retaining wall next to Max and the pair were firing over the top at the incoming troops.

An explosion rang out behind them and Max turned back to see the shed go up in a huge ball of fire. In the glow of the orange flames he saw the group with Blake fall to the ground. He wasn't sure but he thought he saw a couple of their team closer to the shed hit by the explosion.

Bullets raked the house and the garden bed on top of the retaining wall. Dirt and concrete kicked up into the air around him, and he knew he was pinned down.

At the rear of the house, Blake was crawling through the thick grass towards Black. She'd taken a huge concussive wave. He could see blood coming from her ears. He shook her awake and spoke to her, but she couldn't hear him. Her eardrums had burst. She was panicking and yelling. He held a finger to his lips and gave a reassuring smile. He mouthed it's okay.

He looked to his left and saw two men in full military fatigues crossing the paddock. He couldn't be sure if they were military or terrorists, but he knew they were there to kill everyone, so he shot first.

The two men fell as one of his paramedics stood up to come help him. She was hit with a volley of bullets and died before she hit the ground. He knew the two doctors from AIS were dead. They had run ahead to open the shed doors. He saw the explosion hit them. There was no way they survived.

He crawled to the other paramedic who was a few metres back clutching a huge piece of wood which had punctured his stomach. Blood was pouring from his wounds and his mouth. Blake held his hand as he slipped from the world.

He rolled onto his back and saw two more men stalking across the field. He opened fire as they ducked behind an old fence. Bullets hit the dirt to his right and he spun back to see another man running towards him. He pulled the gun around and fired four shots. The third hit the terrorist centre mass and he fell.

The distraction was enough for the other two to reappear from behind the fence and open fire. A bullet caught Black in the leg and she screamed out in pain.

Blake turned the gun and opened fire, until it clicked dry. Black saw the look on his face and saw the pistol slide back. She'd seen enough movies to know that meant the gun was out of bullets. Her hopes completely faded when she saw him toss it in the dirt.

He crawled forward and took her by the hands. He mouthed that he was sorry. Tears fell down her cheeks as she confronted her mortality.

In the distance, Max could hear a helicopter coming in hard and fast. He knew the end was near. His guilt was choking him. First Lachlan, now Blake. He had failed the men he loved.

The big chopper hovered in low overhead and the side door slid open. Brave swung his machine gun out the door and started firing wildly at Max. Max couldn't hear what he was saying but he could see he was yelling. There was a lot of hate behind the words.

"You fucking killed her!" Brave was yelling from the door, referring to the Wild Woman who Max had killed in the plane. "Die you piece of shit!"

The bullets tore into the house and the gardens.

Max stole a look back to search for Hulk, but he wasn't there. He must have moved when the big bird arrived. Then Max saw him. He hobbled fast out the side door and into the driveway and opened fire at Brave and the chopper. The bullets harmlessly pinged off the metal aircraft.

"Move us around so I can get a shot at this prick!" Brave demanded.

The pilot manoeuvred the chopper in over Max's house and Brave smiled sighting in Hulk. He was just about to fire when something caught his attention out the corner of his eye. He looked towards the white trail streaking across the sky towards him and knew his time was up.

The air-to-air missile exploded on impact and the huge, wrecked chopper burst into flames, before it fell towards Max's roof.

Max and Mike leapt the retaining wall firing wildly at any remaining terrorists in the grass land. Max lined up two attackers and shot them one after the other as the wreckage smashed through his roof and the whole house was engulfed in flames and billowing black smoke.

Hulk was thrown off his feet as the second Blackhawk swept in over the property and the gunners on both sides raked the grasslands taking down the last of the terrorists.

Max was on his feet and running before the first shots were fired from the doors of the chopper. He was moving fast covering the metres quickly. He neared Hulk, but the old man just waved him on, so he didn't stop. He found Blake and Black, and slid to a stop beside them. They were still holding hands and Black was weeping in pure terror and pain.

Blake was semi-conscious, but he was alive and that's what mattered. He helped them both to their feet as the chopper landed. Mike arrived to help Black and they made their way over to the helicopter. Hulk was already climbing on board when they arrived.

They helped Black and Blake in, and as soon as Max was in the door the big chopper rose into the air, banked hard and sped off into the evening sky.

Max looked back at the burning ruins of the house that never became his home.

Chapter Thirty-One

"How the fuck did they get away?" Timms screamed.

"They had a back up plan," William said. "We didn't account for it."

"And what was that?"

"They had a Blackhawk on standby."

"How'd they get a message to them? You said you took out the communications networks around the house."

"We think they must have had a failsafe, like if they didn't hear from them, then they had to come investigate."

"You think? I haven't seen much of that lately. You are a failure."

"You might think you are powerful now you're sitting in that chair, but it isn't real power."

"Oh and I guess you know what real power is."

William drew his pistol and pointed it at Timms' face.

"One small squeeze on the trigger and you're dead," William said. "That's real power."

"You forget your place," Timms spat.

"No, you forget yours."

"I beg your pardon."

"We're partners in this. We've got some overlapping goals, but don't think for a moment you're in command."

"I've given you everything you've wanted. We're disbanding the AIS. What more do you want?"

"I want them all dead!"

"Well, that's on you. Your team has had plenty of chances."

"He's going to die with all his little minions and I'm going to piss on the ashes of his legacy."

"You've never told me why you hate him so much."

"Where do I start? He killed my mother."

"What?"

"He was fucking some other woman and I found out. I confronted him and he broke my wrist. My mother was coming to see me in the hospital and she was in a car accident. She wouldn't have been in the car if not for him. He killed her."

"I'm sorry."

"Don't be, he's the one who will be sorry. He ruined my life."

"That's how you ended up on the street?"

"Turning tricks for cash. Blowing old rich guys to pay for more drugs. Every dick and every needle was his fault. Destroying his precious AIS and all those who he held close to him is retribution."

"I can't even imagine how he would have been as a father even before all of this."

"He was absent most of the time. Working. He always cared more about his work than me. When he was there, he was a brutal dictator. When I came out to him in my early teens, he tried to get me to do manly things to somehow get it out of my system. Join the AIS and let the testosterone cure the gay."

Timms was silent for a few seconds as William realised he had just come out to another elderly conservative.

"Get over it," he said, waving his hand. "Anyway, now you know why."

"Indeed."

"Want to tell me what else is in this for you?"

"What do you mean?"

"This office wasn't your endgame. There's more to it than that."

"Maybe."

"I'm guessing it's got something to do with the microprocessors we stole from the Americans. The rest of the shit we've pulled was just to cause chaos, but those chips, that was all for you. What are you up to?"

"Not all of us have personal reasons for what we do like you. I wanted this job and I want cash, it's as simple as that."

"Hmm, well we'll see I guess."

Chapter Thirty-Two

It had taken the best part of two hours for the chopper to reach the Wool Shed. No sooner had it touched down on the dry lawns of the old training facility then Blake was whisked into the building's medical centre for urgent treatment. Black was also carried in on a stretcher and the medical team set about cleaning and repairing her wounds.

Hulk, Liddle and Max sat in Hulk's office drinking whiskey.

"So what's their next move?" Liddle asked, swirling the amber liquid in his crystal tumbler.

"They're starting to shut us out of all our own systems," Hulk said. "Timms has started replacing people at the AFP, AIS and even in the senior ranks of the defence forces. He's trying to isolate us by getting rid of our friends, replacing them with those loyal to him."

"So this is what a coup feels like?"

"We've seen plenty from afar and that's how I'd rather keep them, as far away from here as possible."

"Did we do the right thing?" Max asked, quietly looking into his glass. "Timms might become unstoppable."

"We didn't know how far this thing went, kid. We didn't know who to trust. Now we do."

"How do you figure?"

"Everyone he has sacked or replaced or demoted is one of the good guys. He's shown us his hand."

"So what do we do now?"

"Blake needs to wake up and start making phone calls and we need to start rallying our team."

"He's still under."

"We'll give him us much time as we can, then we'll need to bring him around and put him to work."

"Who does he start with?" Liddle asked. "The Governor-General?"

"Yes, but the good Admiral needs to work quietly behind the scenes. If Timms finds out he's working with us, he'll have him removed from office. He's probably already planning it."

"How do we protect him?"

"We can't. He'll have to protect himself."

"So we start making some lists?"

"Yes. Who's with us, who's against us and who we're not sure of. We start with the most senior positions in Cabinet, the Ministry, public service and military."

A phone started ringing. The men each retrieved their phones and looked at the screens only to see the blank black glass staring back at them. Hulk frowned, then unsteadily climbed to his feet and shuffled to his desk. He pulled open the second draw and the ringing was instantly louder.

He paused for a minute to look at Max and Liddle, but decided to let them stay in the room and pressed he answer button.

"Sir," Hulk answered.

Max and Liddle exchanged a questioning look. There weren't many people in the world Hulk would call sir on the best of days, let alone today of all days.

Hulk listened for a full minute.

"I'm going to put you on speaker," Hulk said, lowering the phone and resting it on the table. "Mike Liddle and Max Shaw are in the room, sir. Do you mind repeating what you just told me?"

"I'm guessing that since you're in that room, you're on our team?" Governor-General Anthony Mills asked, more to himself than to the men in the room.

"To trust me is to trust them, sir," Hulk answered on their behalf.

"What's this about?" Max asked. "Are you okay?"

"I'm safe, Max. Thank you. I know Timms has taken control and is replacing personnel. I also know he is full of shit. This is a coup plain and simple."

"So what's the plan?"

"I've made a call to the King. Steps are being taken. Your commissions are still in effect and when we get a list of who's who, I'll reinstate those on our side to help you out. But, Max please listen, that's not why I'm calling. I've just gotten off the phone with the American President. The microchips weren't the only thing stolen from that transport in the Northern Territory."

"What else was in that truck?"

"Thirty kilograms of enriched plutonium or to be more specific the payload section of a nuclear weapon."

"What?"

"The important bit," Hulk said. "Fucking Americans."

"We don't have nuclear weapons in Australia."

"No, we don't." Mills said. *"But apparently they do."*

"And they didn't tell us?"

"I certainly had no idea and I'm assuming from Hulk's reaction he didn't either."

"I had no clue," Hulk said as Liddle stood and paced.

"So, why did they call?"

"They thought they'd be able to locate it by now and that it would be handled quietly."

"And they obviously haven't. So they want our help."

"They've been watching the turmoil, including two dead Prime Ministers," Mills said, instantly regretting the coldness in his voice. *"I'm sorry, Max."*

"He's not dead, Admiral. He's with us here at the Wool Shed. He's recovering, but he's alive."

"What? That's fantastic. Why did you let Timms takeover then?"

"Someone is still after Blake and clearly this is bigger than we knew. We needed to get him to safety and as you said find out who's with us and who's against us."

"When will he be ready to take back control?"

"We can't be sure just yet, but he's a fighter and he'll do whatever he can. Tell us more about the weapon. If it's just the material, they won't be able to do anything without the rest of the weapon."

"Well, that's why they called. The rest of the weapon is here too."

"What? Where?"

"Some of it was stored at the Reserve Bank. Their vault was until recently supposedly impenetrable. The rest of the weapon was at that defence base they had set up camp in. They saw the report of the plane explosion and breathed a shy of relief thinking it had become harmless debris over the desert."

"Don't tell me."

"Yeah, it was in one of the crates which made it to the ground."

"Shit," Max said, recalling the crates he had used to send more than one terrorist flying out the back of the Globemaster. "Where is it now?"

"It's missing."

"Fuck."

"That's what I said too."

"Where do they think it is?"

"Best guess is one of Timms' people smuggled it out of the warehouse."

"Jesus Christ. We should assume William and his crew have it. So what do we think is they're plan, set off of the weapon or use it against someone else?"

"There's something else, Max," Mills began to say, but was cut off.

The unmistakeable sound of gunshots echoed through the tiny speakers on the phone.

"Jesus, they're here," Mills said.

"Are you okay?" Hulk asked.

There was a hollow clunk on the end of the line, before a gunshot and the sound of a door slamming hard against a wall rang out.

"Who are you?" Mills asked, clearly a small distance from the phone which he must have hidden. *"What do you want?"*

"Shut the fuck up," a man said in the distance. *"Stay where you are and put your hands in the air."*

"Why do you need those weapons, I'm unarmed?"

There were footsteps echoing through the room.

"Hello, Your Excellency," William said, walking into the room.

Hulk froze, and Max and Liddle exchanged looks, before they heard the metallic thud of Wiliam's Ned Kelly helmet placed down on the Governor-General's desk.

"I don't suppose I need the mask anymore, I'm sure you're aware of who I am and that we've taken over the country."

"Why are you doing this?"

"Do you believe the bushrangers were bad people?"

"They killed police officers and robbed banks, that would certainly put them on that side of the equation for most people."

"For most, but it's not that simple, is it?"

"Like most things in life, they aren't always black and white."

"Precisely. I, for one, think they were heroes. They started with nothing, the sons of convicts ripped from their homes and shipped off to a foreign land on the other side of the world. Never to see their homeland and never to be treated as anything other than second class citizens. Sure, they had land to farm, but not to own. It was the great squattocracy. They had to squat on Crown Land and farm it, without any legal rights. Forever kept in the downtrodden ranks of society."

"They were eventually given land rights."

"Not our friend, Ned Kelly."

"He and his band of bushranger brothers stole cattle and robbed banks. They did raids on towns as outlaws and murdered police informants."

"Fucking government snitches!"

"I take it you see yourself as a modern version of your hero, stealing from the government?"

"We're righting a wrong."

"And what wrong would that be?"

"Government."

"Government is the wrong?"

"Yes. People like you and my father. You seek to control the people and keep them locked forever in their place in society. You hold people back with your rules and your lies. Constant oppression. You force people into the streets to do unspeakable things just to live."

Max looked to Hulk. The colour had drained from his face and he looked like he was going to collapse. He placed his hand on the old man's shoulder. Tears welled in his mentor's eyes showing the gut-wrenching pain and sadness he was feeling.

"I know you've had a hard life, William," Mills said.

"Do you?!" William spat. *"How could you? You're one of them."*

"One of who?"

"The oppressors. The man. The government. You are part of the problem and you'll never understand the pain and heartache you cause, and the destruction your bullshit spreads. You spout equality and fairness, and freedom, but how can anyone be truly free while chained to the structures of capitalism and class. You of all people should understand it. You represent a system which is designed to preserve the rights of the ruling classes – power and privilege for the King and his family, and his friends. Unbelievable wealth, while the rest of us are supposed to bow and toil only to see our labour and our efforts filling their bank accounts and not our own. We struggle

to pay our bills and feed ourselves, while they live in mansions and castles."

"And, what, you're the reckoning? You and Timms?"

"Timms, ha," William laughed. "He's just a tool. He's one of you. So eager for power and wealth, and to be accepted as one of you elites. His ego has helped us achieve our goal."

"And what is that goal?"

"Anarchy. We believe the world has to burn so a new world can rise from the ashes of the old. Pro humanitate et terra."

"For humanity and the earth."

"Exactly."

"And he clearly has no idea?"

"You've met him. Do you seriously think he is capable of considering anything beyond himself?"

"So why involve him?"

"His ambition blinds him. He's helped create chaos and now thinks he'll be the one to right the ship and his leadership and power and genius will put us on the right course."

"But I'm guessing you're one step ahead of him?"

"At least."

"And I'm also going to go out on a limb here and say that's why you need the weapon."

"I knew you were smarter than him. The Americans called?"

"Where is it, William?"

"It's safe. For now."

"You going to use it?"

"That won't be up to me."

"Timms?"

"I'm sure he'll comply with our demands to stop it from detonating, but it'll be his choice. If he doesn't do what we want, well let's just say one of our cities is going to be uninhabitable for ten thousand years or so."

"You'll kill the very people you claim to represent."

"They are collateral damage. Martyrs for our new world."

"You're crazy."

"I used to think so, but my thoughts have never been clearer. This is my journey. My purpose. My destiny. To free to world from oppression."

"You'll never win."

"Look around you, Admiral. I already have."

"So what do you want from me?"

"I need you to speak to the President again."

"To what end?"

"I need you to find out where they've hidden the trigger."

Mills actually laughed at the revelation and suggestion.

"You can't set it off?"

"Not yet, but you're going to help us."

"Absolutely not, because like your father, I'm willing to sacrifice myself for this nation," Mills said, his voice cracking slightly as he looked to the stationery box on his desk where he had dropped his phone.

"We have your family," William said, walking over to the desk and pulling out the satellite phone to see it was connected. *"Very clever, Admiral."*

The phone clicked off leaving Hulk, Max and Liddle in stunned silence.

"They have his family," Liddle said. "They'll kill or torture them to get his cooperation. Christ, it's only a matter of time before they find the trigger."

"Unless we get to it first," Max said, marching out of the room.

He walked into the recovery room where Blake was silently sleeping in his induced coma. An AIS doctor was checking Blake's vitals and making notes on a clipboard.

"Wake him up," Max said.

"We can't," the doctor said. "We could kill him."

"There is no one on this earth who cares more about that than me. Don't stand there and tell me the risks. I know them. Do you think I would be in here if I didn't have to be?"

"No, sir."

"Then do it!"

The doctor begrudgingly walked to a nearby storage cupboard and retrieved a small glass vial and a needle. He loaded the clear liquid into the syringe and flicked it to remove any trapped air. He walked over and smoothly slid the needle into the drip outlet attached to Blake's arm.

"How long?" Max asked.

"He'll be awake any second," the doctor replied.

"And how long will I have?"

"Only a few minutes."

"Get me his phone."

The doctor left the room.

Max waited, hoping he'd made the right call.

He watched as Blake's eyelids began to flutter, then lent in to whisper in his partner's ear.

"Blake, it's me. Don't try to speak, please just listen."

Max ran his hand down the side of Blake's face and he felt Blake press his cheek against his hand.

"Just nod if you can hear and understand me."

Blake nodded weakly.

"A lot has happened and I don't have time to explain it in detail. I just need you to trust me. I need to give you a shot of adrenaline, then I need you to make a call to the American President. We need to know where the trigger is for a nuclear weapon."

The heart monitor in the room began to beep louder as Blake's heart fluttered in obvious recognition of the threat.

He tried to speak, but Max cut him off.

"You need to hear me out, Blake. Don't speak it's too hard on your system right now."

Blake's eyes opened softly and tear rolled down his cheek as his eyes screamed trying to communicate with Max.

"It's okay, Blake. I'm here. I love you."

Another tear dropped from Blake's eye and Max whipped it away lovingly with his thumb.

"The problem is Blake, the doctor's not sure what effect the adrenaline will have on you. He's confident it'll be enough to help you make the call, but he's worried it'll cause more damage. He thinks it could react with the other drugs in your system and could affect your heart. It might even be enough to give you a stroke. I wish we had another way, but we don't and we can't wait. Wiiliam has taken the Governor-General hostage and it's only a matter of time before he gets the location of the trigger. If he gets it, he'll have a working nuclear device and he's threatened to level a city to start a nationwide anarchy."

Max saw the recognition in Blake's eyes, but also the determination. There was certainly sadness, but also a strength which was burning behind his eyes.

"If there was another way, you know I would take it, Blake. I love you so much."

Blake managed to nod very weakly and his eyes burned as if willing Max to give him the shot.

"Thank you, Blake," Max said, plunging the needle into Blake's arm and depressing it as the doctor re-entered the room with Blake's mobile phone.

Max took the phone and pressed Blake's finger on the scanner. It unlocked and he scrolled through to find the private mobile phone number of the leader of the free world. He was about to hit call, when Blake reached over and stopped him.

"What are you doing?" Max asked, genuinely confused.

"He can't help us," Blake choked out.

"What do you mean? We need him to tell us where the trigger is."

"He doesn't know."

Chapter Thirty-Three

The helicopter swept in low over the grounds of the Royal Military College, Duntroon. As it swung around the large glass building, he sighted two men standing guard. They had multiple soldiers dead at their feet on the surrounding lawns.

They were wearing matching black special ops fatigues and Max knew they weren't soldiers or AIS personnel. They were William's men.

"Shit," Max said, mostly to himself knowing they'd beaten him to the AIS complex which was hidden in plain sight on the grounds of the military's training base. "Bring it closer, then take us down."

"Yes, sir," his pilot said as the big chopper immediately began to swing into action.

Max lined up the door's mounted gun and opened fire.

The two men were cut down in a spray of blood, before Max wheeled the big gun around and unleashed a wave of bullets into the two idling SUVs. The men sitting inside and the vehicles themselves were sliced through with searing hot rounds destroying them where they sat.

Four men ran out into the open from the AIS building and fired up at the chopper. Max swung the barrel around and opened fire. Dirt and grass exploded all around the men, before Max's gun found its mark. The four men danced on the spot as the bullets ripped through their bodies and into the ground around them.

"Bring us in," Max yelled over the sound of the gun and chopper blades.

The helicopter dropped fast as Max grabbed his MP5 and stood by the open door.

Max jumped before the skids even touched the grass and started for the door.

He ran fast with his MP5 pressed hard against his shoulder. He shot the glass window and stepped into the AIS foyer. He saw another two AIS personnel dead on the cold concrete floor and his blood began to boil. He was going to kill every last terrorist in the building.

He kicked open the fire doors and checked the stairwell. He looked up the stairs, but knew there wasn't much on the upper levels. They were mostly for show. The actual building was underground, including the office he needed to find. He wasn't sure if the terrorists knew that though and he could hear several men upstairs. He bounced up the first short flight and placed a trip wire, before bounding back down the stairs and starting his decent into the concrete bunker.

Max easily dispatched several men in the stairwell. Their lifeless bodies dropping to the concrete before they even knew he was there. When he found the door for the executive office level, he breathed deeply, then flicked it open.

He dived through and rolled in behind a lounge as bullets racked the wall and doorway. He rolled into a crouch with one knee on the ground and his body rolled over into a hunch. He waited.

When the bullets slowed, he sprung up and fired three impossibly quick shots, before ducking back behind the couch.

The bullets hit two targets killing them.

A third man began screaming and firing wildly at the lounge and Max had no choice but to move. He darted out, firing in the direction of the firing terrorist. Two bullets hit the attacker in the stomach and his shots stopped. Max saw him reach down to clutch his bloody wounds. He saw the blood on his hands and looked up in shock. Max fired one bullet and it hit the terrorist between the eyes. He stood for a few seconds before the weight of his body collapsed at the knees and dragged him to the ground.

Max loaded a new magazine and started clearing offices.

He made his way through the modern concrete maze and saw for the first time his own new office. It had a small glass plague with his name and title on it. New furniture had been arranged neatly, but it otherwise looked completely untouched.

There was a pile of briefs in an in-tray, but otherwise it was completely free of personal effects or anything that said it was an office which was in use.

Max heard shouting and refocused. He spun the MP5 towards the voices and marched silently towards them.

As he rounded the corner, he heard the voices more clearly.

"Come out and bring the device," the terrorist demanded.

Max couldn't quite make out the reply, but he did make out a couple of words which sounded like 'fuck yourself.' He didn't know who was in the office, but it looked like they were the final line of defence.

The terrorist began giving orders to his men, when he saw a small cannister land at his feet and his eyes widened.

"Fuck me," he said as it exploded with blinding light and an ear-splitting bang.

The four remaining terrorists all started firing wildly. Two of them ended up killing each other in the confusion. Max stepped out and fired his MP5.

Two bullets each, including for the two who had shot each other. Can ever be too sure.

Max quietly made his way along the corridor and as he approached the doorway to the office he was looking for, he paused.

"Whoever's in there," Max said, turning his face towards the door from cover. "This is Max Shaw and as of this morning, I am your boss. I need you to put down your guns and let me into the room."

"Boss my arse," Kate said.

Max recognised the voice immediately and darted into the room. He saw his old friend, one he thought was dead from the attack on the Lodge, and was overcome with emotion.

"No time for tears, Prince Charming, especially if they're because you aren't getting promoted today," Kate laughed.

"I'm happy to see you," Max said.

"Likewise, kid," she said, clutching her side.

"Are you okay?"

"Not exactly, but I'm alive."

"How?"

"The AIS team found me and got me out, after you left with Blake. Apparently, I was gone for a few minutes, long enough to make everyone think I was dead, but they got a faint heartbeat back and here I am."

"I'm sorry."

"Don't be. I would have done the same thing. I was dead, but I'm not now, so let's move on. How's our boy?"

"He's back under. I had to give him adrenaline and after he told me to come here, he went into convulsions. They put him back in a coma to take the pressure off his brain."

"He'll be okay, Max. He's got your strength, but more importantly, after all these years of waiting, he finally has you. No way he's going to say goodbye to that."

"I hope you're right."

"You know I am and you shouldn't be fucking surprised."

"Do you have the trigger?"

"Yes, it's in there," Kate said, pointing towards her bookcase.

"So we did know they had a device on our soil?"

"Blake figured it out when he was Head of AIS. He started to track their movements and realised they were up to something. He intercepted the trigger and two mechanisms for the bomb, and hid them. One piece at the Reserve Bank, the other at an abandoned base and the trigger he kept here locked in the safe."

"And the yanks were pissed no doubt?"

"Fucking oath, but since they had smuggled a bomb into the country without telling us they didn't really have a leg to stand on. He made a deal. They'd keep the warhead and material, and we'd keep the mechanism and trigger. If a time came when we needed it as a deterrent, we'd reassemble it and make a joint decision on its use."

"You didn't think we should know this after the attacks?"

"We planned to bring you and Hulk up to speed after the cabinet meeting at the Lodge, but obviously that didn't happen."

"I've been racking my brain trying to piece it all together."

"I'm sorry about that, you know I am. I fucking hate having secrets from you."

"And the rest of the leads we were following?"

"As far as we can tell, it's all been part of William's plan to create chaos and anarchy. Each incident is fuelling the idea we're out of control and people should be in fear. Plus with the deaths of our country's leaders and attacks on all of us and on civilians. Well, they are winning."

"And Timms?"

"He has no idea. Just a power hungry prick. He sent over my replacement already."

"Really?"

"Yeah, he's just there," Kate said, pointing casually to the body of a man in his late fifties who had bled out on the carpet of her office. "He wasn't very happy to see me. Fucking terrorist piece of shit. He was here to sack everyone and turn the fucking lights off."

They both sprung towards the door, raising their weapons as an explosion rang out in the distance.

"Get the device," Max said, marching towards the door to provide cover.

"What was that?" Kate asked, entering her pin number and swiping her ring on the sensor to unlock her safe.

"I rigged the stairs. It'll give them something to think about, but won't hold them for long."

"Got it."

Kate spun around and lost her balance. She grabbed a nearby chair to steady herself, but not before Max saw. She looked pale.

"Are you okay?" he asked.

"I'm fine. Nothing like significant blood loss and near-death experience to fuck up your day."

"Can you make it to the carpark?"

"I could carry your arse up there without breaking a sweat."

"Well, stay close to me anyway."

"I should be asking you the same thing. You look like shit. Are you okay?"

"I've had better days."

"So, the attack was worse than you let on earlier?"

"Yeah. The doctors are giving me doses of painkillers and adrenaline, among other things. It's doing the job for now, but I'm sure for how long."

"Jesus. You should be in hospital."

"Look who's talking."

"Here," Kate said, tossing Max the remote trigger for the nuke. "Just in case."

Max holstered the small device in his tactical vest. They both just nodded at each other. Neither would heed the other's advice to go to the hospital. They were going to see this through to the end, regardless of what happened to them personally.

The pair fell into their well-rehearsed formation and headed for the door. Max ducked his head around the corner and saw an empty hallway. He nodded briefly, then headed out in the sterile corridor. He hugged the left wall, while Kate darted around to walk along the right. They both moved in unison, silent and efficient, with their guns pressed to their shoulders. They scanned the path waiting for any sign of an incoming attack.

At the end of the corridor, Max raised his fist. The pair stopped in their tracks and listened. Their senses heightened.

Max flicked his head and gun around the corner, and fired two bullets into the unsuspecting terrorists. They'd been arguing quietly about who would go first. In the end, it didn't matter. Max's precise shots hit them both in the centre of their foreheads. Two neat red holes sat perfectly between dead eyes as they collapsed to the ground.

The two senior leaders of the AIS quickly made their way through the hallways, until they reached the stairs. Kate grabbed a railing to steady herself.

"You okay?" Max asked.

"Don't worry about me, Prince Charming," Kate said with a small laboured smile. "You just focus on getting that fucking thing out of here."

"After what happened, of course I'm going to worry about you."

"I've been dead once, what's it matter if I go again?"

"It matters to me."

"I'm your boss, Max. Your orders are to get that device to safety."

"I've never been very good at taking orders," Max said, stepping back and putting Kate's arm over his shoulder to support her weight.

"Leave me."

"Shut up, boss."

Max helped Kate to the steps and they began the climb. Max had his gun in one hand pointing up the stairs and Kate in the other. He couldn't help but feel her normally strong and athletic body starting to slump slightly as they made their ascent.

They crossed the charred remains of the stairway entrance. It was stained with blood and black burns from the boobytrap he'd set.

Kate sighted a lone attacker running across the foyer. She pushed Max aside and fired a line of bullets from groin to head into terrorist.

"Thanks," Max said. "We need to get out of here."

"My car is next door," Kate said, throwing Max her keys.

Max led Kate out the door and down the concrete path to the carpark. Her car was closest to the entrance, one of the perks of being the boss he guessed.

Max climbed into the driver's seat and started the big black SUV as Kate struggled into the passenger's seat.

"We need to get that as far from here as possible," Kate said, pointing to the device in his jacket.

"We've got a stop to make first," Max said, reversing out of the space and heading for the exit.

"I don't suppose you're going to listen to me," Kate said, blinking hard and slightly slurring her words. "Fuck it."

Kate's head slumped into her chest. Max reached over and felt her pulse, relieved to find it. Given her trauma and blood loss, it was likely she was running on pure adrenaline and her body couldn't avoid passing out.

Max let her rest as he sped out onto the street and headed across Canberra.

The streets were eerily empty as Timms' curfew had come into effect and people were staying home. He wound his way through backstreets as much as possible to avoid any patrols, but as he got closer to his destination, they were getting harder to dodge.

He rounded the corner and came to a solid police roadblock. They'd parked their cars across the road and had their pistols out at the ready.

He had no choice but to approach the roadblock and try to talk his way past.

"Good evening, sir," the young officer said. "There's a curfew in effect. No one is supposed to be out tonight."

"Yes, hello," Max said. "I know about the curfew. I'm the deputy head of the AIS. I need to get through."

Max showed his ID to the officer. It was embossed with the Australian Government seal and simply the words Australian Intelligence Service.

"I've been told AIS has been shut down," the officer said. "I'm sorry, sir, but I don't think I can let you through."

"What's your name?" Max asked.

"Carl."

"I don't know what you think about all this, Carl, but you seem like a pretty bright guy. Does any of it make sense to you?"

"No, sir. Not really. I've worked a couple of missions with AIS and it's pretty hard to believe to be honest."

"I know you've got a job to do and I won't hold it against you, whatever you decide. But, I need to get through. It's a matter of national security."

Carl was clearly thinking about it, when he noticed Kate slumped over in the passenger seat.

"Jesus," he said. "Is she okay?"

"Not really," Max admitted.

"Did you kill her?"

"No. She's alive."

"What did you do to her?"

"I abandoned her. She nearly died, because I wasn't there to save her, even though she's saved my arse a hundred times."

"Is that who I think it is?"

"Yes."

"I heard she was dead."

"Don't fucking count me out yet," Kate said, raising her head. "A bunch of arseholes have tried, but I'm still here."

Carl visibly straightened his body in a sign of respect for the Head of the AIS.

"You need to let us through," Kate said, taking in their location. "And, I need you to delay any response that comes over the radio in the next few minutes."

"I'm not sure," Carl started, but Kate cut him off.

"I know you're worried, but trust me, things aren't what they seem. AIS isn't going anywhere and all of this will be cleared up soon. We could use a man like you."

Kate rummaged around in the centre console and found a small white business card. It just had her name, Kate Matthews, and her phone number on one side and the Australian Government crest on the other.

"Give me a call on Monday," she said, passing the card to the young officer.

He looked the card over and quickly put it in his pocket, as one his fellow officers started to approach.

"Stand down, everyone," Carl ordered, turning to his crew. "Let them through."

The officers all exchanged looks, but followed the order. One of the cops jumped in the middle car and reversed it out of the line, creating a gap for their vehicle to pass.

"Thank you," Max said. "You did the right thing."

"I hope so," Carl said, before waving them through.

Max accelerated off the spot as Kate gave a short nod to Carl.

They drove through the barricade and sped along the wide street, before taking an exit ramp off to the left.

"You didn't let me down, Max," Kate said, after a few minutes of silence. "You never have."

"I thought you were dead," Max said. "I should have been there."

"You're here now, so stop kicking yourself. Also, I'm not some wilting flower. Just because I sit my arse behind a desk more than I'd like to these days, doesn't mean I can't handle myself in the field."

"Even death fears you, Kate. There's a reason your codename is Alpha."

"Too fucking right. Now, am I going to have to fight you to let me come with you."

Max shared a brief look with his colleague.

"I need you to wait in the car," Max said, trying to sound as confident and authoritative as he could, knowing what was coming.

"Bullshit!" Kate snapped. "I'm fine. I just needed a minute."

"You need to protect the device and if I don't come back out, you need to get it to safety."

"Who's going to have your back?"

"You are. By getting the trigger far away from here."

"There could be dozens of them in there."

"I know," Max said, pulling the car into the scrub a few hundred metres away from their destination.

Kate grabbed his arm and felt her grip tighten, but quickly lose strength.

"Stay here," Max said, handing her the small trigger. "If I need backup, I'll call you."

Kate was going to argue, but she felt the wave of unconsciousness spreading over her again. She grabbed the trigger and placed it in the glove box, and locked it with a four digit pin code.

"Thank you," Max said, climbing out and checking his ammo. "I won't be long."

He clicked the door shut and bounded into the scrub as she pressed a small comms unit into her ear, before locking the door and passing out again.

Chapter Thirty-Four

Max ran hard through the thick bushland. He ignored the branches swatting his face and slapping hard against his body.

It was getting dark. The sun had sunk behind the Brindabella range in the distance and the last of the light was fading fast.

As he approached the security fence, he slowed in case there was a patrol.

The sprawling grounds of the Government House estate run through the suburb of Yarralumla. The leafy streets and proximity to Lake Burley Griffin made it a stunning location in the nation's capital.

Government House was formally an 1830s farmhouse, but over many years had been updated and replaced to become the official residence of the Australian Governor-General. The one hundred and thirty acre property was lined with an eight foot security fence and was frequently patrolled by the federal police.

As well as being the Governor-General's house, it hosted international leaders, held events for outstanding citizens and was the place Prime Ministers, Ministers and senior officials and military personnel received their commissions and were sworn into office.

Max had joined Blake on the very grounds to be sworn in as Deputy Prime Minister. The coffee and cakes, and celebration of the event were like a dream of a distant past as he looked across the sweeping lawns to mansion, which was now occupied by William's forces.

He raised a small pair of binoculars to his eyes and scanned the grounds. He could see several men milling around. They were armed, but seemed too casual.

Another man exited the massive home and started shouting at the men. They all very quickly sprung to attention, having been busted by their boss letting their guard down.

Max recognised the new man. It was Tom.

Max's blood boiled as he sighted the recruit, the turncoat, the traitor. He felt his grip tighten on the binoculars.

He watched for a full minute, before tossing them into the scrub and retrieving a small set of metal plyers from his vest. His hands were trembling and he needed more strength than expected to cut along the bottom of the fence, snipping the steel wires.

When he had cut enough, he tossed the plyers next to the binoculars and rubbed his hands together willing them to work. He didn't think he'd need the plyers or binoculars again, and every other bit of dead weight he could afford to lose he did.

He dragged his vest off and emptied out some of the compartments, then pushed it under the fence, before dragging himself through the narrow gap. He felt the wire scratching and grabbing at his clothes, but managed to get through.

He knelt and redonned his vest. He screwed on his silencer and clicked off the MP5's safety, taking a moment to check the grounds.

He heard the crush of gravel to his left and ducked into some nearby bushes. An electronic golf cart was inspecting the perimeter of the complex. The motor's sound was barely audible, but the noise of the tyres displacing the light stones continued to grow.

Max sighted the two men riding on the cart. They were silent. One was driving as the other studied the fence. He would undoubtedly see the drag marks Max he left and trace them back to the cuts in the fence. He would have to act.

He took a minute to study the men and realised they were William's men, not federal police. The feds wore distinct uniforms, these guys didn't.

He stepped out of the bushes into the headlights of the golf cart. The stunned driver didn't have time to react. A bullet slammed into his face, sending blood and brain matter spraying out the rear of the open cart. His colleague hadn't been looking, but quickly spun to see his dead colleague tumble out of the cart. He turned looking for the source of the shot, only to see a brief muzzle flash before his life left his body.

Max pulled out two long cable ties from his vest. He put the first around the passenger's head and fastened it to the pole holding up the roof of the golf cart. The second he tied around the passenger's belt and the small armrest. Once he was satisfied the body wasn't going anywhere, he jumped into the driver's seat and accelerated off the spot, matching the former driver's pace.

He wound the little cart along the fence line. Anyone watching the cart, would think it was just the patrol doing the rounds. As he drove the cart, he tried to formulate a plan. Every idea led him to the same conclusion. He had the element of surprise. He'd need to use it and move fast.

He drove down the gravel path towards the front of the homestead. The guards didn't take much notice. They were expecting two men in the golf cart and that's what they saw approaching.

Max flicked on the overhead searchlight as he got closer. It's bright high beam blinding the assembled guards, then he dragged the dead man's foot over and wedged it down on the accelerator.

The little cart shot off the mark, rushing at pace towards the guards as Max leapt from the side.

He slid to a stop on the gravel, raised the MP5 and began firing.

Three men fell, before the golf cart barrelled through the group knocking them down. A few screams and yells filled the air, as the cart slammed into the front of the mansion. Max sighted the terrorists now laying on the ground and picked them off one by one until they were all dead.

He heard footsteps running on the floorboards inside and dashed down the side of the house. He ran harder as he heard several men bust out of the front door shouting wildly as they took in the scene.

Max rounded the back corner of the house and dropped two more men, then ran up and into the house. Bullets slammed into the walls around him as Tom spotted him.

Max could feel another convulsion beginning. His arms weren't steady and nor were his legs. His vision was starting to blur, but he pushed himself forward.

"Pretty ballsy, old man, I'll give you that," Tom said. "But, you're fucking dead!"

Max had slid in behind a wall for cover. He saw his former trainee in the reflection of the window. He watched as Tom realised the window was acting like a mirror and shot it out. The glass shattered and fell at Max's trembling feet. He had to admit it was impressive, but not good enough.

Max dropped to one knee and fired around the wall, not at Tom, above Tom, as he found a bigger target.

The opulent chandelier exploded in a shower of glass and crystal. Tom fled backwards, out of the room, shielding his face and firing blindly as it rained down over the room.

Max used the quick retreat to run for the stairs. He bounced up them three at a time, falling at the last as his feet and legs gave way. Bullets traced the wall behind him. At the top of the stairs, he crawled across a small gap to cover behind a wall as two more men began firing, tearing up the carpet in the gap he'd crawled over.

He pulled a small flashbang out and tossed it over the low wall in their direction. He heard them swear as it ricocheted off the wall seconds before it exploded in mid-air. The two men were immediately incapacitated and Max stepped out and put two bullets into them, before clicking out the magazine, letting it down to the floor. He pushed a fresh one into the chamber as a door to the left swung open. He dropped and spun instinctively and fired three shots. The first two missed uncharacteristically, but thankfully the third hit the charging terrorist in the neck. He fell clutching his neck as blood started to ooze out of the gaping hole.

Max got back to his feet and looked into the room. He steadied himself against the wall.

Anthony Mills was taped to a chair in the middle of the room. The man Max knew as Joe Byrne was shielding himself behind the Governor-General with his gun pressed against the Australian leader's temple.

"Don't come any closer, you fucking psychopath," Joe said. "I'll kill him."

"You and I both know, you need him to get out of here," Max said. "Because if you kill him, you'll be dead a moment later."

"Put your gun down. We're walking out of here. You're going to stay right there."

Max knew it wouldn't be long before Tom and any other guards would be behind him. He needed to move.

"Kill this prick, Max," Mills said. "Don't worry about me."

"I'd love to, Admiral," Max said. "But we need you alive."

Byrne dragged a defiant Mills to his feet and Max saw the opportunity to step inside the room to the right. He was now behind the wall, behind cover, so no one could shoot him in the back, but he was also using it to steady himself.

Byrne kept the Governor-General in a tight grip between them.

"Stay there," Byrne yelled. "Let us leave or I'll kill him."

"Are you sure you're going to be able to hobble down the stairs with that limp you've got," Max asked, smiling.

"A limp you gave me by gutting off two of my toes you deranged fuck!"

"Oh that's right. That must have hurt. Tell me, did William think you were any less of a man when you turned up with pieces missing?"

"Stop talking!"

"Okay, I was just wondering," Max said as he heard movement in the hallway.

"Wait there," Joe said to Tom who was standing just outside the doorway with a stupid grin on his face. "Agent Shaw, my backup has arrived. You're a dead man. We're leaving now."

As Byrne started for the door, Max heard the unmistakable sound of metal on metal, followed by the hard acceleration of a large car getting closer. Then the catastrophic sound of a car crash. The whole floor shook and Byrne lost concentration for the briefest of seconds.

Mills took that precious time as the gift it was and stamped down hard onto Byrne's injured foot. The pain was immediately evident on his face and it was enough for him to lose his grip. Mills dropped to the ground as a bullet flew over his head from Byrne's gun, thankfully missing him.

Max took those precious seconds to brace himself against the wall, widen his stance and take aim, then he fired three shots. The first into Byrne's gun wielding hand, sending it back and helping the shot miss the Governor-General. The second hit Byrne in the cheek just under his left eye and the third slammed into his chest tearing a hole right through his heart.

Tom watched as Joe fell to the floor, then he dived for the open stairwell tumbling down the stairs as Max swung around and opened fire in his direction.

"Are you okay?" Max asked.

"Yes, thank you," Mills said. "Thank you for coming for me."

"Of course, sir. I'm sorry we weren't here sooner."

"We?"

"Alpha's here too."

"Kate's alive?"

"Sure is. She was in the car that just smashed through your front room."

"How'd you know?"

"She's been swearing at me for the last few minutes over my comms unit," Max said, pointing to his ear. "We need to move."

"After you," Mills said, letting Max lead him out into the hallway.

They found Kate unlocking the glovebox of the ruined SUV. Smoke and steam were pouring out of the big four wheel drive. It was fully armoured and bulletproof, but it was a complete write off. She must have hit the house at quiet a pace.

"Jesus, Alpha," Max said. "Are you okay?"

"The airbags work," Kate said, dismissively, pulling the small trigger out of the compartment. "We need to get out of here."

"Where's Tom?"

"Little fucker got away. He tried to get into the car with me, but when he saw I was alive he bailed."

"We can take my car," Mills offered.

"Lead the way," Max said, following Mills out of the house.

"I just have to get something," Kate said.

"We don't really have time," Mills said.

"It won't take a minute," Kate said, opening rear door on the wrecked car to find an unconscious and bleeding Mad Dog and she dragged him out onto the ground. He was pretty beaten up thanks to the crash.

Mills opened the garage and they saw the luxury BMW sedan. It didn't have a registration plate like other cars in Canberra, instead it simply had a red and gold crown.

"Mind if I drive?" Max asked, after he shoved Mad Dog in the boot.

"Be my guest," Mills said, climbing into the back of the car as Kate took the passenger seat.

Max drove the big statesman GT out and onto the long parkway which led towards the house. Police lights were flashing in the distance.

Instead of following it back to a main road, Max jumped the gutter to his right and headed along the bike path which ran around the length of Lake Burley.

Chapter Thirty-Five

Blake was sitting in a chair by the window when Max walked in.

"How are you feeling?" Max asked.

Blake didn't respond. He was lost in his thoughts, staring out the window across the open grounds of the Wool Shed.

"Blake?" Max prompted.

"Oh, Max," Blake said, getting to his feet gingerly. "I didn't hear you come in. I'm sorry."

"It's okay. How are you feeling?"

Max hugged Blake and held him closely.

"I'm better now you're here."

"Me too."

"How's Kate?"

"She's in with the doc. They're giving her some blood and a handful of drugs to help her out. Doc says she took a shitload of adrenaline over the past hours to get through after everything that happened. It's basically the only thing that's kept her going. They're worried she might have done some serious damage to herself."

"She died in my arms, Max," Blake said, stepping back to look into Max's eyes with tears welling in his own. "She was gone."

"I can only repeat what I said to her, Blake."

"What's that?"

"Death fears her."

Blake laughed and nodded his head.

"Sounds about right, fucking Alpha indeed."

"How are you?"

"I'm recovering fine, Max. I'm just worried about the country. We need to get control again as soon as we can. The news is running some bullshit about your assault on

Government House. Can you believe that? Assault. They say you've kidnapped the GG."

"They're trying to force us into hiding."

"It's working. We're hold up out here. Fucking helpless. We can't do anything."

Blake paused and thought about what he'd just said.

"What is it?" Max asked.

"We're stuck here and they know it," Blake said as his eyes hardened. "I mean it's the only place we can all go. Off the grid and remote. They know it's the most likely place."

"What's your point?"

"They're coming."

Max's heart started pounding in his chest. Blake was right. It was the most logical conclusion. They needed Blake and Mills dead, and Kate and Max out of the picture. They were the only ones stopping them from achieving their goals. And, of course, Hulk was here too. William wanted his old man dead. Max had been so fixated on getting them to safety, he'd fail to consider he may have done the terrorist's work for them. By corralling them all in one location, they were now sitting ducks.

"What have I done?" Max asked with fear showing behind his normally unshakeable, cold gaze.

Liddle burst into the room.

"We've got three choppers coming in hard and fast!" he shouted breathlessly. "They're only twenty minutes out."

"You need to get Blake to safety, Mike," Max said.

"No, Max," Blake said. "I'm staying with you."

"You can't, Blake. You need to get out of here and get back to Canberra. Retake the reins and stabilise the country."

"I'm not leaving you."

"You don't have a choice. The country needs you."

"But I need you."

"And I need to know you're safe. That's all that matters to me."

All three men knew Max's heartache at losing Lachlan. They helped him through that trauma and the complete devastation it had had on his life. They saw him spiral out of control and had helped him rebuild his life. It was pushed down deep, but Blake in particular knew the absolute love Max had for him and the lengths he would go to stop history repeating itself.

"I love you, Max," Blake said. "I've loved you since the first time I met you."

"You're everything to me, Blake. I love you with every fibre of my being."

The pair embraced and kissed, holding the feeling in their own world, before Liddle interrupted with a small cough. Blake and Max stepped back, letting their hands, then fingers slowly slip away from each other. They both knew it could be the last time they saw each other. They both wanted time to stop so they could be together.

"Get him to the bunker," Max said. "Take Kate and Hulk. Go now!"

Liddle just nodded.

"Good luck," Liddle said, grabbing Blake and helping him out of the room and down the hallway.

Max ran from the room to the armoury. He found Kate and Hulk gathering weapons.

"You need to go," Max said. "Mike's taking Blake to the bunker. You need to go too."

"As if," Kate said. "I ain't fucking hiding down there. I'm going to be right here by your side."

"Blake's going to need your help putting the country back together," Max argued. "Please."

"He needs you more than me, Prince Charming, and I don't see you going with him to the bunker."

"I can't."

"Sure you can."

"I've got to see this through."

"I told you, boss," Kate said, turning to Hulk. "He was always the best person for the job."

"You were right," Hulk admitted. "He's never let me down once."

"Never will," she said.

"I don't suppose I can convince you to go?" Max asked Hulk.

Hulk just clicked a magazine into his pistol and shook his head.

Max gave up. He didn't have time to argue and wasn't likely to win in any case.

Liam marched into the room. He was one of only a handful of recruits who had made it through the course. The others had been sent home, but he had decided to stay. He wanted to help.

"What are you doing here, kid?" Max asked. "I thought I sent you home."

"You did," Liam said, walking over to the weapons rack.

"Why doesn't anyone take my orders seriously?"

"I didn't think it was a genuine order."

Kate and Hulk laughed.

"His turn," Hulk said, laughing to Kate.

"Think he'll have it as bad as we did with our new recruit Max?"

"Worse. They are cut from the same cloth."

"Just like the two of you," Kate said with a smile to the old spymaster.

"What are you talking about?" Liam asked.

"Max never listened to me either," Hulk said. "I trained him and mentored him, and led his first missions. All I got was backchat and insubordination. I'm laughing because it's come full circle and now he's got you to deal with."

"If you're going to stay," Max said. "You need to do as I say and keep your head down."

"You got it boss," Liam said, jogging out of the room with his weapons.

"Where the fuck's he going?" Max asked.

Hulk walked over to Max and grabbed his shoulder. The old solider just stood there for a moment in the half embrace, before he started to smile.

"Welcome to my world," Hulk said, before tapping Max on the shoulder. "You've got this, kid."

Once they'd gathered their weapons, they headed for the control room. Liam was watching the three choppers.

"They're splitting up," Liam said. "One's heading straight for us. The other two are splitting left and right."

"I need you to get to the bunker," Max said. "Protect Blake."

"Sir?"

"I trust you. Go."

Liam nodded and bolted for the door.

Max saw the red chopper dots drawing closer, as a blue light showed Blake's location. He wasn't far from the bunker which was hidden under one of the many training courses on the base. A few seconds later, another blue dot sped away from the farmhouse. Liam on a dirt bike.

Max watched the screen trying to calculate times.

Tom would likely have given them a description of the base, but he didn't know where the bunker was. The most obvious places were the homestead, the gun range and the assault tower, and that's where the choppers were going.

"You need to get to the trigger," Hulk said as he watched Max weighing up his options.

"I know," Max said with pain in his voice.

"He'll be okay. He's nearly there and you've sent the kid to help. You need to move."

"I'm going."

"Take Kate with you."

"No," Max said turning back. "You need her here."

"The trigger is what matters. If he gets hold of that, he could kill millions."

"He's right, Max," Kate said. "We've got to move."

"Are you up to this?"

"I've been through worse than this kid."

Max didn't reply. They all knew they'd likely be dead soon anyway. They had to try. They'd been here before and there wasn't much to say that they didn't already know.

"Let's go," Max said, taking a brief moment to look at his old mentor for what they both knew was likely to be the last time.

"I know, kid," Hulk said. "Get out of here. You've got a job to do."

Kate nodded to Hulk, before following Max out the door.

Hulk saw another two blue dots light up on the screen as Max and Kate's dirt bikes tracked towards the gun range to the right of the screen. He saw Blake and Liddle's dot stopped outside the assault tower. Hopefully that meant they'd be inside the bunker before the chopper arrived. Liam's dot was moving fast, but not as fast as the helicopter. He wasn't going to make it before it did. He hoped he'd see it and slow his approach.

The righthand helicopter was moving fast. It would be at the gun range in minutes. Max and Kate were going to get there a few minutes after that.

Then he turned his sights on the final chopper. It was only a few minutes away. He breathed out as if preparing himself for what was to come, then stepped back drew his pistol and fired it into the screen shattering it.

Hulk typed several commands on the computer next to the smashed screen. When it confirmed the order, he stepped back and shot both the screen and hard drive, then walked out of the room.

He leaned hard on his cane as he walked across the lawn of the homestead. He could hear the chopper approaching, but wasn't fussed. He just walked as quickly as he could towards the old barn.

He slid open the door and ducked inside, just as the chopper made its final approach.

He walked through the cold old shed to a modern control room at the rear. It was designed to monitor recruits going through the torture training part of their initiations, but it also doubled as a control room for the holding cells on the property.

They had two guests, Mary Ann Bugg and Daniel 'Mad Dog' Morgan. Two members of the modern age Kelly Gang. Hulk knew at least one of the incoming attackers would be looking for the woman. She was his wife after all. That was one surprising bit of information he had been able to extract from her.

Hulk walked into the room and turned on the monitors. The two criminals were still cuffed to their chairs, but they were awake, no doubt from the rotor wash of the incoming chopper. Mad Dog had a smile from ear to ear and he was just staring at the camera. The woman was a bit more subdued, but she still looked happy.

Hulk locked the door and turned to the other monitor. It showed the massive chopper setting down on the lawns of the big old farm which he had called home for decades.

He saw the team of six jump down. Three ran for the house, while the other three were running towards the barn.

One final man and the pilot stayed in the chopper.

The men arrived at the door of the homestead and kicked it open. All three went in.

Hulk counted in his head. Three, two. As he hit one, the old house was violently ripped to pieces in an explosion of flaming debris. Chunks of wood and metal from the house he'd called home for years rained down over the yard, and slammed into the chopper. Its rotating blades were making short work of most of the debris, but the occasional fragment hit it hard.

Hulk saw a massive chunk of the roof falling, then slamming into the rotors. One of the blades broke away and was sent flying towards the barn. It narrowly missed the other three attackers who had turned to see what was happening. It pierced the side of the old shed and stuck with a flutter.

He smiled knowing he'd taken out some of the terrorists. He didn't think he'd see combat again and he had to admit he missed it, the byproduct of a lifetime of war and conflict.

The final man jumped from the chopper as it began to rock and sway. The pilot was wrestling with the controls, but it would be no use.

Hulk watched as Willam ran as fast as his legs would carry him from the helicopter towards the barn. As he got to within twenty metres of the barn, the chopper finally shook itself apart. The remaining blades flew off and speared into the ground as the engine began spurting oil and fuel. The stream of avgas hit the searing hot engine and rotor, and ignited. For the second time in a matter of minutes a huge explosion rang out over the normally peaceful training base as the helicopter exploded.

William was thrown off his feet by the force of the blast. His men ran to his side to help him up.

Hulk saw him steady himself, then begin barking orders.

The four men marched across the lawn with the burning wreckages of the house and chopper behind them. They cautiously opened the door of the old barn, then waited. When it didn't explode, they hesitantly entered.

William saw the one way mirror at the end of the big space and walked towards it. He watched his own reflection as he walked. His comrades scattered, searching the barn.

"Are you in there, old man?" William asked the mirror. "Clever trick with the house. Pity, looks like the old place had had a few upgrades over the years. I didn't think you'd have it in you to blow it. You spent more time out here than in our own house. I remember coming out here to train and seeing the love you had for the place. More than you had for me, that's for sure."

The mirrored glass instantly lost its mirrored side and William and Hulk came face to face for the first time in years.

"That's not true," Hulk said. "Of course, I loved you, William. You're my son. I know I wasn't always there for you, but I always loved you."

"Is that why you threw me out?"

"It's more complicated than that and you know it."

"You cheated on my mother."

"I didn't. Not even once."

"I saw you."

"You still don't get it. I loved your mother and I loved you. I would never do anything to hurt either of you."

"You killed her!"

"She died in an accident, but yes I take responsibility for my role in the circumstances which led to her death. I've lived with the pain and sorrow of it since that day."

"Putting me in hospital you mean?"

"You didn't leave me any choice."

"Bullshit!"

"Look, son."

"I'm not your son. I stopped being your son the moment you turned your back on me."

"The drugs rotted your brain. You were a walking disaster. I didn't know how to help you."

"No, you didn't want a gay son turning tricks in the street to survive."

"I don't care if you're gay, William."

"Maybe not now, but you did then."

"It was a different time. I was scared for you. Scared of what others would think. I didn't understand."

"That doesn't justify it. I was your son!"

"You were."

"So why?"

"I didn't want a drug addict who stole from me and threw away everything I had worked so hard to give him."

"All you did was try to turn me into you, here on this pathetic empire you've built. You and your boy scouts are responsible for countless deaths and global disfunction. I didn't want anything to do with it."

"I failed you, William. As a father. I'm sorry."

"You're sorry? Do you have any idea what I went through out there in the streets? The things I had to do? The things people did to me?"

"I can't imagine."

"You should. Maybe you'd get a small glimpse into why we are here today."

"Why don't you just tell me?"

"Too hard to imagine?"

"I can't imagine how my boy could do the terrible things you have done. You killed and hurt innocent people, and tried your hardest to completely destroy the country."

"I won't be lectured by you about killing people. You are one of the country's biggest murderers. Just because you wrap yourself in the flag to do it, doesn't excuse what you've done. And, as for the country, it's lost its way. It has allowed you to do what you've done. It's kept people in the streets and out of homes. It's enshrined poverty on masses and forced millions to be working poor, while the rich continue to get richer. There is no equality, no fairness, no freedom. Capitalism is just legalised slavery with a false promise that working hard will help people get ahead."

"And you think you have the answers, do you? Think you've got some other way to run the world?"

"We're going to burn it to the ground and let it rebuild itself from the ashes."

"So anarchy?"

"It's the only way to break the cycle."

"And what about the innocent people who will get caught up in your revolution? Millions will die."

"They are a tragic sacrifice on the road to our new world."

"Listen to yourself. You accuse me of murder, for killing terrorists, while standing there justifying genocide."

"One man's terrorist is another's freedom fighter."

"Or zealot."

"Call me what you want. It won't change the fact that I have won. You have to see that? I've killed Prime Ministers and unleashed fear across the population. When I rid the world of Kevin Timms and his government, and detonate my nuclear weapon in downtown Canberra the world will see this country is done. Then we'll move onto the next one and do the same thing until the existing power structures are gone and the people can rise up and take control."

"You are insane."

"Maybe, but you can't stop me now."

"You're right, but my team will."

"Your precious team will be dead any minute, then there'll be no one to stop us."

"I wouldn't be so sure about that if I was you."

Their conversation was interrupted as Thunderbolt ran back into the room.

"I found them," Thunderbolt said. "Tell him to release them."

"Break down the doors," William replied.

"They won't budge."

William turned back to the glass to see Hulk smiling.

"We made some upgrades to our holding cells after a few attempted breakouts," Hulk said. "There's only one way to open those doors and it's in here with me."

"Open the fucking door now!" Thunderbolt demanded, firing a single round into the glass.

Hulk watched the small blister appear in the bulletproof glass.

"Yeah, I don't think so," Hulk said, pressing a different button on the control panel.

"Fuck, Fred!" one of the men yelled from the side room which housed the cells. "She's being electrocuted!"

Thunderbolt ran to the room and saw his wife, Mary Ann, shaking violently in the chair. He started frantically bashing the glass, before firing his gun dry trying to break the glass.

He ran back into the shed.

"He's killing her!" Thunderbolt yelled. "Get him to stop!"

"Put your guns down," Hulk said. "Lay on your stomachs and interlock your fingers behind your heads."

"No," William said.

"She's going to die if you don't," Hulk said, pushing another button.

"Fuck, now Mad Dog's getting it too!" came the shout from the other room.

"They are both going to die slowly and painfully, almost like a weak electric chair, unless you do as I say."

"Let her go!" Thunderbolt yelled.

"It's your call. Drop your guns and get on the floor."

"No," William said.

"What do you mean, no?" Thunderbolt asked in disbelief. "He's going to kill her."

"What do you think he'll do to us if we throw down our guns?"

"I don't know, but at least we'll be alive. She'll be alive."

"I should never have allowed you to get your partner involved. It makes you weak."

"Oh please, we all know about you and Joe. If he was here, he'd tell you to live to fight another day. Get him to stop, please Will. She's dying. If it was Joe, you'd throw down your guns to save him."

"I wouldn't."

"What?" Thunderbolt said, raising his gun and aiming it at William. "You're a cold bastard. He fucking loves you and Tom."

"Shut the fuck up!" William spat, noting Hulk had frozen hearing Tom's name.

"You don't know, do you?" Thunderbolt asked smugly. "Tom's your grandson."

Hulk felt his heart pounding in his chest. He had been training Tom for months, before he fled. He had felt something he couldn't put his finger on. He thought it was a gut instinct that the boy had what it takes, but it was deeper than that. He had a grandson.

"How is that possible?" Hulk asked.

"You mean how'd your fag son end up with a son?" William asked.

"That's not what I meant. I just…"

Thunderbolt pulled the trigger and his gun clicked. Empty. He had William in his sights, but no bullets in the chamber.

William's eyes went wide in pure anger. He drew his own gun and fired one round right through Thunderbolt's face.

The lifeless body fell to the cold concrete.

"Electrocute them all you want," William said. "I'm not putting the gun down and I'm not going anywhere until you come out here and get what you deserve."

"And what would that be?" Hulk asked.

"A bullet from this gun."

Hulk pushed the buttons on his panel and the two prisoners stopped shaking and slumped in their chairs, exhausted, but alive.

"I knew you couldn't do it," William said. "It goes against your code to kill an unarmed prisoner. It's your weakness."

"My weakness is that I've been a terrible father and grandfather," Hulk said. "I've failed you both and our country."

"You have. And the world too. Joe, Tom and I are heading to America next, then Canada and the UK. We're going to bring them all down."

"You don't know, do you? I hate to be the one to tell you, son, but Joe's dead."

"You're lying."

"You haven't heard from him for hours, have you? Were you expecting him to be here?"

"It doesn't matter. I loved him sure, but like I said to Fred here, they only create weakness. It's better he's gone."

"Jesus Christ. Your friend there was right, you are a cold bastard."

"Fuck you!" William spat, marching up to the glass and firing his pistol dry in rage.

Hulk saw his chance and unlocked the door. He swung it open as William retreated trying to load a new clip in his gun.

Hulk ducked to his right and found the other two terrorists trying to find weaknesses in the holding cell doors. He shot them both with marksman like precision before unlocking Mary Ann's door.

"He killed Fred," Hulk said. "I'm sorry."

"What?" Mary Ann said in a daze from the electrocution.

"William, Ned Kelly, out there. He just shot your husband in cold blood. All Fred did was try to get him to let you go, but he wouldn't."

Hulk released the hidden blade in his cane and cut the tape, before unlocking the cuffs and letting her go.

Fred's gun is lying next to him in the shed out there.

Mary Ann got to her feet. She stopped for a moment to consider taking the old soldier out. It was no doubt he who had been responsible for her torture, but Fred was dead and it was William's fault. The old man would die soon enough. William was another story. She fled the room without looking back.

Hulk walked out and unlocked Mad Dog's cell. He held his gun to the back of the man's head with his right hand, while using the cane to cut the tape free, before unlocking his cuffs.

"Big mistake," Mad Dog said, but Hulk pressed the gun into his skull.

"Don't even think about it," Hulk said. "Now walk."

Mad Dog begrudgingly complied. They walked out into the shed to find Mary Ann and William firing wildly at each other.

"You crazy bitch," William yelled. "He electrocuted you. It's his fault Fred's dead."

Mad Dog dodged left. He was fast. Back in the day, Hulk would never have let it happen, but he was far from his best these days. The younger man spun and grabbed Hulk's gun hand and slammed it down on a table. When he didn't drop it, Mad Dog smashed it down again. This time Hulk lost his grip.

As the pair fell to the floor wrestling for the weapon, William sprung up from behind an old piece of farming equipment he'd been using for cover and put six bullets into Mary Ann's head and chest. She fell backwards and landed only a few feet from her husband's body.

Mad Dog got to the gun first and climbed to his feet. He spat blood from his mouth thanks to Hulk's headbutt. Hulk knew he was defeated and just laid there waiting for the shot.

"Wait," William yelled, stopping Mad Dog from pulling the trigger.

Mad Dog looked back to his colleague in disbelief, but did as he was asked.

Hulk watched as William made his way towards them winding through the junked farming gear.

"I guess this is goodbye," William said, with cocky arrogance. "See you in hell, Dad."

"You sure will," Hulk said, pulling the pin on a grenade and letting the lever flick into the air between them. "I'm sorry I failed you."

William's eyes locked onto the thin metal tumbling through the air and instantly jumped back to run for the door.

Hulk saw the fear in Mad Dog's eyes as he realised he had nowhere to hide.

The explosion was catastrophic. The doors blew off the shed and fire quickly spread throughout the building. Mad Dog and

Hulk were both killed instantly as their bodies were torn apart by the ball bearings and shrapnel.

William was thrown violently across the barn. His face and hair were on fire as he hit the concrete floor with a sudden loud thud.

Chapter Thirty-Six

Max saw the chopper set down outside the gun range.

Six men climbed out of the military aircraft and ran towards the range.

Max gunned the engine on the dirt bike. It was trailing dust, but the night sky would make it hard to see. The chopper blades were still rotating, so Max knew it would be loud enough to muffle the sound of their bikes.

Kate was only metres from his back wheel. The blood and drugs had obviously worked wonders, because she was matching him with relative ease.

Although he was still feeling the effects of the chemical attack coursing through his body, the doctor had begrudgingly given him another dose of whatever the compound was he needed with adrenaline and painkillers, but he knew that the was the last one he'd get. The doctor said anymore could kill him or risk permanent damage.

Max eased off the throttle and came level with Kate. He pointed to himself and made a whirl in the air, signalling he would take out the chopper crew. Then he pointed to her and a made a sweeping gesture, telling her to go around to the far side and make entry. She nodded, then sped off to the right starting her big arc around to the back of the multimillion dollar facility.

Max hit a small levy and the dirt bike jumped into the air. As it landed, he put it onto its side and slid on the dirt track letting go of the bike and it spun off the road to the side. As he slid, he pulled out his pistol and opened fire on the chopper's cockpit.

He saw the pilots both convulse as they were assaulted by the bullets.

He started to lose momentum, so scrambled to his feet and began to run. He was at the helicopter in seconds and raised the gun. When he saw the pilots were dead, he kept running.

One of the terrorists was waiting outside the complex. Max locked onto him over his pistol sights, then squeezed the trigger as he ran. Two bullets hit the man centre mass, but he didn't fall. Max started to sidestep as the man raised his own weapon and started firing at Max.

As Max got closer, he goose stepped, then took the milliseconds he needed to get a clean shot. He pulled the trigger and a bullet raced across the shortening distance, slamming into the nose of the terrorist. His brain exploded out the back of his head and smeared down the big metal wall.

When he reached the side of the complex, he took a moment to get his breath and steady himself, then he flung open the door and was confronted with two of the terrorists.

One fired and the bullet hit Max in the side. He returned fire killing the terrorist who shot him. The second man was going for his gun, but Max was in reach and caught his hand. The two men wrestled, both trying to get their guns into a position to take a shot. A few stray bullets flew from the guns as they grappled for supremacy.

To the terrorist's surprise, Max dropped his pistol and solely focused his strength on trying to take the other man's. He grabbed his attacker's wrist with his left hand, pulling it left. As the terrorist tried to pull it back towards Max, Max drew his hunting knife and stabbed it violently into his neck. Max felt the blade enter and slice through muscle and tissue, and lodge in the man's spine. The man didn't die instantly, his horrified eyes locked on Max's and Max twisted the knife. The terrorist's legs buckled beneath him as his eyes rolled back in his head.

He pulled the knife back as the dead man fell to his feet.

"Freeze!" came the call from a man to his right. "Drop the knife."

"Okay," Max said, turning his head to get a look at his new attacker. "You got me."

"Drop the knife!"

Gunfire rang out from the far side of the complex and it was loud enough to make the other man turned to see what was happening. He realised his mistake too late. Max hurled the knife and it flew end over end until it sliced through the man's throat.

He fired wildly at Max and he felt another bullet graze his arm as he dropped and rolled on the floor. He grabbed his gun then turned to fire at the terrorist, but he was falling to his knees clutching with both hands at his throat. He'd be dead in a matter of seconds.

Max heard gunshots ring out on the other side of the range, then silence.

"You still with me, Prince Charming?" Kate called out.

"I'm here," Max replied. "All clear."

"Hoorah. Let's get the trigger and get out of here."

"Agreed."

Max met Kate in the centre of the complex. It was huge. Multiple gun ranges ran away from the control centre end to targets. Max had learnt to shoot on this very range. It had been a technological marvel then, and even more so now, capable of transforming from an outdoor range to an indoor one, and from a hot sunny day to a cold windy and rainy one with the push of a few buttons.

He'd brought the recruits in on one of his last trips out here and knew the complex had been upgraded further since his training all those years ago. Targets were electronically controlled and much more realistic. It could also simulate real life targets using AI and projectors.

"Where's the trigger?" Kate asked.

"In the safe," Max said as they both instinctively turned for the door. "Let's move."

Max grabbed two of the sniper rifles, throwing one to Kate. They slung them over their backs, then ran onto the range away from the control or shooting end of the complex as they heard another helicopter coming into land. They weren't sure if it was one of the others they'd seen on the radar earlier or a fourth one which had hung back to provide support.

It didn't matter, it would be full of terrorists just aching to kill them.

They headed down the range until they came to a spot about halfway where a panel was cut out of the floor. Max opened it and quickly unlocked the little floor safe.

"We don't have a choice now," Kate said. "Do it."

"Agree," Max said, removing a small piece of plastic explosive and pressing it onto the glass screen of the remote trigger.

He slid the small detonator into it and shut the safe door again, just as the door he had used earlier flew open in the distance. They saw the flash bangs go off, but they were too far away for them to be effective.

Max and Kate took up positions in the darkness and waited. The first three men burst through the door and were shocked to find no one was there waiting for them.

Max breathed out, paused and pulled the trigger.

The massive rifle kicked back hard against his shoulder as the round was expelled. When the scope tried to resight his target, there was just a cloud of red mist. He moved to the second man, but heard Kate's rifle fire and the man's head exploded. He moved slightly to his right and saw the third target turn for the door. He squeezed the trigger and saw the round hit the terrorist in the back and launch him through the door back outside.

The two agents got to their feet and started slowly walking towards the door. They weren't sure anyone would be brave enough to enter the complex after three men were gunned down so quickly.

Halfway back to the door, Max pressed the small detonator in his pocket and the plastic explosive destroyed the nuclear trigger device, the small safe and a good chunk of the gun range's floor.

When they reached the door, no one had entered. They heard the helicopter revving up and ducked out to see it starting to climb.

Two pilots and three men were in the chopper.

Max raised the sniper rifle to his shoulder. He saw a man in the back going for the door gun, so he took him out. The bullet hit him in the chest and blood sprayed all through the cabin. Kate shot her rifle and hit one of the pilots. She saw his brain matter coat the windshield as the panic set in and they were all yelling at each other.

Max ran for the first chopper. He opened the door and dragged the pilots out before climbing in and taking the controls.

Kate jumped into the back and got behind the massive door canon.

The helicopter had been idling, so Max just revved it hard and it lifted off. As it was climbing the other crew were fighting about who would take the door gun, while the remaining pilot was frantically trying to remove his colleague's blood and brains from the window and controls, so he could see what he was doing.

As Max lifted the chopper into the air, he began to rotate it to bring Kate around.

The terrorist pilot finally got control and saw Max climbing beside him. He tilted the aircraft forward trying to put some distance between them.

Max followed still swinging the big bird around. When Kate came around Max was flying sideways. They rose higher than the fleeing chopper so Kate could fire down on them. As soon as she had them in her sights the big gun unleashed. The rounds exploded rapidly from the gun and tore through the air. They pinged off the helicopter and sailed past it.

She lined them up again and pulled the trigger. Bullets danced around sparking on the fuselage, before black smoke started pouring out of the engine, just below the main rotor.

Max quickly saw it was losing power. He swung their chopper around and gunned it, until they were flying side by side. One of the terrorists went for the side gun, but Kate was already in position. She fired and the gun spewed thousands of rounds into the air and into the enemy helicopter. The bullets tore the men and the aircraft to pieces, punching holes in everything and everyone.

The enemy chopper exploded and fell to the ground in a ball of flames.

Max accelerated hard heading for the homestead.

He saw the smoking wreckage of helicopter and the completely engulfed remains of the old home, then he saw the smoke pouring from the doors of the barn.

The two agents both knew in that instant their old boss, mentor and friend Patrick 'Hulk' Scott was dead.

Max's hands griped the controls so tightly his knuckles went white and his eyes filled with tears.

William and his whole team were going to die.

Chapter Thirty-Seven

Liam revved the dirt bike hard. It was kicking the red dirt up in a cloud behind his rear wheel. He took gravel roads and dirt cut throughs that he and the other recruits had made on the bikes in their down time. He hit small jumps with ease after months on the sprawling country farm. It was all starting to feel natural. In fact, he wasn't sure how he would settle back down in the city now he'd been out here for so long, but he guessed that's where most of the work would be. If he survived that long.

His heart was pounding behind his ribs as he drew closer to the assault tower. He'd been there countless times, abseiling in and smashing through the windows, before running various scenarios. From cardboard cutout terrorists to trainers impersonating terrorists holding hostages.

When all of this had started, he assumed it was just another training exercise. But he quickly realised this was real. Since then, he'd felt his demeaner change, somehow more focused. Certainly more serious. And, when he had seen Max, he had known. The spy had taught him so much in the time he'd been at the Wool Shed. Sure, Hulk was clearly talented and had a lifetime of experience, but the old man had lost his edge. Max brought an intensity to the role which made it all so much realer. Yet in the down times he could be so friendly and caring.

It was the change in his face when Blake had been injured. Liam wasn't sure if it was a need to protect the man he loved or a burning hatred of the terrorists behind the attack. He figured it was probably a bit of both. Whatever it was though he knew with certainty he didn't want to get on the wrong side of him. He almost felt bad for the men Max was going to kill. They would be outmatched and outclassed, and quite simply dead, often going out in pure agony.

Liam wasn't sure he could ever match Max's ruthlessness or strength, but he knew he wanted the man's respect. He felt like he had something to prove, but mostly he just didn't want to let him down.

Now, the pressure was really on. He'd sent him to protect Blake. Blake was the Prime Minister, sure, but it was more than that. He'd heard stories from Kate and others about the pair's love and friendship for each other. The pain and heartache, and the warmth and love they had shared. Now Max had put Blake's life in his hands. He said he trusted him.

He was scared shitless. His palms were sweating at the thought and his heart jumped into his throat when the bike slid out on the lose fine powdery dust.

He managed to get it back under control, just as an enormous helicopter flew over him. The side of the big bird opened and he saw one of the terrorists smiling broadly as he brought the barrel of the door gun around to aim at Liam. He wasn't sure, but thought it looked like Tom.

Liam gunned the bike into the scrub, darting between the trees as bullets slammed into the trunks and dirt around him.

The sound of the gunfire and roar of the beating chopper blades, plus the whine of his dirt bike, was deafening. It was all he could do to try to keep the little bike on whatever open enough piece of land he could to dodge the trees and fallen branches, let alone to escape the bullets.

Leaves and branches were torn from the trees as the rounds ripped their way through the bush trying to find their mark.

Liam guessed the chopper must have seen the dust trail. He should have stayed off the main tracks. It must have set down some of the men, then come looking for him.

He figured at least some of the men were focused on him, which meant a smaller number were trying to get to Blake. That's a positive. So he wondered how can he keep them distracted.

He braked hard and skidded to the left, then sped off at a right angle. The chopper overshot, but quickly came around and the gun started up again tearing leaves and smaller brunches from the canopy.

Liam saw his destination up ahead. The giant obstacle course.

He powered along a narrow dirt track until he sped through the clearing and into the course.

He saw the low barbed wire stretched tightly over the swamp like pool, which he'd crawled through numerous times. The wooden poles for overs and unders. And the climbing ramp.

He let the back wheel kick left and right as the spotlight from the helicopter hit him. The bullets started again pounding into the dirt only inches from his back wheel.

He couldn't see it, but Tom was smiling and laughing. He was toying with Liam. This was just a big game to him. The two of them had been evenly matched throughout the course, but it was more than a friendly rivalry. Liam felt Tom's jealousy anytime he beat him and his overconfidence and ego when he'd beaten Liam. Over the final days they'd spent together, before Tom turned traitor, they'd felt the anger rising between them.

Liam found a small track between one of the obstacles and a deep muddy pit which he'd laid in for hours as a test of endurance and patience only a week ago.

He balanced the bike along the little grassy patch, before speeding off towards the ramp. His front wheel hit it and he raced up, launching from the top.

The bike flew through the air and Liam let go. It sailed in an arc beneath him as he reached and grabbed one of the ropes suspended with monkey bars and other climbing equipment, high above an icy cold pool.

The bike made it to the other side of the pool and hit with a thud, before rolling up the chicken wire fence and revving hard, then stalled.

The rope slid through his hands and he felt the burn on his palms and fingers. He flailed about with his feet, until finally his boots caught the rope and arrested his slide.

He watched as Tom yelled directions to the chopper pilot. He wanted him to circle around so he could get a shot. Liam didn't have long.

He started to climb, trying to ignore the pain in his hands.

The chopper was cycling fast and he could see the delight in Tom's eyes. His former colleague was smiling broadly in anticipation.

Liam's hands felt like they were on fire, but it helped him overcome the pain in his arms as he climbed.

He reached the top of the rope and grabbed the metal pole it was attached to, instantly feeling the cold steel soothing his palms. He couldn't linger though, it would only be moments before Tom opened fire.

Liam dragged himself up onto the gangway beside the monkey bars and began pulling on the rope. Like a fireman dragging in a hose, Liam quickly started gathering the thick rope. Several metres of it were quickly rolled onto his left arm.

He tied a quick knot at the end as the helicopter lowered, bringing the blades down to his height. They were going to try to cut him up with the rotors.

Liam started swinging the end of the rope around getting it up to speed, before he launched it. The heavy knot shot up into the air above the chopper. The pilot saw it too late. The rope pulled tight and started to fall.

The rope fell into the rotating blades and quickly tangled itself. It pulled taught and the chopper began to stall. Tom came into view and loosened a handful of bullets towards Liam. Liam jumped back down towards the other ropes as the chopper rapidly pulled itself towards the climbing structure as the rope wound its way around the rotor.

He looked up and realised it was too late.

The chopper slammed into the metal, tilted onto its side and its flimsy blades ripped from their housing, flying off at tremendous speed.

Liam looked down to the freezing water and knew it was his only hope. He let go of the rope and gravity instantly did its job. He fell for a full three seconds before slamming into the fridged water.

Tom had made the same assessment. He hit the water only a second after Liam.

Liam saw the explosion of bubbles and heard Tom hit the water. As Tom righted himself, the pair locked eyes and began swimming for each other.

They met in the middle and began wrestling each other in the water. Tom got the upper hand and quickly locked his legs and arms around Liam's body and throat. Liam tried desperately to get free, but Tom's grip was too strong and he was exhausted and fading from the lack of oxygen.

There was a loud explosion above them and they both managed to steal a look, as the chopper erupted in flames and began falling towards them.

Tom let go and started swimming fast. Liam sank, but found the strength to kick his legs and will his arms to move.

The helicopter had crashed into the climbing structure and its weight was too much to bear. The whole metal climbing apparatus and the burning aircraft dropped like a stone towards the pool in a tangle of hot metal and flaming ropes.

Liam heard the wreckage hit the water only metres behind him, but then he looked up to see a large scaffold sized chunk of metal falling towards him. It hit the water and a large metal monkey bar drove into his side, dragging him deeper into the pool.

He started to panic. His oxygen was already low and his lungs were screaming at him to take a breath. He knew soon enough his body would overrule his thoughts and take an involuntary breath for him.

He kicked hard and pushed trying to get out from under the bar. He was almost free when the whole steel frame hit the bottom of the pool.

He was pinned by the ankle. He desperately kicked with his free leg trying to pull his leg out, but it was caught on his boot.

He grabbed his hunting knife and started hacking at the laces, then he felt it loosen and he pulled hard.

His leg came free and he used his last remaining strength to push up from the bottom of the pool towards the surface.

When he reached the top, he burst through into the cold air and took in several long hard breaths, coughing and panting as the air hit his lungs.

"Neat trick," Tom said as he stood on the side of the pool with his pistol aimed at Liam. "Pity you're still going to die."

"You first," Liam said.

He kicked hard enough for the top half of his body to come out of the water and he threw his hunting knife with everything he had. It flew through the air, tumbling end over end, until the blade pierced through Tom's throat.

Tom's eyes widened and he managed to squeeze the trigger in his last act on earth.

Liam fell back into the water as the bullets sent two trails of bubbles screaming through the water right beside him, but thankfully missed.

Tom's body hit the water and blood began pumping out of his neck and into the pool.

Liam swam to the side and climbed out, dragging Tom's body to with him.

He took Tom's boot to replace his own, then pulled his knife free from Tom's neck.

He left the former recruit's body laying beside the training pool as he ran for his bike.

Liam grabbed the bike and after a minute kicked it to life. He climbed onto the seat and revved it hard, before shooting off back down the dirt track towards the bunker.

Chapter Thirty-Eight

"I understand, Mister President," Timms said. "In only a matter of days, I have killed two Prime Ministers and have taken over the country."

"But you are still weak," Aleksandr Novikov, the Russian President said. "And you have yet to show me any evidence that your agent, Max Shaw is dead."

"He will be shortly."

"That's not good enough! He is responsible for the downfall of my predecessor and the collapse of our economy. The Russian people demand retribution and either you handover the component and kill Prince or we will have to come and get it in person. How long do you think your country could hold off the might of Mother Russia?"

"I'm trying to make it right, Aleksandr."

"It will only be right when he and his boyfriend are dead, and I have the component."

"The microchip will be delivered."

"You said that earlier."

"Agent Shaw got in the way of the transfer."

"I am sick of your excuses, Prime Minister. Get me the chip and kill Max Shaw or else."

"Or else what?"

"I have many people in your country. I would hate to see them lose a third Prime Minister."

"I understand, Mister President. There'll be no need for that to happen."

"Good. It would be tragic."

"Any news on your device?"

"I have a woman who is working on it for you now. She will deliver it in exchange for the microchip."

"Thank you."

"You can thank me by getting it done."

"It goes without saying the Americans can never find out how you got it."

"I won't be telling them."

"You know what I mean. They have to believe you stole it. They can't find out I willingly handed it over."

"Like I said, I won't be telling them. You better cover your own tracks."

Chapter Thirty-Nine

Max swung the big helicopter in over the training tower. Only days before, he had the recruits abseiling into the building and running drills.

From the outside, it just looked like a plain concrete building and that was mostly right. But underneath the structure was a large concrete bunker. It was one of three additional operations bunkers AIS had built to support and provide back up to the primary one, and ensure its missions and the country's leadership would be safe in the event of terrorist attacks.

The primary bunker was in Canberra. There was also one under a storage facility in Sydney. One in Perth. And this one at the Wool Shed.

Max wheeled the chopper around allowing Kate full views of the area around the building.

There were two terrorists in the open near the rear of the tower. They had incorrectly assumed their team was on the chopper and Kate cut them down with the machine gun, before they even registered what was happening.

When they were satisfied, Max started lowering the bird. He brought it down fast, but with a surprising level of control. It landed in a cloud of red dust.

As the blades began to slow, a faint high pitch rev could be heard approaching. Kate swung the gun around to lock the sights on Liam as his dirt bike skidded along the road, kicking up dust.

She lowered the gun as Max climbed out of the pilot's seat.

Liam stopped the bike a metre from his two bosses.

"I'm sorry," Liam said, out of breath. "I'm sorry I didn't get here soon enough. They chased me with the other chopper."

"Where is it now?" Kate asked.

"At the bottom of the training pool on the obstacle course."

"You brought down a chopper with a rifle and a dirt bike?" Kate asked, looking to Max with an impressed expression.

"With a rope actually, but we can talk about it later. Have you heard from the Prime Minister? I'm sorry I couldn't secure him sooner."

"You don't have anything to be sorry for, kid," Max said. "You did what you had to do and it sounds like you did it well."

"Thank you, sir."

"Let's move."

The three agents fanned out, MP5s and assault rifles to their shoulders. They quickly covered the distance to the building. Kate circled around to the rear as Max and Liam waited near the entrance.

Max waited for the count of twenty to give Kate enough time to get to the back of the building, then nodded to Liam.

Max went through the door first and broke right. Liam quickly followed and broke left. The pair scanned the area with their rifles for targets, but it was clear.

There was a gunshot at the rear.

"Clear," Kate yelled.

"Clear," Max replied.

They met at the stairs and Max signalled for Kate to head up with Liam. They didn't need to be told twice, they simply took to the stairs and started climbing.

Max swung his MP5 down the stairs and started making his way down towards the bunker.

Outside the solid metal door, two of William's men were working on the locks. Max heard a solid clunk and the two men stepped back as the big door fell from its hinges and slammed down onto the concrete.

Max couldn't believe his eyes. How could they have broken into the vault so fast? There was only one explanation, they had been given the specs. It's the only way they could have known where to place the charges and where to make the cuts.

The two men grabbed for their weapons, but before they got the chance, Max put two bullets in each of them. They fell to the cold concrete without even seeing him.

Max walked down the remaining stairs and swept the entrance to the bunker with his MP5 making sure no one was hiding in the corners.

"Clear," he said, loud enough for them to hear him in the bunker.

He walked into the bunker to find Blake, Liddle and Mills with rifles trained on him, and the remaining AIS staff huddled in the conference room with guns at the ready.

"Stand down, everyone," Max said, calmly. "It's over."

Mills was in shock. They had been watching the live feed from outside the bunker and knew the terrorists were getting close to making entry, but then the signal went dead. One of the men must have cut the camera's circuit. The last person they had all expected to see enter was Max, but Blake knew his voice straight away and told the others to lower their guns.

"You expecting someone else?" Max said, smiling.

"You really are something else," Blake said, standing and walking around to hug Max. "Thank you."

"I won't let them hurt you again," Max said, before kissing Blake.

They held each other for a full minute until he heard boots on the stairs.

Blake, Liddle, Mills and Max all raised their weapons and aimed for the doors.

"That you, Alpha?" Max called out.

"Yes, Prince," Kate replied. "All clear up here."

"All clear down here too."

Kate climbed down the stairs and walked into the bunker. She noticed the door as she passed and made a mental note of it.

"Looks like you made it just in time," Kate said to Max.

"Thanks to you and the kid," Max said. "Where is he?"

"He's keeping watch."

Max just nodded, but quickly turned back to face Blake as he felt the strengthen go out of his arms. He grabbed Blake under the arms and helped him to a chair. Blake had sweat through his shirt.

"Are you okay, Blake?" Max asked.

"He's been fighting it since we got here," Mills said. "He wouldn't let us fight without him."

"Couldn't let those arseholes take me down without a fight," Blake said. "I'm fine, Max. I just needed a second, but I'm okay."

Max wasn't so sure of that, but he wasn't going to argue and make it worse.

"What are we going to do now, Max?" Mills asked.

"We need to get you and Blake to safety, and evacuate the rest of the team," Max said. "Mike you'll need to get the team to vehicles."

"Can do, Max," Liddle said. "We've got several on the base."

"Good. We don't know if anyone else is coming, so split up and head in separate directions."

"Understood."

"Someone will have to go get Hulk," Blake said.

Max stopped in his tracks and looked down at the floor.

"He's gone?" Blake asked, quietly.

"Yes," Max said with tears welling in his eyes. "The homestead and the barn were completely destroyed. No way he survived."

"I'm sorry, Max."

"Me too."

The whole room took a moment in silence to remember the old spymaster.

"Where will we take Blake and the Governor-General?" Kate asked, breaking the silence. "He'd want us to push on. Job's not done yet."

"Sydney," Max said. "It's the only secure location we can get to."

"Not sure how secure it'll be, given how fast they got in my new door."

"I'm not going to Sydney and I'm not running off to hide," Blake said, getting to his feet. "We're going to Canberra and we're taking back the government."

"Are you sure you're up to it?" Mills asked.

"Are you?"

The country's two leaders just nodded in complete understanding with each other. They would do whatever it takes to reclaim control of the country.

"I'd rather get you to a safe location," Max said. "We can live to fight another day."

"No. You can take us in the chopper. Let's move."

Blake started for the door and was quickly flanked on all sides by his friends and colleagues. Mills took the lead up the stairs. The old military man seemed to relish the chance to get back into the action.

Max helped Blake up the stairs, wielding his gun in his left hand.

Kate, Liddle and the AIS team followed.

As they climbed, they heard the chopper starting. Liam was the only one out there and as far as Max knew, he couldn't fly the big aircraft.

Kate and Liddle had drawn the same conclusion and shouldered past Max and Blake, rushing up the stairs ahead of them.

Kate, Mills and Liddle all burst through the door and out towards the chopper, just as it was leaving the ground.

A badly burned William was in the pilot's seat. He swung the chopper around as Max and Blake made it to the door. Max saw Liam bound and beaten, tied to the rear bench of the chopper.

They all raised their weapons, but Max ordered them not to
fire. He didn't want to risk Liam's life.

As the rotor wash cleared and the helicopter sped off, they
all turned to Max.

"He has Liam," Max said.

Chapter Forty

"I made it out," William yelled over the noise of the chopper.

"Good," Timms said. *"Our Russian friend called. He's threatening all our war."*

"I'm listening."

"You need to get to Canberra and find Mila Basov."

"Who is she?"

"A Russian asset. She needs one of the microchips."

"We tried that already. It didn't go very well."

"We don't have any choice, William. He's holding the country responsible for what Max did. He says he's responsible for collapsing their economy and if he's not dead soon, he's going to come over here and do it himself."

"Well, you leave the Prince to me. He won't be able to help himself. He'll come for me."

"How do you know that?"

"I've got one of his precious team," William said, turning back to see Liam listening intently. "He'll come for him."

"What else aren't you telling me?"

"Nothing."

"I don't believe you."

"I don't care."

"Who do you think you're talking to?"

"Who do you think you're talking to? I've been through hell. I'm covered in burns from that arsehole, Hulk, he set off a grenade and I was caught in the explosion."

"Where is he now?"

"He's in hell."

"You killed him?"

"He killed himself. Not as satisfying, but at least he's dead."

"So, now that's done, will you be able to focus on the mission at hand?"

"I've never stopped focusing on my mission."

"You mean our mission?"

"Where is Mila Basov?" William asked ignoring the quip.

"Canberra. Glebe Park. She's waiting for you."

"I'll be in touch," William said, ending the call.

William opened his phone and connected to the government servers he now had access to thanks to Timms. He searched for Mila Basov across the intelligence systems.

A minute later it returned the results of his search. He read the file and smiled to himself. He's plan was back on track and the Russian was the answer.

Chapter Forty-One

The engine was roaring as it was pushed to its limits.

The car skidded around on the loose red dirt.

Max had driven the road may times before, but still he was operating at the very limits of the car's performance and his own.

Blake was in the passenger seat and Kate and Mills were in the back.

Liddle had taken two groups of AIS staff to other vehicles and they had sped off in the opposite direction, then he had remained behind with two loyal AIS crews. They were in the bunker trying to get the system back online.

Max sighted the tarmac finally and knew they were making good progress.

The big car's tyres hit the bitumen and gripped hard. Max put his foot down harder, now he had more control.

They were rushing towards Canberra. It was their best shot at where William was heading given the direction the chopper had flown.

Blake's phone rang and he raised it to his ear.

"You were right," Liddle said. "We got the network back online. He made it to Canberra."

"Any idea of where he is now?" Blake asked.

"We are back tracing radio signals to see if we can pick up his phone signal."

"It'll be making a straight line over several towers."

"Exactly. If we can find it, we might be able to track him on the ground."

"Keep us posted."

"Yes, sir."

Blake ended the call and confirmed the location was Canberra.

Max gripped the wheel and pushed his foot to the floor.

After around thirty minutes they came to the closest town to the Wool Shed. It was a barren and sparsely populated little village a long way removed from the capital.

As they drove into town, a few locals yelled and gave wild hand gestures as they clocked Max's speed. He ignored them at first, but then began to slow as he neared the local rugby club.

Sitting on the dry lawn was a brand new Westpac Rescue Helicopter.

The government was still compromised and they couldn't call for another helicopter without alerting their enemies, so Blake called in a fake accident to get the chopper on site. He had reminded himself that when this was all over he would make a considerable donation to the charity.

The red hot Land Cruiser skidded to a stop next to the chopper and the paramedics rushed to help their patients out of the car, but stopped when they saw the Prime Minister and Governor-General climb out.

"Sorry for the deception," Blake said, apologetically. "But we need your aircraft."

"Umm, sir," the pilot said. "I'm not sure we can do that."

"Listen, this is a matter of national security. You can take it up with me in a few days, unless I'm dead. Then all I can do is apologise for stranding you out here."

The paramedics looked around at the small town and didn't seem too thrilled with the idea of staying there.

Max threw them the car keys as he walked for the pilot's door, but paused when he reached it. Kate was standing in his way. She'd seen his hands trembling on the drive and could see difficulty he was having even just walking to the chopper. He tried to hide it, but it was no use.

"It would be best if you gave us a couple of hours before calling this in," Kate said, aiming her pistol at the paramedics. "Say the chopper has an issue and that the accident wasn't as bad as originally thought. You've taken care of the patient, but need some time to address the chopper issues. Nothing more, understood?"

"I don't," the pilot started to say, before Kate put a bullet into the dirt next to him.

"Understood?"

"Y-yes."

"Good."

The two paramedics backed away as Max, Blake, Mills and Kate climbed into the chopper. Kate revved the engine up to speed, then lifted off and headed fast for Canberra.

Max sat beside Blake in the rear of the bird. They were both far from their best physical shape and simply exhausted. They rested their heads together and fell asleep for the short journey.

Chapter Forty-Two

"Yes, Agent Shaw, we've seen him on the security footage from the Canberra Centre," one of the AIS Analysts said through his comms unit.

"Do you have him now?" Max asked.

"No, sir. He went into the rear of one of the shops and we lost him."

"Which shop?"

"David Jones."

"Did he have anyone with him?"

"No, sir."

"Copy that."

Max marched quickly through the massive shopping complex in the centre of downtown Canberra. His gun was holstered as he didn't want to frighten the local shoppers. And, if he was honest with himself, his hands were still giving him grief.

"Are you sure you don't want us to alert the security guards and start evacuating the centre?"

"No, it might spook him and he could set off the weapon."

"Roger that."

"Has he met with anyone?"

"No, sir."

"Direct me to the area where we lost him."

"It's in the back of the store, near the electronics section. There's a staff only door back there on the right."

"Got it. Where's my back up?"

"Bravo is two minutes out."

"Let him know where to find me, would you?"

"We're on it."

Max had a slightly faster pace than a shopper on a mission. A couple of shoppers looked at him inquisitively, but didn't get in his way.

"Hello, man on a mission coming through," an older gentleman said over his glasses in the big department store. "Just joking with you sir. Anything I can help you find today?"

"No, thank you," Max said and kept moving.

"Well, you just give me a little whistle if you need a hand."

"Will do."

The retailer gave a little delighted grunt as he watched Max powerwalk away.

Max made it to the electronics section and walked through the aisles of televisions and computers. He spotted the door, then quickly glanced around the room. He couldn't see any lookouts or anyone paying him too much attention, other than the overly friendly staff member who was still watching him from a distance.

As he turned the handle, the door burst open. He stepped back quickly, as he locked eyes with William who had open it from the inside.

William was standing, in shock from seeing Max, next to a lanky eastern European woman.

William leapt forward and tackled Max. The pair slammed into a shelving unit. One of the overpriced eighty-inch televisions tumbled from the shelves and shattered on the carpet.

The Russian woman decided she didn't need to hang around, so she put on her glasses and headed for the nearest exit.

Max and William exchanged punches and kicks, much more like a street brawl than two highly trained spies.

William pulled a second television forward and its momentum toppled it off and hit Max. It didn't do any damage, it was more of a distraction. Max pushed the big unit to the floor, and it too shattered glass and plastic over the fading and worn carpet.

Max turned to face William, when a laptop came rushing for his face. Just before it hit, a small wire running from the underside of the computer pulled taught and William's swing was arrested midair. Both his laptop wielding hands were up over his head. Max took the opportunity and slammed his fish into William's blistered face.

Max felt the pain fun up his forearm and through his fist. His legs were starting to shake and he felt unsteady.

William stepped back as Max threw another punch, but William moved the laptop into the path of Max's fist. It hit hard and cracked the plastic cover, but did more damage to Max's hand. The pain instantly returned, radiating up his arm again.

"Bravo, if you can hear me there's a Russian woman heading for the Bunda Street exit," Max said. "Pick her up would you?"

"Any more details on her, boss?" Jonnie asked. *"We're just pulling up now."*

"Five, eight. Blonde. Aviator glasses."

William dropped the laptop and it swung hard against the shelving unit as the security wire caught. A thin black electrical wire popped out and the space was suddenly filled with a shrill alarm.

The sales assistant from earlier came briskly towards them.

"You can't do that in here," he yelled. "Take it outside you neanderthals."

Max grabbed William around the neck, trying to get him into a chokehold, but William was strong and wasn't about to let Max overcome him. Max sensed it and knew his strength wasn't there, so instead dragged the terrorist headfirst towards a third epic television set. Max rammed the big TV with William's head. The screen cracked and fluttered.

William pulled his head out from under Max's arm and used Max's momentum against him. Max had been moving in to slam William's head against the TV again, this time, William grabbed Max by the scruff of the neck and slammed his head down onto the metal shelf. Max stumbled back and William capitalised by throwing a savage right hook.

The blow set Max back into a shelf full of DVDs and games, sending them cascading to the floor with a hundred plastic cracks.

"You know, I never understood how he could love you, when he hated the sight of me," William said. "We're the same, yet he'd give his life for you, but not for his own flesh and blood."

"He did give his life for you, William," Max said. "He's laying in a smouldering shed, dead, trying to give you the world he promised you as a boy. One safe and free from terror."

Max ran forward and the tackled William through a cardboard display. The headphones and gifts which had been assembled on the display flew off in every direction as the pair fell through it and started wrestling on the carpet.

"Where is Liam?" Max asked.

"I don't know who that is," William said.

"The guy you left the Wool Shed with, where is he?"

"Oh, that Liam. Yeah, I don't know where he is."

"You're going to tell me where he is or I'm going to make you suffer."

"Enough of the speeches, you're worse than Hulk. I'm so glad he's dead."

"You killed him and now I'm going to kill you," Max said, throwing a violent headbutt into William's nose.

William laughed as blood started pouring from the split skin on his nose.

"I killed him because he deserved to die. Everything I've done for the last few months and in the years leading up to today has been to destroy his legacy and to destroy him."

"You've lost," Max said, punching William hard in the face.

William's head cracked as it hit the concrete and his vision blurred, but even through the obvious pain he began to laugh.

"What could you possible find funny?"

"You have his fire, but you've also got his arrogance. I haven't lost. You have, Max."

William passed out, his head fell back and hit the concrete as Max pondered that last comment. It was so sure for someone who was now unconscious, the fight gone from his muscles at least for now.

Max began patting down William and checking his pockets. He found his gun and sat it to the side, before finding his phone and small black device about the size of half of a smart phone.

Max wasn't sure what the device did, so he didn't dare push any of the buttons which sat around the side of the screen. As he moved it though, the little screen lit up. The display had only one thing on it.

A countdown timer.

Twenty-five minutes and one second. Twenty-five minutes. Twenty-four minutes and fifty-nine seconds.

"Jesus, Bravo," Max said into his comms unit. "Please tell me you found the Russian."

"En route to you now, Max," Jonnie said. *"We've got her and the microchip."*

Max dragged William into the staff only area of the shop and cable tied him to a chair.

Jonnie arrived and did the same thing to the Russian woman.

Max stormed into the room with the Russian and waved the device in front of her eyes.

"Did you do this?" Max asked.

"I don't know what that is," Basov said.

"My colleague found the microchip on you. Did you give William this new trigger in exchange?"

"If your friend found something in my pockets, he must have planted it there."

"Cut the bullshit, we've not got long to disarm it."

She looked hesitant.

"How do I disarm it?" Max demanded.

"I have no idea what you are talking about," she said nervously.

"You don't seem like the type of woman willing to die for this piece of shit's cause."

The Russian seemed to momentarily flutter an eyelid.

"He didn't tell you, did he?" Max asked, flashing the small screen towards her, his hands visibly shaking. "He only gave you half an hour to live."

"Govnosos, Pidaras," she spat.

"Shit sucking arsehole?" Max translated. "I'll take that as a no."

"He told me I would have two hours to clear the city. I told him I needed to collect some things. He told me I had time. Yobanaya suka!"

"I agree, he is a fucking bitch. Help me disarm it and get your revenge."

"I can't. He reset the password. It'll take me more than thirty minutes to pull that unit apart."

"No way to speed that up?"

"No. It could blow."

"Any other way to stop the device?"

"If you know where the weapon is you could remove the remote trigger sensor. That way when the signal is sent from the device in your hand, it's got nowhere to go. But, I doubt you'll be able to do it with those hands."

"Where is the weapon?" Max asked, rubbing his hands willing them to stop shaking as Jonnie looked on in concern.

"I don't know."

"Can you remove the sensor?"

"Yes, but I want something in return."

"You're not really in the position to be making demands."

"Nor are you. We will both die here in twenty minutes if you don't meet the demands."

"What are they?"

"I want immunity and safe passage to a country of my choosing."

"Call it in," Max said to Jonnie, before leaving the room.

Next door he found William groggily coming around.

"Where's the device?" Max asked.

"It's safe," William smiled. "For a few minutes anyway."

"Where's Liam?"

"He's safe. For another twenty minutes or so anyway."

Max took out his hunting knife and stabbed it down through William's forearm. William screamed in pain. Max twisted the blade and felt the bones moving in William's arm as the muscle and ligaments and soft tissue sliced apart.

"You're wasting your time, Max," William said through bloody, gritted teeth. "I won't tell you where it is."

"This can't all be because daddy didn't love you," Max said. "There has to be more to it."

"He killed my mother."

"No, you did. Your fight started it. You didn't have to fight your father, just like now, you don't have to let the weapon harm innocent people. How many people will lose their mothers today if you let it explode?"

"Nice try, Max, but you won't get under my skin that easily. I want this country to suffer. I want them to know loss and pain, I want the economy to crumble so every one of these pricks can see and feel what it is like to have nothing. Only by destroying the nation, can we rebuild it into a fairer and more just society. One without you and your precious mentor. Pro humanitate et terra."

The door flung open and Jonnie entered.

"We found it, Max," Jonnie said. "The satellites have been sweeping over the cities looking for radiation. It's here in the city."

"Get the woman," Max said and lead the way.

"It's too late, Prince," William yelled. "You can't possibly disarm it in time. You're dead! Do you hear me? You're dead!"

"No, William. Your father's dead. Your son is dead. And, your lover is dead. You have nothing and your plans have failed."

Max walked out of the room as William screamed in anguish hearing Tom and Joe were both gone. He was shouting and hurling abuse, but Max just walked off down the corridor after Jonnie.

Max checked the countdown timer as he moved. There was only ten minutes left on the clock.

He noted the scared faces of the children, and the men and women shopping in the retail precinct. Jonnie was all but carrying the Russian to move faster. It must have been a strange sight, but it didn't matter. All they could do was get to the weapon and try to disarm it. They could evacuate the mall, but there wasn't enough time for the locals and tourists in the building and in the city to get to safety.

Jonnie kicked open a side door near the food court and the trio ran down the stark white hallway, which was scuff marked from years of delivery trolleys damaging the walls.

Jonnie's Geiger Counter crackled and started getting louder. He aimed it at a storage cupboard door and knew the device was inside.

He opened the door and they saw it sitting on a table in the centre of the room.

"Tell me how to remove the sensor," Max said to the Russian. "You fuck it up, we're all dead."

"Has my immunity been sorted?" she asked.

"It's not going to matter in a few minutes anyway."

The Russian looked at the countdown clock in Max's hand. She didn't want to die, but she equally didn't want to spend the rest of her life in gaol.

"I know what you're thinking," Max said, holding the wall to steady himself. "I give you my word, I'll honour the agreement if you help me."

She took a long moment to consider her options as Max fell to his knees and started convulsing.

Jonnie rushed to him, but Max managed to shake his head and point to the nuclear weapon.

Jonnie looked to the Russian.

"We're running out of time," Jonnie said. "You have my word too. I'll honour what Max told you. Immunity, the works. Let's just stop this thing."

The Russian was sweating, but nodded.

"Okay, open the small flap on the righthand side near the cylinder," she said.

Jonnie opened the metal lid and saw three wires.

"Red, blue and orange," he said.

"Cut the blue wire."

Jonnie cut the blue wire without even a moment's hesitation.

A small glass case clicked open exposing a series of wires and metal buttons.

"Move the first two buttons into the up position," she said. "Then the fifth one to the down position."

Jonnie used the tip of his knife to move the tiny buttons into position.

The trigger device began to beep and buzz, and the countdown sped up.

"What the fuck did you do?" Jonnie asked as Max laid still on the ground.

"It is okay, it was always going to do that," she said. "I should have mentioned it."

"Time's running out. What next?"

"In the original compartment, cut the orange wire."

Jonnie flicked the knife and cut the small wire. The countdown timer raced away towards zero.

"Hurry up!" Jonnie said.

"That is the last step," she said, stepping forward and grabbing a small black box on the lefthand side of the weapon.

She tore it free seconds before the clock hit zero.

Chapter Forty-Three

The AIS medical team arrived.

Max was conscious and alert, but in significant pain. He'd sweat through his shirt and the colour had drained from his face.

Jonnie was pacing in the back of the room as Max argued with the doctor.

"Just give me a dose, Doc," Max said. "I accept the risk. I've just got one thing left to do, then you've got my word I'll head straight to the hospital."

"You could die, Prince," the doctor said. "I've already given you too much."

Max looked back to Jonnie for support.

"We've got this, Max," Jonnie said. "Get yourself taken care of. We've lost enough good people today."

"I appreciate all you're both saying, but I'm not going to let this go," Max said. "Give me the shot. I'll finish this, then go to the hospital."

"Max," Jonnie started.

"He killed Hulk and he's got Liam. He tried to kill Blake and Blake's still in danger. I'm not going to let that slide. Do either of you seriously think I ever would?"

"No, Max. But."

"But nothing, Jonnie. I'm going to finish this, even if it kills me."

"That's what we're worried about, Max. You could die."

"I'll be fine," Max said, turning back to the doctor. "Just leave me the shot. I'll do it myself. If I die, it'll be on me, not either of you."

The doctor and Jonnie both exchanged worried looks, but they knew there was no convincing him.

The doctor loaded the syringe and handed it to Max, before leaving the room.

"Are you sure, Max?" Jonnie asked.

"If it was your fiancé, your family, would you just sit around and hope for the best?" Max asked as he plunged the needle through his skin and depressed it, sending the clear liquid into his veins.

"No, I couldn't, Max."

Within a minute Max felt the liquid going to work and he pulled himself up with Jonnie's help.

"Just so you know, Max," Jonnie said softly. "I consider you and Blake family. Hulk too."

Max stopped dusting himself off and looked up at the younger man with a sadness in his eyes. He'd been so wrapped up in his own issues, he hadn't stopped to think about Jonnie's feelings and he regretted how he'd spoken to him.

"I'm sorry, Jonnie," Max said. "Thank you. We feel the same way about you too, kid. I appreciate your concern and I know you've only got my best interests at heart. I'm sorry for challenging you just now."

"It's okay, Max. I can only imagine what you're going through. But I hope you know I'm here for you and for our team."

"Our family."

"Indeed."

Max patted Jonnie on the arm.

"I've got your back, boss," Jonnie said.

"Then let's go finish this," Max said starting for the door.

Max and Jonnie left an AIS clean-up crew with the nuclear device and the Russian.

They walked back towards David Jones.

"I'm glad you're okay, kid," Max said. "I felt sick to the stomach when your team was taken out. I thought you were dead too."

"Kicking these guys' arses will go in someway to thanking them for their sacrifice."

"Yes it will."

"I'm sorry about Hulk."

"Yeah, me too. He went out how he would have wanted to go. Taking a couple of those arseholes with him in a big explosion."

"Perfect."

The pair shared a brief look at each other as in unison they both felt a change. Something was wrong.

They picked up their pace and drew their pistols.

The eerie silence in the mall was deafening.

When they reached the doors of the massive department store, they knew why. The first two of Jonnie's team members were laying dead, bleeding out onto the carpet.

They started to run dodging dead bodies and destroyed merchandise displays.

Max saw the sales assistant who had offered to help him earlier. He was lying holding a gushing wound in his stomach. He was trying to speak, but the pain and shock had taken over.

"Go check," Max said as he knelt down with the dying salesman.

Jonnie ran off towards the back room to find William.

"I'm sorry," Max said to the dying man.

Tears welled in his eyes as Max took his hand. He checked the wound, but it was too late. He squeezed the man's hand tight and saw the realisation wash over his face. He had been fighting it, but Max watched as his face relaxed accepting his fate. A tear fell down his cheek and he smiled one last time, thankful Max was with him at the end.

Max felt his hand go limp and the life disappeared from his eyes. He closed the man's eyes with his free hand.

"He's gone," Jonnie said, out of breath beside Max.

"There's only one place he could be going," Max said, the anger noticeable in his voice.

"Where?"

"Same place as us," Max said. "Call Kate and tell her to hold off until we get there."

"Yes, boss," Jonnie said, pulling out his phone.

Max and Jonnie headed for the doors. Their cars were parked up on the footpath. Worried onlookers were gathering, drawn like moths to the blue and red lights flashing from their windows.

Jonnie's crew had locked down the nuclear device, but teams of federal police were arriving and they couldn't be sure who they were taking their orders from. The most likely scenario was Timms, so they had no choice but to flee. They didn't want to get into a shootout with police just following orders.

Max drove the big four-wheel drive slowly through the sea of people. They moved to the side as the vehicle approached, but stayed close trying to catch a glimpse of the mysterious men in the car.

Jonnie hit the siren and they jumped back, clearing more room for Max. He pushed the accelerator a little harder and the big V8 roared, pushing the car forward. He steered it around the merry-go-round, which was a permanent fixture of the outdoor mall, then down over the gutter and onto the road.

He drove through the streets, then over the Commonwealth Bridge, heading up towards Parliament House.

They could see the flashing lights of the police roadblocks on the on ramp for Parliament. They weren't getting through there.

He took the sweeping circle road to the left. When he found a gentle sloping grassy hill he turned the Land Cruiser hard to the right, jumped the gutter and used the four-wheel drive to climb the hill. He drove on an angle following the road, tearing up the grass out of sight of the police roadblocks.

A few hundred metres along the road they spotted Blake and Kate in the tree line and came to a stop beside them.

"You're not supposed to be here," Max said, climbing down. "You were supposed to stay with Mills."

"You can't do this by yourself, Max," Blake said.

"He's right, Prince," Kate said. "We don't know how many of these arseholes are inside. We're all going in together."

"You've all been through resent traumas," Max said, looking to each of the members of his team. "It's lucky you're all alive."

"Look who's talking, Max," Blake said. "You've been suffering the effects of the chemical attack. I'm not going to argue with you about going to the hospital. I know you too well. You wouldn't be dragged out of here. That's why we're coming with you. We've got some scores to settle, and we've also got your back and we know you've got ours."

"Too fucking right," Kate said, clicking the slide back on her MP5 chambering a round.

"I'm with them," Jonnie said, as his fingers danced down the stiches on his neck from the explosion. "Call the play, boss."

Max took a moment to look at them all. He knew there was no way he could do it without them, but still felt the sickness in the pit of his stomach that he was putting them at risk. After a moment, he nodded reluctantly.

"Any idea who we'll be dealing with inside?" Max asked.

"We checked the rosters," Kate said. "Looks like the crews outside are legit. They're not involved. Just normal cops doing their jobs."

"Okay, so we don't want to start any trouble with them. How about the ones inside?"

"They're fair game. Timms and Willams' crews and those loyal them are guarding the building from the inside."

"Good. Weapons free inside."

"How will we get in? We tightened the fuck out of security after that assault years ago. It's basically impossible to get in."

"Not for me," Blake said.

"No," Max said.

"It's not your call, Max," Blake said, taking his hand. "I'm the Prime Minister and I'm pulling rank."

"There's got to be another way."

"There's not. Take the distraction and go in. Clear the building, then come get me."

"They'll shoot you on sight."

"Maybe."

"I can't let that happen."

"We don't have any other choice."

"We could come through the top."

"As Kate said, it's impregnable. The glass is reinforced, bullet, drone and bomb proof glass. No abseiling in this time. And we can't just kill the police outside, they aren't on Timms' payroll."

Blake leant forward and softly kissed Max.

"I've loved you since the day I met you at the Wool Shed," Blake said. "The most handsome recruit I've ever seen and still the most handsome person I've ever met. We've been through so much shit, Max, but I've never stopped loving you and never will. If I die today, I'll die happy knowing I had you in my life."

"You're not going to die, Blake," Max said. "We've been through too much. We've fought everything and everyone who has stood in our way, and today is no exception. I will kill every fucking one of them."

"One last time for you to come and save me," Blake said, squeezing Max's hand, before sliding his access card into it. "See you soon."

With that he turned and marched up the hill.

"Let's move," Max said, tearing himself away from watching Blake climb the grassed slope.

Kate, Jonnie and Max all ran hard. They hurdled small shrubs and used the walls and plants for cover as they quickly moved.

They found the road they were looking for and changed out their magazines. The blue tape wrapped metal ammunition holsters all clicked into place.

As the three agents all took a moment to catch their breaths, Blake arrived at the front door of Parliament House.

A very nervous looking federal police officer approached him and called for her team to lower their weapons when they saw who it was. She looked like she'd seen a ghost.

"Mister Prime Minister," the officer said. "Are you okay? We heard you were killed."

"Not yet, sergeant," Blake said. "I need to see the pretender Prime Minister."

"Of course," she said, before catching herself. "I don't really know what the protocol is here. Timms has been sworn in, so technically you're not the Prime Minister anymore."

"Actually, I just left the Governor-General. He ended Timms' commission and reinstated mine. I'm going in to tell him myself."

"You should know there's some weird shit, sorry, weird stuff happening here."

"Like what?"

"They threw all the feds out and the normal security guards. I've never seen the crews they brought in."

"This is going to come as a shock, but Timms has been behind everything that has happened. Killing the former Prime Minister, the attempted assassination on me and all of the terrorist activities in recent days. He's responsible for a coup d'état."

The massive glass doors of the Parliament opened and William walked out with a team of ten. They fanned out around Blake.

"Bring him," William ordered.

The police sergeant raised her pistol at William and the other cops all raised their weapons and aimed for William's various crew members.

At the delivery entrance of the Parliament, Max, Kate and Jonnie all popped up from behind the small brick wall and opened fire. The almost silent puffs from their rifles rattled out one after another in quick succession as the police officers fell to the concrete with small tranquilizer darts hanging from their necks and chests.

Kate and Jonnie covered Max as he ran across the driveway. He clicked the release and let the blue magazine drop to the ground as he pulled a fresh mag out and clicked it into place. This one didn't have any blue tape.

Kate and Jonnie followed, checking their flanks as they moved. Max shot out the security cameras, then threw a small device at the massive roller door. It hit and stuck to the metal, before exploding and tearing the door to shreds.

Max ran through the jagged opening and slighted two very confused and coughing terrorists. He dropped both with ruthless efficiency, before leaping up the small set of stairs and running for the door.

Kate and Jonnie clicked out their mags and swapped over to the live ammo, then headed in after Max.

Out the front, Blake watched as William listened to the report coming in over his comms unit. His face twisted in anger.

"Stand down, Sergeant!" William yelled. "You don't want to get yourself and your team killed. The Prime Minister has issued an order. You are relieved of your duty."

"I don't think so," she said, clicking the safety off on her pistol.

"You don't want to try me."

Blake stepped forward and put his hand on the top of the officer's pistol and forced her to lower it.

"It's okay," he said, sliding a business card into her hand as they lowered their hands. "You know what to do, I'll be fine."

William's men grabbed Blake roughly and dragged him into the building, leaving the sergeant and her officers in shock on the forecourt of the government building.

She looked down and saw a mobile phone number roughly scrawled on the card as the doors to Parliament locked and she saw them drag Blake deeper into the building.

She pulled out her phone and rang the number.

After only one ring, it answered.

"Hello," she said. "Who is this?"

"It is Admiral Anthony Mills, Governor-General of the Commonwealth of Australia," Mills said. "And who is this and how'd you get this number?"

Chapter Forty-Four

Max swiped Blake's access card on the small reader and the door clicked open.

He ducked into the corridor, taking a knee as Kate and Jonnie followed him in and went left and right.

Kate fired once taking down a terrorist who was leaning against a walk smoking.

The concrete maze of white concrete and tiles, and sterile lighting stretched out for hundreds of metres. Max had been into the basement of Parliament House many times, but each time was still surprised at how confusing the layout was. Everything looked the same. He saw a street sign painted on the wall and headed down the corridor he was looking for.

As they moved, the AIS leadership team took down a handful of William's crew who were busy trying to fortify the basement. They looked like they were preparing to bunker in for the long term.

Max could only think William was smart enough to know this was the hill they were likely to die on. No doubt Timms had other plans, but William wasn't an idiot. This was his endgame. If all his other plans failed, this would be his last stand. The symbol of Australian democracy falling.

"Keep a look out for anything out of the ordinary," Max said. "I've got a feeling we've walked right into his trap. Bravo, take a look around, will you?"

"Sure, Prince," Jonnie said. "I'll let you know if I find anything."

"Be careful, kid."

"You too."

Jonnie peeled off and headed down the next corridor searching rooms as he went.

Max and Kate had walked under the House of Representatives and were now nearing the centre of the building.

Upstairs, William was dragging Blake through the Great Hall. The polished wood glistened under the lights. The Great Hall sat just behind the opulent marble foyer. It was used for functions with visiting Heads of State and Government, and for official dinners and ceremonies.

The focal point of the room is the epic tapestry at the rear. Measuring twenty metres wide by nine metres high, it is one of the largest tapestries in the world. Blake knew Arthur Boyd had created the original artwork it was based off depicting the Australian landscape – colours and textures of the scenery under the canopy of a eucalypt forest. It was truly magnificent.

The doors that sat under the tapestry, which were normally locked separating the public area from the security-controlled area were wide open.

William dragged Blake through the doors, followed closely by his ten guards.

Blake started to fidget and William pulled him in closer trying to control him.

"Enough," William said, grabbing Blake tighter around the back of the neck.

Blake elbowed William hard in the ribs. He felt the grip on his neck loosen and he drove the elbow in again. His hands were flexicuffed in front of him, so he couldn't throw a punch, but the elbow had done the trick.

William let him go to clutch his ribs. Blake ran to his right and looped his arms over the head of one of William's men. He kicked the gun free from the man's hands, then pushed his knee hard into his back and pulled his cuffed wrists back hard against his neck. Blood started trickling down the terrorist's neck as the plastic cuffs sliced the skin.

"I see you still have some skills," William said.

"Step back or I'll kill him" Blake said, circling around so his back was towards the Great Hall.

William's crew all had their weapons trained on him.

"Look around, Mister Smyth," William said. "You're out numbered and have nowhere to go."

Blake looked around and saw what he already knew. He looked at the incredible Members' Hall. It sat at the very centre of Parliament House. The floorboards around the massive square had all been cut onsite for that specific spot and they echoed like the creaking deck of a Queenslander house as your walked on them. The rest of the ground floor space was tiled with massive white marble slabs polished to a high shine. In the very centre of the room, sitting square under the mammoth glass pyramid and stainless-steel flagpole which sat on the roof of the Parliament, was a square fountain. It was perfectly square and its edges were cut to laser precision from black marble.

Normally, the fountain had a perfectly flat layer of water on the top which rolled over the sides and down into the well beneath. The sound was supposedly to disrupt the conversations of the House of Representatives to Blake's left and the Senate which was through the large glass doors on the right, symbolically at least.

But today, there was no water in the fountain. Blake could hear the incessant tick of the thousands of synchronised clocks echoing through the building, but there was no water flowing into the well.

The terrorist Blake was holding dropped one of his hands down and grabbed a small knife from his belt. Blake tried to pull him back, but he wasn't a little man and held firm long enough to cut the flexicuffs on Blake's wrists.

Blake's arms sprung apart as the terrorist fell forward clutching his throat and coughing to get air.

"You were going to let him kill me," he said, searching his neck to assess the damage.

"Yes," William said coldly, raising his gun and shooting him in the top of the head.

The terrorist fell to the floor and the blood started to pool on the floorboards.

"Have you finished?" William asked Blake with an unimpressed look on his face. "You've got nowhere to go."

Blake reluctantly raised his hands as two of William's men grabbed him and they started for the far side of the hall.

As they walked past the fountain, Blake stole a quick look inside.

They were heading towards the doors of the cabinet room, which sat on the other side of the Members' Hall.

As William's feet left the marble and hit the floorboards, gunshots rang out from behind him. He turned back to see the two terrorists who had been escorting Blake dead on the ground. Blake was going for one of their guns.

Then he saw them.

Kate Matthews, the head of the AIS, was firing a MP5 from the foundation. She was standing so only the top half of her body was sticking out of the hole in its centre. And, Max Shaw was running for Blake, firing his pistol at any of William's men who stood between them.

His world slowed down watching the two agents cut his team to pieces.

William saw the unrivalled determination in Max's eyes and knew there was only one way to break the man. Blake had to die.

He raised his gun as Max reached Blake. He levelled his pistol and fired.

Max tackled Blake to the floor and the first bullet sailed over their heads as they slammed into the hard marble.

Kate took aim and fired. The bullet hit William in the chest and he staggered back. He darted to the right and behind one of the huge pillars as Kate put three more bullets into it, splintering the wood panelling.

Max dragged Blake onto his feet and they ran for the row of pillars to their left. Kate provided cover, taking down the last two of William's crew.

Max pushed Blake behind the pillar and stood in front of him, checking him for wounds.

"I'm fine, Max," he said, panting. "Go get him."

Max gently touched Blake's cheeks as William opened fire. His bullets smashed through the wood and into the concrete behind Blake's back.

Max stole a quick look and saw William moving his gun back towards Kate.

"Cover me," he said to Blake.

Blake ducked his head and arm around the pillar and fired at William's pillar with the gun he'd taken from his dead terrorist escort.

Max ran the length of the Members' Hall as William realised what was happening and started raining bullets down towards Max. They slammed into the pillars and sailed through the glass windows behind Max as he ran.

When he got to the last pillar, he turned and ran hard along the echoing floorboards.

William heard him coming and fired his last two bullets.

The first hit Max in the side, slicing through an inch from his left, beside his abdominals. The second grazed the edge of his right forearm and he dropped his MP5.

William ran for the door of the cabinet room as Max arrived. He tackled William, hitting him hard in the lower back.

The pair collided with the cabinet table with a heavy thunk. The massive wooden table didn't budge an inch. Instead, William folded over its rounded edge and the air rushed from his lungs.

Max started throwing violent punches into his back and kidneys. William's anger started rising and he managed to push off the table enough to turn around.

Max was relentless. He threw punch after punch into his enemy. William tried to block as many of the blows with his hands and forearms, but Max was a machine.

William for the first time in years felt overcome and outmatched. He was running out of options. His blistered and burned skin was aching more with every blow.

He dropped his guard, exposing his face to Max. Max went to throw a punch, but William took the precious moment to push back off the table and shove Max back. It was enough to break the onslaught and for him to throw his own punch. It hit Max square in the jaw and broke the trance Max had been in.

William tripped on a chair, but managed to pull himself towards the side wall. Max focused in again and ran for William. He slammed into him and they crashed into the sideboard. National treasures from all over the country and gifted by visiting world leaders, tumbled to the floor and clattered down the shelves.

William grabbed a heavy pot, about the size of a soccer ball. He swung it towards Max's head, but Max was fast enough to just lift his shoulder in time to take the force of the blow. The ancient vase shattered sending broken clay shards scattering across the carpet.

Max threw a right hook as his left arm dropped to his side. He'd felt the pain before, he knew the pot had dislocated his shoulder.

William stumbled over another chair and fell. Max moved in quickly, but William was already in motion. The shard of clay sliced into Max's leg and stuck in place.

Three of William's men burst through the door which led into the anti-chamber and beyond into the Prime Minister's office.

William scrambled to them, then pushed past them.

"Kill him," he said as he stumbled to the door, taking one of their guns.

Max dropped to the ground, as the two men opened fire. Their bullets smashed the cupboards and precious antiques, drawing lines down the room, then into the cabinet table.

He ripped the chunk of clay from his leg and tossed it to the side, thankful the cabinet table was as solid as it was.

He looked around for anything he could use as he popped his shoulder back into place with a painful groan.

He heard the first gun click empty. This was his only chance. He couldn't wait for them to reload.

He threw a small plate up into the air. The second man opened fire and smashed it, before his gun clicked out of ammo too. Max leapt to his feet and grabbed the only thing resembling a weapon in the room – the gold mace which sat in the House of Representatives when it was in session as a symbol of the Monarch's power.

It was ornately crafted with crowns and symbols of the realm. On the top, four slender gold bands curved up to crown and cross. It was over a metre long, solid and heavy.

Max grabbed it as he ran, spinning on the spot as he did. He used the momentum of his pivot to swing the mace with as much energy as he could muster. The big mace whistled through the air and shattered the face of the man who given his gun to William. Blood exploded from his face and Max heard the sickening sound of bone and scull breaking.

The two other men were both in shock at the horrific sight of their fallen comrade.

Max wound up the mace, swinging it from up over his head as he leapt forward. He brought it down with tremendous force onto the top of the second terrorist's head. The whole top section broke off the mace, leaving Max with only the handle in his hands, but it had done the damage. The impact had broken the man's scull and his neck. The crack was loud enough to echo in the room.

The third guy was panicking and trying desperately to chamber his fresh magazine. Max jumped onto the table and took two massive bounding steps, as the terrorist clipped the magazine into place. He was swinging the gun towards Max as he leapt from the cabinet table with the handle of the mace pointed at the terrorist.

Several bullets sailed past Max, tearing into priceless artworks, the wall and roof. The final bullet the terrorist managed to get off, hit Max just below the hip, as the jagged metal end of the mace handle tore through the terrorist's neck. He fell backwards as all Max's weight and strength pushed the mace handle through his neck and severed his spine. As they hit the ground, the mace ripped through the back of his neck and pierced itself in the plasterboard. His mouth was wide and so were his eyes, as blood poured from the gruesome wound.

Max took the fallen man's gun, clicked in a new clip, then busted into the anti-chamber. Two guards were stationed there waiting for him. He dived to the right and rolled behind a sofa. He swung out the other side and fired five shots. Three missed, but two hit the terrorists. One hit a knee of one of the men and one hit a shoulder of the other. It was enough to distract both men.

Max got to his feet and shot the man in the face who was clutching his shoulder. The second man's pained face gave way to shock and fear as he fell to carpet, clutching his knee. As his arse hit the ground, a bullet hit his brain.

Kate and Blake came into the room behind Max.

Blake ran over and helped Max to his feet.

"Are you okay?" Blake asked, assessing each of Max's wounds.

"I'll be fine as soon as I kill that son of a bitch," Max said, nodding towards the door. "Time to reclaim your office."

Max limped ahead of Blake and Kate. He used a broken piece of mirror to check the corridor running along the outside of the Prime Minister's office. It was clear.

The trio crossed the blue carpet and entered the plush suite. They walked through the empty offices and made it to the door to the PM's office.

Kate kicked open the door.

Timms was standing behind the large wooden desk. The bookcase was still full of Blake's books and ornaments. Timms obviously hadn't had the time to fill it with his own yet.

William was standing at the glass doors which led out into the courtyard.

"Drop the gun," Max said as both he and Kate took aim at William.

William smiled and threw his gun onto the side table.

"What the fuck are you doing?" Timms asked. "Kill them."

"Oh, shut the fuck up," Willam said, raising his hands to show his mobile phone. "Thank fuck I won't have to listen to your bullshit any longer."

"What are you talking about?"

"The building is rigged. If my thumb comes off this screen, the whole place will be turned to rubble."

"That was never part of the plan."

"Not your plan, but it was always part of mine."

"What? Why?"

"Because one thing my dear old dad did teach me was to always have a contingency. He told me it was always wise to have a backup plan. I was always going to destroy his legacy, destroy the image of AIS through their failure to stop me and to bring down democracy by blowing up Canberra and killing all the politicians. The contingency won't take out Canberra, but it'll take down this building, the very symbol of corruption this parliament represents. I couldn't care less about you or the Russians. This was all about my plans. I was just using you and I'm thrilled you're about to die in this pile of stone."

Max's anger was pulsing through his body at the mention of Hulk and his legacy. The man had dedicated his whole life to saving people, protecting Australia and its allies, and to making it a safer country for everyone. He wasn't perfect and would have openly admitted that to anyone, but his heart was in the right place and the grumpy old prick would have killed to fix the relationship with his ungrateful and corrupted son.

"I see your pain, Prince," William said. "I'm just sorry I didn't get to kill him myself."

"He beat you at your own game," Max said.

"Why because he killed a couple of my men going out the coward's way?"

"No, because he taught me the same lessons. Only I'm better at it than you."

Max ran across the room and dived for William. William frowned and simply let go of the phone. The screen turned red, but nothing happened. No explosion. No building collapse.

William was puzzled and looked at the phone, but before he could do anything else, Max hit him and the pair crashed through the glass and tumbled out into the Prime Minister's courtyard.

"What the fuck?" Timms asked. "Get the phone, quickly, before the building explodes. What have you done?"

"William wasn't wrong," Blake said, removing the small comms unit from his ear and throwing it onto the conference table. "That's an AIS comms unit. We have one of our best agents in the basement. He found the control unit on William's explosives. He disarmed it and radioed it in. See Max's contingency plan was our colleague, Bravo. You should also know the building is being retaken as we speak. The last of William's crew are being wiped out, thanks to a combined force from AIS and the federal police on direct orders from the Governor-General who just happened to get a call from a very good police sergeant who I passed his number to out front. That was my contingency plan. Hulk died a national hero. One who trained us all to stop people like you and William."

"I just wanted what was best for the country. You have no place being in this office."

"No actually, you don't have a place in this office. The good Admiral swore me back in as Prime Minister and this is back to being my office."

Out in the courtyard, Max and William had both exchanged punches and were wrestling on the tiles. William drove his knee into Max's wounded leg and Max groaned in pain before slamming his forehead down on William's nose busting it. Blood sprayed from his nostrils and from the broken skin on the bridge.

"I'm going to fucking kill you!" William yelled. "You've taken everything from me. You've ruined everything."

"You did that to yourself," Max said as he wrestled on top of William and threw a short elbow into this face.

He grabbed William by the head and slammed it back into the tiles.

William laid perfectly still and Max breathed a sigh of relief through the pain which was shooting through every inch of his body. His heart was beating erratically and he was struggling to control his breathing. He felt like he was about to have a heart attack.

He got to his feet and staggered over to C1 the Prime Minister's luxury car. He leaned heavily on the doorframe to steady himself, then he heard footsteps. He turned just as William arrived and slammed him into the side of the big BMW.

They wrestled against the side of the car. William grabbed Max's head and bounced it off the roof, then Max kneed William in the balls and did the same thing to him. William's head collided with the polished white steel. The blow clearly dazed him after the hit to the head on the tiles. Max saw it and capitalised. He grabbed William by the face and slammed his head into the car's window. It was bulletproof glass, so there was no way it would shatter, it would have felt like hitting the steel or tiles all over again.

William swung at Max, but Max caught his arm. He tried the other side, but Max was ready for it and he caught it too. He twisted William's arms up and out, getting them into an awkward position, before headbutting him. William dropped to his knees.

Max broke William's left arm and as he was about to break the other, but William headbutted him in the balls. Max fell to his knees, involuntarily releasing William who reached behind him and opened the door.

He shoved Max, who fell backwards into the open doorframe. William used all his strength to swing the big bulletproof door towards Max's head. Max caught the door before it hit him. His back pressed awkwardly against the bottom edge of the doorframe and his hands pressed into the door, holding it off.

William opened the door again, then swung it harder. Max braced his arms for the impact, but as he did, he kicked out in a stomping motion and wrecked William's kneecap. There was a stomach-churning crack as William's leg folded the wrong way.

The door lost all momentum as he fell. Max dragged himself out of the doorframe, then pushed William into it. He swung the door with an anger that seemed to rise from the pit of his stomach and it smashed into William's upper body. It broken several ribs and Max heard the rush of air from William's lungs.

He swung the door fully open, then slammed it against the terrorist's chest again. William coughed blood onto the tiles. His lungs punctured by the heavy steel door.

Max took a step back and let the anger wash away. He didn't need to kill him. He wanted to, but didn't need to. William could spend the rest of his days in a maximum-security prison thinking about his failures.

He turned to walk away, but stumbled. He felt his heart beating out of his chest.

"Pathetic," William coughed. "You know I'll never stop. Do you really think a gaol cell will stop me? My men will find me and we'll finish what we started."

"What men?" Max asked. "They're all dead."

"Are they? I'll find Blake, you know. I won't rest until he's dead. Oh and it won't be a quick death. I'll take my time. I will make him suffer beyond anything you can imagine, then when he's begging for death, I'll redouble my efforts until he can't even beg anymore. When he's nothing, but a shell of the man he once was I will film his final moments and let you witness it. I will see your pain and suffering, and know I've broken you.

I'll destroy both of you, pissing on Hulk's legacy, before I wipe this country from the face of the earth."

William struggled to his feet.

"I will never stop," he said as blood poured from his mouth and he hopped forward on his good leg. "You killed my son and my partner. Do you really think I could let that go? I'm going to return the pain I feel to you tenfold. Blake is fucking dead, do you hear me?!"

Max's anger came flooding back. He jumped forward and drew back his right fist and slammed it into William's face. As he landed, he sprung up letting all the power he could muster drive up from his heals and out through his left shoulder. His fist broke William's jaw on impact. William hoped back trying to get his balance, but his broken knee was useless. Max grabbed him by the back of the head and drove his face down as he exploded up with his knee.

William took the full impact and fell back onto the car. He laid against the side of the car in semi-consciousness as Max pulled the survival bracelet from his own wrist.

"Do you remember this?" he asked, waving it in front of William's face as a hint of recognition flashed in his eyes. "It was your father's. He gave it to me as a memento of our friendship. But it was more than that, he was like a father to me."

Max slipped the small knife out of the bracelet. He stepped forward, grabbed William by the jaw, then slipped his knife welding hand behind William's head. William's fight had left him. He was ready for what was to come. Max pushed the knife into the space between the top of William's spine and the base of his skull. After a few seconds of pain, the life drained from William's eyes and Max removed the knife and let his body drop into the fountain.

Max watched as the water turned pink, then red.

"I'm sorry, Hulk," Max said, letting his eyes well with tears.

Max limped back into the Prime Minister's office as the sergeant and her police squad arrived behind Blake. He held his chest, tried to focus his breathing and control his heartbeat.

"Director Matthews, take this piece of shit into custody, will you?" Blake said, nodding towards Timms.

"Yes, sir," Kate said.

Kate stepped forward as Timms surveyed the scene. He was beaten.

Timms reached down and drew a pistol. Blake, Kate and the police officers all raised their guns at the Senator.

"Don't do it, Kevin," Blake said. "You've got nowhere to go."

"My family will be destroyed by this," Timms said. "You'll tell them I'm a traitor, even though I'm a patriot."

"You are a fucking traitor," Max managed to cough out through critted teeth as he fell into one of the lounges in Blake's office still clutching his chest in pain. "I'll make sure the whole world knows it."

Timms raised the gun and aimed for Max, but before he could pull the trigger Blake fired and sent a single bullet through the Senator's forehead.

His lifeless body hit the desk, then fell to the carpet.

Max smiled and let out a small laugh, before passing out.

Epilogue

In the weeks following, Blake had stabilised the government and parliament. He had reassured world leaders that Australia was once again secure and at peace. The terrorist threat had been neutralised.

The Americans were still angry about the microchips, even though Blake was now confident they'd all been destroyed. Jonnie had led a team to sweep all the known locations William and his team had been. They recovered the remaining chips and destroyed them.

He also reassured the Americans that their nuclear weapon was in a safe place and promised it would stay that way. Blake was renegotiating the alliance terms, particularly the clauses around national and Five Eyes secrets, including the chapters on nuclear weapons storage and logistics.

Kate had immediately reformed the AIS and put her agents to work assessing the damage and ensuring William and his team's efforts to destabilise the country had in fact died with them. She led the arrests of dozens of people who had enabled Timms and William's coup to take hold. She cleared a massive investment from the off-the-books AIS budget to rebuild the Wool Shed and put Liddle in charge of the project.

Max had sent a good chunk of time in the hospital. His wounds were heeling and thankfully he'd only done some minor damage to his heart with the injections. It would take some time, but the doctors said he'd fully recover.

The ANU professor had finally cracked the chemical compound and had created a vaccine, which put Max and the other victims of the attack on the path to recovery. They were all mentally scarred, but would physically get better in time.

The team had all gathered at the construction site at the Wool Shed with a huge contingent of men and women who had worked with Hulk over his decades of service in the military and with AIS. There were even a couple of world leaders and heads of spy agencies, generals and senior military officers from Australia and the Five Eyes countries, among others, who turned up to commemorate and celebrate the achievements of their old friend and colleague.

Max had stood in silence as they unveiled a small brass plaque on a rock formation, not far from where the old homestead had stood. It was a simple, understated reminder of his old mentor.

It read 'In recognition and memorial of General Patrick 'Hulk' Scott. Australia will never know your sacrifices in its name, but it is forever thankful.'

Max had rubbed his fingers over the survival bracelet Hulk had given him as he remembered the old man. He cried quietly to himself as the others exchanged war stories of Hulk's exploits on the front yard of the Wool Shed only metres from where the man had sacrificed himself to remove a terrorist from the world. A selfless and heroic final act, that Max knew the old man would have loved. Going out in a literal blaze of glory and taking a terrorist with him. Max smiled at the thought of his mentor laughing notching a final bad guy onto his kill sheet.

When the travelling party had left, Max sat at the firepit sipping a beer and watching the flames as Kate walked out onto the grass.

"Mind if I join you?" she asked.

"Not at all," Max said. "Want a beer?"

"Got one," Kate said, showing him the bottle. "I've actually got something for you."

"What is it?" Max said, taking the small tablet.

"It's a message from Hulk."

Kate handed Max the tablet and started back towards the temporary living quarters.

"You don't want to watch it?" Max asked after her.

"He didn't leave it for me," she said, smiling softly. "He left it for you."

Max had watched Kate walk away and felt sadness rising in his throat. He couldn't look at the tablet. His eyes welled with tears.

He took a moment to gain control, then sat down his beer.

He held the tablet and pressed his thumb to the unlock button. The little screen lit up and showed a white screen with a play button.

After taking some time, he pressed play.

The screen changed to a shot of the old spymaster's room in the Wool Shed. He walked into the shot and sat in his big chair. He took a minute to rest his cane against the bookcase and to catch his breath, then looked down the lens of the camera. Max felt his hair stand up on end and a cold shiver ran through his body as his mentor looked right through the screen at him.

"I've never been very good at this," Hulk said. "You probably know that better than most. I just felt I owed it to you. Jesus, I would never have guessed all those years ago we'd be here like this. I remember the day they passed me your file. You ticked all the boxes. Intelligent, athletic. By all rights, you should have been a cocky son-of-a-bitch, given your natural talents, and you were to some extent, but you had heart, kid. You had empathy and emotion, and a dose of common-fucking-sense. I knew from that minute I wanted you in the program."

"I staked my whole career and reputation on being able to find and recruit the best of the best, and they thought I was mad for choosing people outside the defence and police forces. But you proved them all wrong. You made it through training at the Wool Shed and we threw everything at you. You just fucking ate it up and kept going. You weren't perfect, but none of us are. Fuck, I know I'm not. I've done some shit in my life I regret, Max. I didn't always have all the answers and I still don't. Anyone who walks around saying they live without regret is either a liar or oblivious."

"My biggest regret is out there now, terrorising this country, this nation that I love and have sacrificed everything to protect. I loved him, like every father loves his son. I didn't handle his coming out well at all and I handled the death of his mother even worse. I tried, Max, but I didn't know how to be a father to him and I lost him. I regret not trying harder and not finding him and helping him find the answers he was looking for. If you're watching this video, it's very likely that my son is dead. I want you to know if you killed him, which I have no doubt you did, that I forgive you. William brought this on himself and you did the right thing. You always do the right thing, Max. You saved the country from another terrorist and we are all in your debt."

"I told Kate to give you this video when I died. So, there's that, I guess. I'm dead. I hope I went out with some dignity, not of this slow and long debilitating disease that's robbed me of my strength and ability. May no one ever have to experience their own slow demise. But that's not the point I wanted to make. I've lost track of what I was saying. Fucking disease. What was I saying? I know men like us don't usually get to have long lives and I should be thankful, but I don't want to go like this."

Hulk took a drink of scotch and Max joined him taking a sip of his beer.

"From your first day on the job, you were dealt a shit sandwich," Hulk continued. "I still owe you for saving my life that day. Fuck, you want to talk about regrets, I regret fucking up your life so badly. I grieved with you when Lachlan died and I still feel responsible for his death. If I hadn't gotten you involved, maybe he'd still be here. Maybe you wouldn't have gone through the pain and suffering you've had to endure. But then what would the country look like now? You have single handedly saved our arses more times than I can count. Australia will never know the full extent of what you have given to save them. But I do and I can't thank you enough. This isn't a job anyone can do. And, no one can do it like you. Thank you, Max."

"One thing I don't regret is that this job led you to Blake. I've never been so happy and so proud to see the two of you together. It's taken me a lifetime to learn that love is love, but

I get it and I see it in your eyes. The strength and passion, and unyielding bond between the two of you is something not everyone will get to experience, and I'm so happy for you both. I want you to both live a happy and full life together. Hopefully he sees the light and gets the fuck away from those wankers up the Hill. I still can't quite believe that career move. But I do know he loves you. He has since the first time he saw you. Kate was beside herself with joy when she chose your codename. Fucking Prince Charming. I thought Blake's head was going to melt off his shoulders, he went so red from embarrassment."

Hulk started laughing and coughing, reminiscing. He took another sip of scotch and regained his breath.

"Anyway, I've taken up enough of your time," Hulk said. "You've got a fucking job to do. Pull yourself together, kid. I'm gone, but life goes on. Try to remember what I've taught you. Look after yourself and Blake. Keep having Kate's back, she needs you. The whole AIS needs you. I'm leaving it to you all. It is my legacy and I'm happy to be leaving it to you, my friends. You've been like a son to me and I love you, kid. Good luck and Godspeed."

The screen went black and Max wiped the tears from his eyes.

He had sat for hours watching the stars that night drinking in the warm glow of the fire and remembering his friend.

In the days following, Max had focused on his recovery. He had taken his place as Deputy Head of the AIS and he had begun the recruitment process for the next round of potential recruits.

He sat on the bulldozer and drove it forward collecting the last bucket of burnt wood and rubble. He lifted the bucket and took the load over to the semi-trailer and tipped it into the back of the truck he'd rented. He shook the bucket, then reversed back and lowered it, before shutting off the little workhorse.

He stood for a minute looking at the concrete slab which once held his house. The home he'd bought with Lachlan and they had hoped to spend their lives in. Now, like Lachlan, it was gone, but Max felt at peace. It had been years since

Lachlan's death. He would always have a place in his heart, but he knew Lachlan would want him to move on. And he had, Blake was the best man he knew and he loved him more than anything in the world. He smiled thinking about the life they have left to live together.

As the sun started its slow descent, a speeding motorcade rushed over the hill in the distance and quickly tracked along the road towards the now vacant block.

It arrived and turned into the property.

Max was instantly surrounded by federal police protective agents. They took in the surroundings and waited a full minute before the lead agent opened the backdoor and Blake stepped out.

He walked over to Max and hugged him tightly.

The dirt and sweat from Max's skin pressed into Blake's new suit, but neither of them cared. They embraced as if no one was watching, locked in their own little slow dance on the rural property in the setting sun.

Blake pulled a folded piece of paper from his pocket and led Max to the front of his limousine. He unfolded it out onto the bonnet to reveal a large blueprint.

The pair began pointing excitedly to it, then to the concrete slab and old shed.

As the sun began to set, they walked hand in hand around the property, listening to the birds and taking in the view of the rolling mountains. On a small hill, not far from the boundary fence they hugged and kissed passionately as the pink, purple and orange streaks washed across the twilight sky.

The End.

Max Shaw will return in *Shaw Transition*.

www.jwpublishing.com.au

www.ingramcontent.com/pod-product-compliance
Lightning Source LLC
Chambersburg PA
CBHW030600170726
48283CB00002B/414